THE AMBASSADOR'S DAUGHTER

Also by Pam Jenoff

The Kommandant's Girl
The Diplomat's Wife
The Winter Guest
The Last Summer at Chelsea Beach
The Orphan's Tale
The Lost Girls of Paris

THE AMBASSADOR'S DAUGHTER

PAM JENOFF

PARK
ROW
BOOKS

PARK
ROW
BOOKS

Recycling programs
for this product may
not exist in your area.

ISBN-13: 978-0-7783-0913-0
ISBN-13: 978-0-7783-0998-7 (Library Exclusive Edition)

The Ambassador's Daughter

First published in 2013. This edition published in 2019.

ParkRowBooks.com
BookClubbish.com

Printed in U.S.A.

In loving memory of Dad.

THE AMBASSADOR'S DAUGHTER

The sun has dropped low beneath the crumbling arches of Lehrter Bahnhof as I make my way across the station. A sharp, late-autumn breeze sends the pigeons fluttering from the rafters and I draw my coat closer against the chill. The crowds are sparse this Tuesday evening, the platforms bereft of the usual commuter trains and their disembarking passengers. A lone carriage sits on the track farthest to the right, silent and dark.

I had been surprised by the telegram announcing Stefan's return by rail. There were hardly any trains since the Allies had bombed the lines. At least that's what the newspapers write— the defunct trains and the British naval blockade are the excuses given for everything, from the lack of new pipes to start the water running again—a problem that has forced us back outside as though it were a century ago—to the impossibility of getting fresh milk. Looking around the desolate station now, I almost believe the excuse.

Stefan's face appears in my mind. It was more than four years ago on this very platform that we said goodbye, the garland of asters I'd picked hung freshly around his neck. "Don't go," I pleaded a final time. Stefan was not cut out to fight—he had a round, gentle face, wide brown eyes that said he could never hurt anybody. But it was too late—he had gone down to the enlistment center two weeks earlier, ahead of any conscription, and come home with papers ordering him to report. The war was going to be quick, everyone said. The horse-mounted Serbs, with their swords, were no match for the Kaiser's tanks and planes. The fighting would be over in weeks, and all of the boys wanted a piece of the glory before it was gone.

I peer back over my shoulder past the closing kiosk, which gives off the smell of stale ersatz coffee, at the station doors, creaking open and closed with the wind. Someone more important than me should have been here to meet Stefan. He is a soldier, wounded in battle. More to the point, he is the only young man from our Jewish enclave in Berlin who had gone off to fight and come back at all. I don't know what I expected, not a marching band and reporters exactly, but perhaps a small delegation from the local war council. The once-proud veterans' group had been disbanded, though. No one wanted to be identified as a soldier now, to face the glares of reproach and the questions about why they had not gotten the job done.

Fifteen minutes pass, then twenty. I clutch tighter the fine leather gloves that I've managed to twist into a damp, wrinkled ball. Fighting the urge to pace, I start toward the station office to inquire if there is news of the next arrival. I navigate around a luggage trolley, which has been upended and abandoned midstation. My skirt catches on something and I pause, turning to free the hem. It is not a nail or board, but a filthy, long-haired man sitting on the ground, a fetid mass of bandages where his right leg had once been.

"*Bitte...*" a voice rasps as I jump backward. "I'm sorry to startle you." He is a soldier, too, or was, his tattered uniform barely recognizable. I fish a coin from my purse, trying not to recoil from the hand that reaches out for it. But inwardly, I blanch. Will Stefan look like this sorry creature?

I lift my head as a horn sounds long and low from the darkness beyond the edge of the station. A moment later a train appears, threading its way onto one of the tracks. It moves so slowly that it seems to have no engine at all, nudged instead by some slight tilt of the earth. Great clouds of steam billow from its funnel, filling the station. As I walk toward the platform, straining to see through the mist, my heart begins to pound.

The train grinds to a halt. The doors open with painstaking slowness and a few men spill out, some in uniform and others street clothes. I search those walking toward me for Stefan, knowing that he will not be among them.

When the platform has nearly cleared, a nurse pushes a wheelchair from one of the train carriages. I step forward, and then stop again. The chair does not contain Stefan, but an elderly man, hunched over so only the top of his bald head shows. The nurse struggles with the chair and as its rear wheels catch on the door, I hasten to help her.

The man in the chair uncurls, straightening slightly as I near. It is Stefan, I realize, biting my lip so hard I taste blood. A giant slash across the right side of his face from temple to chin combines with the lack of hair to make him almost unrecognizable. But the worst part is his arms, skeletal and shaky. My mind races as I try to fathom the horrors that could age a man decades in a few years.

Stefan gazes up with vacant, watery eyes, not speaking. "Hello, darling," I manage, bending to brush my lips against his papery cheek.

He reaches for me with a quivering hand. "Let's go home," he croaks, and as his fingers close around my wrist like cold death, I let out the cry I can hold back no longer.

My eyes fly open and I sit up in the darkness, still screaming.

PART ONE

PARIS, DECEMBER 1918

I cycle through the Jardin des Tuileries, navigating carefully around the slippery spots on the damp gravel path. The December air is crisp with the promise of snow and the bare branches of the chestnut trees bow over me like a procession of sabers. I pedal faster past the park benches, savoring the wind against my face and opening my mouth to gulp the air. A startled squirrel darts behind the base of a marble statute. My hair loosens, a sail billowing behind me, pushing me farther and faster, and for a moment it is almost possible to forget that I am in Paris.

The decision to come had not been mine. "I've been asked to go to the peace conference," Papa informed me unexpectedly less than a month ago. He had previously professed no interest in taking part in "the dog and pony show at Versailles," and had harrumphed frequently as he read the details of the preparations in the *Times*. "Uncle Walter thinks..." he added, as he so often did. I did not need to listen to the rest. My mother's older brother, an industrialist who had taken over the electron-

ics firm their father founded, could not attend the peace conference himself after contributing so much to the war machine.
He considered it important, though, to somehow have a voice
at the table, a presence before the Germans were formally summoned. So he had secured an invitation for Papa, an academic
who had spent the war visiting at Oxford, to advise the conference. It was important to be there before Wilson's ship arrived,
Papa explained. We packed up our leased town house hurriedly
and boarded a ferry at Dover.

Papa had not been happy to come, either, I reflect, as I reach
the end of the park and slow. The street is choked thick with
motorcars and lorries and autobuses, and a few terrified horses
trying to pull carriages amid the traffic. He had pulled forlornly
on his beard as we boarded the train in Calais, bound for Paris. It
was not just his reluctance to be torn from his studies at the university, immersed in the research and teaching he loved so, and
thrust into the glaring spotlight of the world's political stage. We
are the defeated, a vanquished people, and in the French capital
we loved before the war, we are now regarded as the enemy. In
England, it had been bad enough. Though Papa's academic status
prevented him from being interned like so many German men,
we were outsiders, eyed suspiciously at the university. I could
not wear the war ribbon as the smug British girls did when their
fiancés were off fighting, because mine was for the wrong side.
But outside of our immediate Oxford circle it had been rela-
tively easy to fade into the crowd with my accentless English.
Here, people know who we are, or will, once the conference
formally begins. The recriminations will surely be everywhere.

My skirts swish airily as I climb from the bike, thankfully free
of the crinolines that used to make riding so cumbersome. The
buildings on the rue Cambon sparkle, their shrapnel-pocked facades washed fresh by the snow. I stare up at the endless apartments, stacked on top of one another, marveling at the closeness
of it all, unrivaled by the most crowded quarters in London.

How do they live in such spaces? Sometimes I feel as though I am suffocating just looking at them. Growing up in Berlin, I'm no stranger to cities. But everything here is exponentially bigger—the wide, traffic-clogged boulevards, square after square grander than the next. The pavement is packed, too, with lines of would-be customers beneath the low striped awning of the cheese shop, and outside the chocolatier where the sign says a limited quantity will be available at three o'clock. A warm, delicious aroma portends the sweets' arrival.

A moment later, I turn onto a side street and pull the bike up against the wall, which is covered in faded posters exhorting passersby to buy war bonds. A bell tinkles as I enter the tiny bookshop. *"Bonjour."* The owner, Monsieur Batteau, accustomed to my frequent visits, nods but does not look up from the till.

I squeeze down one of the narrow aisles and scan the packed shelves hungrily. When we first arrived in Paris weeks earlier, it was books that I missed the most: the dusty stacks of the college library at Magdalen, the bounty of the stalls at the Portobello Road market. Then one day I happened upon this shop. Books had become a luxury few Parisians could afford during the war and there were horrible stories of people burning them for kindling, or using their pages for toilet paper. But some had instead brought them to places like this, selling them for a few francs in order to buy bread. The result is a shop bursting at the seams with books, piled haphazardly in floor-to-ceiling stacks ready to topple over at any moment. I run my hand over a dry, cracked binding with affection. The titles are odd—old storybooks mix with volumes about politics and poetry in a half-dozen languages and an abundance of war novels, for which it seems no one has the stomach anymore.

I hold up a volume of Goethe. It has to be at least a hundred years old, but other than its yellowed pages it is in good condition, its spine still largely intact. Before the war, it would have been worth money. Here, it sits discarded and unrecognized, a gem among the rubble.

"Pardon," Monsieur Batteau says a short while later, "but if you'd like to buy anything…" I glance up from the travelogue of Africa I'd been browsing. I've been in the shop scarcely thirty minutes and the light outside has not yet begun to fade. "I'm closing early today, on account of the parade."

"Of course." How could I have forgotten? President Wilson arrives today. I stand and pass Monsieur Batteau a few coins, then tuck the Goethe tome and the book on botany I'd selected into my satchel. Outside the street is transformed—the queues have dissipated, replaced with soldiers and men in tall hats and women with parasols, all moving in a singular direction. Leaving the bike, I allow myself to be carried by the stream as it feeds into the rue de Rivoli. The wide boulevard, now closed to motorcars, is filled with pedestrians.

The movement of the crowd stops abruptly. A moment later we surge forward again, reaching the massive octagon of the Place de la Concorde, the mottled gray buildings stately and resplendent in the late-afternoon sun. The storied square where Marie Antoinette and Louis XVI were executed is an endless mass of bodies, punctuated by the captured German cannons brought here after the armistice. The statues in the corners, each symbolizing a French town, have been covered in laurels.

The crowd pushes in behind me, onlookers from every side street attempting to pack the already choked space. I am surrounded by a sea of tall men, the damp wool from their coats pressing against my face, making it impossible to breathe. Close spaces have never suited me. Trying not to panic, I squeeze through to one of the cannons. I hitch my skirt and climb onto the wheel, the steel icy against my legs through my stockings. *"Pardon,"* I say to the startled young man already on top of the gun.

There are flags everywhere, I can see from my new vantage

point, banners unfurled from the balconies of the columned Hôtel de Crillon, American flags in the hands of the children. "Wilson the Just!" placards declare. A lane has been formed through the square, roped off with great swaths of sky-blue cloth to keep the crowd back. Airplanes, lower and louder than I've ever heard, roar overhead.

A few feet to the right of the cannon, a woman in a blue cape catches my eye. Nearly forty by the looks of her, she stands still in the feverish crowd. She is tall, her posture perfectly erect, with chestnut-brown hair piled upon her head. She is somehow familiar, though from where I cannot say. Abruptly, she turns and begins walking, swimming against the tide, slipping away from the gathering. Who would leave before Wilson's arrival? Surely there is nowhere else to be in the city now. I wonder fleetingly if she is ill, but her movements are calm and fluid as she disappears into the crowd.

The din grows to a roar. I turn my attention back to the square as a row of mounted soldiers canters into view, wearing the bright helmets of the Garde Republicaine. The horses raise their heads high, snorting great clouds of frost from their flared nostrils. The crowd pushes in, twisting the once-straight lane into a serpentine. I shudder as unseen guns erupt jarringly in the distance. Surely that is not a sound any of us needs to hear anymore.

Behind the horses, a procession of open carriages appears. The first bears a man in a long coat and top hat with a woman beside him. Though it is too far away for me to see, I can tell by the whoops that he is President Wilson. As the carriage draws closer and stops in front of the hotel, I recognize Wilson from the photos. He waves to the crowd as he climbs down. But his bespectacled face is solemn, as if seeing for the first time the hopes of so many that hang on his promises.

A minute later Wilson disappears into the hotel. The show quickly over, the onlookers begin to ebb, bleeding down the dozen or so arteries that lead from the square. I glimpse the woman in the blue cape, several yards away now, still fighting her way through the crowd. Impulsively, I hop down from the cannon, catching the hem of my skirt as I do. I free the material, then push toward her, weaving through narrow gaps, heedless now of the closeness as I follow the flash of blue like a beacon.

As I reach the street, I spy the woman fifty or so meters ahead, turning into the park where I'd been cycling an hour earlier. There is nothing unusual about that. But one would not have left Wilson's arrival for a stroll and her gait is purposeful, suggesting an errand more interesting than just fresh air. I push forward, following her into the park. A moment later, she turns off the main path into a smaller garden where I've not been before.

I pause. A gate, tall and tarnished, marks the entrance, elaborate lions carved into either side standing sentry. Ahead, the path is obscured by winter brush. *Turn back,* a voice seems to say. But the woman in blue has disappeared at a turn in the bend and I cannot resist following her.

I step through the gate and into the garden. A few meters farther, the path ends at a small, frozen pond, dividing to follow its banks on either side. I scan the deserted park benches, but do not see the woman. From beyond the bend comes the sound of laughter. I follow the path as it curves around the pond and it opens to reveal a wide expanse of frozen water, nestled in a cove of trees. A group of well-dressed young women in their late teens, perhaps a year or two younger than me, skate on the ice, chatting in loud, carefree voices.

Across the pond, something stirs against one of the trees. The woman in blue. Will she join the skaters? Maybe two decades older, she appears an odd fit, but the conference has brought together all sorts of unusual people, blurring the conventions and distinctions that might have separated them back home. The woman hangs in the shadows, like the witch out of a fairy tale,

watching the skaters raptly. Her gaze is protective and obser-
vant, a scientist studying a subject about which she really cares.

The skaters start for the bank and the woman in blue steps
back, disappearing. I consider following her farther, but the
sun has dropped low behind the trees, the early winter afternoon fading.

Twenty minutes later, having retrieved my bike, I reach the
hotel. Papa chose our lodgings at the tiny Hôtel Relais Saint-
Honoré carefully. Just across the river from the foreign ministry, it keeps him close to the conference proceedings while still
maintaining a bit of privacy. The lobby, with its cluster of red
velvet chairs in the corner, feels more like a parlor.

"*Mademoiselle,*" the desk clerk calls as I cross the lobby. I turn
back reluctantly. He holds out a letter toward me, between his
thumb and forefinger, as though the German postmark might
somehow be infected. I reach for it, my stomach sinking as I
eye the wobbly script.

I start for the elevator once more. As the doors open, I am
confronted unexpectedly by Papa and two men with swarthy
complexions and dark mustaches. "And if you look at the prewar boundaries..." Papa, speaking in French, stops midsentence
as he sees me. "Hello, darling. Gentlemen, may I present my
daughter? Margot, these are Signore DiVincenzo and Ricci of
the Italian delegation."

"A pleasure," I say. They nod and stare at me strangely. It is
my dress, soiled and torn at the hem from where I caught it on
the cannon, as well as my disheveled hair. I may quite possibly
smell, too, from my vigorous bike ride through the park.

But Papa does not seem to notice, just smiles a warm mix of
affection and pride. "I'll be up in a moment, my dear." It is not
just that he is an absentminded academic—Papa has always accepted me wholly as I am, with all of my rough spots and imperfections. He is not bothered by my unkempt appearance, any

more than I mind his predisposition to forgetting about meals or the days of the week.

The attendant closes the elevator gates and my stomach flutters in the queer way it always does as we ride upward to the third floor. I unlock the door to our suite, which consists of a bedroom each for Papa and me, adjoined by a sitting room. I go to the washroom and run the water in the large, claw-foot tub, then pour in some salts. As the tub fills, I remove my soiled dress and the undergarments that have etched themselves to my body. Crinolines may have gone out of style but corsets, unfortunately, are another matter. I turn off the tap and slip into the deep, warm bath, grateful to be enveloped by the steam.

Thinking of the unopened letter, Stefan's face appears. It is hard to remember exactly when we became romantically involved. He had always been present—a boy on the neighboring block and in the class a grade above mine across the hallway at school. We had played together often as children and he'd been beside me at my mother's funeral, taking my hand and helping me slip away from the crowded house after. One autumn morning when I was fifteen and reading on the front step of our home in Berlin, Stefan rode by on his bicycle, slowing but not quite stopping as he passed. This did not strike me as unusual—he had a paper route delivering the *Post* to the houses on our block that ordered it. Half an hour passed and he circled again. I looked up, my curiosity piqued. Stefan's house was around the corner on a nicer block than ours, twice as big but with a drooping roof and cracked steps in need of repair. I'd seen him on our street three or more times a day lately, though the paper came only daily.

"Wait," I called after him, standing up. He stopped abruptly, grabbing the handlebar to stop the bike from lurching sideways. "Did you want something?"

He climbed off the bike and set it down at the curb then walked over to me. There was something different about him. Though his strawberry-blond hair and pale skin were the same, he had started shaving, the peach fuzz that had once adorned his upper lip now a faint stubble. He had shot up in height and stood several inches above me and there was a new thickness to his arms.

"I was wondering," he said, "if you'd like to go to the movies."

I averted my eyes, caught off guard. I'd expected an invitation to join the football game the boys played Sundays in the park, though Tante Celia said I was getting too old for such things. But his tone was different now and when I turned back to him, I noticed that perspiration soaked his collar. He was nervous.

"Yes," I say hurriedly, wanting to ease his discomfort.

"I'll call for you tonight at seven." He stepped backward, nearly tripping over his bike before getting on and racing away.

The night at the movies was unremarkable, an American comedy, followed by an ice cream at the Eiscafé. After that day, Stefan became increasingly present, coming by the house after school, joining us for Sunday lunch at Uncle Walter's villa in Grunewald. One afternoon as we strolled around the lake behind the villa, I looked down at our hands, fingers intertwined, and realized that we were courting. Not that it was so very different from when we had just been friends. Stefan was unobtrusive and left me to my own devices. Being with him was rather like being with myself.

We were at Uncle Walter's for Sunday lunch when news of the war came. One of his aides rushed into the dining room and whispered in his ear and he broke the usual quiet by turning on the radio that sat on the mantelpiece. The men nodded with approval as Germany's declaration of war crackled over the airwaves. Our ally Austria's Archduke Franz Ferdinand had been assassinated, murdered in broad daylight by a heathen Serb. We had to take a stand.

Ten minutes later, I climb from the tub, still thinking of Stefan as I dry and put on a fresh dress. I could have gone back to Berlin after the war, insisted that Papa allow me to be with

Stefan as he recovers. But I had not. I swallow against my guilt. He is well cared for by his family. It is me he wants above all else, though, I can tell from his letters, which always speak excitedly of my return. I have sent packages of French jellies and other delicacies, but answering his letters is harder. What can I say to this man I hardly know anymore?

I rummage through my toiletries for some salve to relieve my hands, which have grown dry and chapped from the air here. It is my insistence on taking off my gloves too often, Tante Celia says. The items in my kit are few—some face powder, a single tube of pale pink lipstick for special occasions, a fragrance that Celia had given me for my birthday last year, too flowery for my taste.

By the time I emerge, Papa has returned, shuffling papers at the rolltop desk in the corner that doubles as his study over a glass of Pernod. Dinner, two plates covered by metal domes and a thick loaf of bread wrapped in cloth, sits unserved as is our preference.

"Papa," I say gently, nudging him from his work. I bring the candlesticks down from the mantelpiece as he pours the wine. *"Baruch atah Adonai..."*

"Celia is at a reception," he says without my asking when we've finished the blessings. I exhale slightly. I would not have been uncharitable and turned away kin with nowhere to go. But spending each Sabbath together is a tradition that Papa and I have observed wherever we have been in the world, bringing our silver Kiddush cup and candlesticks with us, and we continue it here in Paris. No matter how busy he is, Papa always stops what he is doing so that we can have a meal and talk, just the two of us.

I cut the crusty, still-warm loaf of bread. Living in the hotel, it is easy to forget about the shortages the outside world still endures. I hand Papa a piece and notice then that his face is pale. Though he is immaculately dressed and groomed as always, a trim sliver of silver hair circling his head, there are dark circles around his eyes. "Have you taken your medicine?" I ask gently. He gets so caught up in his work that he can forget to eat or sleep much less to take the pills that the doctor said are important for his heart condition. I've been reminding him for as long as I can remember.

Before he can answer, I sneeze once, then again. "It's the dry air," I say hastily, reaching for my handkerchief. Papa's brow wrinkles with consternation, now his turn to worry about me. Spanish flu, like the one that had taken my mother more than a decade ago, has been on the rise since autumn. Though I had also come down with the flu as a child, it had spared me like the angel of death in the Passover story, passing by as if lamb's blood had been painted on the door. I had labored with a fever for days. Then I'd awakened with a permanent crescent-shaped scar on my neck, a reaction to one of the medicines.

But this new flu strain is even more virulent, having taken twelve lives at Oxford alone before our departure. People talked endlessly about how to prevent it—wash out the nose with warm water and soda, wear garlic around the neck, drink a shot of whiskey before bedtime. Some whispered that the Germans unleashed it as a weapon of war, stopping just short of blaming me and Papa personally. "More likely," Papa said once, "it came across the Atlantic with the soldiers." In London, people had all but stopped going out. But here the parties continue on gaily, as if germs were some invention of the science fiction writers.

I sample a spoonful of the rich coq au vin. "I'm fine, really. Tell me about your day."

As we eat, Papa describes his meeting with the men from the Italian delegation, who are seeking his support for an independent Macedonia. "And then there are the West African colonies," he says, jumping topics as always with mercurial speed. "The French are going to put up a fight on granting independence. They want mandates instead."

"So it is only to be self-determination for some."

"*Liebchen*, we must be practical. One cannot change the entire world in just a few months."

Then what is the point of the conference? I wonder. "We have to work within the system," he adds, as if responding to my unspoken question. "Though I know you do not agree. Enough about my work," he says, as I clear the plates and set out coffee and apple cake. "How are you, my dear?"

"Fine. A bit restless."

"Oh? I thought you and Celia might enjoy some of the museums…" His voice trails off and he winces at the gulf between me and mother's sister, a woman he dearly wishes I would accept. "Perhaps if you had a brother or sister," he frets, as he has so many times over the years. Small families like ours are the exception rather than the rule but, for some reason not quite clear to me, siblings had not been possible.

I kiss his cheek. "I would not have cared to share you," I say, trying to assuage his guilt. It is the truth. The two of us have always been enough. I see then our Sabbath meals as a tableau, a scene that has played itself out in various cities over the years. "And I'm fine, really. The parties are all well and good, but the women are just silly." I stop, hearing myself complaining again.

"Would you be happier outside the city?" Papa asks.

I contemplate the question. I have always felt freest when close to nature, like on the hiking trips we took when I was a child. Papa, despite being bookish, had an amazing capacity for the outdoors, an ability to navigate the densest forest without a compass, to find fresh water and sense the weather that was coming. We would climb high with a day's food in our packs and stay in the cabins that populated the high hills, reaching the next before sundown.

But Paris, while cramped, has a certain energy. And I don't want to be exiled to some boring suburb with Tante Celia. "I don't know. I don't think so, anyway."

It isn't the city itself that I dislike, I decide as we eat dessert. I came here every spring as a child, shopping the fine boutiques of Faubourg Saint-Honoré with my mother until Papa joined us at the end of the day for cakes at one of the patisseries. I'd even dreamed of one day studying at the Sorbonne.

No, it's Paris *now* that I hate. On the eve of the conference, the city is bursting at the seams with journalists and delegates from every conceivable cause and country. Hotels empty since before the war have been aired out, their rooms hastily refreshed to accommodate everyone who has come to the show. I don't mind those who have cause to be here, the stuffy clusters of suited men who will decide the future of the world, the scrappy delegates from countries seeking to be born. But the hangers-on, the socialites and doyennes that have come to provide the parties and other window dressing, having stifled Paris to the choking point.

"Well, the question will be out of our hands at some point. When the Germans arrive," he says. My brow wrinkles. We *are* the Germans. "The official delegation, I mean, we'll be expected to go out to Versailles where they are to be housed."

I consider this new bit of information. The conference proceedings are being held in Paris, but the Germans will be housed outside in Versailles. The site where the Germans had imposed their draconian peace terms on France a half-century earlier, it is now where we are to get our just deserts. "Are the conference proceedings to move out there when the delegation arrives?"

"Not that I'm aware."

"But one would think, if the Germans are to participate in the conference that they should be near the meetings..."

"One would think." He pauses for a sip of coffee. "One would think that they would have invited the German delegation here for the early months of the conference if they were really to participate."

How could one negotiate peace without the other side at the table? "Are you familiar with the delegation?" I ask.

"Oh, the usual sorts. Rantzau—he's the new foreign minister—

as well as the defense minister and the ambassador, of course, Uncle Walter's old nemesis." The men in power form a very tight club, raised in the same circles and educated at the same schools. It was a club to which Papa had never wanted to belong, but now he had found himself drawn back in by the conference. "There's a younger fellow, too, a military captain, but I can't recall his name."

"Are they bringing anyone with them? Families, I mean?"

Papa shakes his head. "Hotel accommodations are quite limited in Versailles." It was unusual for delegates, even from the victorious countries, to bring their wives and children. "You still haven't told me what you've been up to today, other than avoiding Tante Celia."

I consider mentioning the woman in the blue cape, but even in my head it sounds inconsequential, my own interest silly. "I saw Wilson's arrival today," I say instead.

"Oh?"

"The crowd was most receptive."

"They have such high hopes. The Fourteen Points, self-determination, a new world order..." He shakes his head. "Wilson is idealistic. It's like the notion in Judaism—*tikun olam* means, quite literally, to repair the world. That's what he is trying to do."

"You don't think he will be able to do it."

"I think it isn't that simple." He picks up his pipe, but does not light it, instead waving it like a pointer in a lecture hall. "Take self-determination for example. What does that mean? Who is the self—a nationality, a religious group or something altogether different?" He jabs at the air in front of him. "Do I believe they will make a difference or reshape the world? I don't know. The world will never go back to what it was—kaisers and czars and kings, but the question is whether we can make something better in its place. I believe the world will be a better place for the trying." He sighs. "Anyway, you'll get to see a bit more of Wilson at the welcoming reception tomorrow night."

I cock my head. "I mentioned it to you last week." The social calendar had been so full with stuffy affairs, I'd stopped listening, rather allowing Papa and Celia to lead me where needed. "It should be quite the occasion."

I groan. "Must I attend?"

"I'm afraid so. It is an important event and it wouldn't do for us to miss it. You've heard from Stefan?" he asks, changing the subject again. Papa has allowed me much liberty as a young woman, but on this one point he pushes. He is nearly seventy now, and eager to see me settled, rather than left alone in the world.

"I have." I do not admit that I've not opened today's letter, instead focusing on things that Stefan wrote last week. "They've apparently got a good deal of snow in Berlin, much more so than here."

He nods. "Uncle Walter said the same. I'm sure you are eager to return to him. Stefan that is, not Uncle Walter." I smile at this. My mother's brother has never been a favorite of mine. "How is he?" Papa asks, an unmistakable note of fondness to his voice. Papa always liked Stefan—their gentle personalities were well suited to each other. Stefan did not share Papa's razor-sharp intellect, but he always listened with rapt attention to Papa talk about the latest article he was writing.

"He's working very hard at rehabilitation. He's even managed to stand up a few times."

"That's remarkable. He wasn't expected to live, so to get out of a chair is really something. Perhaps he'll even get around with a walker someday. What an extraordinary young man."

A pang of jealousy shoots through me. In some ways, Stefan is the son Papa never had. Not that Stefan could follow Papa into academia. The Osters were a once well-to-do banking family that had fallen on hard times. Stefan, as the oldest of four children and the only son, has been expected to somehow restore the family to a better station. We had hoped that he might join

Uncle Walter and run one of the plants. But imagining him trying to navigate around the heavy machinery of the factory floor with a walker seems quite impossible now.

"He is doing really well," I say, but something nags at me. "Do you think he is damaged, beyond his legs, I mean? His letters just feel a little off." Papa wrinkles his brow, as if asking me to say more. But I can't quite articulate my concern.

"It's the war, darling. Give him time." I nod. Stefan is such a good man. My heart breaks for the things he has seen and suffered. I cannot help but wonder, though, whether he will ever be whole again.

"Hopefully the conference will move quickly and we can return to Berlin soon so you can see him."

I swallow over the lump that has formed in my throat. "Hopefully."

"Good night, dear." He walks to the desk and reaches for a stack of papers. Despite his slight size and quiet demeanor, Papa has always been the strongest man I've known. Not just strong: brave. Once when I was about six we'd been walking our German shepherd, Gunther, through the Tiergarten when a large stray confronted us, blocking the path ahead. My first instinct had been to leap back in fear. But Papa moved forward placing himself between gentle Gunther and the snarling beast. In that moment, I understood what it took to be a parent, in a way I might never quite be able to manage myself.

He has given up so much to raise me. After Mother died, it would have been logical for him to leave my upbringing to Tante Celia or governesses. But instead he had cut short his schedule at the university, declining to teach in the late afternoon and evening, and taking his work home so he could read alongside me. He had made me a part of his journeys and declined the opportunities where he could not because the destinations were too far-flung or the travel unsafe or good schools not available. There were times, I could tell, that conversation was too much and he was eager to escape into his work from the harshness of everyday life and the pain that he carried. He made sure, though, that I was never alone.

But now, hunched over the desk, he appears vulnerable. I am seized with the urge to reach down and hug him. Instead, I place a hand on his shoulder. He looks up, startled by my unexpected touch. We have never been very physically affectionate. "Good night, Papa."

I return the dinner tray to the hall, then carry the lamp to my room so that Papa can work in the sitting room uninterrupted. I pull out the volume of Goethe I'd purchased from the bookseller and run my hand over the cover. Stefan would love it—or would have, once upon a time. We had always shared a deep passion for books and our families were frequently amused to find us sitting together under a tree in the garden or in the parlor, reading silently side by side, each lost in our own world. But is he even reading now? And would the book, with its references to death and suffering, just make things worse for him? I set it down on the table.

Stefan's letter sits on the dresser. Reluctantly, I open it.

Dearest Margot—

I can tell from the almost illegible script that he has tried to write himself this time instead of having the nurse do it.

I hope that this letter finds you well. Exciting news: Father is modifying the cottage and building an extension for us so we can live there after the wedding.

I cringe. Stefan is immobilized in a wheelchair—of course he cannot return to the Berlin town house with its many narrow stairs. I recall the Osters' vacation cottage, a two-room house on the edge of a maudlin lake, more than an hour from the city. Are we really to live in the middle of nowhere? How will he earn a living?

I finger the ring that Stefan gave me before leaving for the front. I should have gone to be with him, a voice inside me nags for the hundredth time. I had good reasons for not going—first the war and later the railway lines and now Papa being summoned to Paris. There were ways I might have gone, though, if I pushed hard enough. But I hadn't, instead embracing the excuses like a mantle, shielding myself from the truth that inevitably awaits. I slip the ring from my finger and put it in my pocket.

I fold the letter and put it back into the envelope without reading further.

A scrap of paper falls from the envelope and flutters to the floor. A photograph. I pick it up, wishing he had not sent it. He meant it as a good thing, sitting up in the wheelchair and smiling as if to say, *Look how far I've come.* In some ways it is better than the man I see in my nightmares, but his face is a stranger's to me, the hollow eyes confirming everything I fear about our future together.

Perhaps being in Paris is not the worst thing, after all.

A s we ascend the marble staircase to the ballroom at the Hôtel de Crillon, my impression is one of white—wreaths of lilies and roses climbing the columns, great swaths of snowy tulle draped from the balconies above. "I'll just be a moment," Papa says, heading in the direction of the cloakroom with our coats. I take the glass of wine that is offered to me by one of the servers, then step out of the flow of the crowd. The reception is like all of the other parties we have attended since coming to Paris, only magnified tenfold, the pond of gray-haired men in black tuxedos now a sea. A handful of women in expensive gowns, the deep maroon and dusky-rose shades that are the fashion this year, cling to the periphery. The savory smell of the hors d'oeuvres mixes with a cacophony of floral perfumes and cigarette smoke.

The orchestra at the front of the room breaks from the waltz it had been playing midstanza and bursts into a robust rendition of "The Star-Spangled Banner." The guests hush, turning expectantly toward the entrance and there is a low murmur as President and Mrs. Wilson enter. The crowd parts to let them through. Closer now, he is taller than I thought, with a grimly set jaw.

A man I recognize from other occasions as the American ambassador, Stan Stahl, steps forward to greet the Wilsons. But before he can reach them, an Oriental boy, no older than myself, cuts in front of him and approaches the president. The boy, who wears not the uniform of a formal server but the white shirt and apron of the kitchen staff, holds an envelope outstretched in his shaking hand. An audible gasp runs through the ballroom.

One of the guards flanking Wilson moves to place himself between the president and the boy, but Wilson shakes him off. "He means no harm." Wilson takes the letter and opens it. "Thank you," he says, as solemnly as though he is speaking with one of the other Allied leaders. Apparently satisfied, the kitchen boy bows, then turns and disappears through one of the servers' doors. Yelling can be heard from the other side.

What does the letter say, I wonder. The spectacle over, the crowd closes in to greet the Wilsons. I scan the room for Papa and find him in the corner, shanghaied by someone, undoubtedly a delegate wanting to secure his support for a resolution. Now that the conference is about to begin in earnest, those lobbying for certain issues have dropped all pretense of subtlety, haranguing Papa and others in positions of influence nonstop for their support. I don't mind his being delayed—it is easier to be anonymous on my own, to slip back among the draperies and observe rather than participate. I only hope he will be able to extricate himself at some point. My curiosity at seeing Wilson satisfied, I am eager to escape back to the hotel, out of this starchy gown that Tante Celia selected for me and back to the novel I'd been reading.

The orchestra begins playing a waltz. Watching couples swirl around the floor, a memory flashes through my mind of a night not long after Stefan and I had started courting when he had come to the house to escort me to a school dance. He had arrived too early and as I brushed my hair I could hear him talking with Papa in the parlor below, their conversation somehow more awkward than usual. I came downstairs a few minutes later and Stefan's eyes widened at the sight of me in my pink party dress. His hair was freshly trimmed and he wore a crisp white shirt I had not seen before.

"Here." He held out a small corsage. As he helped me pin it on awkwardly, I smelled the aftershave he had surely borrowed from his father. We did not speak on the short ride to school. Everything was more formal, the way he held doors for me and helped me from the car, and I disliked the stiffness that interfered with our usual easy company. The school cafeteria had been decorated with crepe paper and vases of fresh wildflowers that could not quite mask the lingering smell of sauerkraut and wurst lunches that had worn its way into the cinder-block walls over the years.

As I see Stefan's face in my mind, an unexpected flash of tenderness wells up inside me. He cared for me in a way that no one ever had except Papa—and I liked that. Before him, my world had always been solitary, with my mother gone and Papa ensconced in his work. Stefan's near-constant presence made me feel somehow less alone. But I am longing for the boy I left four years ago. Even if I returned to Berlin this minute, things would be different.

My foot throbs, reminding me of the cracked dress shoe that I've neglected for months to replace. I duck into one of the side salons off the main ballroom, where a handful of people cluster around small tables with tiny white candles at the center, and sink into an empty chair by a potted fern. In the far corner, an older woman sits at a piano, head bowed, eyes closed as she plays.

When the pianist lifts her head I gasp slightly. She is the woman in blue who fled Wilson's arrival, the one I'd followed from the square. That is why she looked familiar—I have seen her playing at a handful of the other gatherings since we arrived. I stand and start toward the piano. She is not beautiful, I decide instantly. The bridge of her nose is curved and her eyes set close, giving her a hawkish appearance. But her cheekbones are high and her hair upswept, making the harsh somehow regal.

I watch, fascinated. It is unusual to see a female musician, or a woman doing anything other than accompanying a man on his arm at these affairs. Of course, there are the cooks and maids and such, but the woman's high-collared silk blouse and straight posture does not bespeak the serving class. She plays with her whole body, shoulders swaying side to side as her hands traverse the keys, partners in a dance.

She finishes playing and the last note resonates throughout the salon, but the guests are too engrossed in their conversations to notice or applaud. "That was lovely," I remark. The woman glances up and I wait for her to thank me, or at least smile. But a flicker of something close to annoyance crosses her face. "Mahler, wasn't it?" I say.

She blinks. "Yes, from his *Sixth Symphony*." Her voice is low and husky, just short of masculine, and her French is accented slightly, hailing from somewhere eastern I cannot place.

"One of my favorites, though I haven't heard it since before the war. I didn't think they would have you play it here." My words come out more bluntly that I'd intended.

"Music is not political."

I want to tell her that everything is political now, from the wine that is served (always the chardonnay, never the Riesling) to the color of the tablecloths (a patriotic French blue). But I do not know her well enough to get into a debate.

"I play what I want," the woman adds. She adjusts the thick chignon of hair, the chestnut color broken by a few strands of gray. "It's not as if they pay me."

"Oh?"

The woman shakes her head. "My parents won't allow it. They think it would be unseemly to take money." It sounds odd, a woman who must be close to forty listening to her parents. But I will always care about Papa's approval.

She points through the doorway toward a cluster of silver-haired men in the main ballroom. "My father. He's a diplomat."

"Mine, as well." I leap too eagerly at the commonality, ignoring the fact that Papa's title is in fact only a formality, conferred to credential him to the conference.

"Mine is with the Polish delegation." My excitement fades. The Germans and Poles had been on opposite sides of the war, enemies. We could not, in fact, have less in common. "I'm Polish, or will be if they ever get around to making us a country again," she adds. I nod. Poland had been partitioned among Germany, Austria and Russia for the better part of a half century. "Hard to see how they'll have the time with all of this socializing." She gestures toward the larger gathering. "You're German, aren't you?"

I flush. I had worked so hard to remove any trace of an accent from both my French and English. But a musician with a trained ear, the woman can hear the slight flaws in my speech and discern their origin. "Yes." I hold my breath, waiting some sign of disapproval.

Her expression remains neutral. "Or at least you are until they get around to making Germany no longer a country," she says wryly.

I cringe at this. It is the great unanswered question of the peace conference, whispered about in the salons, debated openly in the bars and parties: What will happen to Germany? "Back home they believe that it will be a fair peace."

"Yes, they have to, don't they? I'm Krysia Smok," she says, extending a hand.

"Margot Rosenthal. A pleasure." I want to mention the fact that I have seen her before but that would beg the question of what she was doing in the park, too intrusive of someone I've just met.

"I didn't think the German delegation was coming until late spring," she remarks.

"They aren't. That is, we aren't part of the delegation. My father is a professor, he teaches at Oxford at the moment..." I can hear myself babbling now. "And he's detailed to the conference, not the delegation." I study her face, wondering if she is impressed by the distinction.

From behind the column comes tittering laughter. "Really, even the kitchen staff have political aims," a woman comments in English. "Are we to have soufflé tonight or a political rally?"

"They say the Japanese will demand a statement of racial equality, too," her companion replies in a hushed tone, as though saying it aloud might make it real.

"Americans," Krysia scoffs as they walk away. "They think they're so progressive. And yet women in the States still do not have the right to vote." I consider her point. Women were only given the vote in Germany a year ago and I haven't been back to have the chance.

Papa is at my side then. "Darling, I'm sorry to have left you. I was waylaid by a Dutchman."

"It's quite fine. Did you hear about the kitchen boy?"

"Yes, Indochinese, by the sound of things, and seeking Wilson's support for some sort of autonomy."

"Do you think he lost his job?"

"I think," Papa replies gently, "that he did what he set out to do at the conference and..." He stops midsentence and turns to Krysia. "Forgive my manners." Papa is not like some of the men at the conference, seeing through the staff as though they are not here. "I'm Margot's father, Friedrich Rosenthal."

"Papa, this is Krysia Smok."

She tilts her head. "Rosenthal, the writer?"

He shifts, uncomfortable with the attention. "I've written a few academic books, yes."

"I'm more acquainted with your articles." How is Krysia, a pianist from Poland, familiar with my father? "I particularly enjoy your work on the interplay between the suffragist cause and socialism," she adds, animated now.

Papa bows slightly. "I'm humbled. And I'd be delighted to discuss the subject with you further if you'd like to come around for tea tomorrow. For now, I must excuse myself. Margot, I'm afraid I need to stay to speak with one of the British representatives after this." He pats my cheek. "The car will be out front for you. Don't wait up for me. I shall see you in the morning."

When he has gone, I turn back to Krysia. "How do you know my father's work?"

"His writings on the advancement of women in the communist system have been very helpful to the suffragist cause."

"Papa isn't a communist," I reply quickly, though I've never read Papa's work myself.

She doesn't hear me, or pretends not to. "I detest pure academics. But your father, well, he was quite active in the protests in his day." Papa out of his study is an animal removed from natural habitat; it is difficult to fathom him on the streets, chanting angrily like the Serb nationalists in front of the foreign ministry on the Quai d'Orsay. There is much about him, I realize, that I do not know.

Her gaze travels the room and stops on the catering manager who has entered the salon and is staring at us. The reception is winding down and Krysia is meant to be playing as the guests leave, not talking. "It was a pleasure meeting you," she says, shuffling through her sheet music.

"Come to tea tomorrow," I press. I'm lonely for company beyond the superficial chatter of the parties and I've enjoyed these few brief moments of conversation more than any since our arrival.

She shakes her head, demurring. "Is it because we are German?"

"Of course not." Her tone is sincere. "I have a prior obligation. Another time."

"Here." I reach into my pocket and pull out one of the calling cards that Tante Celia had insisted I need. They seemed so frivolous at the time, but I'm glad to have them now. "In case you change your mind."

"Thank you." Krysia puts the card in her pocket in a way that tells me she will never use it.

She resumes playing and I walk from the salon, deflated. In the main ballroom, the gathering has begun to dissipate. I make my way to the cloakroom and when I return, the piano bench is empty.

Outside, I scan the line of cars and find ours. There is a dampness to the frosty night air that I can almost taste. As I get in, I see Krysia walking from the hotel with her parents. She kisses them each on the cheek and starts in the other direction, her blue cape radiant in the sea of black. I watch as she slips away, quiet as a cat, then ducks into the alleyway before reaching the boulevard.

Where is she going alone at night? It is after ten and there is still a curfew. I climb from the car once more. "I'll make my own way," I say to the driver, shutting the door before he can protest.

I weave my way through the departing crowd, breaking free and turning down the alleyway where I last saw Krysia. The street is dark and I fear that I have lost her, but I hear footsteps ahead and quicken my pace. A moment later the passageway opens onto a wide avenue and Krysia appears in a yellow pool of streetlight. She moves swiftly, almost seeming to fly beneath the billowing cape. I struggle to stay back far enough so as not to be noticed.

Krysia reaches the corner and stops. Then she turns, facing

me before I have time to hide. "You again!" I freeze, an animal trapped. "Are you following me?"

"No—" I protest too quickly.

"I was joking, of course. You're staying in the area?"

"My hotel is nearby, but I am going to visit some friends." I regret the lie as soon as I have spoken, the notion that I would be calling on anyone at this hour of the night hardly plausible.

She does not respond but continues walking, shrugging her shoulders in a way that suggests I am welcome to join her. We travel wordlessly along the rue Royale, the swish of her cape giving off a faint hint of lilac perfume.

"Did you come to Paris before the war?" I ask, hoping she will not mind conversation. My breath rises in tiny puffs of frost.

"Yes. There was not so much work for pianists in southern Poland." She unfurls detail a bit at a time, like a kite string, or thread off a spool. "When the war broke out I found myself stranded here." There is something deeper beneath the surface, a longing in her voice that belies a part of the story she is not willing to share with me. "But I miss home terribly. Do you?"

"I suppose." I have not until just this moment thought about it. Our town house in Berlin's Jewish quarter is not large— even as a child, I could touch both walls of my bedroom at the same time if I stretched my arms out sideways. But it is cozy and made beautiful by all of my mother's decorations, the floral trim and slipcovers that Papa never would have thought to do himself and that he has left untouched since she died. There's a tiny garden with a fountain in the back, a park down the road for strolling. It's been years since we've actually lived there for any period of time, though. "We've been abroad for so long. Now home is wherever Papa and I land with a place to lay our heads and books to read."

She smiles. "The vagabond lifestyle." We reach the steps of the metro, a dark cavernous hole I've passed before but never entered. Krysia stops. "Your friends," she says suddenly. For a moment I am confused. She is referring to my alibi for being out walking, the fact that we've long since left the neighborhood I purported to be visiting. "You really were following me." It is not a question.

"I just…" I falter.

"What is it that you want from me?"

I try to come up with another excuse and then decide to be honest. "Company. I'm bored," I say, my voice dangerously close to a whine.

Krysia arches an eyebrow. "Bored, in Paris?"

My statement must sound ludicrous. "Not with the city, exactly. It's all of the parties and silly gossip."

"So don't go. Play your own game. No good can come from idleness. Come."

The metro steps are damp and slick and I take care not to fall as I follow her down. Below, my senses are assaulted by the dank odor of garbage and waste. I avert my eyes from a pair of rats scurrying along the tracks, fighting the urge to yelp. The ground rumbles beneath our feet and a long wooden train rolls into the station, looking not unlike the trolley cars that travel the streets above. The car we board is empty but for an old man sleeping at the other end. It begins to move swiftly through the darkness. I try to act normal, as though accustomed to this strange mode of travel.

"I saw you at the arrival parade for Wilson," I say, unable to hold back. Krysia stares vaguely over my shoulder and for a minute I doubt my memory, wondering if the woman at the parade had been someone else. "You left in the middle," I press. The statement comes out abrupt and intrusive.

"I had somewhere to be." She does not elaborate.

Two stops later the doors open and I follow Krysia back up onto the street, breathing in the fresh air deeply to clear the dankness from my lungs. We are on the Left Bank now, with its narrow, winding streets. This is Paris as I knew it as a girl, buildings leaning close, whispering secrets to one another. Parisians, still in the habit of conserving from the war, have shuttered and darkened their houses and only every other streetlight splutters in an attempt to save electricity. A low fog has rolled in from the river now, swirling eerily around us.

A few minutes later, we reach the boulevard du Montparnasse. The wide avenue is as bright as midday, light spilling forth from beneath the café awnings. A door to a café opens and a woman's high tinkling laugh cascades over the music. *La Closerie des Lilas* reads the painted sign on the glass window of the café, smaller print advertising the billiards and rooms available on the floors above.

I follow Krysia inside, where she weaves through a maze of tables without waiting to be seated, steering toward the high mahogany bar with red leather stools. Shelves filled with bottles climb to the ceiling of the mirrored wall behind it. The room is warm and close, plumed with clouds of cigarette smoke. Ragtime music from an unseen gramophone plays lively in the background, mixing with boisterous conversation in French, German and a handful of other languages.

Behind the bar, a skinny brown-haired boy, eighteen or nineteen maybe, with coal-black eyes, stacks beer steins. Feeling his gaze follow me, I flush. I'm still not used to the kind of attention young women receive in Paris, so much more admiring and less veiled than in London or Berlin.

We reach an alcove behind the bar, not quite set off enough from the main part of the café to be its own room, a few tables with an odd assortment of chairs thrown haphazardly around them. A half-decorated Christmas tree lists in the corner.

Krysia pulls up two chairs to one of the tables, where a handful of men are gathered. I await the introductions that do not come, then sit down beside her. The marble table is littered with overflowing ashtrays and empty wine bottles and an untouched carafe of still water. Two candles in a brass dish burn at the center, melting together in a molten pool. The only woman, Krysia looks out of place in this group of rough men. But she chats easily, as if among family. The gathering crackles with conversation. Across from me two men are debating how the war will be remembered in the literature, while to my left there is a lively discussion about the future of Palestine. Ideas rise like champagne bubbles around me and I struggle to keep up, to grasp one before it is displaced by the next.

"Is Marcin coming?" one of the men asks in accented French. His sideburns, wide and deep, lash onto his cheeks like daggers. He wears a red silk scarf around his neck, knotted jauntily.

Krysia shakes her head. "He's playing a wedding at Chartres."

The man snorts. "That's a disgrace."

"One has to eat," Krysia replies vaguely, then turns to me. "Marcin is my husband."

"Oh." Krysia seems so solitary and stoic, an island unto herself. It is hard to imagine her needing or living with anyone.

"He plays cello."

An older man, fiftyish and portly with a shock of white hair, pads over to the table and places fresh, foaming mugs of beer in front of us. "She's too modest." His vowels are rounded, as though his cheeks were full, a Russian accent unmuted by his time in France. "Marcin is one of the foremost cellists in Europe," the man informs me. He begins twirling a coin between the knuckles of his left hand, index finger, middle, ring, pinky, and then back again without stopping. His fat fingers, each a sizable sausage, are surprisingly nimble. "He should be playing filled concert halls, not background music for wedding guests munching on canapés and cheap wine."

The red-scarfed man beside me raises his glass. "Hear, hear." His words are slurred.

Krysia pats the arm of the man who has handed us our drinks. "Margot, this principled fellow is Ignatz Stein." I am surprised to hear her introduce the barman as a friend. "He owns this place." I take a sip too large, caught off guard by the full, cold taste of hops, carrying me back to the fields of Bavaria in late harvest when Papa and I hiked there years earlier. The extra liquid spills out of the corner of my mouth. I reach for a napkin and, seeing none, furtively blot at the moisture with my sleeve, hoping no one will notice. Krysia turns to the man seated beside her. "And this is Deo Modigliani."

"The artist?" I cannot help but blurt out, awestruck. I have studied his work, seen it in the finest galleries and museums. Yet here he is sitting in this nondescript café and drinking beer like everyone else. I've heard of this Paris, artists and writers gathering in the Montparnasse cafés to drink and share ideas. It exists beneath the surface, separate and secret from the pomp and formality of the conference and everyday life overhead.

Krysia does not answer but turns her attention to a debate on the future of Alsace-Lorraine that has heated up at the far end of the table. "Surely the territory will be returned to France now." I have not been introduced to the man who is speaking.

"If the Americans and the French don't tear one another apart first," Krysia interjects. I nod. The conference is just days old and things had reportedly gotten quite contentious already.

"But the Americans…"

"It is quite easy to have views from halfway around the globe." Her observation is unfair and yet at the same time true. The Americans came to help with the fighting and they are here to help make the peace. Yet they will return home, largely unscathed by what is decided here. So why are they at the center of it?

She continues, "If the conference is to be democratic, then why is so much being done by the Big Four behind closed doors? And where is Russia?" I watch in awe as Krysia speaks her mind in a forthright way, mixing logic and passion in the way of a woman long accustomed to debate. Holding court, she appears ethereal, bathed in light. I have seldom heard women offer up opinions and have never seen them received with such respect. There is a keen intensity to the way she speaks, her voice low and melodic and commanding, that makes her somehow beautiful.

"Did you hear a kitchen boy from the Orient sent Wilson a petition for his country's freedom?" Modigliani offers, changing the subject.

"Ask Margot about it," Krysia says, gesturing toward me with her head. "I was playing in one of the salons, but she saw the whole thing."

"You were at the Wilson reception?" The barman, Ignatz, comes up to my chair, regarding me with newfound interest.

"Yes, my father is with the conference."

"Her father is Friedrich Rosenthal," Krysia adds with emphasis. Heads nod in recognition.

"Your father doesn't write under a nom de plume," Ignatz observes, still twirling a coin.

"No, why should he?"

"I think Ignatz only meant that not every writer has the courage to speak of such things in his own name," Krysia clarifies. *Courage.* I recall the news from back home in Berlin, the violence that had erupted as a result of the civil unrest. Politicians has been shot for no more than their views. Could Papa and the other academics be in similar danger?

Modigliani leans in, his artist eyes soulful. "And what are you, *ma petite?*"

"Deo," Krysia warns in a low voice, protective like an older sister.

I am uncertain how to answer. "I'm engaged," I offer. My response is met with blank stares around the table.

"I believe," Krysia prompts gently, "that he was asking what you are planning to do now that the war is over?" Krysia's clarification is of little help. Before the war, my future was clear—marriage to Stefan, the biggest question being whether to live with Papa indefinitely or save for an apartment of our own. That world is gone now. But still the old ties and expectations remain.

"I don't know," I confess finally. The room is warm and wobbly from the beer.

"How exciting." I search for sarcasm in her voice and find none. "Starting fresh, reborn out of the ashes. The war was horrible, but it has shaken things up, given each of us a chance to stake a claim for what she wants."

"They say that Kolchak's Whites are making gains at Perm..." Ignatz offers, turning the topic to Russia. I sit back, grateful to no longer be the focus. But I find the topic unsettling. Russia has become a wild land since the czar was taken down, his whole family murdered. The Bolsheviks are in charge, or at least most think so—the country has largely been cut off from the West and so only rumors trickle out.

"Papa says we need to engage with the Whites as well as the Bolsheviks," I say, speaking up in spite of my own desire to remain inconspicuous. I fight to keep the uncertainty from my voice. But I sound childish, falling back on my father's opinions as if I have none of my own. "That is, perhaps we can help them to form some sort of coalition government..." I falter, unaccustomed to the eyes on me. Even the dark-eyed boy behind the bar appears to be listening with interest. I have discussed politics with Papa all my life, but never in a public forum such as this.

"What else does Papa say?" Ignatz asks from where he stands behind Krysia, a note of chiding to his voice.

"That the conference will move quickly to act before Russia can subsume too much territory." I speak quickly now, too far gone to stop. "With a quick vote on recognition of the new Croat-Serb state, for example. The vote is to take place as soon as the conference opens. And it seems that Wilson and Lloyd Georg are favorably predisposed to a Pan-Slavic nation. But Clemenceau is likely to side with Orlando and the Italians and hold it up..."

"They can vote all they want. Lenin will not compromise on any sort of coalition," Krysia remarks. She is talking about the Bolshevik leader not with the same fear I've heard at the parties, but with a kind of hushed reverence.

"You're communist?" I ask, recalling her description of Papa's work.

"I detest labels," she replies coolly. "I'd say socialist, really, though there's nothing wrong with communism as an ideal."

Thinking of the stories I've read about Russia, I shudder. "It's anarchy. They destroy businesses and overthrow leaders. They murdered the czar's whole family, even the children."

"That's the problem with Germans," one of the men scoffs derisively. "No stomach for reform. As Lenin says, revolution will never come to Berlin because the Germans would want to queue up for it."

"It's a shame that social change has to be accomplished by such violent means," Krysia says before I can respond to the insult. "Though the previous rulers were hardly saints. Really, the ideas behind communism of equal contributions and distributions are good. But they're being corrupted for power just like any other ideology."

One of the men snorts. "Bah! The socialists are too weak to act on their principles. We can sit around here talking all night and it will do nothing. We need to do something."

"Raoul..." Krysia says, and there is an undercurrent of warning to her voice. "We should go," she adds abruptly.

I've offended her, I fret. But the gathering has begun to break up, and around us everyone is gathering their coats and reaching for their pockets for a few loose francs. I picture guiltily Papa's allowance money folded neatly in my purse. Should I offer to pay? Only Modigliani sits motionless. "Am I to accept another drawing from you?" Ignatz asks him chidingly. I notice then that the wall behind the bar is covered with artwork, framed paintings and hastily pinned sketches to pay for food and drink. The artist does not answer, but stares into the distance, his eyes heavy lidded.

"You'll see him home?" Krysia asks Ignatz, then turns to me without waiting for a response. "Spirits help the creative soul to a point," she says in a low voice, as we make our way through the main room of the café. The crowd has ceded to the curfew, leaving beer bottles and overflowing ashtrays in their wake. "And then they destroy it."

"Monsieur Modigliani, will he be all right?"

She nods. "Stein will kick him out at some point. Otherwise a good number of them would stay all night—these days, it's cheaper than heating their flats."

"So many artists. I'd heard of such things, but I had no idea..."

"They suffered during the war like everyone else with lack of food and money. But now they're trying to recapture the lost time, the frenzy of life. And art is such a solitary business. Coming together like this gives them a sense of companionship. Though with all of the drinking and such, it's a marvel they get any work done at all."

Outside the night is icy. "What did that man, Raoul, I believe you called him, mean about 'doing something'?"

She hesitates. "Nothing. They all like to talk big when they drink. What could a few artists do, anyway? It's just that the way the peace conference is being conducted, it will still only be justice for some, a gift from the powerful if they choose to be beneficent. But true freedom is innate—given not by man but from God herself." My jaw drops slightly at Krysia's reference to God as a female.

Krysia hails a taxi and holds the door for me. I slide across the seat to make room for her. She does not get in, but starts to hand the driver some bills. "My flat is nearby," she explains.

"I have money," I say.

"Well, get home safely. And Deo is right. You should figure out what you want to do."

"Do?"

"With your life. Self-determination isn't just some abstract political notion, intended for the masses. Each of us must decide whom she will be, what we want for ourselves." I had not thought about it in such a manner. "You're not bored," she observes. "You're restless. Bored suggests a lack of interest in the world around you. But you drink in everything and can't get enough. The world has come to Paris and you're at the center of it all," she adds. "The question now is what you do with it."

I see myself then as undefined, a lump of clay. "But I'm just an observer." In that moment, I grasp my own frustration—I am tired of just watching things play out in front of me like a performance on a stage. I want to take part.

"Why?" she demanded. "Why not allow yourself even for a minute to step outside the box into which you were born?"

"My father. And there are other reasons. My fiancé was wounded..." I falter, swept by the urge to tell Krysia how I feel about Stefan.

"We all have pasts." Her tongue seems loosened by the alcohol and I think she might say something about her mysterious errand to the park. "There's a new world being born," she observes. "We each might as well make what we want of it."

I look up at the dark slate of gray sky above, picturing the kitchen boy from the Orient, the one who was fighting for his country's independence among the dirty dishes and food scraps. If he was not daunted in his quest, then how could I be? I hadn't until this very moment seen the opportunity in all of the change, rules and norms discarded.

"Make Paris your own," she exhorts again. "Do something, write something, take a class. You are young and unattached, at least for the moment." I hold my breath, waiting for her to ask about my fiancé, but she continues. "You're in one of the

world's greatest cities at the dawn of the modern age. You have
resources, wits, talent. There's no greater sin than to waste all
of that. Find your destiny." Before I can ask her how, she turns
and disappears into the night.

I sit in the stillness of the study, the room dim but for the pale light that filters in, silhouetting the windowpane. Beyond the lattice of dark wood, the robin's-egg-blue sky is laced with soft white clouds. A rolling wave of slate-gray domes and spires spills endlessly across the horizon, poking out from the haze that shrouds the city like a wreath. Bells chime unseen in the distance.

I wrap my hands around the too-hot cup of tea that sits before me on the table, then release it again and gaze down at the front page of yesterday's *Le Journal*. The early mornings have always been mine. Papa loves to work long into the night, a lone lamp at the desk pooling yellow on the papers below. As a child, I often fell asleep to the sweet smell of pipe smoke, the sound of his pen scratching on the paper a familiar lullaby.

I eye the letter I'd started writing to Stefan the previous evening. I had written to him regularly when we were in England, of course. But I have not put pen to paper since our arrival in

Paris simply because I did not know what to say about the fact that I had come here instead of going home.

I reread my words. *I attended the welcome reception for Wilson and it was quite the affair...* I crumple the piece of paper and throw it in the wastebasket. I feel foolish talking of parties and Paris while he lies wounded in a hospital bed. Why had I not returned to Berlin straightaway to be with him? Stefan is so loyal. Once, when I was laid up with a sprained ankle, he faithfully brought me my school assignments each afternoon and carried my completed work back to school each morning for a week. He would not have left me alone if the situation was reversed. I am not abandoning him, though. I will go back as soon as the conference is over.

Starting on a fresh sheet of crisp stationery, I decide to be more forthright: *I'm sorry not to be there with you. Papa was summoned to the conference and I did not want him to travel alone.* Then I pause. Stefan has never begrudged me my relationship with my father, the way that Papa seemed to come first and would always be central in our lives. But he would know that Papa had Celia here to look after him. I try again: *Papa had to come directly to Paris and did not want me to travel back to Germany alone.* Though the explanation is still unsatisfactory, I set down my pen.

I stand and pick up Papa's hat from the chair. Wrapped up in his thoughts, he's prone to dropping things and leaving them where they fall. I run my hand along the felt brim, too wide to be fashionable now. *With love, Lucy,* reads the now-faded embroidery along the inside band. It was a gift from my mother, worn beyond repair.

Reflexively, I continue straightening the room, moving books to piles in the corners, sweeping a few missed crumbs from the table. We've managed to accumulate a sizable bit of clutter, even in the short time we've been here. There are a handful of cozy touches—a small vase of gardenias on the windowsill, a throw across the settee—all courtesy of Tante Celia, who is domestic in a way that I could never be.

In the corner are the discarded boxes that had contained Uncle Walter's Hanukah presents. The holidays had passed quietly, Papa so immersed in work before the formal opening of the conference he had scarcely paused. Too much celebrating would have been unseemly, anyway, with all of the suffering, the homeless and wounded that linger at every corner. But Uncle Walter, unaware of the subtle context here, had sent boxes of gifts: slippers and a wrap for me, new ties and shirtwaists for Papa. He'd sent money, too, more than we had seen in some time, with special instructions that I was to have my wedding gown made. Included was a remnant of lace and a picture of my mother's dress for the tailor to copy.

Picking up the lace now, my throat tightens. The gift contains a silent message—that I am to do what is expected of me, play along as I always have. This time in Paris is not a license to step out of line, but merely a brief sojourn before I marry Stefan.

Stefan had proposed the Sunday after the war broke out on a walk by the lake behind the villa. "If you'll marry me when I get back…"

I hesitated. Stefan and I had been formally courting for just over a year, the transition from friendship to romance marked rather unceremoniously by a brief conversation between him and Papa. Yet despite the exclusivity of our relationship and the time that had passed, I hadn't given thought to the future. But the war had sped up the film, bringing the question to the glaring light of day. "Why rush things?"

His eyes widened with disbelief. "I'm going to war, Margot." For the first time then I saw real fear, portending all that was to come.

"I know. But they say it will be quick—weeks, maybe a month or two at worst case. Then you'll be back and we'll decide things properly." He did not answer but continued staring at me, pleading. I swallowed. Marriage felt so adult and constraining, so permanent. Stefan asked little of me, but he was asking for this now.

I thought of the dance Stefan and I had attended months earlier. At first it had been an awkward affair—most students had not come as couples and boys and girls lingered separately back against the walls, barely speaking. Then a few people shuffled to the middle of the dance floor and gradually others joined them. I had gazed at Stefan hopefully and, seemingly encouraged, he extended his hand. But before he could speak, Helmut, a thick-necked boy, walked over. "Would you like to dance?" he asked me, so forcefully it was hardly a question. I looked up at Stefan helplessly—I had come with him and I wanted to dance with him, at least for the first song. But he shrugged, unwilling to struggle. If Stefan could not stand up for himself at a dance, how would he ever survive war? He needed the promise of our marriage to keep him strong.

The war was coming, I told myself; we would all need to make sacrifices. "Well, then," I said. Marriage was to be my own personal conscription. "Yes, I would love to be your wife."

We walked back to the house to share the good news. "You don't mind, do you, that he didn't have time to ask permission?" I asked Papa. "I mean, with the war and all."

"He had asked my permission some time ago," Papa confided. So Stefan had this planned all along. The war had just been an excuse to move things up.

The quiet clicking of the door leading from Papa's room into the hallway stirs me from my thoughts. Tante Celia keeps her own apartment in a town house in the 16th arrondissement that I've not visited, a fiction designed for public appearances as well as for my benefit. Once, when I was not more than twelve, I spied her leaving our house in Berlin before dawn, head low beneath the hood of her cloak. At the time I was incensed: How dare they soil the memory of my mother—how dare he? Older now, I do not begrudge Papa company and warmth. He seems so much happier with her nearby than he had been in England, where Celia could not get a visa to join us. She is just so plain and uninteresting, a shadow of her beautiful older sister. Though perhaps that is why Papa likes her—she is the closest reminder of my mother.

My gaze travels to the photograph of the tall, willowy woman on the mantelpiece, taken in our Berlin garden before I was born. My mother had been an actress before marrying my father, leaving home at the age of sixteen and performing around the world to great acclaim against her family's wishes. Papa had seen her in a performance of *As You Like It* in Amsterdam and had been so taken with her portrayal of Rosalind that he had sent flowers backstage with an invitation to dinner. Six months later they wed and she left the stage for good.

I study the photo, which Papa brings with him wherever we go and puts out as soon as we arrive. Her pose, one hand on hip, the other outstretched slightly with palm upward, is beguiling, yet somehow natural. Mother and I shared the same pale skin and almond-shaped eyes, but her dark hair was smooth, not kinked and unruly like mine. Ten years have passed, and my actual memories of our time together are dim. To me, she is a shadowy figure with a sad expression and hollow eyes, a woman who never seemed to sit still or truly be present.

I return to my chair and wrap my hands around the warm cup of tea, watching as a flock of starlings rises from one of the cathedral spires, startled by a noise I did not hear. My thoughts turn to Krysia. It has been weeks since she put me in the taxi. I had hoped she might call or send word inviting me out to join her circle of friends again. The longing for company is strange to me. I've never had female friends. Even in school, I tended to play with the boys, enjoying the pure physicality of sport where it was permitted. But the excitement of the evening I spent at the bar with Krysia has left me hoping to see her again.

She has not contacted me, though. Did I embarrass her with

my lack of substance? A few nights earlier there was a gala and I attended more eagerly than usual, urging Papa to dress promptly. But a string orchestra played waltzes, the piano in the corner deserted and silent.

Restless, I finish my tea and dress, then scribble a note for Papa before putting on my coat and gloves and leaving the apartment. On the street, I pause. It is January now, the pavement altogether too icy for biking, so I begin to walk, making my way toward the river. As I near the wide expanse of water, the wind, no longer buttressed by the buildings, blows sharply. Drawing my coat tight, I cross the arched pont de la Concorde. On the far bank sits the wide expanse of the Quai d'Orsay. Though it is not yet seven o'clock, the crowds of demonstrators, protesting for their causes and seeking to be heard, have already begun to form outside the tall iron gates of the foreign ministry where Wilson and the other powers labor to re-create the world.

I press forward, head low against the wind. Past the ministry and away from the water now, the streets begin to narrow. At the corner I pause, peering uneasily down a side street. Rue de Courty is one that I have avoided for months. The center of the block is taken up by a wide building with columns that suggest it was once a government administration building of some sort. I passed it once shortly after our arrival in Paris, taken aback by the improbably young men in wheelchairs, who sat forlornly by the windows looking as though they are just acting parts in a play and in fact might jump up and walk at any second. Would they ever leave the hospital? What if there were no families to claim them? I had run from the block, haunted.

Now my guilt rises anew: Should I have gone back to Berlin and taken Stefan from the hospital, cared for him myself? The hospitals themselves could be as dangerous as war—nursing care was short and supplies minimal even in the best hospitals. Influenza and tuberculosis were rampant. If I went back to Germany now, perhaps I could get him out.

Unable to bear the cold any longer, I walk to the corner and hail a taxi. "Montparnasse," I say to the driver and it is only then that I fully realize I am going to try to find Krysia. "Rue Vavin," I add, recalling one of the major intersections. A few minutes later, I pay the driver and step out onto the pavement. The boulevard du Montparnasse is quiet at this early hour, the bars and cafés that seem to never sleep now briefly at rest. At La Closerie des Lilas, I peer through the glass into the darkened café. I push against the door expecting it to be locked, but it opens.

"Bonjour."

"Oui?" I step inside, adjusting my eyes to the dim lighting. Ignatz is behind the counter, alone in the otherwise deserted room. Last time I was here the café felt almost magical, but in the crude light of day it is a dirty room, trash from the previous evening still littering the floor, ordinary in a way that makes me wonder if I imagined the revelry of the earlier night. "Ah, the ambassador's daughter." His tone is mocking.

I consider pointing out that the title more aptly describes Krysia than me, then decide against it. "Margot Rosenthal," I correct.

"Mademoiselle Rosenthal." He gives a mock bow, then throws a handful of spoons into one of the bins with a clatter. "Of course. How can I help you?" His voice is gravelly.

"Krysia…that is, I haven't heard from her in a few weeks and I was worried."

"I haven't seen her. She's sick. The grippe, or some such thing."

So that is why she hasn't contacted me. I'm relieved and concerned at the same time. "Is it serious?"

He shrugs. "I shouldn't think so, or I would have heard. She's got Marcin to look after her."

His answer does little to assuage my fear. "I'd like to check on her if you'd be so kind as to provide her address."

I hold my breath, expecting him to object, but he pulls out a scrap of paper and scribbles on it. "It's not far from here. If you walk up rue d'Assas, you'll find it just before you reach bou-levard Saint-Germain." He starts to slide the paper across the bar, then stops, leaving my hand dangling expectantly in mid-air. "I'm glad you're here, actually."

"Oh?"

Ignatz steps out from behind the bar. "*Oui.* You had so many interesting things to say the other night." He is larger than I re-membered from last time I was here, reminding me of a griz-zly bear.

Warmth creeps up my back. I never should have spoken about Papa's work. I replay that night in the bar in my head, my tongue loosened by beer, too eager to say something meaningful and curry favor with the group. "It was nothing."

"No, you had real views."

I flush. "I never should have spoken at all."

"Nonsense. Your wit added much to the discussion. But it also caused me to think, your contribution can be of most use to our cause."

"I'm afraid I don't quite understand."

"As you may have gathered the other night, we're interested in politics quite a bit. We're more than just a ragtag group of artists and innkeepers. Some of us—not all but some—are ac-tually doing something to further our beliefs in a just world." What could they do, I want to ask. Write about freedom? Lobby for it? "You do believe that people should have the right to self-determination, don't you?"

"Yes." But I remember then my conversation with Papa about the limits of what could be done at the conference, the fact that not everyone's claim to autonomy could be granted.

"We gather information, pass it on to Moscow or others who might be in a position to further those aims. You can help us if you'd like."

I hesitate. What could I possibly do? He continues. "The information you shared about the Serbia vote was most helpful. If your father should say anything else…"

I cut him off. "He seldom speaks about his work."

"Your father would not mind—ours and his cause are one and the same. I daresay he would want to help us himself, but for his position."

Krysia had been so excited about Papa's work. Maybe their interests really are aligned. "Perhaps…"

"So if you hear something of interest about what the Big Four might do…"

"I'll tell Krysia," I finish, regretting the words almost before they are out of my mouth.

"Oh, I wouldn't burden her," he interjects hurriedly. "She's so caught up in her music. Best to let me know personally."

Not answering, I snatch the paper with Krysia's address and make my way out to the street, half-expecting him to try to stop me from leaving. The fractured cobblestones point in different directions, beckoning me to follow. Did Ignatz seriously think that I could—or would—help him?

Soon, I stop before the address Ignatz had given me. I step forward, studying the narrow four-story building. There is an iron gate overgrown with ivy, a small courtyard behind it leading to an arched wood door with carvings and a brass knocker at its center. The note indicates that Krysia lives on the top floor, but when I peer upward the shutters are drawn tight. Musicians, like artists, I suppose, work long into the night, and shut out the indecency of early morning. It is not yet ten o'clock, my arrival unannounced. I turn away, suddenly aware of the impulsiveness of my coming here. I should have asked Ignatz if Krysia had a telephone or perhaps had him forward a message. But I continue to stare upward, wishing I could somehow reach her.

"Hello," a familiar voice says behind me. I turn to face Krysia in her blue cape. Contrary to what Ignatz had said, she does not look ill.

I notice then the rosary beads clutched in her right hand. "You were at church?"

She nods. "The old parish church at Saint-Séverin."

"You're devout," I marvel. How does her faith mesh with her communist political views?

She ignores my remark. "Come in." If she is put off by my unexpected visit, she gives no indication, but opens the door then steps aside to let me in. The lobby is dim and in disrepair but the banister carvings are ornate, belying a once-fine home. Paned windows swung inward to let in the fresh air, which carries a hint of smoke.

I follow her up the winding staircase, hanging back as she unlocks the door. She does not speak but walks to a tiny kitchen in the corner and puts on the kettle. The flat is just a single room, tall narrow windows overlooking a stone courtyard. The space is cozy, large pillows, everything in a maroon and gold reminiscent of something from India. There are books stacked in the corners, rich paintings on the wall. There is no table and I wonder where they eat. A candle, now extinguished, gives off a cinnamon smell.

I stand in the entranceway, clutching my gloves. To have shown up unannounced is bad enough, but I do not intend to overstay. A moment later, she carries two cups of coffee to the cushioned seat by the window. "Please, come sit."

I take off my coat. "Your flat is lovely," I remark, as I perch on the edge of the settee.

She waves her hand. "It's a fine little place. We've been here since before the war, when the neighborhood was less in fashion."

What might my own apartment be like? A vision pops into my mind of a garret like this, with lots of windows and light, a nook where I could drink my breakfast tea and gaze out the window. I'm not sure of the city in which my fantasy apartment exists—back in Berlin just steps from Papa, or somewhere farther away?

A cat slips quietly around the base of the chair before jumping up and folding itself into Krysia's lap. I'm surprised—I've seen almost no pets since we've been back in Paris, none of the poodles and little terriers on leashes that littered the parks before the war. There are the strays, of course, animals too large and mangy to have been anyone's pet for long, hurrying busily between the rubbish piles in the side streets. But there wasn't enough food for the people during the war, much less animals, and it was a mercy I'm sure to put one's beloved pet to sleep rather than let it starve. Some were probably eaten.

Through the floorboards comes a lively, unrecognizable tune from a gramophone. "I'm so sorry to intrude," I apologize again.

"Not at all. Artists are a bit reclusive, but back home in Poland there are none of these formalities. Guests are always welcome at a moment's notice."

Relaxing somewhat, I take the cup she offers. "I hadn't seen you. And then I heard that you were sick."

She waves her hand dismissively. "Just a bad cold. These things get so exaggerated." But there are circles beneath her eyes that suggest something more. She takes a sip of coffee, savoring it with relish. Coffee, like so many things, was scarce during the war, the ersatz mix of ground nuts and grains hardly a substitute.

My body goes slack with relief. "I was worried." The fullness of my voice reveals my concern.

"It's good to know that someone might notice if I dropped off the face of the earth." She smiles faintly, her tone wry.

The cat hops across into my lap, purring low and warm. "She doesn't like most people," Krysia observes approvingly.

We drink our coffee in silence. Something about her absence and her tired expression do not make sense. I take a deep breath, then dive in. "Krysia, I wanted to ask you about the young women in the park."

She blinks. "How do you know about that?"

"When you left Wilson's reception, you went to the park…"

"You followed me then, too?" she asks, cutting me off.

"No. That is… I was curious where you were going and why." I falter. "I guess I did follow you."

"And I should ask the question—why exactly?" She has a point. We've spoken twice, spent a few hours together—hardly the kind of intimate friendship that warrants such probing questions.

"I was concerned."

"You were curious," she corrects. I was both, I concede inwardly. Of course I wanted to know what she was doing, understand her mystery. But I feel a certain kinship to Krysia, more so than I should for a woman I've only just met.

"Years ago I had a child," she says, her voice a monotone. I stifle my shock. Whatever I had expected Krysia to say, it wasn't that. "I was twenty-two when I got pregnant." Just about the age I am now, though I cannot fathom the experience. "Old enough to make my own choices. The father—it wasn't Marcin back then—was long since gone." I struggle not to reach for her. "My parents wanted me to have it taken care of, to avoid the scandal that would have devastated them socially. I made the appointment and even went. I couldn't go through with it, though. I had the baby." Her voice cracks slightly. "But I was too afraid to try to raise her on my own. So I gave her up."

Her. I remember the young women skating. One had been taller than the rest, with chestnut hair not unlike Krysia's. She continues, "I go to the park each week to see her. Just once a week. Any more would only raise suspicion."

"Have you ever spoken to her?"

She shakes her head. "I have no wish to intrude and complicate her life. I've tried to do the right thing—letting her go when I couldn't support her, keeping an eye out for her safety. Yet it all gets twisted somehow. I mean, I had to give her up.

But I can't just abandon her, can I, and go on as though she doesn't exist and this piece of me isn't out there in the world?" She sounds lost, no longer confident and strong but a child herself somehow. Krysia is caught in a kind of purgatory, unable to leave the child but unable to be with her.

"She's no longer a child. Perhaps if you spoke to her now, you could explain."

"There are some doors that are not meant to be opened." Her tone is firm.

I recall the girl, so similar to Krysia, except that she was slight, a thin slip of birch beside Krysia's oak. "She looks well cared for."

"The people who adopted her are good folks," she agrees. "A bit more materialistic and less cultured than I would have wanted. But there's time for that later, perhaps a year abroad, study at the Sorbonne." She sounds as though she is planning a future that she will somehow be a part of, though that, of course, is impossible.

"Perhaps," I soothe. I have no idea if she is right, but it is what she needs to hear. "Perhaps you'll have children of your own. More children," I add as she opens her mouth to protest that the girl is her own.

"Having Emilie nearly killed me." *Emilie.* I do not know if that is the child's actual name by her adopted parents, or just one Krysia uses in her mind. "She's seventeen. But she hasn't settled on a suitor that I can tell, I think because she is still studying." There is a note of pride in Krysia's voice, as if through her estranged child she could correct the mistakes of her own youth.

"I've never told anyone." Underlying her voice is a plea that I not judge her choices. "I don't know why I'm telling you." *Because I caught you,* I want to say. But she could have lied to me, made up a story about the girls in the park. No, there is something about me that she trusts almost instinctively. I've always had that way about me, that makes people want to talk and share.

"What about your parents?"

"There was a time they would not speak to me. Now we're civil since we've put all that behind us." She places heavy irony on the last two words, as though acknowledging that it is anything but in the past.

"This week she didn't appear at the park. Listening to the others, I learned that she'd been taken ill." I understand then Krysia's absence, the circles beneath her eyes that came not from her own sickness but worry about her child. "It was the worst thing in the world. I wanted to go to her in the hospital but, of course, I couldn't. So I've been in church, praying almost nonstop for her recovery." No, madly liberal, communist Krysia was not religious. It was the helplessness and despair of a sick child she could not be with that had literally brought Krysia to her knees. "She's turned the corner now and is recovering."

Yet Krysia still prayed. "When I didn't see you for a time, I thought maybe I had said or done something to offend you," I say, changing the subject. Then I stop, realizing how insecure I sound.

"Not at all. I'm glad to know you. I have Marcin, of course, but I've forgotten how pleasant the company of another woman can be."

I nod. "Me, too." I am not comfortable in the company of women. I dislike their gossipy talk and the way they eye one another as if in constant competition. But Krysia is different somehow. For a minute I consider sharing Ignatz's request that I help provide information. But Ignatz bade me not tell her about our conversation, almost as if he considers her too vulnerable and weak to be trusted. I do not want to bother her now, while she is so worried about Emilie.

She picks up some knitting needles and yarn beside her. Her hands are so often in motion, playing the piano, knitting—like two birds she needs to keep occupied so they don't fly away.

"So have you made any decisions?" she asks abruptly.

"Excuse me?"

"When we last spoke, you were trying to figure out what you were going to do." She watches me expectantly, as though I was supposed to have remolded my life plan in a few short weeks. Why must I *do* at all? As a girl, no one expected me to do or be—I just *was*, a happy state of affairs that I should have liked to carry on indefinitely. In truth, our conversation and Krysia's challenge had prickled at me nonstop since our last meeting. But I have no new answers. There have always been expectations: I will be wife to Stefan, a mother someday if his condition still permits it. Those things just meant being an appendage to the lives of others, I see now. Could that possibly be enough?

"You have a real gift with words," she adds when I do not answer. "Have you ever considered being a writer?"

I laugh, toss my head. "A writer? What would I say? You have to have more than just words—you need life experience and I have so little of that."

"Where will you go after the conference?" she asks, trying an easier question.

"Back to Berlin with Papa, I suppose."

She scrutinizes her knitting, then pulls out a stitch. "Why? Why not see a bit of the world now, while you can?"

"But my fiancé..."

"Ah yes, you mentioned him the other night, fleetingly. Once you go back to him, there will be a wedding, then children. There will always be something to stop you. You only have right now. Go while you can."

"I'll go back to Stefan after the conference," I say stubbornly.

"You sound enthralled."

"I didn't mean it that way." But it isn't my tone that she has taken issue with—it is the fact that I am going back at all.

"Is that what you want?"

I start to say yes, then stop. It is a lie.

"Then why go?"

"Because he is my fiancé. And he was badly wounded."

I expect her to ask how he was hurt, the seriousness of his injuries. "Do you love him?" I'm not sure what love is, really. When I was fifteen, Stefan and our tiny neighborhood, the park where we would walk together, and our quiet cinema dates, were the only world I had ever known. Stefan would have changed during the war.

"I care for him."

"That isn't the same."

"I know." I turn to gaze out the window at the courtyard below. "I feel so differently now."

"Or maybe you feel the same, but you've changed and so those feelings are no longer enough."

I consider this. Part of me has always sensed that there were differences. I recall a conversation Stefan and I had once about my mother. I'd found an old playbill from a show she'd done in Morocco and shown it to him. "How exciting," I remarked, "to have traveled the world."

But Stefan had looked at me blankly. With everything he wanted right here in Berlin—his family and me—he had no desire to leave. "It must have been terribly difficult," he replied, "not to mention dangerous."

I could see it in his eyes, too, the day he left for the army. "You'll get to go so many places," I'd offered as we stood on the platform and said goodbye, trying to force optimism into my voice. "Belgium, Holland, maybe even France." But Stefan had never wanted to leave in the first place, whereas I could not wait to go. No, the differences were there even before the war, but it had taken the years apart to make me perceive them clearly. Now they are magnified, not just by time, but the ways in which I had changed, as well.

"Maybe," I reply to Krysia. "We were so young and four years apart feels like a lifetime. Sometimes he seems more like an idea than a person. I hate feeling this way. And he needs me."

"A sense of obligation is no way to start a life," she presses.

"Loyalty is important." My voice sounds tinny and weak.

"So is happiness. Would you want someone to marry you for such a reason?"

"No, of course not." But I am not lying wounded in a hospital bed, with no prospect of a future. I am suddenly annoyed. I barely know Krysia. Why is she asking me such things? "I should go." I stand and put on my coat. "Thank you for the coffee."

I half wish she will try to stop me, but she nods, rising. "Thank you for calling. I hope to see you again soon."

Outside it is warmer now, the late-morning sun taking away some of the chill. The sidewalks are now lively with pedestrians, merchants and deliverymen unloading crates from lorries. As I make my way toward the metro, Krysia's questions about Stefan prickle at me. I hear her voice, exhorting me to see the world now, while I still can. A thousand objections roar through my brain: I can't leave Papa. I can't travel alone.

Nothing has changed—my problems loom as large as ever. But despite my earlier annoyance, it felt good to share my fears about Stefan and a life together with Krysia, to verbalize to somebody the thoughts and feelings I'd barely dared to acknowledge to myself for so long. And Krysia confiding her story of Emilie helped, as well. Learning that someone as strong and self-assured as Krysia also wrestles with the past and the right thing to do makes me feel somehow less alone. She seems to enjoy my company, though perhaps I am simply a proxy for the daughter she so desperately wants to know but cannot. Squaring my shoulders, I start down the street with a lighter gait than I've had since before the war.

Forty minutes later, I reach our suite at the hotel. I open the door and stop. The curtains are drawn and only faint daylight filters in. A rustling noise at the desk startles me and I jump. Papa is here, hunched over the desk in the darkness, when he should have been at the ministry. "Papa?" Alarmed, I rush forward.

He does not move. I put my hand on his shoulder, fearful that it is his heart and the worst has happened. "Papa, are you well?"

He straightens but his expression is dazed as though he does not see or recognize me. Before him on the desk sits a newspaper. "There's been an attempt on Clemenceau's life." I pick up the paper. My breath catches as I take in the photograph of the would-be assassin. The dark-eyed boy from the La Closerie des Lilas stares back at me.

"The attacker possessed information from the conference that was not public, information that prompted him to act." Papa drops his head to his hands once more. "And I'm afraid they're going to blame it on me."

PART TWO

VERSAILLES, APRIL 1919

I peer out the window down the road at the Hôtel des Réservoirs. The six-story building, with its aged yellow facade and arched doorway, stands behind hastily erected barbed wire, giving it the feel of a fortress or prison, depending upon whether one is to be kept in or out. Either way, it looks as if the German delegation is to be quarantined, defeat a virus that no one wants to catch. Apple blossoms frame the hotel in a defiant lush pink.

The road leading to the guarded hotel gate is lined three deep with onlookers, reporters and photographers and townspeople and those who had packed the trains down from the city. There is no official party as there had been when Wilson arrived, no military band or other pageantry to herald the Germans' arrival—just hordes of the genuinely curious, waiting to see those who are to be held responsible for the world's suffering.

I turn back into the room where Papa sits working at his desk, oblivious to the spectacle taking place across the road. Our apartment in Versailles is located not in a hotel, but a tall

row house that has been converted into apartments to accommodate the sudden influx. It is laid out much like our previous
quarters in the city, two bedrooms adjoined by a common space.
Everything, from Papa's piles of books to the photograph of my
mother on the mantelpiece, is in the same location as in Paris.
It is as if we travel in a shell, I'd decided when we first settled
in, re-creating the identical living environment for ourselves
in each city. But the rooms here are smaller and oddly shaped,
the parlor something of a trapezoid, walls with faded flowered
paper slanting inward from the windows.

"They should be here soon," I say. Papa does not answer. He
had not wanted to be here today—or at all for that matter. He
had tried to lure me away with an excursion to Paris. But I had
insisted that we stay, despite his derisiveness of what he called
the "circus of shame." He does not stand at the window himself,
but busies himself at the desk. How can he not look?

The topic had come up at a dinner party three weeks earlier when it was announced that the Germans had finally been
summoned to the conference. "You'll move over to Versailles
now, of course, and stay with the delegation?" someone asked
Papa. Until that point we had enjoyed our neutral status, not
being identified too closely with any one camp, including the
defeated. But when a telegram came from the head of the delegation inviting us to relocate, Papa could avoid it no longer. So
we left the city for this dreary little suburb of Versailles, though
he still commutes almost daily to the conference proceedings at
the ministry in Paris.

Our apartment is just across the road and down a bit from
the hotel. The location, close by the German residence but not
within, reflects the delicate role Papa must play. The conference
does not trust him because he is German. The German delegation will surely not accept Papa because he has been part of the
conference. We are an island.

"I'm going to market," I say, unable to stand the confinement of the apartment any longer and eager to get a closer view. Unlike the hotel in Paris, there's no kitchen to deliver our meals and the town's few remaining restaurants are dismal affairs, so it falls to me to procure what we need.

I hold my breath, waiting for Papa to see through my excuse—the shops are likely to be closed now with the arrival. But he does not. Papa has been more preoccupied than ever these past few months since the attempt on Clemenceau's life. Though the French prime minister recovered quickly and the story faded from the newspapers, it continued to hang over Papa and me, a silent dagger.

I almost told Papa that night that it was my fault. "Quite a shock," he'd remarked. "Clemenceau will be fine, even joked as they were taking him to the hospital about the madman's poor marksmanship. But it is a sobering reminder to us all that even while we are here working toward the new world, there are those who would derail it." His brow furrowed.

"What is it? Is there something more?"

"Not at all."

"You don't need to shield me. I'm not a child."

He smiled. "No, of course not. I never like to trouble you and give pause to your beautiful smile, even for a moment. It's just that this may cause trouble for me. Cottin—the would-be assassin—was upset about French opposition to the Pan-Slavic state. We had been trying to keep it a secret so the media controversy would not keep us from getting the matter done. The assassination attempt, the timing of it, gives rise to suspicions that someone had leaked information about the vote."

"But surely no one could think that you had a role."

Papa, the only German detailed to the conference, not to mention a Jew, feared himself a likely scapegoat. I watched his face, wondering if he suspected me, or was perhaps even hinting. But he could not imagine that I would have betrayed him in such a fashion. "I appreciate your outrage on my behalf. It will be fine."

Though the accusations had never become overt, there had been a quiet distancing between Papa and some of the other conference advisors that made our sojourn to Versailles almost a relief.

Studying Papa now, my guilt rises anew. Only I know the truth—that it was my careless remark, overheard at the bar, which gave Cottin the information to act. I have never been good at keeping secrets from Papa and I have struggled for months not to blurt out what I had done, to seek his forgiveness. But he has enough to deal with right now and I won't strain his health further.

Down on the street, the morning air is warming and a bit stale with gutter stench. Across the road the hulking Versailles palace sits with its endless fountains and gardens, swallowing the tiny town below.

I walk around the side of the apartment building to the garden I planted. When we'd arrived, the dirt patch had been overrun by weeds. "I could tend to it," I suggested. "Make the place come back to life a little."

"A fine idea," Papa said quickly. Gardening, if done properly without too much strain, is an acceptable avocation for women. "Though we're hardly likely to be here long enough to see things grow."

"Then it will be here for others," I replied stubbornly. I'd planted flowers, tulips and other perennials that I hoped would blossom for years even after we were gone, something beautiful to leave behind. One of the plants has fallen, I notice. I dig my hands deep into the soil, savoring the buried warmth. Then I stand too quickly, my hands creating a smear of dirt across my dress.

I make my way down the cobblestone lane in the opposite direction from the crowds at the hotel, in case Papa is watching out the window. I head toward the market, skirting the edge of the park that sits at the end of the street. I have come to know the quiet rhythm of this part of the town through my days here—the old woman who sits at the corner with her poodle as if waiting for a bus that will not come, the two men who appear every morning at seven to slip schnapps into their coffees and sit wordlessly for twenty minutes before getting up and going in opposite directions. Are they brothers, cousins, friends? Was their routine always like this or was it disrupted during the war?

Gazing down the path into the park, I am reminded of Krysia. I've not seen her since we came out here. Versailles is at least twenty-five kilometers away from Paris, too far for an impromptu excursion into the city.

Stopping short of the market, where most of the stalls are indeed closed, I double back around the block to the hotel. The crowd has thickened now, a low murmur of expectancy crackling through the onlookers. Moments later, three buses appear on the road, old coaches belching smoke and making such noise that it seems questionable whether they will make the last ten meters of the trip. A truck rides ahead of the buses. It lurches to a stop then dumps a bunch of boxes in the hotel courtyard as unceremoniously as though they are garbage. Studying closer, I can see that it is luggage, once-fine suitcases now covered with dust and grime.

The bus doors open and the German delegation begins to emerge. They are bureaucrats, stooped older men, thin and paunched, bald and bearded, indistinguishable from the other nations' delegates, but for their low shoulders and downcast eyes. They shuffle forward to face the indignity of sorting through the luggage, each to find and carry his own.

A boy lets forth a jeer. I brace myself for the rest of the onlookers to join him. Instead, the crowd is silent, their eyes boring into the Germans with pure hatred. Insults would have almost been better. This is why Papa sits at his desk, why he cannot bear to watch. This is not peace or even armistice, but rather the thinnest of truces, scarcely concealing the hatred of the war still bubbling beneath the surface.

A man steps from the last coach behind the others. He is younger, I can tell, even beneath the cloak of his naval coat and hat. Papa had mentioned someone military. My first impression is of a hawk. Steely blue eyes take in the crowd. I'm reminded of the soldiers I saw so often on the Paris streets. Even out of uniform I can spot it—the anxiousness, searching the corners for a cellar or other hiding place, as though the air before him might at any moment explode with grenades and mustard gas.

He starts forward, walking with his shoulders squared, seeming to clear the path ahead of him as he goes. Then his head lifts slightly and his eyes flick in my direction and I can swear, though I am one in a crowd of hundreds, he is looking directly at me.

My breath catches. I step back and, as I do, my scarf drops. Suddenly the German breaks from the procession. He steps toward the crowd, which parts. Then he bends down and picks up my scarf and holds it out to me.

I recoil. There is something chilling about him, militaristic and terrifying. Stefan is a soldier, too, I remind myself. But that is different—Stefan is an ordinary man, called into war by circumstances and patriotism. This man is a high-ranking officer, a soldier by nature. I look down, suddenly conscious of the garden dirt on the sleeve of my everyday blouse.

The people around me glare with accusing eyes as if my receipt of this act of kindness somehow makes me complicit. I tilt my head upward but the soldier does not meet my eyes. Should I thank him in German or French? I take the scarf but before I can say anything, the man has rejoined the procession and is gone.

I can hear the party before I can see it, laugher spilling forth down the streets of Neuilly-sur-Seine. We turn the corner and a house in the middle of the street stands as a beacon, light beaming from within. It is not the largest on the block of this affluent Parisian neighborhood, but it gives the impression of being the most grand—flower boxes overflow with blooms too early in the season to be native and great ribbons of silk batting adorn the balconies, as though Armistice Day was last week and not months ago.

I stop midstreet, drawing my flimsy shawl against the evening, which is pleasant but chilly enough to remind me that it is not summer yet. Normally I would have dreaded such an affair. But after weeks locked away in dreary Versailles, I somehow welcome the return to the city and its bustle, even with Tante Celia as my host. There is no room in Versailles for Celia, a woman without official status, so she has remained behind in Paris. Papa is lonely for her, I can tell, by his quieter than usual demeanor, the excuses he has found to stay over in the city after dinners.

Celia touches my elbow as we climb the stairs. "You've heard of Elsa Maxwell, *n'est-ce pas?*" She jumps indiscriminately between German and French.

"Of course." I reply in German, not bothering to lower my voice. It's not as if anybody will be fooled into believing we are someone else. Elsa Maxwell is ubiquitous. A reporter in the softest sense of the word, she is in fact a social doyenne whose real fame came from hosting soirees such as this. "She threw parties in London during the war." I neglect to mention that I had not been to any of them.

Inside, the house is hot as August, too many bodies pressed close, trying to move in all directions. The party has been going on for hours, the festive atmosphere a train we had missed. A far cry from the stuffy receptions I had attended with Papa, there is no pretense of restraint. The men have loosened or in some cases removed their ties. The women have kicked off their shoes and those who have not bobbed their hair have let it loose from its pins. The women who had come to Paris were of an

unusual sort—would-be writers and entertainers and journalists whose free-spirited nature surely gave consternation to the
wives who had been left at home. Their dresses are the latest
fashions, Oriental-themed shifts, Bohemian frocks without any
pretense of a corset. I feel positively frumpy in my staid rose
party dress, though not as much so as Celia, who with her high
collar and crinolines stands out like a peacock, or a jester in an
Elizabethan play.

Bodies fill the makeshift dance floor in the center of the great
room, moving in strange new ways to the lively jazz music that
blares from a gramophone. Two women dance as though one
was a man, pressed close together. A strange scent, something
strong like burning flowers, mixes with the faint odor of sweat
in the air. There is a kind of desperation to the revelry, especially among the women. It is more than just the wiping away
of cobwebs and sorrow of a world struggling to live again. The
chance for a normal life with a husband and children has been
denied to so many, a generation of would-be suitors gone to the
trenches. The men who were left were the oddities, those who
had escaped the military for some sort of infirmity, and those
like Stefan who came back broken.

"All of this immorality," Celia remarks in French, "everyone's roles confused, the lines between men and women gone,
brought about by women going into work."

"You really think that's the cause of all of this?" My voice is
incredulous. "There are so many other reasons. What about the
desperation of the war, not to mention the influx of large numbers of soldiers now with too much time on their hands, so far
from home?" Celia sniffs, unpersuaded.

"It's a sight, isn't it?" a woman next to me remarks idly. I
nod, my eyes traveling toward the dance floor where the two
women are locked together now, nearly kissing. There is something about being in Paris here, away from familial and societal
expectations back home, that has given people license to act

this way. "Austrians at the party, as if they were our friends," she adds. I step back, stung. The woman had not been referring to the outlandish behavior at all, but was incensed by our kind being here, the enemy treated as equals.

"Come." I follow Celia through the packed room. She disappears into the crowd ahead of me and, after searching above the sea of heads in vain, I give up trying to keep up and instead make my way to one of the open windows. The cold, crisp air is a welcome relief against my face, a reprieve from the swaths of perfumed smoke.

Outside a woman in a tattered work dress picks through the rubbish in the alley adjacent to the house. Though the homeless have become an increasingly common sight in Paris, I am taken aback by the woman, not much older than myself, searching the garbage for food. What does she think of us being here with all of our parties and revelry and noise? I imagine a husband taken at the front, hungry children back home. Sensing me, she looks up and her eyes widen with alarm, fearful that I will reproach or report her for being there. Desperately, I reach into my purse and fling coins through the window, ashamed by the callousness of the gesture, as well as the inadequacy of my aid.

Celia is at my arm again, this time with our hostess, a buxom woman with short brown hair and a broad smile I recognize from the society pages of the newspaper. "Elsa, you remember..." I hold my breath, waiting for the woman to deny our having met in London.

But Elsa Maxwell, accustomed to traveling in wide circles and knowing people less often than she is known, sweeps me into a firm hug that has none of the airiness of the kisses so often exchanged here. "Darling!" Celia watches, eyes wide, apparently having bought the subterfuge. Elsa releases me. "If you'll excuse me, I must get everyone started on the game."

"Game?" But she has already moved on, leaving a burst of Chanel in her wake.

A moment later a bell rings and Elsa appears on the landing of the broad staircase in the middle of the foyer, commanding a presence well beyond what her rather plain appearance suggests. The din in the room instantly dulls, but there is still too much noise for me to hear well. She makes an announcement, holding up papers of some sort. A whisper of excitement blows through the crowd. Then she throws the papers into the air with a flourish and they scatter like confetti.

I turn to Tante Celia, confused. "A scavenger game," she exclaims excitedly, scrambling to grab one of the sheets. "It's a treasure hunt," she explains, placing great importance on each syllable.

She scans the paper, then passes it to me. It is a shopping list of the oddest sort: a pair of opera glasses, a man's swimming costume. Some of the items are phrased in riddle. "I don't understand. How are we to buy these things if the shops are closed?"

She titters with superiority, staring toward the door. "We don't buy them. We find them," she replies, gaily as a child. Are we seriously to run around the streets hunting in the darkness?

"I don't..." I start to beg off, following her outside. But Celia has already formed a foursome with two Swedes and together they set off toward the dense trees of the Bois de Boulogne.

As I start toward the massive park, my ankle twists, a sharp but fleeting pain. Celia turns back impatiently. The heel of my shoe, which caught the cobblestone, is cracked and, sensing my moment, I pull intentionally until the heel snaps. "It's broken," I lament, trying to fill my voice with disappointment. "You go on."

Celia hesitates. "If you're sure you'll be fine." Not waiting for my response, she follows the Swedes, who have already run off into the night, intent on the errand of finding a newspaper that is more than a month old. As she disappears into the trees, I sigh. I do not begrudge her excitement when she has so little to call her own. And she would not have left me if I was in real distress.

I limp back toward the house. The party has faded, the salon empty except for a rowdy group of men in the smoking room, a couple kissing shamelessly on one of the settees. I find the butler and ask him to call a taxi.

It is nearly midnight when the cab reaches Versailles. I pay the driver and step out, then peer across the road toward the Hôtel des Réservoirs, where lights still burn on the ground floor despite the late hour. Curious, I walk down the street. In a first-floor library, a man works intensely behind a desk, head low, bathed in yellow light. It is the German naval officer who picked up my scarf. I watch him, transfixed. He looks to be about thirty. He lifts his head and catches my eye, holding my glance for a second longer than he had earlier at the arrival. Then he stands and walks from the room. I step back into the shadows. How rude of me. He obviously minded the intrusion. But then the front door to the hotel opens and I see him silhouetted against the light.

"Can I help you, *mademoiselle*? We are not a zoo."

I flush, seized with the urge to run. "No, of course not." Then I take a step forward, out of the shadows. "It's *fraulein*, actually." I am quick to identify myself as a German out of the earshot of others, as if our kindred citizenship might excuse my watching him. I shift my weight awkwardly to my right foot. "I mean, Margot. Margot Rosenthal."

"The professor's daughter?" I nod. "I'm Georg Richwalder. I'm the military attaché to the delegation."

"I'm sorry if I disturbed you. I broke my heel and was just pausing." I hold up the shoe as evidence, take a step through the gate. He walks down the steps toward me. He is taller than I thought and I crane my neck upward to meet his eyes rather than stare at his chest as we speak.

"May I?"

I hand the shoe to him.

"I can fix this, I think."

I eye him skeptically.

"You learn to be handy in a great many ways when you're at sea. Would you like to come in for some tea while I try?"

I hesitate. The library behind him looks warm and inviting, the quiet and solitude a welcome contrast to the Maxwell party. But it wouldn't be proper. "No, thank you. I'll just be on my way."

"Wait here," he instructs firmly, a man who is used to giving orders. I shiver at his commanding tone. "I'll bring the tools— and some tea—outside."

I sit down on the step. A few minutes later he emerges with two cups of tea and a small kit. "I'm sorry to have disturbed you," I say.

"Not at all." He smiles and in that instant seems not at all the terrifying soldier I'd glimpsed during the delegation's arrival. A chink in the armor. "After so much time on the train, the fresh air is refreshing. The trip was exceedingly long. We sat at one point for eighteen hours for some reason known only to the French." He is wearing the same dark blue uniform as earlier today, but the jacket is unbuttoned, the shirt loosened at the collar.

I run my hand along the step, the stone hard and rough beneath my fingertips. "And the hotel...is it quite dreadful?"

"It's not bad, really. I mean in its heyday I'm sure it was quite grand. But I spent the better part of the four years on a ship, so I may not be the best judge of comfort."

"You were in the navy, weren't you?"

"I was on the *SMS König*, the crown jewel of His Majesty's High Seas Fleet." The pride in his voice is reminiscent of the prewar days, taking me back to the parades down the Unter den Linden, young girls pressing sandwiches and sweets into the hands of newly minted soldiers as they made their way to the station. "Even as a senior officer, my quarters were no bigger than a closet. The hotel has reasonably clean linen and fresh water and I'm not awakened to the sound of gunfire each morning." He smiles. "It's paradise. And the library is wonderful. I shall enjoy working there at night after the rest of the delegation has retired. They're mostly older, and we don't have much in common. But it's not a social occasion."

"And your family—did they mind being left back home?" The question comes out more prying than I intended. "I mean only that I've heard some of the men lamenting that their families couldn't enjoy Paris."

"No." An image pops into my mind of a Frau Richwalder, elegant and well coiffed, keeping the house running back in Germany. "That is, there's no one. I'm not married. Not so much to enjoy here these days, anyway."

"I suppose not." The German delegation was almost entirely confined to the hotel except for sanctioned meetings and a lone excursion.

"There." He hands me my shoe, neatly fixed.

"It's good as new. *Danke.*" He watches me, as though lost in thought. Between my mud-streaked dress earlier and broken shoe now, he must think me a wreck.

"Aren't you cold?"

I shake my head stubbornly.

"That's hardly a suitable coat."

"It's the fashion." I struggle to keep the sarcasm from my voice.

"Well, no one is here to see." He takes his coat and puts it around my shoulders in a strange, too-familiar gesture.

A mixture of soap and wool wafts upward from the collar. "Now won't you be cold?"

"I'm something of a polar bear actually. All of those nights on the North Sea."

My eyes travel to the contour of his shoulder, dark against

the lighted window. "Papa mentioned that there's a trip to the battlefields scheduled for Sunday. Are you going?"

"Not if I can help it. I've spent the past four years on a battlefield of another sort. I'd like to see them, of course, and pay respects, but on my own, not from the window of a motor coach. I came here to work, not sightsee."

"I suppose you won't be going into Paris for the plenary session tomorrow, either?"

He shook his head. "We weren't asked." How odd, to be summoned all of this distance, only to be sequestered in a hotel, excluded from the very meetings for which you were invited. But then he forces a smile. "It's no matter. So much better to have the time to work and not be shut up in stuffy proceedings all day."

"True. What are you working on?" His eyes widen and I wonder if he minds the question.

"It's quite dry," he says apologetically. He is not offended, just surprised that I might take an interest. "I'm the delegation's military officer and I'm studying plans and proposals as to what the treaty might look at, reading up on what the French and British experts are advocating in order to develop a counter position." He continues, "There's going to be a whole new world, a way for nations to coexist and to form strong alliances that will ensure we never face such destruction of man like that again." His shoulders straighten. "I can be part of that, I think, by helping the navy to find its place. It's slow going. Not the technical parts—I'm familiar with all of the engineering concepts from the ship. But languages were never my strong point and the delegation can't spare a translator outside of the sessions."

"I can help you," I blurt out, without meaning to. "My French and English are quite good. I've got no technical training but with the aid of a dictionary I could muddle through."

He looks at me dubiously. "It's tremendously dull, lots of engineering reports."

"I studied maths and science through the progymnasium

level," I reply. His jaw drops slightly, making his lips even more full. "I know it isn't the typical curriculum for a girl," I add, my words flowing more easily than usual. Back home girls are typically schooled in the gentle arts of music and literature at the high school level. But I had gravitated naturally toward the sciences and Papa had let my curiosity direct my studies.

"There's nothing to be paid for it."

"That's fine."

He coughs slightly. "Then why would you want to?"

"For the chance to do something—" I fumble for the right words, replaying my talks with Krysia "—meaningful. Real." Because I'm sitting here in the middle of the world being formed, I add silently, playing at dinner parties and treasure hunts.

"Fine," he acquiesces. For a moment I am annoyed—I'm trying to help him, but it sounds as if he is doing me a favor. "It's quite late tonight but if you'd like to come by tomorrow evening at eight, we can work after the delegation retires. You'll need clearance, of course, but that shouldn't be hard to get with your father's credentials."

"So we're agreed."

"*Ja*. If..." he adds, "your father approves."

I bristle and open my mouth to tell him that I am an adult and my own woman. But I can tell by his tone that it is not subject to debate, and that he will not cross another member of the delegation. "I'm sure it will be fine. I will see you tomorrow." I stand and hand him his coat. "Thank you for the shoe, and the tea." He stands. I wait for him to offer to escort me home, but he does not.

Back at the apartment, Papa is hunched over some papers in the study, reading so intensely he does not hear me come in. Smoke curls upward from his pipe, giving off a sickly smell. Seeing me, his brow furrows. "Is something amiss? I thought you were with Celia."

"I was. I came home. Are you working?"

He shakes his head. "Just composing a cable to Uncle Walter." I worry sometimes that Papa reports back to his brother-in-law too much, as if beholden to a superior. But Uncle Walter is just curious, a child being kept from the adults' table, eager for every detail he is missing, as well as an assessment of how the Germans will fare. He has always imagined himself a political thinker. I suspect that in reality he is just an excellent prognosticator of what is to come, and he sorely needs details to do that.

"Papa," I begin tentatively.

"Ja, liebchen?" He looks up and smiles. My father, an absent-minded academic, can fairly be accused of spending the better part of life in a hazy bubble of his own thoughts. But he has always had a way of knowing when my tone was serious and required his actual focus and attention.

Which was not the effect I am going for here when I was hoping to pass this by him before he ever had the chance to focus on it. "I've been offered an opportunity to do some work." He raises an eyebrow, and I continue. "Captain Richwalder from the delegation, you know him?"

"The young military officer. We met earlier."

"He needs someone to help him with translations. Please, Papa, I'm just so terribly bored." I don't tell him that the work will need to happen in the evening or in the library of the hotel. "I just want to help."

He rubs his chin. "I see no harm in it. It will be good for your linguistic skills." He turns back to his papers.

Dismissed, I walk to my room. Across the road, the massive expanse of the palace grounds, trees and fountains are shrouded in darkness. I press my head against the window, craning my neck to glimpse the hotel. The light in the library still burns yellow on the first floor and I imagine Captain Richwalder hunched over his papers. I wonder what the work will be like. Will my language skills be sufficient? Remembering his imposing gaze, I shiver. Then, I turn off the light and climb into bed, anticipating with excitement and more than a little dread the day that is to come.

CHAPTER FIVE

I
t is just shy of eight o'clock and the lamps glow behind the curtains at the hotel as I approach. I knock and a few seconds later the door opens. Captain Richwalder wears no jacket this evening, but his dress shirt is pressed crisply, the short hair above his ears still damp from washing. "Thank you for being prompt," he says, sounding as though used to people being otherwise. I had, in fact, loitered a good twenty minutes at our apartment, not wanting to arrive too early, checking my reflection with more care than I otherwise would have to make sure I look capable. My clothes are simple, a starched cream blouse with a scalloped collar and a navy skirt a shade longer than is fashionable these days.

Taking in his stiff, formal demeanor, I am suddenly uneasy. What if he is difficult to work for, even unkind? Though I volunteered to do this and am not receiving pay, Papa will expect me to honor the commitment I've made and see the job through.

Captain Richwalder leads me through the lobby of the hotel,

which is nicer than I might have expected from the drab exterior. The maroon curtains are just a bit faded and the chandelier overhead is every bit as elaborate as the one in our Paris hotel. He opens the door to the study. "Please make yourself at home. I'll just be a moment." As he closes the door behind him, I remove my coat. The library is modest in size, no bigger than our parlor down the street, but pleasant, with soft, overstuffed chairs and book-filled shelves that climb to the ceiling. The air carries the same damp, musty smell that permeates most of the town.

Captain Richwalder returns a moment later with two cups of tea and sets them down on the low table. "It's a bit warmer now. The weather, I mean." His attempt to make small talk is awkward, simple conversation strange on his tongue.

"Indeed." I smooth my hair, which is pulled back in a loose, low knot. Then I decide to be direct. "So what is it that you need me to do?"

His face relaxes at being given permission to turn to work and he motions for me to follow him over to the desk in the corner, where he holds the chair out for me to sit. "There are a number of military matters related to the peace treaty that are to be proposed, and I've been asked to work on those, not surprisingly, that involve the navy. The Imperial Navy is one of the finest in the world," he adds, unable to keep a note of pride from his voice. Or was, I cannot help but think. "And I believe there's a real role for the navy as a peacekeeper in the new world order."

His suggestion is the first I've heard of such an idea. "Do you think that's what the Allies have in mind?"

"Surely some sort of partnership. Remember what Wilson said at the cease-fire, peace without blame." It was true that in the desperate efforts to stop the fighting, Wilson had made such hasty promises. But the rhetoric since we've been in Paris has been far more pointed.

He continues. "So I believe such an arrangement is possible. But we've got to make the case." He is animated now, gesturing broadly with his hands to illustrate his point. "There's a vast amount of correspondence about the role that naval fleets might play, drawn up before and during the war. Synthesizing it will give a sense of what the Big Four are thinking and help to frame any proposal. But we have to work quickly."

I nod. The other nations have been meeting for close to six months, inviting the German delegation only at the final hour. Captain Richwalder's idea makes sense, but the window for providing any sort of input and making a difference is slim. "I would have started earlier, of course, but I was given access to the materials just days before leaving Berlin," he adds.

"Of course."

"I've prioritized the documents most in need of translation." He spreads the papers out on the desk before me. I would have expected the hands of a soldier, thick and crude. But his fingers are long, more artist than warrior, delicate half-moons at the cuticle.

He retreats to one of the chairs by the low table, which is piled high with papers, and I turn to the first document. It is a report on the structure of the smaller vessel fleets, and though once or twice I consult the dictionary I brought with me, to be certain of the exact words, it is not altogether difficult. My translation settles into an easy rhythm. Working alongside Captain Richwalder is not so different than reading in the study with Papa.

When I've finished the first page, I glance up, studying Captain Richwalder out of the corner of my eye. He is as imposing as he'd appeared at the arrival ceremony, with strong features seemingly etched from granite. But close up, there are little things I can see now—long eyelashes, almost impossibly so for a man, a bottom lip much fuller than the top. Faint, end-of-day stubble covers his cheeks.

He looks up unexpectedly. "Do you need something?"

"No." Heat rises from my neck as I fumble to find an excuse for my staring. "I was just wondering, how are things in Berlin?"

"You've not been back?"

"Not since the start of the war. We were in England."

"England?"

"Yes, Papa was on a teaching fellowship." My own explanation sounds uneasy. At the time, our departure had been too rushed to ask. But afterward I had questioned it silently myself: Why had we gone to an enemy country right after the war broke out? Papa could have postponed the fellowship. But there had been an urgency to our leaving. Had he been worried for our safety? The war never reached German soil, and surely at Uncle Walter's palatial mansion in the countryside we would have been fine. Had he been afraid of something else?

Captain Richwalder shakes his head. "Very bad, I'm afraid," he says, returning to my original question. "The Social Democrats nominally hold power in Berlin, but the south, Bavaria especially, has become a hotbed of communist activity. There are rumors that the government may have to retake Munich by force to restore order."

"That I've read in the press. But what is it like on the street?"

He pauses, struggling to fashion a description beyond the political. "Strikes, protests, rioting. Neighbors who lived in peace their whole lives taking sides and fighting one another. It's anarchy. You will find the city much changed. Immigrants have poured in by the thousands from the east, living in these cramped apartments, entire families in a single room. And there's no food, not for them and not for the people with money to buy it. The war is over, yet women and children continue to starve because of the blockade." His tone is harsh.

"Oh!" I bring my hand to my mouth. I hadn't understood it until then. Removed from the continent, safely tucked away in England, war seemed a remote thing, fought in the trenches by men who were strong enough to withstand it. Maybe that's why Papa accepted the appointment in England. He must have sensed the horror of what was to come and wanted to spare me.

While I was bemoaning the rainy British weather and lack of things to do, people back home were dying from hunger and cold. I shudder. "Your description of the chaos makes it sound like Russia."

"Perhaps, but I don't think it's going to go that way. The SDP is so divided within that they can't organize to get anything done, much less form an effective government. The right is taking advantage of that, capitalizing on all of the anger—they've managed to convince lots of people who weren't there that the new government was responsible for our ultimate defeat in the war. It's not true, of course, but people back home don't know that and it makes for an attractive, simple story. So the right has some popular appeal but they don't have the numbers. Things will settle somewhere in the middle. It's terribly dissatisfying."

"Maybe." To me, there is a kind of comfort in the inertia, a safeguard against any one extreme taking too much.

He picks up one of the cups of tea from the low table and walks over. Our fingers brush as he hands it to me. "Forgive my bluntness. All of the time on the ship has made me forget how to speak to a lady properly."

"Not at all. I much prefer plain speech." I take a sip of tea, then set the cup down well away from the papers. "Captain Richwalder..."

"Georg," he interjects. "If you don't mind."

"Georg," I say, the name unfamiliar and awkward on my tongue. "What will you do after the conference?"

He retreats to his chair, stretches his legs out before him. "Return to the battleship, I suppose, or a different craft if that was needed."

"You haven't seen enough of war?"

"There is no peace without war," Georg says. "There's a concept in Asia called yin-yang, two opposite halves of the whole. War and peace are just that. And soldiers are needed. Without the military, there would be no order."

I want to protest that man's nature would allow him to coexist peacefully, but I know that he is right. "I mean, what would you do if you couldn't go back to a battleship?" I ask, shifting topics slightly.

Georg cocks his head, as though he had not before contemplated the question. He had always assumed that there would be a navy and a place for him in it.

"Would you join the new government?"

He shakes his head. "I've got no patience for bureaucracy, and the capital makes me feel as though the walls and buildings are closing in around me. No, I'd probably return to Hamburg and oversee the family shipping business. If I can't be on the sea, at least I could be near it."

"Your family ships goods?"

"No, we build ships." I had not realized until now that Georg is wealthy. I've always been oblivious to matters of money and class—too oblivious, Tante Celia remarked once. But with his uniform and haircut, it would have been impossible to tell. "There isn't much of a 'we' anymore, unfortunately. My parents both died some time ago, and my brother Peter was killed at the Battle of Jutland."

"How terrible."

"He was on a ship not far from mine that was torpedoed. I saw him go down and I could do nothing to stop it." His recounting is factual and precise, but his eyes cloud over at the memory. "Eight ships and nine thousand men at that battle alone. We joined the navy together, but it was really more his dream to be a great naval officer. I just went along."

Now Georg had picked up the mantle, fulfilling the career his brother could never have. "Tell me more about Hamburg," I say, trying to gently steer the subject away from war. The sadness on his normally strong face is somehow unbearable.

But he will not be dissuaded. "I think Peter wanted to escape to the sea. You see, our parents were terribly strict and they had such high expectations."

"Yes, of course." I nod.

"I have a sister, too. My parents had plans for her to marry someone rich and fairly dreadful, so she ran away to Austria. She lives in a cottage in the Obersalzberg with her husband, someone she actually wanted, cared for, and they have about a dozen children. I see her occasionally, send money. They have a modest lifestyle but it's very happy."

"And noisy, I'm sure, with all of those children," I remark.

"I don't mind," he replies, surprising me. Quiet and order seem better suited to him. "I would have liked children."

"You talk like you're eighty!" I exclaim. "You can still have them."

"I'm twenty-five," Georg replies. "I will be twenty-six, to-morrow, in fact." There is something grave and imposing about his demeanor that makes him appear more than just a few years older.

"There's still plenty of time." Though it is not at all hot in the room, my skin feels suddenly moist.

"I suppose. And you?"

"I do want children," I reply with more certainty than I'd planned. It was not something I'd thought about on a conscious level until now.

"No, I was asking about your family. Are there many of you?"

"Oh." For the second time in an hour, I feel myself blush. "A small family, also. Just Papa and me." I do not count Tante Celia or our other extended relations. "My mother died of flu when I was younger."

"I'm sorry." His voice is full with the empathy of shared loss.

"Growing up an only child, Papa working all of the time, was sometimes a lonely existence. That's why I'd like to have children. How many, I don't know, but definitely more than one." I feel myself talking too fast and saying too much. I have not felt this comfortable speaking with anyone since Krysia. "With siblings you always have each other..." I stop, realizing my error. Georg had his brother until he died at war, in front of his very eyes.

But he does not take offense. "I understand what you mean. My sister, Alice, is my dearest friend, though I don't see her that often."

"And you, do you get lonely?"

He shook his head. "There was a time when Peter was gone, and my parents, too, that I didn't want to go on. But I've made my peace with it now." Solitude had become his default state, such that he did not know how to be otherwise.

"There are so many things I want to do before having children."

"Like what?"

"Well, travel mostly. Not just England and France, but the whole world. Africa, maybe. Or take that railway that's been constructed to China." I'd thought about it so often since my conversations with Krysia a few months earlier. Talking about it now with Georg, the fantasy journeys I've constructed in my head feel almost possible.

"The Trans-Siberian?" He chuckles as though the idea is far-fetched.

"No, really. I want to see the world, not just the cities, but the edges and frontiers before they are developed and changed into looking just like everywhere else."

"Then you would have loved the navy. I've been to some of the places you mentioned—Japan, for one. But I've never been far from harbor to the really deep inland bits." Georg has seen great swaths of the world but always from a great distance, just scratching the surface. But I want to delve deeply into such places—to see the children walking to school and the way the people eat, how they live. "There's nothing better than standing on the deck of the ship as the coast disappears behind you, a clear horizon ahead." A dreamy, faraway look comes into Georg's eyes. "Do you enjoy the seaside?"

"No. I fear the water," I confess. Growing up in landlocked Berlin, I had not seen the ocean until I was six, when we'd taken a holiday to the Dutch seaside during Papa's visitorship at Leiden. I found the dark, murky waters and the rough, churning current unsettling. Since then, I've had terrible nightmares about it—a giant wave rising and swallowing me whole. On the ferry crossing I stayed inside the cabin, reading a book, pretending I was elsewhere and trying not to see the endless water that surrounded us on all sides. "It just feels so ominous." I'm not sure why I'm sharing this confession with a man I barely know.

He looks puzzled, as if the idea of someone not liking the water is unfathomable. "Can you swim?"

"I don't think so. I've never tried."

"I could make you love the water." An image flashes through my mind of Georg and I on a seaside promenade. The cool sea breeze and taste of salt air almost seem real. "Or at least not to be afraid. The thing is to understand that it is a different world—we are visitors in the ocean, not in charge of it. So you have to treat it with respect, come to learn the local customs, so to speak." His words make sense. But I doubt that I could ever love it as he does, or even be comfortable.

"Of course, being on a sailboat is one thing. A naval fighting ship is quite another." He cringes as the memories press over him. "You should give the ocean another chance. It's the only place to really be free," he adds.

"I don't know about that. The mountains can be most liberating." Papa and I have always taken our holidays in the Alps. We would pack simple cheese and fruit that would keep for a day, setting off into the woods as the sun broke. We might not speak for hours, each lost in our own thoughts as we wound between the trees. It was a kind of quiet meditation and a peace I'd not found elsewhere.

I'd suggested hiking when we were in England. "We could go north to the Lakes." But Papa had shaken his head. "Two Germans disappearing into the middle of nowhere might provoke suspicion." And anger. There were stories of a mob beating up a few German expatriates in Leeds just as the war had broken out. Papa insisted that we stay in the cities where help was available and we would not be isolated, protested every time I went out alone.

"Margot..." It is the first time Georg has used my name.

"Yes?"

But before he can continue, there is a creaking sound and the library door, already ajar, opens farther. Papa stands there in his overcoat. I look at the clock. It is nearly ten. Georg and I have talked for most of the time and I've scarcely done any work. "I'm sorry to interrupt, but I'm headed home and I thought that perhaps I could escort you." I smile inwardly. Papa is nowhere near finished work—midnight is only a starting point for him. But he was concerned enough about my being with Georg to break from what he was doing and come to check on me.

"I'm fine, Papa. Though..." I turn to Georg. "I'm afraid we didn't get very far."

Georg nods with recognition. "It's no matter. We can resume tomorrow."

"Same time?"

"I should be most grateful." He turns to Papa. "I trust you'll be at Ambassador Bossart's dinner party Friday?" Papa had mentioned the dinner in passing, a rare occasion for the German delegation to leave the confines of the hotel and enjoy dinner in the city as a show of good faith.

Papa smiles wryly. "Is there any choice?" The men chuckle, bonding over their shared dislike for social obligations and their preference for solitary work.

"Good night, Captain." Though he has bade me to call him by his given name, doing so feels too intimate in front of Papa.

"An odd chap," Papa remarks when we are well clear of the hotel. "So quiet." His description does not sound at all like Georg, who chatted so easily we scarcely made it through any of the translation. But I think back to how scary and imposing he seemed the day the Germans arrived. Knowing him now, it is hard to picture him as the same person. "Some say he's a bit touched in the head."

"He's not," I protest, too defensive of the man I've only just met. "I mean, perhaps he's a bit shaky from battle, but otherwise he appears quite normal." How can Papa and I look at the exact same man and see such different things?

We cross the street to our apartment building, not speaking as we walk up the stairs. "Make sure you don't stay up too late tonight," Papa cautions as he unlocks the door to the flat. "Tante Celia rang that your appointment tomorrow is at nine, which means you'll need to be on the seven-forty train."

"Appointment?" The dress shop, I remember. My wedding gown is ready for its first fitting. I do not want to go, and consider rescheduling. But best not to make waves—it is a gift I've always had, knowing when to go with the current and stifle my rebellious impulses. "The little diplomat," Papa joked, more than once. "Oh, yes, the fitting." Going into Paris will give me an excuse to visit Krysia, as well. I've missed her mightily since our move. "Good night, Papa."

In my room, I change into a nightgown and robe, then pull back the drapes. I strain to glimpse across the road, pressing my head against the window frame. The light in the hotel library still burns. Georg. Though I cannot see him, I imagine him hunched over the desk, studying one of his reports. He so believes in what he is doing, the ability to make a difference and convince the Allies that there is a place for us in this new world order. I hope, for his sake as well as for Germany's, that he is right.

There is a knock at my door and I jump back from the window. "Yes, Papa?"

"I'd almost forgotten. A letter came for you." My stomach sinks as I take the envelope. Another missive from Stefan, no doubt, when I still had not answered the last. But if it was from Stefan, Papa would have said as much. Instead, he looks quizzically at the blocky, unfamiliar script on the coarse brown envelope. When I do not answer, he hands it to me and leaves with a slight shrug, unwilling to pry.

I drop to the edge of the bed and turn the envelope over, suddenly uneasy. Then, too curious to hold back, I rip it open.

Please come see me about a matter of utmost importance.

It is signed by Ignatz Stein.

CHAPTER SIX

_____

"Turn to the left, if you please," the dressmaker says. I shift, cringing as the stiff material scratches against my skin.

"Perhaps just a bit more lace at the neck," Tante Celia offers, rising from her chair and squinting with an appraising eye. Inwardly, I groan. The too-tight collar already creeps against my chin, making me want to gag.

"I don't know..." I demur.

"Your mother," Celia replies firmly, "would have loved the lace."

I open my mouth to protest. The woman in the photos was natural and soft, her flowing clothes nothing like the elaborate frocks Celia favors. I am quite sure she would have preferred my gown to be simple. But the argument is pointless. Celia invokes my mother's memory frequently as both shield and sword, and my own vague recollections of her provide little ammunition for countering Celia's assertions.

As the seamstress pins the fabric around my waist, I see my

reflection behind her in the wide mirror. The solemn, dark-haired woman in the white dress seems a stranger. Behind me, Celia's image appears. My aunt is immaculately coiffed as ever, her hair in a flawless chignon. But the latest fashions cannot mask her too-weak chin and wide nose. Celia has always been about the appearance of things, as if she is trying to plaster over the imperfections and defects of her life, like the man that can never quite be hers because his heart still belongs to her beautiful, dead sister.

An hour earlier, I'd followed Tante Celia reluctantly into the boutique, which was tucked on a side street in the Faubourg Saint-Honoré district, eyeing the satin-and-tulle-clad mannequins with unbridled dread. I imagined then the weddings those dresses represent, the breathless anticipation of a shared future. Would it be different if I was excited about the prospect of marriage and was picking a dress of my own accord, unfettered by the expectations of others?

Expectations. My thoughts turn to the note from Ignatz Stein. What could he possibly want from me? He could not be hoping, these many months later, that I might convey some information to him about Papa's work. I should go to see him today while I am in the city and find out. I shiver, seeing his dark eyes. "Be still, please," the seamstress admonishes.

I stand motionless for what seems like forever, feeling the seamstress's soft rustling hands as she pins the bottom. Finally, she is finished and, with Celia's help, carefully extricates me from the dress. "Are you hungry?" Celia asks a few minutes later as we step onto the street of grand shops, their wide-paned windows displaying jewelry and furs and fine silks that no one can afford anymore. I inhale deeply, clearing the stuffiness of the dress shop from my lungs. "We could go to the food hall at the department store," she offers.

I hesitate, then nod. I am eager to try to see Krysia while I am in the city. But Celia's expression is so hopeful I cannot refuse. And I am hungry, having not eaten this morning at Celia's behest in order to remain as slim as possible for the fitting.

We make our way down the boulevard des Capucines with its rows of fashionable stores and restaurants, past the newspaper kiosks and the stalls selling fruit. Spring has broken in earnest, the trees that line the pavement in full bloom, crocuses sprouting purple from the flower beds. The outdoor cafés overflow with patrons, women in fresh spring fashions and men in blazers with carnations in their lapels. They spill from the tables onto the sidewalks, making it difficult to pass. Above, every shutter in the city has been flung open to let in the fresh air.

Soon we reach the Galeries Lafayette, its grand staircase and glass dome more reminiscent of an opera house than a department store. The ground-floor food hall appears much like I remember it before the war, but the space is too big for the goods that are now available. There is a subtle pride to the way the sellers have laid out the breads, and a reverence with which the shoppers accept their parcels of food that suggest the years of hunger and doing without will not be easily forgotten. "Not so many vegetables," Tante Celia remarks critically. I cringe at the obviousness of her German accent.

"Perhaps when the fields can be tilled with fertilizer instead of the blood of Frenchmen," a woman beside us replies haughtily, then turns away. Suddenly I am not hungry.

Tante Celia lifts her chin with surprising defiance. "Why don't you find us a table?" she suggests to me.

I navigate my way through the crowd toward the seating area. *"Pardon,"* I say as a man bumps into me. I step aside to let him pass. But he brushes against me again, this time pushing me toward the wall. The assault was intentional, I realize, as I look up into the face of Ignatz Stein.

He removes his brown fedora and tips it in my direction. "Hello, Margot," he says, and there is something predatory about his tone. He looks strangely out of place away from the café.

"Monsieur Stein…" I lick my lips uneasily. "This is a coincidence."

"You didn't answer my note."

"I only received it late last night. There was hardly time."

He clucks his tongue. "I understand. Fittings and parties and all. It's a busy life."

He must have followed me, but why? I decide to ignore his sarcasm. "What is it that you want?"

"You had said you would keep your eyes open." No longer the affable café proprietor, he looms over me, menacing.

"I've not seen or heard anything from my father that might be of interest." I fumble for an explanation. "We're so much more removed from everything since moving out to Versailles."

"But you're working for the German officer now, aren't you?"

How had he known? It was a development not two days old, so recent I'd not even had time to tell Krysia. "That should prove useful," he continues, not bothering to wait for me to confirm. "Information about German military operations is scarce and valuable."

I raise my hand. "I have no interest…"

"Pity, isn't it, about Cottin? Poor fool really thought he could stop Clemenceau from voting against his beloved Greater Serbia. One only hopes he can be persuaded to remain silent…" Ignatz knows that I will do anything to protect the truth about Cottin's source, to keep the blame from falling to Papa.

I stare up at him with revulsion. Stein is Jewish, too, but he is a crude caricature, greedy and manipulative, the way the anti-Semites would paint us all. "If it is a question of money…" I don't know why I have said this. I have none of my own, but I could figure out something.

"Don't insult us. We don't want money from you or any of the bourgeoisie scum." He spits this last word. "Your contacts and position make you far more valuable to us than any compensation."

I open my mouth to protest—I cannot possibly steal from Georg. Then, thinking of Papa, my shoulders slump. "What is it you want me to do?"

He drops his voice. "The Germans have claimed they've de-militarized." I stare at him in disbelief. We've scarcely begun to recover from the war—how could Ignatz possibly be contem-plating another one already? I recall uneasily Georg's insistence the previous night that a strong military is essential for peace. Perhaps Ignatz is not that far off. He continues, "We believe they've stockpiled munitions in the east—and those could be used to support the Whites in their fight against Lenin and the Bolsheviks. Keep an eye out for anything about the German military plans, particularly those on the Eastern Front. Reports, cables—get copies if you can."

"Who is the work for?" I press. "Really, if I'm to risk things and help…"

"A small group of us gather information to help counter the fascist influence back home. The head of the group is known covertly as Red Thorn."

"Can I meet him?"

"I'm afraid not. Just deliver the papers to me."

But before I can protest, Tante Celia is at my side. "Is some-thing wrong?" I turn back toward Ignatz, but he is already cross-ing the hall, enveloped by the crowd. "Who was that odd man?"

"A friend of Krysia's. I was asking after her."

"Oh, the Polish woman," Celia's tone was dismissive, as if talking about one of the maids. "The pianist."

"You've heard of her?" For once, I am almost impressed.

"Of course. Anyone who is anyone has Krysia Smok play at their party, and her husband Marcin, too, if one can get him." To Celia, Krysia is a commodity and a sign of status, not a person.

"She's the daughter of an ambassador, actually," I reply, fight-ing to keep the annoyance from my voice.

Her expression remains skeptical. "This is Paris. Anyone can reinvent themselves here."

A waiter brings the tray of assorted cheeses Celia had selected to one of the tables and I take a cracker. "So, I was thinking of salmon terrines for the starter course," Celia says, turning to the wedding menu as though we were in the middle of a conversation about it. No one is more excited about my engagement than Celia. Though they had fallen on hard times of late, the Osters are an old Berlin family and the fact that they are socially well-placed made Stefan a palatable choice in Celia's eyes. And it is the wedding she never had the chance to plan for herself. I nod as she continues speaking, still shaken by my encounter with Ignatz and what he has asked me to do.

"Would you like to go shopping?" she asks when we've finished eating. "The boutique over on rue Fleury has reopened. Or shall I just have the car take us back?" *Us.* She has no reason to come to Versailles. Escorting me back to the suburb is merely a pretense to wait and see Papa.

"Actually, I'd like to go see a friend," I reply. "Here in the city."

"The Polish woman?" Her nose wrinkles as she tries to comprehend my preference for spending time with Krysia over her. "Suit yourself," she says quickly.

Celia's jealous. For years, she has been trying to be some sort of surrogate for my mother, an older sister perhaps. Celia is closer to my age than my mother's. We might have been friends, if only we shared some mutual interest or concern beyond Papa. But then Krysia came along and our friendship was instantaneous. I'm not trying to be callous with Celia's feelings. Who can explain why we bond so readily with one person but not another? It is human nature, some odd makeup of our biology perhaps, or a sense that we were destined to be with some people.

Celia really tries to be there, though, not just for Papa but for me, in a hundred little ways that are missing without my mother. I am so ungrateful. "I'll come in next week and we can go shopping then," I offer. Her face brightens.

Twenty minutes later, I step out of a cab at Krysia's. Perhaps I should have called ahead. But she had said Poles did not mind drop-in guests. I ring the bell.

"You again," she says teasingly when I reach the top-floor landing, kissing me airily on both cheeks. She wears a gauzy blouse, flat laced slippers that give the impression of a ballerina. "I haven't seen you at any of the salons."

"I've been working." It had not occurred to me that Krysia might wonder about my absence the way I once had hers.

Behind her there is a shuffling noise and a man appears in the doorway. "You must be Margot."

Krysia's husband looks nothing like I might have expected of a world-renowned musician. In sharp contrast to the brooding artists I'd met at the café, Marcin has a wide grin that lifts his pink, cherubic cheeks close to his eyes. He is a good foot shorter than Krysia, with a full stomach and salt-and-pepper hair, a premature gray. Somewhere between playing Saint Nicholas, if he'd been a bit taller, and one of the elves.

I flush, flattered that Krysia had spoken about me. What had she said? "I hope I'm not intruding."

"It's fine," Krysia says. "Marcin was just leaving."

And whether that is true or said out of politeness, Marcin picks up his coat. "Goodbye, my love." Marcin's expression leaves no doubt as to his adoration for Krysia.

She gazes at Marcin and there is a softness to her eyes that I have not seen before. Her attachment to her husband is not a contradiction to the independent woman I've come to know. Marcin's love supports her and gives her that strength. He is clearly devoted, but yet she still seems so alone. It's the child who has left a hollow place within her that can never be filled.

"So you've found something to occupy your time?" Krysia

asks when the door has closed. She pours two cups of coffee, brings them to the settee.

I sit down. Sunlight streams in through the lace curtains, creating dancing patterns of shadows on the parquet floors. "I'm just translating some documents for the delegation." It goes without saying that I am referring to the Germans, and I study her face. Will she be offended that I am helping them? "It's hardly a life makeover, I suppose." My tone is apologetic now.

"But it's a start."

"Perhaps. Only…" Picturing Ignatz looming above me in the food hall, my stomach twists. "You remember the attempt on Clemenceau's life?"

She nods. "That idiot Cottin thought he was helping his cause. Instead he just gave those in power an excuse to be less benevolent."

"Oh, Krysia!" Suddenly I am telling her everything about Stein's request that I look for information, first from Papa and now Georg, his threat to expose the truth if I did not. "I'm so sorry I didn't say anything earlier. But I didn't know what to do. He was your friend and so I thought…"

"He put you in a very difficult position and that was wrong." Her lips set grimly. "I long suspected that Stein was up to something. He's a wild card—he lost his parents in Kiev pogroms as a child, made his way on his wits since he was nine years old." She takes a sip of coffee, gazing out the window. "The war produced all sorts of would-be spies like Stein. Intelligence is everywhere. All of the information that was once locked up in vaults at ministries is now out, making it that much more enticing for opportunists and rogues." Suddenly I see a whole underworld to the conference. "Most likely he's just acting on his own, like Cottin."

My hope rises. "Do you really think so?"

"Let me make some inquiries and find out if there's something to be done about it all."

"You have contacts?"

"Nothing personal, of course. But I've got a cousin who is involved with the Cheka."

Cheka is the intelligence arm of the communist party, rumored to be operating on behalf of Russia throughout Europe. I shudder at the notion, foreign and ominous. Somehow, though, it does not surprise me that Krysia has connections everywhere. "You won't tell Ignatz that we've spoken?"

"No, of course not."

"If something should happen to implicate Papa, I couldn't bear it." My voice is pleading now. "He's in a terrible position as it is, suspected by the Allies because he is German, and by the Germans because he is a Jew."

"What about you? Do you consider yourself Jewish German or a German Jew?" she asks.

I tilt my head, puzzled. "I'm both," I insist. I've certainly never felt as though I had to choose.

"Marcin is Jewish," she informs me.

"Oh." Gentle and refined, he is nothing like Ignatz or the other Jews I've seen from Poland and other places to the east. And he is married to a Gentile. Though we live among our non-Jewish neighbors and see them socially and do business with them, intermarriage is just not something that happens.

"His family has not spoken to us since the wedding." Her lower lip droops, pulling her whole face downward.

"I'm sorry."

"It's a hard thing to be rejected simply for being who you are." She laughs. "There are a great many reasons to dislike me, but usually people at least meet me first."

"Nonsense." To me, Krysia is wonderful, mysterious and sure of herself. But there is something about her quiet confidence, the way she challenges people, that could be off-putting.

"Anyway, I'll take care of Stein," she says, patting my hand.

"Try not to think too much about it." Her tone is so reassuring that for a moment I almost believe she is right.

By the time the train pulls into Versailles, it is nearly dark. I'd lingered longer than I had intended at Krysia's and there is no time to go back to the apartment to freshen and comb the dust from my hair before I have to be at work. As I near the hotel, my step quickens. Georg is waiting by the door when I arrive. Warmth rises in me, and I am more glad than I should have been to see him again. "I'm sorry if I'm late," I apologize. "I had an errand in the city and…"

"Not at all. The library's not available this evening, I'm afraid. It's being cleaned. But I've cleared a spot in my rooms for you to work." Pushing a vision of Papa's disapproving stare from my mind, I follow him down the corridor. He unlocks the door and lets me into a small sitting room with a desk and two chairs and a hat stand. A second door sits ajar, revealing a bedroom on the other side.

I stand in the center of the room, looking around uncertainly. Georg has cleaned in preparation for my arrival, I can tell, and opened the windows to try without success to clear some of the mustiness from the dank gray space.

He coughs once, then a second time stronger. "Are you unwell?" I ask.

"Not at all. I've had this blasted cold ever since I came back from sea."

"Have you seen a doctor? Papa has a physician in the city on rue de la Rochelle."

He shakes his head. "There's no time. It's just a cold." He gestures to the cardboard box I carry. "What's that?"

I open it, revealing the small cake that I had picked up for him on impulse before leaving Paris, yellow with just a touch of whipped cream on the top. "Happy birthday," I say.

Several expressions cross his face at once—uncertainty, then

bewilderment and finally joy. "I cannot remember when someone last celebrated my birthday."

"Would you like some?"

"No, thank you."

I set down the box, feeling foolish.

"Not just this moment," he amends. "I need to leave you for
a short while to confer with one of my colleagues," he apologizes. "But if you wouldn't mind working on without me, perhaps we could have some cake when I return."

"Of course." In fact, I am uneasy at the notion of staying here
alone in the desolate hotel room. I consider asking if I might take
the documents with me to our apartment, then decide against it.

"I'll be back as soon as I can."

Watching him leave, a strange sense of longing floods through
me. It's the room, I tell myself, the fact that I don't want to be
alone here. The space feels even colder and darker without him.

My eyes drift to the pile of binders and notes over by the desk,
the ones that Georg has not given to me. Now would be the
perfect time to search for the information Ignatz has insisted that
I procure. But I cannot. It is not just that I am nervous, uncertain when Georg will return. There is something in the way he
looks at me, filled with such trust. I don't want to betray that.

Tea, I decide. I peer into the bedroom. Unlike the sitting area,
it has not been tidied for my benefit and the feeling of Georg
is everywhere, in the still slightly tousled sheets, the smell of
his aftershave, which lingers in the still-wet brush by the basin.
Searching for tea, I open the cupboard, which is well stocked
with crackers and dried fruit. Georg does not, I surmise, like to
stop working and leave the hotel to eat.

I set the kettle, then walk to the basin, peering into the egg-
shaped cracked mirror above it. Georg stands here each morning, washing and getting dressed. Does he ever think of me?

Alarmed by the thought, I step away from the mirror and
closer to his bed. I run my hand over the pillowcase, imagining

him there, asleep. This is silliness, a schoolgirl's crush. But I'm twenty years old, and I have a fiancé waiting for me.

A sharp whistling jars me from my thoughts and I leap back. The kettle. I pour the tea with shaking hands, then hurry back to the front room.

I thumb through the pile of memos, sorting before starting on one about the German battleship fleet. The language is complex and I frequently turn to the dictionary, but I soon become engrossed and the translation flows more smoothly.

The door opens and Georg walks in. I look up, surprised at the time that has passed and the fact that it is nearly ten o'clock.

"How's your progress?"

"Good, I think." In truth, it is easier to work without Georg and the temptation to talk. I push the notes toward him, smelling as I do the faintly sour odor of wine on his breath.

He stands behind me and reaches down. "This passage here." Georg gestures as if to demonstrate his point, and I find myself staring as his hands—the long tapered fingers, soft nail beds almost improbably well-manicured. He bends closer, his warmth against my back.

Then he straightens. "Shall we have some cake?" Not waiting for an answer, he cuts two pieces and passes one to me. He drops to the seat across from mine and takes a bite. "Delicious. Thank you."

I set my plate aside and finish augmenting the translation to include the paragraph he indicated, then pass it to him. He leans over to read it. There is a space between his collar and hair where the skin is exposed, and I am seized with the urge to put my lips there. What is wrong with me?

I clear my throat. "Let me know once you've had the chance to review these if you have any questions."

"I shall." But his eyes glaze over the notes, seeming not to see them. He yawns and sets down his plate. "You said you had an errand in Paris. Where did you go?"

The question is perhaps intrusive, but I do not mind. "To a dressmaker," I say. "I had a...fitting."

"Not for one of those formal dresses, I hope. After all of the makeup and ruffles the women wear around here, you are positively refreshing."

"Thank you." I shift uneasily.

He stands again, walking to the mantelpiece and picking up a framed photograph of a ship, a row of men lined up neatly on the gangplank. "Your men?" I ask.

"They were. It all fell apart at the end." His words run together now, slurred slightly by drink. "We received orders to move north and engage the British navy there. We knew it was futile—the war was all but over and we were defeated. But we commanded the men to proceed. They refused. They were starving and demoralized. They didn't want to die, too. It was madness, Margot." The full sorrow of the sentence crashes down on my name. "Sailors fighting sailors. Two of my own men killed one another."

"The war cost me everything," Georg adds abruptly, setting the photo back down unsteadily. He is open and exposed in a way that I have not yet seen.

"Your brother..."

He nods. "I lost my father when I was on the ship, too. I received word that he was dying but it was a matter of hours and we were at sea. There was nothing that could be done. It was just days after Peter died at Jutland so he never even knew, which I think was in itself a blessing."

He continues, "I was studying at university when the war broke out." His eyes have a faraway look and his voice sounds like mine when I speak of travel. I see him then as a boy, wide-eyed and bright with a future in front of him. He is so broken now, like so many others. I am seized by the urge to take him into my arms. Can he be healed or is he too far gone?

"You can still go back."

He smiles, as though talking to an indulgent child. "That's kind of you to say. But what school would have me? I'm twenty-five, no, twenty-six." He gestures toward the rest of the cake, which sits uneaten on the table. "My hands shake like an old man's and I can't concentrate. That was a younger man's dream." He leans back resigned. "But if we can get this right, that is, if we can come up with an order of things that makes sense, that would mean it was all for something. It has to have meant something, doesn't it?" He searches my eyes and there is a kind of desperation in his voice.

Our conversation is intimate now, as though we have known each other years and not just days. "The war took so many good men," he adds. "I suppose that is why you are on your own?"

I swallow, uncomfortable at his abrupt shift in focus to me. "There was someone."

"You were engaged?"

I nod. "My fiancé was at the Marne."

"A tragedy. So you understand, then, what it was like with my brother." I realize, too late, that he has come away with the impression that my fiancé died. There was a time when I thought that Stefan was dead. Papa had come back to our rooms at college at midday when I knew he should have been holding supervisions. A telegram was clutched in his hand and his face was the strangest shade of gray. "Darling," he said. We'd both taken to speaking more English while here, part of our futile quest to fit in, and it spilled over to the times when we were alone. "It's Stefan...he's missing."

"Soldiers go missing all of the time," I said, my voice wavering at the end, me comforting Papa when it should have been the reverse.

He shook his head, and I took the paper from his outstretched fingers to spare him from having to tell me the rest. Words leaped from the page piecemeal, rising up and forming a tapestry of images in my mind. A bomb had blown a crater a quar-

ter of a mile wide, decimating the trench he'd been in. Stefan
and his whole unit were gone, and the severity of the attack had
left no hope of survivors.

Stefan was dead. I had imagined it secretly in the places so
dark I could scarcely acknowledge them. Had I brought it on
him? Even through my sadness, I knew that such things were
not possible, that the universe did not operate according to the
whims of my mind.

In the days that followed, my sadness mixed with new ideas.
I could remain in England and take classes, or perhaps travel
farther abroad as a governess. Surely in my grief and my search
for a new direction, I'd be allowed more than the usual latitude.

Word that Stefan was alive did not come for nearly six weeks.
"Found in a hospital in Belgium. But, darling, he's been quite
badly wounded. His legs have been hurt, there may possibly be
other injuries, as well. You must prepare yourself."

I was silent for several minutes, overwhelmed by a combination of shock and relief and, to my shame, a tinge of disappointment. "Will he make it?"

"I believe so. He's very strong of will, according to Walter."
My uncle had been using his contacts at the ministry to procure information. "It must be the thought of coming back to
you that kept him alive."

"That's wonderful news." But my voice was flat and without
meaning. I had come to accept Stefan's death in recent weeks.
I'd been sad for him, of course. But freed from the expectations
of marrying him, I'd begun to make plans. Now he was back
and the visions of a life for myself crumbled to dust and blew
away with the breeze, as if they'd never been there at all. The
old world began to tighten around me like a noose.

"Do you believe in God?" Georg asks, drawing me from my
memories. I tilt my head at the sudden shift in conversation. His
tone is philosophical now. "You're a Jewess, aren't you?"

"Yes." His words strike me as somehow abrupt, just short of rude.

"Are you religious?"

"I suppose." Mine is the naive and childlike sort of belief that comes from things taught rather than deeply considered. Religion isn't something I ever questioned; it was just something that we did, part of the expectation of who I was to be. But it was not something I thought about on a deeper level. "You?"

"I stopped believing, really, the day I saw my brother swallowed into the sea." He is asking whether my faith was shaken, as well, by losing someone I loved.

"The men were awful to the Jewish sailors, I'm afraid," Georg says. "They hazed them, beat them, took their food. Once there was a particularly grievous assault of an, ahem, sexual nature." He is clearly uncomfortable but unwilling to shield me from the truth.

"Oh!" Stefan's letters had given no hint. There had been only cheer in his writing, bright talk of the future we would have, building a house. It was as if he had to doggedly persist in his belief that he would return unscathed—a belief that was shattered nevertheless at the Marne.

My guilt rises. After all Stefan has been through, he deserves a life full of joy, a hero's welcome or at least a woman who wants to be by his side.

"It was a horrible thing, the way they treated the Jewish lads," Georg says. "That's why Palestine is so important."

"Oh?" I flare. "You want to ship all the Jews off to the desert?"

"No, of course not. But a home of their own, a safe haven."

"Germany is our home," I persist. My family came to Prussia in the seventeenth century, when only a few Jews were allowed in, and stayed, our lives interwoven with the fabric of the non-Jewish Germans who were our neighbors and friends. I cannot identify with some strange Semitic land I've never seen.

Georg sits, staring wordlessly over my shoulder. "And you?"

I find myself emboldened to ask, pushed by the need to change the subject. "Do you have a fiancée?" He shakes his head.

"I've never been involved with a woman," he confesses. "I noticed them, of course, like any young man would, but there was work and my studies. And they always seemed interested in the most superficial things. I've never found one I could speak to as I do you." This last comment, too intimate for the short time we have known each other, catches me off guard. Yet I feel exactly the same.

"I thought there would be time. And then well, war changes a person. Have you ever been to a carnival, one of those with the merry-go-round that spins so very fast that afterward when you lie in bed at night you feel like you are still spinning?" I nod, trying to follow the story without letting images of Georg in bed intrude. "I lay awake at night and I hear the cannon fire against the ship and the screams of the men around us as they sank to a cold watery death while we stood hopelessly by."

He buries his head in his hands and I start toward him, seized by the urge to comfort him with more than just words, to wrap him in my arms and rock him like a child. But as I near he stands and takes a step back. "And that is why I will never marry or be of any good to any woman." His eyes are steely, as though he regrets having let down his guard and confided in me. "Good evening, Margot." He gets up and walks into the bedroom. I stare at the now-closed door, stunned.

I take my coat and start for the hallway. "Margot, wait…" I turn back as the bedroom door opens again. I wait for him to apologize for his outburst. "We won't be able to work tomorrow," he says instead. I wonder if I have done something wrong, whether my work is not pleasing to him. "The dinner party," he explains. I recall the gathering in Paris that both he and Papa are dreading.

"Of course. If you'd like, I can keep working on my own."

"It's not that. Rather, I was wondering…" He is gazing at

me squarely now. "Would you like to accompany me?" It takes me several seconds to comprehend he is asking me to go as his date. "Perhaps if I ask your father…"

"No!" I say, too vehemently. Papa will never approve and then he will tell Georg the truth about Stefan. "That is, I told Papa I would go with him." It is a lie. "I will meet you there." Better, too, to avoid the many questions from Papa that Georg's invitation would provoke.

I walk from the hotel hurriedly. The feelings Georg stirs in me are unlike any I have ever known. But until now, at least I could take comfort in the fact that they were one-sided, a pretense that has been shattered by his invitation. How is it possible that someone as attractive and worldly as Georg could be interested in me?

A few minutes later, I barrel into the flat. "I should like to join you for the dinner party, if you don't mind," I say before Papa can look up. Papa does not respond, but his eyebrows lift. For so long I have tried to avoid the social obligations of the conference.

"I hadn't thought you would want to." He had mentioned the dinner party previously only to ask my forbearance in missing our usual Sabbath meal together, not with any serious thought that I would want to go.

"I'd enjoy an evening in the city."

"I'd love you to join me." He smiles at the prospect of my escorting him. Celia's lack of any official status and the quiet nature of their relationship makes it impossible for her to attend such functions with him and so he often goes alone. Then a light dawns in his eyes, as if he suddenly understands my newfound interest in the occasion. His brow furrows with consternation. "Margot, *liebchen*. About Captain Richwalder…"

"I'm helping him with the translation, that's all. It's good for my language skills." He dips his chin in that way that signals he isn't convinced by what I've said. "You don't like him," I observe, trying to hide my disappointment.

"He fights for a living. He must be at least ten years older than you."

"Five only," I counter. *Technically six.*

"And he's odd," Papa continues, undeterred.

"It's the combat, Papa, that's all. The things that he saw and he heard…" I stop, realizing that my words are revealing the extent of our conversation, an intimacy that goes well beyond just work.

"That may be the case," he concedes. "The war changed people in so many ways and we all have to live with who we are now. But Georg's not Jewish." Finally, we are getting to the heart of the issue. Why, I wonder, thinking of Krysia and Marcin, should that matter? We have become so assimilated. Papa doesn't even wear a yarmulke anymore. There are some things, though, that are still sacrosanct. Intermarriage would mean children that might not be raised Jewish. But I cannot engage in this debate with Papa without admitting to him that there is something to his question.

"Of course not," I say quickly, avoiding the confrontation any other answer would bring. I swallow over the lump that has formed in my throat. "Anyway, I'm engaged to Stefan." The explanation hangs hollowly and without conviction.

His brow wrinkles. "Maybe we should get away for a bit when the conference is over." He fears that he has been neglecting me and that I've gravitated toward Georg out of loneliness. "Perhaps this summer we should rent a villa on the coast." Does he expect us to be here that long?

Not waiting for a response, he turns back to his papers, our conversation apparently over. I walk uneasily toward my room, then stop, turning back. There is no one in the world to whom I feel closer than Papa. Yet despite our deep affection, there are vast areas of darkness, things unsaid, parts of ourselves that we cannot share. Once upon a time the idea of keeping secrets from Papa was unfathomable. There was the unspoken between us—the fact that he and Celia were together—but that was not quite a lie. Our trust is a thread that, once pulled at, is swiftly unraveling.

Later that night I lay awake thinking about Georg. Why hadn't I told him the truth about Stefan, the fact that he is still alive and waiting for me back home? It would have been the natural response, but now it is too late. Georg is a man of principle and ethics. I feared that if he knew I am not by Stefan's side, he would judge me less than honorable. But it is not his judgment I am feeling—it is my own shame.

I remember Georg, standing too close behind me. Warmth rises from my legs and I bring my hand low, trying to silence the feeling, but this only increases my longing for him. I have no business thinking such things. I know so little of matters between men and women. With Stefan there had been a few innocent gropes. I've heard whispers of the other girls at school and learned a bit from novels, the ones I did not let Papa see. But the rest is a gaping hole in my comprehension, a curtain I cannot pull back. My secret thoughts have always been nameless and faceless until now. I press harder and my desire crests, then ebbs. Finally, I turn and close my eyes, still seeing Georg's face in my mind.

CHAPTER SEVEN

"Are you ready?" Papa stands at the door to my room, waiting patiently.

"Just another minute, please." As he retreats, I pull back a lock of hair for what feels like the hundredth time, but it breaks free once more. I throw down the pin, frustrated. I have never been any good at dressing and polishing and I always wind up looking as unkempt as before I started. It seems a waste trying. "The lack of a mother's touch," I heard Tante Celia remark once when she thought I wasn't listening. She tries to help in her own clumsy way, buying me lipstick and powder for my nose, but they reflect her own taste, stiff and heavily scented. I imagine my mother here, smoothing my hair, giving some advice on what I should and should not say at dinner. A rare and unexpected wave of longing for her shoots through me.

I take a final glance in the mirror, patting with resignation the tangle of curls that have ceded into a tight ball from the dampness and fog. My eyes peer out, too large for my face, making me appear something of an owl.

An hour later, we arrive at the Swiss ambassador's residence, a Le Marais town house double the usual width with carved wrought-iron balconies. The drawing room where drinks are being served is a staid affair, with plain beige drapes and a hardwood floor that shows its scuffs through the polish. In contrast to the wild galas I've attended previously, the mood is quiet, even somber. The German delegates cluster on the opposite side of the room from their hosts, like adolescent boys and girls at a dance back home, too shy to mingle.

As Papa hands our coats to the butler, I scan the room but do not see Georg. Perhaps, since I'd declined his invitation to come as his guest, he has decided to defy expectations and remain at the hotel working. I am seized with the urge to flee back to Versailles and do the same.

A moment later I sense him, lifting my head as his square frame fills the doorway that separates the foyer from the great room. It is the first time I have ever seen him in his dress uniform, resplendent with the rich blue fabric that contours to the gold-braided shoulders. Medals of valor adorn the broad expanse of his chest. Suddenly it is as if the air has been sucked from the room, making it impossible to breathe.

All female eyes turn toward him. A handsome man, even an enemy soldier, is an oasis in the desert that was left behind by those who went to the front and never returned or who came home broken like Stefan. The room shrinks around Georg as he surveys the room, his expression grim. He was late intentionally, I decide, wanting to spend as little time here as possible. His steely eyes take in the gathering. There is a seriousness to him, a wisdom and worldliness beyond his years. The things he has seen have worn grooves in him, like driftwood pounded by the water, making him fascinating in a way that other men simply are not.

His head turns then in my direction and as our eyes meet, a light dawns within him. I hold his gaze, mindful that I am staring but unable to look away. His face breaks wide open then with the vulnerability of a young child. The people and sound fade, leaving just Georg and me and then endless space between us. In that moment, the walls crumble, revealing the attraction that should not exist, but nonetheless does.

Papa is at my side now, but my ears buzz with such a din that I cannot hear what he is saying. I pretend to listen, still watching Georg out of the corner of my eye as he crosses the room. I am filled with shame at the way my pulse quickens. But the daughter of a British viscount whom I've encountered at a few social functions intercepts Georg and takes his arm. She leads him to the fireplace, a ravenous dog about to devour a steak dinner. My heart sinks. Leigh Arrington is an alabaster beauty, with a tall, willowy grace I could never hope to match. I feel silly and childlike by comparison. How I wish we were back in the drafty study at the hotel, just the two of us.

Georg shifts slightly and his expression is pained. His eyes meet mine over her head and the look of longing is unmistakable. He would rather be alone with me, as well, I realize, suppressing a flutter.

The sound of a piano, its cadence familiar, blossoms from the corner of the room. I turn, delighted to see Krysia seated at the keyboard. I had not known she would be playing tonight. The sound is more fulsome than usual, Marcin at his cello beside her. I start toward Krysia, but a tuxedoed man I do not recognize reaches the piano first. He pages through the sheet music over her shoulder and I expect her to be annoyed, but she does not appear so. A moment later, the man whispers something, then walks away. Krysia begins playing a Chopin piece, presumably the one the man requested.

As the last note fades to a smattering of polite applause, I approach. "You didn't mention you would be here tonight."

"You didn't ask."

"I've never heard you two play together. You sound wonderful."

"Marcin is the real artist," she remarks. He smiles but does not look up from tuning his instrument. "I'm going to take a break, my dear," she tells him. She steps away from the piano as he begins to play a solo, her eyes wide with adoration. Krysia always seems so strong; it is strange to watch her step back and let Marcin take center stage. But she is right, there is a poetry to the way his fingers move over the strings, a fluidity to his bowing that even a neophyte such as myself can recognize as world-class.

"I'm glad you're here," Krysia says. "There's something I need to... Good evening." She switches topics abruptly, glancing over my shoulder. I turn and find Georg standing behind me, too close.

"Captain Richwalder." There is a note of playfulness to my formality. He does not answer, but stares at me. It is the gown, one that Celia had picked out for me. The pink material clings long and lean to my torso and the neckline is much more daring than the everyday blouses I wear to work for him. My mother's drop pearl necklace circles my throat.

"Margot." He recovers, then leans forward and kisses me on the cheek, the scent of his aftershave reminiscent of his rooms, only more intense. I freeze—though not improper, it is hardly the traditional kiss on the hand. His lips are warm and fleeting on my cheek, high and close to my ear. He pauses, breath lingering in my hair, and I fight the urge to move even closer. As he straightens, his expression is confused, as though he had not himself quite planned to behave in such a manner.

Beside me, Krysia clears her throat. "Please excuse me," I say. "Georg, this is Krysia Smok."

"A pleasure," she says, but her voice is devoid of its usual warmth and her hand remains at her side.

"Krysia is Polish," I offer, trying to break the ice that has formed suddenly.

"From Krakow to be exact."

He grimaces. "Southern Poland is a hotbed for communists. The traitor Rosa Luxemburg for one." His voice is harsher than usual.

Krysia stiffens at his reference to the recently killed activist. "Rosa and I were classmates in school. She was shot like a dog, her body dumped in a canal. Is this the world we've come to?"

"I certainly don't condone such violence. But the communists are a great menace to our society back home. Law and order is needed," he adds firmly.

"But in a democracy, the ideals of different groups—"

"All have their place in an orderly forum." I understand now why Krysia and he instantly dislike each other.

Krysia looks away, unable to continue the debate calmly and unwilling to rise to the bait. "Krakow is beautiful," she says, returning to more neutral waters. "The City of Kings, we call it. Castles and churches and the mountains close by. You should try to see it someday."

Georg shakes his head. "It's landlocked. I'm afraid my love pulls me toward the sea."

"'One may find beauty where one least expects it,'" Krysia prods. "'There are more things in heaven and earth…'"

"'…than are dreamt of in your philosophy,'" he finishes for her. There is an awkward silence between them. Georg's expression is uncomfortable, Krysia's icy. "Margot, I need to speak with your father about some matters. If you'll excuse me." Without waiting for a response, he walks across the room, leaving me deflated by his departure, as well as the realization that the two people I've met and like best since coming to Paris do not seem to at all like each other.

"So that's your German," she says, a note of disdain to her voice.

"He's not 'my' German," I correct, annoyed. "He's German—as am I. What was that last bit about?"

"It's from Shakespeare's *Hamlet*. It means that one should not profess to know all of the answers—and that the world holds a great many mysteries and wonders for one to see." Her bottom lip curls. "Not that he would understand."

"Krysia, you've hardly met him."

"He's a fascist soldier and—forgive me—a German."

"It is a hard thing to be rejected for who you are," I say, throwing back at her the words she'd used to describe the pain of being shunned by Marcin's Jewish family.

"Perhaps." But I can tell from the way her jaw is set that she will never accept him.

Over Krysia's shoulder, I watch Georg and Papa together, heads bowed low in quiet conversation. The two could not be more different—the scholar and the warrior—yet I love them both so much. *Love.* I stop, caught off guard by my thought. It is the first time I have ever allowed myself to think of Georg that way and now it has leaped out and I cannot stop it—like trying to put paste back into a tube. Is such a thing possible after just a few days? My feelings for Georg are undeniably real, but at the same time they change nothing—not the fact that I cannot be with him, or that Stefan is still waiting for me.

"He should be thanking God for the Bolsheviks," Krysia mutters under her breath.

I turn to her, grateful for the reprieve from my thoughts. "How can you say that?"

"Because the red menace, as they call it, is the only thing that's keeping the Big Four from destroying Germany entirely. They need your country strong enough that communism cannot spread across Europe like wildfire, but not so strong that it can cause trouble again. If it weren't for Russia, the Western powers would send Germany back into the nineteenth century. Of course, he would not understand that." Before I can respond, Krysia returns to the piano and joins Marcin as he plays.

Standing alone, I scan the room for Papa and Georg. Across the party, one of the servers, older and more portly than the others, catches my eye. I gasp. Ignatz. He makes his way over to fill my wineglass. "What are you doing here?"

"Working. My cousin is a catering manager and I fill in sometimes for a bit of cash."

"Oh," I reply flatly, unplacated by his answer. There are dozens of parties in Paris each week—it makes no sense that he happens to be at this one.

"And I wanted to see you," he continues, getting to the heart of the matter. My stomach sinks. "Have you gotten the documents for me?"

"You only asked me yesterday. There's hardly been time." I study his face wondering if he believes me. Could he possibly have known that Georg had left me alone in his rooms the previous night with full access to his files?

He does not press the point, instead gesturing across the room with his head. "That's him over there, isn't it?"

His question is not in earnest. The only military man in the room, Georg would be hard to miss. "Perhaps I shall speak with him myself." Ignatz's tone is menacing. "Or maybe your father…"

"No!" I yelp, more loudly than I intended. A woman standing behind me turns to look over her shoulder. Ignatz could reveal everything before all of these people and destroy Papa.

"Don't play games with us, Margot," he says, his voice low with menace. "Time is of the essence and…"

"Darling," Papa says, coming to my side, "is something wrong?"

"Not at all," I say, searching for an explanation for my extended conversation with a server. But when I turn around, Ignatz has disappeared. "I'm going to freshen up before we are seated." I make my way from the reception, then double back around to the piano. "He's here," I whisper to Krysia from behind.

She does not stop playing. "I know. That is what I was trying to tell you. It is just like that fool. Remain calm and I will see what I can learn."

A bell rings on the far side of the room, signaling dinner. At the door to the dining room I meet Georg, who is standing to one side, trying without success to adjust his tie. "May I?" I offer. It is something I have done as long as I can remember with Papa, smoothing out the knot, tucking the corners just so.

His face relaxes. "Please."

I struggle to keep my fingers from trembling against his skin, the lump in his throat moves slightly beneath my touch. "There. Much better."

"Thank you." He coughs once, then again. "How are you enjoying the party?"

Our eyes meet and we laugh, understanding just how much we both hate being here. Then his expression turns serious. "It's good, I suppose, to be out. I'm sorry if I offended your friend the pianist with my political talk. Spending so much time at sea has robbed me of all sense of polite conversation."

"Not at all."

"There you are." Papa comes up behind us.

"I've taken the liberty of arranging to be seated near you," Georg says. My breath catches. "There are some matters related to the Ruhr proposal that I'd like to discuss." He was talking, of course, to Papa, not me. But when we reach the table the placards indicate that the seating is the customary man-woman-man insofar as the lopsided numbers permit, and I am nevertheless sandwiched in between Georg and my father. Seeing the arrangement, a frown flickers across Papa's face.

The table is set plainly, I notice as I sit down in the chair that Georg has pulled back. The cloth napkins are crude, the knives and forks just a step above everyday kitchen silver. But this is more than just the lingering austerity of the war. Rather, the message from our hosts is clear—we will sit down with you Germans because we must, but we will never accept you as equals.

As the first course, salmon croquette, is served, Georg engages in conversation with a Swiss military attaché across the table. "If we can make them see that the German navy can help maintain peace and stability in the new order," he begins doggedly. It is not the first time I have heard him express his views, and there is an optimism and hope in his voice that lightens my heart. But the faces across the table are skeptical.

"Surely you are aware of Weber's writings on the subject of the military-economic nexus in Germany?" a Dutchman at the far end of the table asks. Georg falters. Though he speaks well about matters in which he has experience, he is self-conscious about having not completed his education.

"Will there still be a Germany?" I blurt out, trying to help him by changing the subject. All eyes around us turn in my direction.

"Pardon me?" a startled older woman to Papa's right asks.

I clear my throat, too far gone to turn back. "It's just that the country is so young." Though Germany has been unified for all of my life, it is easy to forget that just half a century ago, when Papa was a boy, it was a series of fragmented states. Prussia, Bavaria and the other regions are still in many ways more distinct that homogenous. "The strain of the treaty, if it doesn't go well, may be more than the republic can bear."

"How can you speak of such things about your own country?" Leigh Arrington asks.

"Our remaining silent will not make the issue disappear. We must meet the question head-on."

"My dear, is it your place to trouble with such things?" The question, from a monocled man I do not recognize, is condescending.

"I, for one, am most interested in what Fraulein Rosenthal

has to say," Georg declares, coming to my defense. Out of the corner of my eye, I see Papa nod slightly with approval. His reservations notwithstanding, Papa is pleased that Georg respects my views and treats me as an intellectual equal.

The main course, mutton in too-rich gravy, is served. The conversation turns elsewhere to a debate about North Africa about which I have no knowledge or views. Beneath the table, Georg's fingers skim the back of my hand. I wonder if it is an accident, but then his fingers close firmly around mine. I can feel his eyes on me, trying to catch my gaze to ask if I mind. But I am unable to look up. Papa continues speaking to Georg above my head, noticing nothing.

With my free hand, I sample a piece of baguette, savoring the buttery flavor. Passover had ended just a few weeks ago and it had been nearly torture to walk past the patisseries only to face the dry, sawdustlike matzo Papa had procured from the city's only functioning Jewish bakery. As I reach for my water glass, there is a clattering across the room, a silver tray falling from a server's hands and crashing to the floor. Startled, Georg jumps up and reaches instinctively for the pistol he no longer carries.

"Never mind," I soothe, putting my arm on his and willing him to sit down again. But he is shaken, a gray pallor to his complexion. Though he is not outwardly wounded like Stefan, Georg is broken in quieter ways. There are other signs, as well—he eats quickly, as though food might be taken from him, drinks each mouthful of water as if it might be his last. "Perhaps we should get some air," I suggest.

"This room is infernally warm," he agrees. "I've heard there are some lovely gardens. Do you think we might take a stroll?"

I hesitate, glancing at Papa, who is ensconced in a conversation with a man on his far side. "I'm going to powder my nose," I say, gesturing slightly with my head toward the door, prompting him to meet me.

A moment later, I slip into the garden where Georg waits in

the shadows. Outside the spring air is cool, but not unpleasantly so, the smell of fresh honeysuckle coming from the side of the path. A fountain trickles unseen in the darkness.

"This is much better." He chuckles as we walk down the path, the voices inside fading. I hope he might offer me his arm, but he does not. "I thought that woman, LeeAnn…"

"Leigh Arrington," I correct, secretly pleased he does not remember her name.

"Yes, that's the one. I thought she might faint when you offered up your views."

"I never should have said anything."

"Nonsense. You spoke your mind forthrightly and well and the conversation was better for it. You were only voicing what the others were thinking but were too cowardly to say. I admire your courage."

Courage. If only he knew. "I hold my tongue as often as I can. Women where I come from aren't encouraged to speak or do much, you see. We're meant to go to the parties and salons, to look nice and act pleasant." I comprehend fully for the first time the truth of my words. Even Papa, who encouraged me to read and learn, did so just for the sake of knowledge—but what good was it all if I didn't use it? "That's why I enjoy our work…" I falter.

His lips twitch with amusement. "I'm glad to provide a diversion."

"That's not what I meant at all." What I do, with him and for him, means so much more. But I cannot find the words. "It's just so frustrating, watching the hypocrisy day after day. Wilson came with promises of freedom and self-determination, the very premise on which America was founded. But the reality seems to only be freedom for some."

"Yes, but if we give everyone those rights, it will be anarchy. And right now, when we are among the defeated and seeking our own rights, we must be most careful."

I stop and turn to him. "No, it is exactly now, when we are fighting for our own rights, that we must stand in solidarity with others who seek theirs."

Georg is silent for a moment. "Of course. Sometimes, amid all of the political struggles, I forget why we are here in the first place. You are like true north on a compass, Margot, and you help me find the way back." The statement, too bold and naked for the short time we have known each other, hangs awkwardly between us.

"It's been a beautiful spring," I offer, eager to break the tension.

"Yes, though I understand the farmers are quite mad to have some rain." I nod. They've only just been able to return to tilling the fields after years of battle. It is difficult to fathom the disaster a drought might bring to a country just coming back from the edge of starvation.

A breeze blows through the garden then, pulling a piece of my hair from its moorings. Georg reaches out and brushes the lock from my face, then stops, hand suspended midair. It is my scar, illuminated in the moonlight, that has drawn his attention. A small colorless indentation just below my left ear, it appeared suddenly years earlier after the flu had passed, a reaction perhaps to the medicines that they tried. It is normally not visible, but tonight with my hair pulled higher, he can see it for the first time.

I hold my breath, wondering if he will find it distasteful. But he continues to stare at me longingly, eyes wide. "Margot..." He fumbles to find further words but cannot.

We continue walking in silence. Though we work beside each other each day, the air between us is somehow different here. "I'm glad you decided to attend the dinner tonight," he says, then coughs slightly. "I mean, even if it isn't with me."

I touch his forearm. "Georg, about that. It was just easier to come with Papa."

"I understand. He wouldn't approve." He believes my refusal was about him, that he somehow wasn't good enough. I want to tell him that wasn't it at all, but how can I without explaining the truth about my engagement to Stefan?

"Your father doesn't like me." It is not a question.

"That's not true," I protest quickly. I touch his forearm. "He thinks you are incredibly smart." I stop and pull back, a blush creeping into my cheeks. Now Georg knows that we have been talking about him. "It's only that he is a pacifist. He was against the war."

"None of us wanted the war," he replies. "That is, none of the real people. There are old men, of course, in Berlin and Paris and London using the military for their own ends."

"You talk like it is a chess game."

"In a sense, it is."

"And you don't mind being a pawn?"

"If wars are to be fought, they should be led by men who can do it well. Fewer lives are lost that way. A well-waged battle can bring war to a quicker end." I do not answer. Through the window, I see Papa talking to one of the other guests.

"You're quite fond of him," Georg observed. Fireflies flicker in the distance, then disappear into the blackness like shooting stars.

"It's always just been the two of us."

"He's a good man." He turns away to stifle a cough. "Though I fear academia is an ill fit with the cut and thrust of politics. As poor of a fit as time at battle." They are both outsiders here. "You must warn him to be careful. I should not want to see him get hurt." His pupils have grown large in the moonlight, two wide circles swimming in pools of gray.

Thinking of the information I shared with Ignatz and the danger I've brought to Papa, my consternation rises. "You make it sound like war, not a peace conference." Another sharp breeze cuts across the garden then and I shiver involuntarily. Before I can protest, Georg unbuttons his coat and with a swift motion brings it around my shoulders as he had the night we first met. His scent, wool and fresh soap, wafts up around me, and in that moment it is as if he is holding me in his embrace. "Thank you."

"Your necklace is beautiful. May I?" I nod and he brings his finger to my throat, skin warm against mine. The back of his nail grazes my skin as he lifts the gem.

"It was my mother's." Papa had given it to me as a sweet-sixteen present, pulled from the box at the bank that still holds my mother's better pieces, the ones he considers me too impetuous and careless yet to wear.

He lets the gem fall gently back to my throat, and as he pulls away his hand trembles. He's scared, I realize. Georg has always been an island, too remote to let anything touch him. Until now. Am I the same? Though I have been involved with Stefan, these feelings are terrifying.

The back door to the house opens and a silhouette appears. "Margot, are you out there?"

"Coming, Papa."

"I can escort you home," Georg offers in a low voice as we walk back across the garden. "That way your father will not have to interrupt his conversation. Perhaps the driver could take us down the Champs-Élysées to see the lights." A shift from the man who had said a few days earlier that he was not in Paris to play tourist.

Georg's jacket, I remember as we step into the light of the house, which now feels garish. I slip it from my shoulders and try to hand it to him, but it is too late—Papa has already seen. Confusion, then realization and concern, cross his face in an instant.

Inside, the party has broken up at the table, the men retreating to the library for brandy and cigars. "Papa, Georg has offered to take me home." I no longer pretend to call him by his formal title.

"That is, if you'd like me to escort Margot back to the hotel."

Georg steps in to save me from having to ask. A fine layer of perspiration coats his upper lip.

I watch Papa struggle inwardly, his own desire to remain in Paris and see Celia colliding with his wanting to keep me and Georg apart. "You'll take her straight back?" Georg towers over Papa, a giant. But it is Papa who seems somehow larger now, fierce in his protectiveness of me.

"It's just a ride, Papa," I nudge gently. "Georg is hardly a stranger." Something flickers across Georg's face. To him it is something more. A ride back to Versailles, just the two of us, a goodbye on the steps of our building...

"Fine," Papa relents.

Georg coughs once, then a second time harder. "I'll get your coat."

As Georg disappears, I spy Krysia in a vestibule, motioning for me to join her. "I didn't have time to speak with you before with everyone around. I've done some checking, and I'm afraid Ignatz is for real. I should have guessed it. He isn't very subtle. He spends money far beyond what he could earn serving drinks and cakes to a bunch of starving artists. He's gotten in with some folks with legitimate connections. And he's not going to leave you alone, I'm afraid. His taking the risk to come here tonight is proof positive of that. He must consider you a terribly valuable asset. Any step out of line and your father will be revealed as the leak."

Papa's career, I lament, ruined because of my own stupidity. Anger rises up in me, then a sense of futility. Krysia had been encouraging me to be my own person. Instead, I've become a chess piece in the very way I'd criticized Georg of being. But if I don't help, I will discredit Papa. "I hate politics."

"It's always politics, isn't it, unless it is our own point of view? Then it is the truth."

A sharp coughing erupts across the room. Georg. He has stepped from the cloakroom and gasps for air, his face turning red. Suddenly he slumps against the wall and his eyes roll back. He collapses to the floor.

"Georg!" I start forward, but Krysia puts her arm on mine. "Herr Mitten is a doctor. Let him take care of this." A group of men swarm Georg, tending to him, loosening his collar. Let him be all right, I pray. Minutes pass with agonizing slowness. Outside comes the shrill cry of an ambulance siren.

I step forward again, desperate to be with Georg. He needs me.

But Papa is beside me now, holding me back as medics put Georg on a stretcher and carry him from the house. I turn to him frantically. "We should go to the hospital."

"It isn't our place. The other delegation members will look after him."

I press against his grasp. "But…"

"We should go."

I start to protest. The notion of returning to Versailles without knowing if Georg is safe is unfathomable.

"I will check," Krysia whispers. Papa herds me toward the car, the siren wailing long and desolate as the ambulance bearing Georg disappears into the night.

CHAPTER EIGHT

The next morning I've just finished steeping my tea when the bell rings, signaling an unexpected visitor below. Hearing footsteps on the stairway, I wonder if I should wake Papa in case it is official business. But when I open the door to the flat, Krysia appears on the landing. I am surprised; she has not come to Versailles at all in the months since we moved out here, much less unannounced.

"Did I wake you?" I shake my head. Worried about Georg, I'd slept little all night. I look over my shoulder. The apartment is a mess—Papa's discarded notes are strewn across the floor in crumpled balls, and dirty glasses and filled ashtrays litter the tables. Picturing Krysia's elegant flat, I step in front of the doorway, trying to block her view.

"I'm sorry not to have called first," she says, appearing too large in the narrow, crooked corridor. "But I had to catch an early train and I didn't want to wake anyone."

"Not at all. I believe arriving unexpectedly is a tradition I started."

She smiles slightly, but her expression is forced. Has she come in person to bring me bad news? "What is it? Is it Georg?"

"Everything is fine," she replies hurriedly.

"Won't you come in? I've just made tea."

"No, thank you. I have an errand out of the city so I won't be able to stay long. Perhaps we could walk instead? It really is a lovely morning."

Outside the air is unseasonably warm but not unpleasant, with a gentle breeze wafting lavender from the fields to the east, clearing the smells of the street.

"He has pneumonia," says Krysia a moment later.

My shoulders slump with relief. "So it isn't the flu."

"No, but pneumonia is no trifling matter. Apparently he's had it for some time but neglected to get care." I recall the persistent cough that Georg had shrugged off in order to keep working. Ignoring their health is another way in which he and Papa are alike. "Anyway, they've pumped him full of medicine and he should be discharged to his rooms later today."

We round the corner, skirting the edge of the market, where chickens and cabbage and fabric and tools are sold indiscriminately alongside one another from wooden, tarp-covered stalls or cloths spread on the ground. The smell of fish, still alive in murky tubs of water, hangs heavy in the air. Krysia lowers her voice to a whisper. "I spoke with Ignatz after the reception last night," she says, and I understand then her reason for coming here in person rather than ringing. "I thought perhaps I could reason with him, but I was wrong. He's quite dangerous. He came from the Pale, saw his own brother murdered by the czar's army." He had lost a brother like Georg, but he had responded with anger and bile. "He has a criminal past, has done things that I'd rather not know about. In another time, he would be just a common thug. But in this world…" I nod. Paris right now is a free-for-all, the old rules broken. Power and opportunity are there for those who dare take it.

"Perhaps I should just refuse. After all, Papa has been given an ambassadorial title for purposes of the conference. With his diplomatic immunity, surely he would be sheltered from any scandal."

She shakes her head. "I grew up as a diplomat's child, remember? Immunity is easily dispensed with for political purposes. If your father was found to have leaked information, he could be arrested, or simply declared persona non grata and ordered to leave the country." I nod. Even if he weren't formally prosecuted, the scandal and having to face Uncle Walter in failure would be more than Papa could bear. "Ignatz isn't going to let you off until he gets what he wants."

"But I haven't seen any documents," I say evasively. "Georg only has me work on translations, documents given to him by the English or the French. They're nothing like the information on German weapons that Ignatz wanted. Perhaps Georg doesn't even know anything."

"He's a senior military officer and a member of the delegation," she replies impatiently. "Of course he knows something. And now…"

"He's sick."

She swats at a gnat, then exhales, exasperated. "So much the better. He'll be resting, disoriented."

"I'm not going to take advantage of his condition." There is a line I won't cross, even when threatened.

"Why are you protecting him? Is it because you have feelings for him?"

"No, of course not. I'm engaged," I add, pulling Stefan's ring from my pocket and holding it up like some sort of amulet to ward off danger. "But Georg trusts me."

"So does your father," she adds pointedly.

My stomach tightens. How had I gotten into such a mess? But Krysia is right. My loyalties must lie with Papa.

"You asked for my help and I've done what I can. You need to look out for yourself now." She kisses me on the cheek. "I have to go. Come see me when you are in the city."

"Wait…" She turns back expectantly. I search for the words to form a question, and seek extra guidance from her. But I must figure out the rest on my own. "Thank you."

"Not at all. I wish I could have been more help. Take care of yourself. Get some rest. And here…" She reaches in her bag and pulls out a small sachet. "You might give these to Georg in some tea or broth." She knows, even before I've admitted it to myself, that I will be going to him.

"What is it?"

"Just herbs, rose hips and such. They are most restorative." She presses the sachet into my hands and, before I can thank her again, turns and walks down the street.

I return to our apartment where the tea I'd made earlier still sits on the table. I pick up the semi-warm cup, thinking back to my walk in the garden with Georg the previous evening. There had never been a moment like that with me and Stefan. It is hardly a fair comparison, since we knew each other our entire lives before we were together. But even if we had been strangers and met under similar circumstances, it would feel nothing like this. Stefan. Sometimes it is as if he is already gone. But he is out there, wounded yet alive. And I am, or am supposed to be, his.

Papa emerges from his room, dressed for the conference session in the city. "I'm afraid there's a meeting tonight, so I won't be back to dine with you. Would you care to come into the city today? You could shop with Celia."

"I'll just stay here, if you don't mind. I'm quite tired after last night's dinner."

His eyebrows lift. Then he shrugs. "It's your choice. I just thought, now that your work with Georg is on hiatus, you might be bored."

I set the teacup down. "Krysia told me that he's to be released from the hospital today."

"He's sick, darling. He won't be able to work. And surely you aren't thinking about going over there..."

"It's pneumonia, Papa," I answer quickly. "Not contagious at all."

"You can't be certain." But then, seeing my stubborn expression he knows so well, he shrugs. "My car is waiting. Don't stay too long at the hotel."

"I won't," I promise.

"Be careful—and give him my best."

When the door has closed behind him, I race to the window, craning my neck to look down the street at the hotel. It could be hours before Georg returns. I straighten the apartment, then sit down to read by the window. But I glance up to check the street so often I cannot keep my place. Finally, I give up and pace the apartment restlessly.

It is late afternoon when I finally glimpse a flash of white, the top of an ambulance as it lumbers down the cobblestone street below. I leap to my feet in time to see the back doors of the ambulance opening in front of the hotel. My heart twists as Georg is carried motionless on a stretcher through the front gate. When the ambulance has disappeared again, I go to the washroom to freshen. Then, unable to wait any longer, I make my way down to the street. The guard at the front of the hotel, accustomed to my late-day arrival, nods as I pass.

I knock on the door to Georg's apartment and a moment later it swings open, revealing an attractive dark-haired girl wearing a white apron and cap. *"Oui?"*

"Oh." I falter. It had not occurred to me that anyone would be here. It makes sense—Georg is helpless and needs care. Still,

I cannot help resent the familiar way the nurse moves around his room, the ease with which she adjusts his pillow.

From the hulking mass of blankets atop the bed, there comes a violent cough. "Georg?" As I move toward him, my jealousy is replaced with concern. He lies motionless with eyes closed, his skin damp and gray. Was he really well enough to be discharged?

His eyes flutter open and as they focus on me, he smiles faintly. "Margot…" He struggles to sit up.

I press my hand on his shoulder. "Rest, and don't try to move."

He nods slightly in acquiescence, then closes his eyes once more. There is a dark stubble about his cheeks which gives him an unkempt look. Trying not to stare at the top of his chest, the few dark hairs revealed by the open collar of his dressing gown, I avert my gaze. The apartment is tidy, but there are smells of antiseptic and iodine I do not recognize.

He opens his eyes again. "Hello," he says, as though he had forgotten I was there. His faint smile lifts my heart. "Now if you will help me get out of this silly bed, we can get back to work."

"Work? You can't possibly work in your condition."

Frustration crosses his face as he processes for the first time the delay that his incapacitation will cause. "How could I have allowed this to happen?"

"You're human. Humans get ill."

He shakes his head stubbornly. "Not me. Not now."

I take his hand, rubbing it like a child's to soothe him. "Shh. Getting upset will only make things worse."

The nurse appears again and sets down a tray of broth and toast on the nightstand by the bed. "*Merci*, Mildred. That will be all," Georg says.

"But…" She looks confused at being dismissed. "There's a tonic if he starts feeling poorly. I'll check on him again in the morning."

"The delegation insisted upon hiring her," he explains when

she has gone. He coughs again, the spasms indicating that he is the furthest thing from better.

"Drink," I order, holding the cup and supporting his head. His hair where it meets his neck is short, like the fuzz of a baby chick I once held.

"It's awful," he says when he has recovered, frowning so hard I wonder if he is in pain. "You seeing me like this."

"Not at all." But his expression remains displeased. Does he mind that I have come? "I was so worried..." His eyes widen, as if unused to having anyone care about him. "Do you want me to go?"

"No," he replies firmly, almost before I have finished asking. "But if you could help me..." I lean forward in anticipation of his request, another pillow or perhaps some medicine. "Can you bring me my binder from the desk?"

"You aren't nearly well enough to work," I insist again.

"But there's no time." He tries to sit up.

I press him back against the pillow firmly, the skin of his bare chest warm under my hand. "If you get up too soon and relapse, we'll never finish."

"But—"

"I can keep working for you," I interrupt. He relaxes, seemingly mollified. I walk to the anteroom and retrieve the binder he'd indicated and carry it back. "Now I will keep translating as long as you rest. Understood?"

He smiles weakly and closes his eyes once more. "Yes, *fraulein.*"

I shift in the hardwood chair, balancing the binder on my lap. Working like this is awkward, but I can watch him from here in case he needs anything. A fan hums low in the corner, sending the curtains dancing a gentle waltz. I glance up. Georg's head is tilted back and he is snoring lightly, eyes dancing beneath their lids. What does he dream about? His features are so familiar to me now, the way Stefan's should have been, if only I could remember them clearly. His face is relaxed, as vulnerable and innocent as a boy's. My heart twists. Here I am, caring for Georg as I should have been Stefan. But this does not feel suffocating—I belong here and this is where I want to be.

An hour passes. I set down the translation. Georg is awake now and watching me. "How are you?"

"A bit better now, I think."

"Do you want to try some of the broth?" He nods. I move the tray close and start to spoon it for him.

"I can manage." I sit back, watching as he eats with a shaky hand.

He eats in silence, his eyes focused over my shoulder. I follow his gaze to a picture of a group of men on the deck of an enormous ship. "Are you thinking of the sea?"

"The men. They called me a hero after Jutland," he said. "But I just did what was expected of me, and we—most of us, anyway—made it through. Later I was summoned from the ship to the delegation. The sailors—they think I abandoned them." He sets the spoon down as a pained look crosses his face.

"Shh," I soothe.

He continues, as if he has not heard me. "I'm so broken, Margot. And if I can make this work…" His eyes are desperate, wild. He clings to his work for the conference like a raft. "When I'm with you, it all seems possible somehow." My stomach flips. "The day I stepped off that bus and saw you standing by the roadside, I felt as if I had somehow known you my whole life." Can he possibly be saying such things? I search his face but his eyes are glazed, lost in some sort of delirium.

I reach forward and press my hand to his forehead. It is alarmingly hot, his fever climbing as night approaches. Perhaps it was a mistake to let the nurse leave. I walk to the sink and find the tonic she'd indicated. "Swallow," I order, holding a spoonful of the thick brown syrup to his lips.

He obeys, grimacing. "Talk to me…" He pants, eyes closed,

too sick now to care whether I continue working or not. "I should like to have a dog again," he remarks sleepily, jumping topics without reason. "A terrier, most likely."

"Yes," I say, a mother giving permission for such a pet. He reaches for my hand and I let him take it. This will mean nothing, I tell myself. But there is an intensity to his touch and longing rises in me before I can help it.

"The other day, when I told you there had never been a woman…that wasn't entirely true." I hold my breath. "There was someone once. At port in Genoa, I met a young woman." I close my eyes, desperately curious and at the same time wishing he would not continue. "We walked the city and she showed me a great many sites before bidding me bon voyage. She took me as just another sailor, though I could have liked her quite a bit." The book that is Georg opens and words spill forth, forming a picture that I can now see more completely.

"You remind me of her." I stiffen. I do not want to be a substitute for someone else. "She was just an image, there for a few hours. But I've gotten to know you so much more. The way you flare your nostrils when angry." I cringe at this less-than-flattering description. "How your eyes seem to change colors with your temper, like two mood stones…" These last words slur as he starts to drift off. Conflicting emotions rise up in me—jealousy over this woman that once held his heart and relief that he has cared, is capable of it.

He does not speak further. I pick up the binder once more, but I am unable to concentrate. Georg is sleeping deeply now, a snore like a low growl each time he inhales, a whistle more teakettle than train with every release. My thoughts turn to Ignatz and the need to find something to pacify him. But the kind of information Ignatz seeks, if Georg possesses it at all, would not be found in the documents that Georg has me translate. I look toward the study, Krysia's suggestion to search while he is asleep echoing in my mind. If I am going to do this it has to be now. I will check, just once, in order to satisfy Ignatz that there is nothing here. I open the door to the sitting room, then turn back, my guilt rising at the sight of Georg sleeping peacefully. I do not want to betray his trust, but I have to protect Papa.

Trying to step normally but keep my footsteps quiet, I walk through the doorway. On the far side of the sitting room, there is a stack of documents he keeps separate from the other papers, the ones he asks me to translate. I pick up the pile and riffle through, scanning the documents, which are in German. There are cables here about shipbuilding operations, a new line of cargo freighters. I relax slightly. So this is why he has not asked me to translate these materials—they pertain not at all to the conference, but rather to his family's shipping business.

I turn to the next page and stop, my hand suspended midair. It contains technical engineering plans and though the terminology is foreign to me, it is clearly a plan to fit the cargo ships with guns. A shiver runs through me. Was all Georg's talk of peace a lie, intended for my benefit? I continue paging through, then stop at a map. Cities to the east are marked: Archangel, Murmansk, Brest. Though I do not understand the notations, I know this is what Ignatz wanted.

I remove the document from the stack, my hand trembling slightly. I'd done it. In the other room Georg snores, none the wiser. I am flooded with remorse. Georg is so earnest and he has brought me into his trust. I've betrayed him.

Georg cries out then in his sleep, a whimper that breaks open to a scream. I fold the paper hurriedly and tuck it in my dress. With any luck I can show it to Ignatz and return it before Georg notices that it is missing.

Back in the bedroom, Georg is agitated in his sleep. He is on the ship, reliving a battle as his body convulses from side to side—most likely the one that had taken his brother. Sitting on the edge of the bed, I throw my arms around him. His gown is soaked through with sweat, skin hot through the material.

"I'm here and it's okay." He wraps himself around me, holding me tightly as though I might slip away.

A minute later, his grip relaxes and he begins to breathe evenly once more. I look at the clock on the nightstand. It is nearly eleven, and Papa might be back from his dinner, if he did not go to Celia's. He will wonder where I've gone, but I cannot leave Georg and there's no way to send word. I lean back wearily beside him on the wide bed.

I awaken sometime later. Where am I? Georg's rooms, I remember, inhaling the familiar spearmint smell of his aftershave. I had not planned to fall asleep. The room clicks into focus as my eyes adjust to the darkness. I sit up quickly.

He shifts beside me, opens his eyes. "Margot." He smiles, his face as relaxed and happy as I have ever seen. "You are here. I thought it was a dream." He blinks. "Were you here all night?"

"Yes." I study his face. Does he recall the things he said? But his expression is impassive, the awkwardness that would have been present if he remembered his declaration of feelings nowhere to be found.

Then his face clouds. "How improper of me. I never should have…"

"It's fine. I came to you. It was my choice. I wanted to be here."

Then a pained look crosses his face as his head begins to throb, bringing the memories of the previous evening into focus. "I'm so sorry. You should not have had to see me in such a state. You should go."

He does not want me here. Stung by his curtness, I stand and start for the door. "Margot, wait." He grabs my hand to stop me. I am instantly warm. What is it about this man that provokes such a reaction in me? It was never this way with Stefan, no matter how much I liked him.

Then he drops my hand just as quickly. "It's just that when I sleep…" He turns away, embarrassed.

"I have nightmares, too," I say, wanting to ease his embarrassment. "Not about anything as serious as yours, of course."

"What do you dream about?" Before he finished the question, I realize my mistake: I cannot tell him about the fiancé and the inevitable marriage that haunts my sleep.

"I dream that I am trapped," I say carefully, somewhere short of a lie. I hold my breath hoping that he will not press me to elaborate. "How are you feeling?" I ask, changing the subject.

"Much better."

I touch his now-cool forehead. "The nurse said she would check back on you this morning."

"You should go home and rest."

Or at least wash. My hair is pressed flat to my head from sleep and I have a stale taste in my mouth.

"If I may trouble you for one thing before you go, I should like to shave." I notice then the thick stubble that covers his cheeks. He is not used to being so unkempt.

"Certainly." I fetch a bowl of warm water and his shaving kit from the basin. When I return to Georg's beside, he has unbuttoned the collar of his nightshirt further, revealing a wide swath of skin. Warmth rises in me. He drapes his neck in a towel and dampens his face. But as he reaches for the razor, his weakened hand trembles. "Let me." I work the cream into a lather as I have seen Papa do, then bring my hands to his cheeks. His skin is unexpectedly soft beneath my fingertips. I run the razor upward against his jawline, struggling to keep my hand still, not meeting his eyes.

"Much better," he says when I have rinsed the lather. He pats his face dry with the towel I hand him. "Thank you."

"Not at all." I still cannot look at him.

"Margot, I am so grateful for your friendship." I step back, caught off guard by the word. "I'm sorry, was that too forward of me? We've known each other for such a short time."

"Not at all." To the contrary, his description sounded cold

and formal, something well short of how I feel. He does not consider me more. Of course not. Whatever was I expecting?

"I don't think of it as you working for me, you see. I regard us as peers, colleagues, but the way we speak of so many things makes it something more than that…" He fumbles with these last words, then clears his throat. "Now, if you'll bring me my papers."

"You're still too sick. That was our arrangement, remember? I shall keep working as long as you rest."

"Yes, but now you are going."

He has a point. I need to return to the apartment to freshen and make sure Papa is not worried. "I hate being idle like this," he presses. "There isn't any time to waste. Every day that passes decreases the chance of getting the report to the commission and making a real difference."

"I can keep working," I offer quickly. Then I stop. "I mean, not here, of course, but if I take the papers with me."

I watch as he considers the idea. The delegation is worried about material slipping out, concerns about espionage growing by the day, though whether legitimate or just paranoia it is impossible to say. Papa has told me before that they even play the gramophone as they work, symphonies and operas at a decibel that makes it hard to think, to prevent anyone from listening. "I'll take them from here to our rooms and nowhere else," I promise. "I'll bring them back tonight."

"I suppose your suite really is just an extension of the delegation space here," Georg concedes. I wait for him to admonish me to be careful. But he doesn't. He trusts me, something which I suspect does not come easily to him. Something I do not deserve.

"I will check on you later. Stay in bed and rest. I can show myself out." I slip from the apartment before he has the chance to argue, taking the binder with me.

A few minutes later, I unlock the door to our apartment. The

sitting room is still, I note with relief, untouched since the previous day. It is the first time I have ever been glad that Papa had
spent the night with Celia. I set the binder on the desk then pull
out the map I'd taken from Georg's rooms out of my dress. Will
it be enough to satisfy Ignatz?

I place the document in the middle of the stack of papers in
the binder, then walk to the toilet to wash. As I dress twenty
minutes later, I glance over at my bed, the rose duvet bathed
in sunlight. I am tired from my night of caring for Georg and
the pillow beckons invitingly. But I promised Georg I would
keep working.

I put on the kettle in the small kitchenette and a moment later
return to the parlor with a cup of tea, which I set down on the
low table by the divan before sitting. I pull out the sachet of
herbs Krysia gave me the previous day for energy. I'd forgotten
to put them in Georg's broth, but perhaps they will give me a bit
of energy, as well. I tap a bit into the teacup, savoring the floral
smell that wafts upward. I take a sip, then turn to the binder and
remove the documents. But as I start on one of the memos, the
words blur, making it difficult to read. I blink several times and
take another sip of tea. I rub at my dry eyes, then set the papers
down. Perhaps just a quick rest. I tilt my head back.

I sit up with a start, disoriented by flashes of dreams, dark
scenes of the ocean, reaching for Georg's hand before sinking
below the rough surf. How much time has passed? I struggle to
adjust my eyes to the dim room. Though I had meant to rest
only a few minutes, I can tell by the heaviness of my limbs and
the way the scant late-afternoon light filters through the curtains that it has been hours.

The binder has fallen from my lap to the floor, documents
scattering everywhere. How careless of me. I take the papers and
fold them neatly back in the stack. I'd meant to go find Ignatz
this afternoon and show him the report so that I could return
it to Georg's study this evening, but it is too late now. I reach

into the middle of the binder for the loose document I'd hidden there. As my hand closes around emptiness, my stomach tightens. Hurriedly, I page to the middle of the binder.

The report I'd stolen from Georg is gone.

CHAPTER NINE

I stare down at the binder in disbelief, paging through the documents a second, then a third time. The map had been there, I am sure of it. I retrace my route from when I entered the apartment, looking under the divan and table. But it is gone. I race to the window. Could it possibly have fallen in the street? I thought I had been so careful.

I put on my shoes and start for the door. But before I can turn the knob, it opens from the other side and standing there, glowering, is Papa. "There you are!" he exclaims, nostrils flaring as he enters the apartment. I have never seen him so angry. "I tried to ring you last night and then again early this morning and finally was so worried that I came to check as soon as I was able. You were at the hotel, weren't you?"

"Papa, I…" I search for another explanation that would explain my absence at such hours and find none.

"I knew it! You said you were just checking on Captain Richwalder briefly."

"I hadn't planned to stay. But he was so sick, and there was no one else to help."

"And then walking out of the hotel the next morning, like some… I cannot even say. It isn't proper."

"Is that what matters now? It was a very urgent circumstance."

But he is too far gone to back down. "What will the other members of the delegation think?" His voice raises and a vein stands out on the left side of his head.

I should hope that the other delegates have more important things to worry about than my comings and goings, I want to say. Papa has never been one to trouble about appearances, but his tenuous position here at the conference has made him subject to scrutiny. "Papa, your pressure," I remind him instead, alarmed that the fight will be too much strain on his health. "I'm sorry I worried you," I add, trying to calm him.

"Working for Captain Richwalder on some translations is one thing." His tone softens slightly. "But staying out all night and playing nursemaid…"

"Papa, I'm not a child."

"Exactly. And I expect you to make adult decisions." Or if not, decisions will be made for me, is the silent, unfinished implication. For years, Papa has encouraged me to think on my own, but now I see that is intended to go only so far, like an animal perceiving it has free rein because it has not comprehended the contours of its cage. "Spending time with Georg when you are an engaged woman. It isn't proper," he repeats.

"And you and Tante Celia," I spit, unable to hold back. "Is that proper?" He blinks and his cheeks flush as though I have slapped him.

"I'm not…" He stops short, unable to finish the denial. "That's entirely different." But my recriminations hang in the air between us. In all of the years the affair has gone on, it is the first time either of us has spoken of it.

A moment later, he clears his throat. "I have to return to

Paris for dinner now that I know you are all right. You are to stay here."

"I'll not be a prisoner."

"That's rather dramatic. You can leave the apartment. But you aren't to go to Captain Richwalder."

I start to protest. "Papa..." He goes to his room and closes the door hard. I stare after him, defeated. How can he possibly tell me I cannot continue to work with Georg, or to see him when he is ill? And then to assume how I feel... Papa has always tried to guide with a gentle touch. But this seems to be the one exception.

I walk from the apartment, then hesitate. For a minute I consider defying Papa's order and going back to Georg. Suddenly this has become a power struggle. What will happen if I refuse to listen? I am an adult, after all, and a person of my own accord. Papa could turn me out like Krysia's parents initially did when she became pregnant. For all of the conflict, though, he has no wish to alienate me. He could make trouble for Georg with the delegation. But Papa isn't the type to make waves. No, there is not likely to be any tangible repercussions from my going against his will. Still, fighting with him even for a few minutes makes me ill.

Remembering the lost document, I hurry down the street, check the gutters and the scraps of newspaper that blow along the roadside. It is nowhere to be found. What now?

Krysia. She will know what to do. I start in the direction of the train station. It is nearly dark outside now, the shops closing. At the end of the street, I gaze back longingly at the hotel. Georg will be waiting for me, wonder why I have not come. I walk to the guard at the front of the hotel and scribble a note for Georg, making my excuses.

An hour later, I ring the bell at the entrance to Krysia's apartment building. When I reach the top of the stairs, the door opens and Krysia appears in a long flowing robe.

"I'm so sorry. I should have called," I add, repeating our now-familiar refrain without humor.

"I think we're long past that," she replies wryly. Then, noticing my distress, her face grows serious. "What is it?" I twist my hands reflexively around my purse, embarrassed to be running to Krysia with my problems yet again. "Come in."

Inside, I scan the apartment warily, relieved to see that Marcin is not there. Krysia does not prepare coffee as she usually does but instead, sensing the need for something stronger, pulls a bottle of brandy and pours small amounts into two glasses. "Drink," she orders when I look at her hesitantly. I obey, the strong liquor burning my nose and throat. "Now," she says, "what's wrong?"

Hurriedly, I tell her about taking the document. "I tried to do what Ignatz wanted. Only now it's missing."

"You searched your apartment?"

"I looked everywhere."

"It will turn up. These things do." She seems strangely untroubled.

"Perhaps I should tell Georg…"

"No," she replies quickly. "Do you really think he would understand?" She's right, of course. Telling him would mean revealing my deception and he would never forgive me. "There's still time for you to try again and get something else."

"Again?" I explode. I cannot help it. Taking from Georg once was bad enough. But the thought of doing it a second time… "I can't."

"We've been through this before. There's no other way."

"But betraying him like this when he trusts me… I feel horrid."

She raises an eyebrow. "You care for him."

"Hardly." My voice raises a note too high in protest. "We disagree about everything." I search my memory to find an example. "Like the other day we fought about Palestine."

"He didn't see the need for a Jewish state?"

"No, quite the opposite actually. He thought it would be good for the Jews to have a place. But I am a German and I didn't see the necessity." It sounds so trivial now. What is it about Georg that brings out such a strong reaction in me? "What do you think?"

"About Palestine? I believe that Jews enjoy relative calm and stability in Europe right now. Especially in places like Germany." I nod in agreement. Back home we are integrated into almost every part of society, academics like Papa, businessmen like Uncle Walter. "But in the East, where I come from, it wasn't always that way. There were these terrible pogroms where the Jews were forced from villages at best or even beaten or killed, their homes burned, often with no notice at all. In recent years there have been sudden outbursts of violence, even where the Jews had lived peacefully among their neighbors for centuries. I think that's why so many of them don't mind the communists—it has to be better than what they suffered under the czars."

I try to imagine the violence of the world Krysia described. Poland is Germany's eastern neighbor again, or will be now that it has been re-created at the conference. The places where this happened are just hundreds of miles from Berlin, but the barbarity is so foreign it might have taken place centuries ago.

"I suppose it really doesn't matter what we quarreled about," I say, returning to the subject of Georg in spite of myself. "We just don't see eye to eye on anything."

"Why should you? You've got nothing in common."

Is that true? Our backgrounds are quite dissimilar. Yet there is a connection between Georg and me when we speak that makes all of the differences disappear. "I don't know about that, exactly," I say slowly. "He's just so stubborn."

She let out a chuckle, uncharacteristically abrupt, almost a snort. "You're rather headstrong yourself, my dear. And that's a good thing. Headstrong holds its own in a headwind, my grandmother used to say."

"Maybe that's why we argue so much."

"Maybe. Or maybe it's because you like him," she says again.

I stop drinking midmouthful, heedless of the brandy that lingers on my tongue, burning. "Like him?" I repeat the words, buying time in which to formulate a real response.

"Or is this just about rebellion? Because there are easier ways..."

I consider the question. I can see how it might seem that way—a girl from a well-to-do family, rearing back against expectations. Indeed, when Papa and I quarreled my first instinct was to run to Georg. But my feelings for Georg aren't about that—they are real and I would care as much if Papa approved and he fit neatly into my world.

"It isn't that. But how can I possibly have feelings for a man I've known less than a week?"

She shrugs. "Sometimes you just know," and her tone suggests the observation is personal. But is she talking about Marcin or the man who came before and gave her Emilie?

"Even if I did, it's a moot point. He thinks of me as a silly child."

She dipped her head. "One could get in much trouble for looking at a child like that."

"What do you mean?"

"You can see a great deal from the piano bench. Georg watches you with real feeling—and an intensity I've seldom seen."

"It doesn't matter," I insist. "There's no future in it."

"Because of your fiancé? Engagements can be broken. It isn't that hard."

"No, you don't understand. It's so much worse." I pause, and take a deep breath. "Krysia, I'm married!" I bring my hand to my mouth. It is the first time I've confessed this to anyone, the secret I've pushed so far from my mind these recent months. But spoken aloud now, the words are now real, impossible to deny.

The evening before Stefan was to report for duty we'd gone

down to the Unter den Linden. It was a humid August evening and a fine coat of perspiration covered everything. The street was closely packed with revelers, celebrating Germany's certain quick victory, men and women such as ourselves enjoying a last night together in the cafés and dance halls before the men left for war. Outside the Rathaus, a line had formed. A few of the women clutched makeshift bouquets of flowers or Bibles.

"They're waiting to get married," Stefan observed, a note of prompting to his voice. I did not respond. The couples were mostly working class, with their simple dresses and worn coats. Those women sorely needed the benefits that came with being a soldier's wife—or a soldier's widow if things went wrong. I was lucky enough to have not just Papa, but the security of Uncle Walter and the family estate to fall back on. I would be sad, but not destitute, if Stefan should fall.

But as Stefan watched the queue inch toward the town hall, there was a light in his eyes like none I had seen before. "Should we…?" He could not bring himself to finish the question and behind the hope, the fear of rejection flickered.

I hesitated. There were a dozen reasons to decline: I wanted a real wedding (the furthest thing from the truth), I could not get married without Papa being there. Seeing Stefan's face, though, I knew that he needed this if he was to make it through whatever lay ahead. "Let's." Hand in hand we walked toward the courthouse to be married.

The line progressed up the steps of the town hall, couples pressed close behind us. In front of us a woman leaned in and rested her head contentedly on her fiancé's shoulder. Something prickled at me. It was not right. It was all happening too fast. I wanted to tell Stefan that we should wait and do this another time with our families, but he stared straight ahead, shoulders squared, chin lifted with confidence. My palms began to sweat and I wondered if he would notice and ask me what was wrong. He squeezed my hand, oblivious.

Minutes passed, seeming like hours. As we neared the front of the room, a tight grip closed around my chest until I could not breathe. I turned, pulling my hand from Stefan's and searching for the exit. But it was too late—the registrant was taking down our names on a piece of paper and completing the certificate. I could scarcely hear the question she asked over the buzzing in my ears. *"Ja,"* I croaked. Then it was over and we were shuffled to the side to make way for the next couple.

"That's it?" I asked. I had not been a woman who had dreamed of a wedding ceremony, but it was hard to believe that a few words and signatures were the difference between freedom and forever.

"Yes?" His smile dampened. "You don't mind, do you? We'll do the rest after." Armed with our marriage, he could go off to war believing in *after*. "Unless you want to tell our families?"

"No." The word came out more firmly than I'd intended. "Papa would be upset not to be here."

"This should have been so much more," Stefan lamented as we walked down the steps of the Rathaus. "I'm happy we did it, of course. But you deserve a proper wedding, with a reception after."

I shook my head. "Nonsense. You know I've never cared about that. The marriage is what's important, being yours." But a lump grew in my throat as I clutched tighter the piece of paper that bound me to him. Something did not feel right, like a rock caught in one's shoe, pressing down painfully step after step. It was not the lack of a wedding I minded. Rather, the permanency of what we had just done crashed onto me.

After dinner we returned to our house to find a surprise party, a gathering of family and close friends. "A small celebration," Papa said.

He knows! I thought with alarm, wondering if he and Stefan discussed a quick wedding, as well as our engagement. "Since there is no time for an engagement party," he added.

My shoulders slumped with relief. *Oh, Papa,* I thought as he raised a glass and said a few quiet words about me and Stefan, love and hope. *If only you knew.* My heart ached to tell him. We never had secrets when I was a child. "You didn't have to do this," I said instead. "It is really too kind."

"These happy moments are rare, and to be rarer still in the months to come," he replied. There was a darkness behind his eyes that hinted at his true suspicions about the war, that nothing would be as sure and quick as the politicians and journalists were making out. Papa studied war for a living, centuries and centuries of fighting since the Mongols and the Tartars. He knew that if it were really so easy, the war would not have been fought at all but resolved another way.

"At least," Celia said coldly, "if something happens, you would have been engaged." She was not trying to be cruel, just practical. To her, having had someone who really wanted you, enough to make it official, meant everything. What would she have said if she knew the truth about our already-marriage? She surely would have been embarrassed by the crude nature of our courthouse wedding.

"If only we hadn't gone to the courthouse that day," I say, as I finish telling Krysia. "This would have all been so much easier to untangle without the lies. And I'm sorry I didn't tell you earlier. But you see now why Georg and I can never be together."

"Marriage isn't a death sentence. People end marriages. Perhaps in this situation, where it isn't publicly known, it might be easier."

"Stefan would never agree. And even if he did, I couldn't do that to him now that he is hurt."

"Is lying to him any better?"

"It won't be a lie. Once I'm back in Berlin and we have the chance to get to know each other more intimately, I'm certain things will be different."

"You mean you and Stefan never consummated your marriage?"

I shake my head, feeling the blush creep up my neck. "There wasn't time."

Stefan had not come to me that night. I'd lain awake, wondering if he might slip up to my window and find a way for us to be together. We were, after all, married and this one chance to explore the things I'd only read about secretly was perhaps the brightest spot in all of this. "I've got to report at five tomorrow," he'd murmured as he left. "And we should wait until we're properly married by a rabbi, anyway, rather than sneaking around."

Krysia gives a soft laugh. "What?" I demand angrily.

"I'm sorry, my dear. I'm not making light of your situation, not in the slightest. But you aren't married, not in the biblical sense. Even the church might annul a marriage under such circumstances."

"To Stefan we are." And I've never heard of an annulment in Judaism, I lament silently.

"Do you really believe you can just go back to the old life and fit in so easily as though none of this ever happened?" She has a point. I'm not the same girl I was four years ago. "Life has a way of reshaping us." I'm unsure if she is talking about herself or me.

"Anyway, I'm sure you're wrong." I wave away the bottle of brandy she's picked up again, but she ignores me and pours. "Georg isn't interested in me. I'm a diversion, that's all."

"You're attractive and intelligent and articulate. Why do you discount yourself? It's a defense mechanism, I think, to protect yourself from rejection," she says, answering her own question. "Don't let anyone get close and they won't leave or be able to hurt you again. Maybe it's because of your mother." She is not being unkind, just speaking bluntly. "Death is a kind of abandonment," she adds.

"Anyway, Georg and Stefan are two separate issues," she con-

tinues, raising her hands in opposite directions. "Your feelings
for Stefan changed long before Georg came along." But even
if I had truly been in love with Stefan, I would have noticed
Georg—no matter what. Georg did not cause me to stop loving Stefan. But he highlighted the difference between everything and emptiness and made it impossible for me to go back
to a place where the latter was enough.

"Did you love Stefan? Ever, I mean?"

I consider the question. "I think so. I mean, I was so lonely
and well, being with Stefan was company."

"There are worse things than being alone."

"I don't like Georg," I protest again. "He's all wrong for me."

"Yet you haven't told him about Stefan?"

I shake my head. "Not exactly." Why hadn't I told Georg
the truth about Stefan? Now, of course, it would be awkward,
a secret kept too long. But back at the very beginning when
we were discussing our childhoods and families and lives back
home as the newest of acquaintances might, it would have been
the most natural thing in the world to mention. It was more
than just my guilt over the fact that I am here in Paris while
Stefan convalesces in a veteran's hospital. No, there was something about Georg right from the start that made me want to
keep that part of myself hidden.

"Georg isn't the man for me," I repeat stubbornly.

"Nor is Stefan," she adds with a certainty that makes me
wonder if she has met him. I look at her, puzzled. "You have
no warmth when you speak about him."

"No," I admit, unable to lie to her. "It's not because he's in-
jured. It's as though the light has gone out in the furnace inside me with respect to Stefan, and much as I try to blow on
it, I can't make the embers burn. Perhaps it's because I haven't
seen him in four years." My eyes begin to water. "I can barely
picture his face."

"Or because you were sixteen when you became engaged,

scarcely more than a child." She's right. The girl I was before the war was someone I barely remember. "We commit our lives to others when we are still unformed ourselves. I'm glad I met Marcin later—it would not have been the same when we were young. We had to make our mistakes."

But neither Krysia's explanation of age nor mine of the passage of time adequately explains my lack of warmth for Stefan. He is wrong for me. The way I feel when I am with Georg has changed my notion of love and made it impossible to go back to the bland feelings I once had for Stefan.

"What am I going to do?" Tears fill my eyes. Krysia reaches out and pulls me close, her arms warmer than I could have imagined, like the mother's touch I have lacked for so long. I put my head in her lap and weep like a child.

"There, there." Krysia's voice is a warm blanket, her advice wise—like a big sister I never had, or the mother I scarcely knew.

A few minutes later, I sit up and wipe my eyes. "I'm so sorry."

"Don't be. Emotion is human—and good for us. It shows that we care. It is getting late, though," Krysia remarks.

I glance at the clock on the mantel. It is almost eleven. "I'm so sorry," I repeat, standing to leave. I have overstayed my welcome. "I should go."

But she shakes her head, pulls me gently back to the settee. "Not at all. You won't get a taxi this time of night and the trains will have stopped running. Why don't you just stay here? It's nothing posh, but you're most welcome. Marcin is playing an engagement out of the city."

My shoulders sag with exhaustion. Suddenly staying in Krysia's warm apartment seems the most inviting thing in the world. "Thank you."

"Your father won't be worried? There's a telephone booth at the corner."

"Oh." I would rather not speak with Papa after our quarrel, but I don't dare to go missing a second night.

"Why don't I run down and ring him while you freshen up?" she offers, sensing my unease. Gratefully, I scribble down the number on the back of the matchbook she hands me. "The toilet is just down the hall if you need it."

When I return to the apartment a few minutes later, Krysia has fixed up some blankets and a pillow on the divan. "There." I burrow under, inhaling the scent of her perfume and looking around the room in the darkness.

"You don't have a piano to play here," I say, noticing for the first time, as my eyes grow heavy. Of course not. There would have been no way to get it to the garret and no room for it, anyway. No phonograph or radio, either. It seems the oddest thing for a musician to have no music.

"No. There's a music store around the corner that lets me play theirs in exchange for giving the occasional lesson."

"I like quiet," she says, reading my thoughts. "You shouldn't be afraid to be alone with your own thoughts." She dims the lamp, then retreats to the loft bed in the corner of the flat without speaking further, as if to prove a point.

Surrounded by the soft downy bedding and Krysia's lilac scent, I drift quickly to sleep. I dream that I am running down the street from our apartment to the hotel in Versailles, searching for something, perhaps the missing document. No, not something, I realize as I reach the hotel. Someone. I am late for work and I go into Georg's hotel room but the bed is made, all of his personal effects gone, and it is as if he was never here at all. I turn and suddenly it is not his hotel room at all but our house back in Berlin and I reach for the doorknob but it will not open. I am trapped.

My eyes fly open. I blink in the darkness, confused. Krysia's apartment, I remember, hearing her faint snore. I lay awake, shaken and trying to collect fragments of the dream as they scatter.

My thoughts turn to our earlier conversation, my revelation to Krysia that Stefan and I are already wed. What is marriage, anyway? It has been over four years since Stefan and I went to the Rathaus and came out with that piece of paper calling us man and wife, and yet I feel no closer to him than the stranger I pass on the street. Was it supposed to confer some new feeling, or simply recognize what is already there? But if it is no more than acknowledgment of the status quo, then why do we need it at all?

Sometimes it is as if I have two people inside me—the one that knows what is right and the one that does not care and only knows want, desire. She is the one who would cast off these skirts and run wild through the forest, who would hop a freighter for China. My gaze travels to the window and the thin strip of night sky above the roofs of the buildings. I could just leave. I'd head west, I decide, over the rolling hills until I reach the sea and a ship to take me away from it all. How would I survive? I've never had a job, do not have any skills, but I could find work as a governess or tutor. Something tells me I can manage hard work, am perhaps even suited to it. And my needs are simple, a place to rest, a bit of food. But I could not leave Papa any more than I could forsake myself.

"There are some doors," Krysia told me once, "that are not meant to be opened." At the time she was referring to her own situation, my suggestion that she try to talk to Emilie. But remembering the day I met her, the words also ring true. What if I had stopped at the gate of the Jardin des Tuileries that December afternoon, heeded my inner warning and not gone through? I would not have gone to the café and spoken carelessly in front of her artist friends and I would not be embroiled in this whole mess with Ignatz. But then I also would not have known Krysia and she is so embedded in my world I can scarcely imagine it without her. No, it is impossible to take one piece of the puzzle away and try to envision the rest whole.

My eyelids grow heavy and I allow myself to be lulled to sleep once more by a gentle breeze through the open window and the sounds of the street below.

CHAPTER TEN

The next morning I awaken on the strange divan, still in my dress from the previous evening. My mouth is sour from the brandy. "Krysia?" The apartment is still, the sound of her snoring gone. On the table beside the couch sits a hastily scrawled note.

Had to run out on an errand. Meet me outside the station in Versailles today at noon.
—K

The note does not give the purpose of our meeting, nor does it contemplate the possibility of my being unavailable on such short notice.

Just before noon I stand at the entranceway to the Gare de Versailles-Chantiers, having returned home briefly to wash and change. The crowd at midday is a mix of locals making their way into the city. Suddenly I feel as if I am being watched. A chill creeps up my spine and I turn, scanning the travelers who move uneventfully from the ticket kiosk to the platform. It is paranoia, brought on by Ignatz and this spying business—the fear of getting caught, that he is somehow monitoring me all of the time.

In the distance, the cathedral clock begins to chime twelve. Perhaps Krysia isn't going to show. A moment later, I hear the sound of a car engine behind me. Krysia appears, not from the train platform as I thought she might, but through the stillness of the fog, resplendent and surreal, driving a motorcar, a long black Citroën, up the wide thoroughfare that runs perpendicular to the station. She wears a broad-brimmed hat, held by sashes tied under the chin that match perfectly the blue of her cape.

She pulls up to the curb but does not switch off the engine. "Come," she says, gesturing for me to get in the car.

"You can drive," I marvel.

She nods, concentrating as she pulls from the curb. "I can try."

"Where are we going?" She does not answer, but drives with both arms extended as though navigating a great ship as we follow the road that leads away from town. Soon the houses on the outskirts start to thin, giving way to the occasional farm. The fields, knee-high with too-dry crops and wildflowers, sway gently beneath the cloudless midday sky. "Beautiful," I remark. "So peaceful."

"So different now than during the war," Krysia agrees. "There were raids almost every night. Once Marcin and I were out walking and we had to hide in an arch at the Louvre." The war was so far away in London. It is hard to imagine being in the middle of it all.

We come to a roundabout and she follows it three-quarters of the way around, turning onto the spur that indicates towns to the northeast, the road toward Belgium. Great rolling fields of poppies flank either side of the road, an endless carpet of red.

An hour later, Krysia turns onto a smaller road, not much more than a country lane. Through the now-faded black paint that was used to cover the signs during the war, I can make out that we are headed in the direction of Reims. On a hill in the distance stand the remnants of the once-grand Reims cathedral. Though the tallest of its pillars still stands, the stained-glass windows are now jagged shards and its roof is peeled back like an open can.

Krysia slows as we approach the town center. In contrast to Paris or Versailles, Reims is a ghost town. Ours is the only motorcar on the narrow cobblestone street, which is deserted, save for a cart pulled by a sorry, malnourished mare. From the sidewalk, pedestrians eye us with interest. Here one can see the closeness of the war. Buildings the entire length of the street were destroyed by the bombs and only the front walls remain standing, gaping craters behind the facades, which seem ready to topple at any second. The smell of gunpowder hangs in the air as though the destruction took place hours, and not months or years, ago.

But there are small signs of life. At the end of the block, two low garage walls remain, standing opposite one another like bookends. A makeshift roof of canvas and oil paper has been erected between them, and a woman sells bread and fruit on the ground beneath. Krysia pulls the car to the curb and steps out to buy food from her. She hands the woman a fistful of bills, suggesting a desire to help rather than genuine hunger. A moment later, she returns with several fresh young peaches.

She hands me one, then starts the car again. I bite into the soft flesh, blotting at the juice that dribbles down my chin with a handkerchief. On the next block not even the fronts of the buildings remain, just low piles of rubble. *Abri—40 personnes* is painted on the foundation of one of the decimated buildings, indicating that shelter from bombs could safely be taken there, a promise broken.

The road leads us out of Reims and I breathe the air deeply, eager to clear the devastation from my lungs. The sky has begun to cloud over, dampness and fog chilling the air. We cross a low bridge, children wading in the stream beneath. Overhead, birds call to one another in seeming cadence with the car engine.

Krysia pulls to the side of the road and turns off the ignition. As I step from the car, moisture from the ankle-high grass seeps through my stockings and the heels of my boots sink deeper into the sodden earth with every step. A wind begins to blow, sweeping away the fog. We are standing in a rolling field that stretches to the horizon like a great wave before disappearing. It is a battlefield, or was. Now it is a graveyard. Small crosses, some painted white and others crudely handmade from sticks, spring up around our ankles like dandelions among the lush clover. A faint halo of mist lingers inches above the earth.

I stop midstep. I had avoided coming here, and might have demurred if Krysia had told me in advance where we were going. For even as I wanted to know everything, part of me had long suspected that I could not bear the truth. But I am here now and have no choice but to see.

We reach a row of trees that have been sheared at the midpoint. Atop the amputated branches, new leaves have begun to sprout. Krysia unties her hat and removes it somberly. Her hair comes loose, billowing around her face as regal as a lion's mane.

I take a step forward. Krysia grabs my arm and pulls me back as I nearly step on something hard that juts from the earth. "Oh!" I gasp at the sight of naked bone.

She begins to walk up the hill. At the top of the ridge, the terrain that had appeared endless breaks suddenly. The trenches. The long tube of hollowed-out earth is much deeper and wider than I'd imagined, a kind of subterranean city where the men had lived and died, rats in a maze. The smell of peat and earth and human waste wafts upward. About fifty meters to our right, the trench is bisected abruptly by a great crater, maybe ninety feet in diameter. Like the spot where Stefan had nearly died, only so much worse in reality.

My guilt rises up as I see the thousands of Stefans before me, the young men who were killed, or wounded and lay bleeding. Had he called for me? Krysia had brought me here, I suspect, to give me some perspective and show me that life is fleeting. To help me move forward. But, instead, all of the reasons I cannot leave loom larger than ever.

"Such destruction," I lament, my words sounding tinny and inadequate.

"And not a drop of blood spilled on German soil," she remarks, gazing off into the distance. It is not meant as an insult; she is merely stating a fact. Picturing Stefan, I want to tell her that we had suffered, too. "There was enough stupidity on all sides, enough blame to go around," she adds as a concession, reading my thoughts. "But the victors will write history in their own way." I nod—laid out in the panorama before us is the reason the Allies will not be lenient, why the ideals embodied in Wilson's Fourteen Points will not be big enough to include the Germans. How can Georg not see that?

I'd been in the college library when one of the maids came to tell me about the armistice. A few days later, we assembled in the courtyard at Magdalen as the bell tolled, marking the official end to the war. We stood shoulder to shoulder—professors and students and porters and cooks, English and German alike. The war had changed so much—dukes and heirs had died alongside footmen and laborers. Women had worked as nurses and drivers and in the factories. Surely it all couldn't be put together the way it once was, an eggshell cracked in a thousand different pieces.

"The next war, I fear, will be even worse." Krysia's voice pulls me from my thoughts.

I turn to her in disbelief. "The next? Surely you don't think this will happen again."

"Not the men who fought this war, of course. The strongest pacifists are those who have seen battle. But governments have had a taste of the bloodshed and the power—and the weaponry will only get better."

My heart sinks as I realize she is right. They had called it the war to end all wars. But already there are whispers of newer, more sinister fears, gasses and other weapons that could take out the civilian populations of entire cities. Georg said militaries are needed in order to keep the peace. If we cannot end war, then his work to prevent it, what he is trying to achieve, seems more important than ever.

"Some say if women could have voted, the war never would have started," I offer.

"Nonsense. Do you really believe those silly creatures who crow at the salons would have had any more sense than their husbands?" She is right. The war, more so than anything, had been about stupid pride, and the women, with their too-large hats and peacock feathers, had more than enough of that.

"At least one can speak openly of peace again," she remarks. I nod. Throughout the war it was considered treasonous and cowardly to speak of anything other than military victory. Only during the waning months did the word begin to creep into conversation again, a tacit recognition of the weariness and yearning for the end of the fighting that we had all secretly shared but not dared to voice. It was as if no one knew how to behave in peacetime again.

"Marcin wants to return to Krakow." She speaks into the air, not looking at me. "He can't compose here, he says, with all of the noise. He's begged me to come with him. But I can't leave Emilie." She has her own pain, I am reminded, of which she seldom speaks. I want to tell her to go with him, to leave the past behind. But who am I, childless and unable to escape my own past, to give her advice? I reach down and squeeze her hand gently.

"We should go," she says, as the sky begins to deepen at the edges.

"Thank you for bringing me."

"I've been meaning to come. And it can be helpful to step out of one's own world, even for a bit, to gain some perspective." It's true. For a few hours, I've been able to escape all of my worries about the missing document, my questions of Georg and Stefan and the future. But as we wind through the hills and valleys, making our way back toward Paris, my heaviness grows once more.

"You're thinking about Georg." It is not a question and her voice sours as she says his name.

"You don't like him," I say to Krysia, dejected.

She shrugs. "I'm happy for you. It is good to see you wanting something—fighting for something—instead of letting life drag you along. But no, I don't like him. He's the enemy." There is a bitterness in her voice that I have never heard before.

"He's a German. Am I the enemy, too?" I feel again in that moment the gulfs of anger and hate that the war has sown, even in educated and worldly people such as she, pain too fresh for an armistice paper and a few months' passage of time to heal. "Don't you see, if we hate just because of where we come from, we're no better than the fools who started the war in the first place?"

She does not answer but continues driving. I gaze up at the sky, which is clear, but over the horizon to the west, dark gray clouds are forming. "Krysia, do you believe in fate?"

"You obviously do."

Suddenly it seems as though all my life I have been searching for the right answers, some hidden script I was supposed to follow without anyone actually giving it to me. Even my little rebellions, studying English instead of Latin, music instead of art, had been well planned and designed in some way to show that my choices were the right ones. "I think there has to be some kind of order, a path."

But she shakes her head slightly. "I don't. We each have free will. There may be higher purpose, but the actual path each of us takes to get there, and whether we choose to accept it at all, is up to us." She turns to me. "If you can't let go of that fear of making the wrong decision, you will never be able to take the chances you must take to live life fully." She looks back at the road.

I consider this for the first time. I find romantic the notion that there is a purpose to it all, something that we are intended to do, a path—perhaps not unlike the people who preferred the firm constructs of the good old days. But as Krysia says—we each can choose our way. If it was all preordained and we stepped off, then what would happen? "People make choices every day," I say, musing aloud. "Turn right or left…"

"Follow someone out of a party or not…" she chides.

I ignore the joke, nursing the more serious line of inquiry. "And things would be very different if they did not."

"You have a choice. But you have to seize the moment or it may not come again. It is, as they say, now or never."

"But those choices have consequences," I counter, and with that she cannot argue. I could refuse to go back to Berlin, but so many people would be hurt—Stefan, for whom all hope would be lost, and Papa, too.

"I just want to go back to the way things were." But even as I speak the words I am not sure what I mean by them. Back to where? Life in Berlin with Stefan will never feel the same as it once has. London, our temporary stay among the enemy, was not the answer, either. I suppose I mean to some nameless place in time where it is just Papa and I with our books, but that place does not exist in a vacuum. There are others—Celia and Krysia and, yes, Georg.

"There is no back," she says gently. "We must forge on."

I nod. I've been a prisoner not of Papa's expectations or of Stefan, but of my own fears all of these years. "And speaking of forging on, what are you going to do about Ignatz?"

"I don't know." If I don't get the papers from Georg, Papa

will be discredited. I am caught between the two men I care most about. "Talk to him, see if we can figure something out." I cannot keep running from Ignatz.

"I will take you to him." At the roundabout, she exits on a different road, heading to the northern edge of Paris. We reach the city limits and she continues in the direction of Montmartre, the motorcar engine struggling to ascend the steep hills. The neighborhood is ragtag, empty buildings and littered steps. "The artists used to live here before the center shifted to Montparnasse," she explains. She stops the car in front of a dilapidated building. "Stein lives on the first floor." I wait for her to offer to go with me but she does not.

The door to the apartment building is ajar so I enter and climb wood stairs so rickety I fear they will fall through. At the top, I knock. *"Da?"* Stein's voice calls and a moment later he throws open the door wearing only an undershirt and trousers. Behind him the flat is a cavernous space, open and bare, perhaps once an artist's studio. A woman I recognize from the bar sprawls in a chaise longue, clad in a dressing gown. I comprehend then just how far from my world I have come.

His bushy eyebrows pull together in a single scraggly line. "You! Do you have what I want?"

I swallow. "Not exactly. That is, I found it—it was a map and it showed markings at some of the eastern cities…" I falter, unable to convey the significance of what I had seen.

He rubs his hands together. "Perfect. Where is it?"

"I lost it. That is, I got the document but then it disappeared and…"

"Idiot!" Swift as a cat, he grabs me by the wrist and pulls me close. I cry out as great waves of pain shoot down my arm. I have never been struck, even lightly. Papa did not believe in spankings, despite admonitions from Uncle Walter and others that he would spoil me. It is the first time I have ever felt pain at the hands of another and I am frozen, unable to react. "Do you think I care about your excuses?" His breath is foul with vodka and smoke.

I pull away, stifling a cry at the burning of my skin as I wrest myself from his grasp. "How dare you?" I say, trying without success to keep the tremor from my voice. "I could have you arrested." I realize my mistake as soon as I have spoken. Threats will only feed his anger.

"Ignatz…" Before he can respond the woman from inside the apartment beckons.

"Three days," he hisses. "You have three days to get me what I want." He slams the apartment door, leaving me standing in the hallway, shaken.

I walk down the stairs and climb into the car. Krysia does not ask how it went and I do not offer. Instead, we drive silently into the night.

CHAPTER ELEVEN

Papa is at his desk when I return, trying to read with the lamp turned down too low. That morning when I'd returned from Krysia's to wash and change, the apartment had been neater than I remembered leaving it, as if the maid had come on the wrong day. Now, it is a sea of strewn papers once more.

We eye each other warily. "I'm sorry," I say quickly, forgoing my usual stubbornness. I have no energy to argue after my day at the battlefields and confrontation with Ignatz.

Relief floods his face. He does not wish to continue our quarrel, either. "As am I. I just worry about you."

"I'm going to keep working for him, Papa," I say, struggling not to waver, to keep my voice clear and calm. I have never dared to defy my father like this and I can hardly believe my own resolve. Alienating him and leaving for good is unthinkable. But on this point I stand firm. "The work we are doing is important and it matters for the delegation and for the conference and for Germany."

His mustache pulls downward as he bites his lip, unable to disagree. "I understand, but I'm worried, *liebchen*. You seem to be attached to Captain Richwalder in a very strong way. This is not the time for complicated alliances," he adds, before I can protest. More so than fretting about propriety, Papa is concerned about me. He does not want me to get hurt. I should not be surprised—he has always put me first. But there is something more urgent about his worry this time, as if he is standing above me on a ladder, able to see things in a way that I can't.

"And then there is Stefan," he adds. "He's a good man and he cares for you deeply. He's sacrificed much." *I'm your daughter,* I want to say. *My happiness should be what matters.* But to say this would be to admit that my happiness lies with Georg, not Stefan, and how could I tell him that? "Your well being is everything to me," Papa says, reading my thoughts. "I only wish..."

That the things that make me happy and the things that are good for me were one and the same. "I know." I raise my hand, warding off a return to the debate. "I went to Reims with Krysia today to see the battlefields."

He nods. "I saw your note that you'd gone somewhere."

"Do you mind?"

"To the contrary. I'm glad. I've been so busy with the conference, but it's no excuse. We've been remiss in not going and reminding ourselves of the very reason that we are here."

"I had no idea about the extent of the devastation. You had not told me."

"With Stefan fighting, I thought it might be too much. Sometimes I forget that you are not a child." He had been trying to shield my innocence. Still, I am frustrated by his hypocrisy—wanting me to be educated but not aware, teaching me to be curious and yet sheltering me from the truth.

"I was thinking of dinner in the city on Saturday, you, me and Celia," he says, changing the subject. There is a moment of uncomfortable silence between us. While I appreciate his need for her companionship, I have always resisted his attempts to bring Tante Celia closer into our circle. The last thing I want to do right now is sit down at a formal meal with the two of them. But he has conceded to my continuing work with Georg. And seeing the hope in his eyes, I cannot refuse. I smile. "Certainly, Papa."

Our conversation over, I walk to my room and change into my nightgown. Brushing my hair, I go to the window. It is raining now, thick round drops slapping against the window. My gaze travels down the street toward the hotel. I'd wanted to check on Georg, but the late hour, on top of Papa's forbidding me to go there, had stopped me. I undress and climb into bed, then lie awake in the darkness.

My thoughts roll back unexpectedly to the day Mother died. I came home from school that afternoon like any other. We'd been painting with watercolors and I'd done a scene of our garden I thought my mother might enjoy for her study. That the house was quiet was nothing new—she was often in her own quarters, napping or reading. I made myself a snack of cheese and crackers like I'd been taught, started on my homework. Twenty minutes passed, then thirty.

Finally, the door to the kitchen opened but it was Papa who stepped through. This was not unusual, either—he sometimes worked in his home study. But his sleeves were rolled up and his hair disheveled in a way I never saw unless I caught him on the way to the water closet in the middle of the night. "Mama's gone," he said in a hoarse whisper and I thought he meant to the market or tea with a friend, though she had none of whom I knew. Seeing the faint red half circles around his lower eyelids like makeup in a play, I understood then that he meant dead. He had always tried to shield me from the worst, then as well as now.

A noise at the window pulls me from my memories. I push back the covers and as I walk to it, puzzled, the sound comes again, a pebble grazing the glass.

Georg stands on the pavement below, head tilted upward, face illuminated in the moonlight. "What are you doing here?" He does not answer. My stomach gives a little skip. But his standing on the street beneath my window is sure to attract attention. Suddenly I am mindful of my nightgown. "Can you wait a moment? I will be right down."

Quickly I dress and walk through the apartment to the front door. "Is someone here?" Papa calls from his desk.

Unable to bear the questions the truth would bring, I pretend not to hear him. Downstairs, I open the door. "Hello, Margot," Georg says, as though it were perfectly normal for us to meet like this. His eyes reflect like dark pools.

"Are you mad? You should be in bed." Behind him, raindrops lingering from the storm that has just ended fall from the eaves, the dripping sound rhythmic.

He shrugs. "I'm better now." I want to protest that he cannot possibly have recovered so quickly. His color is restored, though, and his face clear but for the faint half circles beneath his eyes. It is as if he has shrugged off serious illness like a bothersome cloak.

I've missed him, I realize, as a faint hint of his aftershave drifts beneath my nose. The past two nights apart have seemed so much longer. Then, remembering the missing document, I am flooded with panic. Perhaps he has noticed and that is why he is here.

"When you didn't come..." He falters. "I was worried."

I slump with relief, then hope he has not noticed. "I sent word." My note had only indicated I'd be gone the previous night, though, not tonight, as well. "I meant to return the papers today. I can get them right now if you need them."

"It isn't that. Rather, I wanted to know why you had not come."

Tante Celia appears behind him unexpectedly in the doorway. "Oh!" she says, mouth agape at the sight of the tall, handsome officer. I stare at her, equally surprised. Though I've long been aware of her slipping into the apartment to see Papa, this is the first time we've encountered each other at such a late hour of the night, when there is no respectable explanation for her appearance.

"Excuse me," Georg says, moving aside to let her in.

Celia steps around him, forgetting to leave her wet parasol outside. Then she turns to me. "Margot?" We stare at each other awkwardly.

"Tante Celia, may I introduce Captain Georg Richwalder? Georg, this is my…" I hesitate, considering a more explicit introduction, then decide against it. "This is my aunt."

He shifts his hat to his left arm and extends his right, kissing Tante Celia's hand as though we are at a ball and not the front door at a wholly improper hour of the night. "A pleasure."

Her eyes travel from him to me and there is a moment of interminable silence, broken only by the drops falling from her umbrella to the marble floor. "I've heard so much about you," she says slowly. She could tell Georg about my engagement to Stefan. I hold my breath, waiting for the next drop to fall.

Upstairs Papa coughs. "I should go," she says, walking past us.

"I shouldn't be here unannounced at this hour," Georg frets when she has gone. "Only I saw these…" I notice then his hat is full of flowers, still wet from the storm. "Honeysuckle. You mentioned you like it and these are the first I've seen of the season. They've just begun to blossom," he adds, his eyes hopeful as a child's.

I step out of the apartment building and close the door behind me, then I reach for the flowers. They are a pretext, of course, an excuse to come and see me. At the bottom of the hat, my hand closes around something cool and metal. The flowers are held together by a finely linked bracelet of pearl, wrapped around the stems. "Oh, Georg. I couldn't possibly accept this."

"It's just a small token of my gratitude for your work, and for your kindness while I was ill. It was my mother's." He takes the bracelet from the flowers and fastens it around my wrist. "She believed that such things were to be worn, not shut away in a drawer from the light."

I open my mouth to protest. Such an elaborate gift isn't proper—I don't know him well enough. And it must hold a great deal of sentimental value for him, if he cared enough to bring it along with him to France. But the bracelet seems to forge to my skin as if a part of me and I cannot refuse it. He lifts my wrist to adjust the clasp. "What's this?" Illuminated in the glow of the streetlight is the scratch, red and swollen, from where Ignatz had grabbed me in threat. I am seized with the urge to tell Georg the truth about everything. There is a calm confidence about his demeanor that makes me want to trust him and I know he could fix this. But I cannot.

"I scraped myself earlier," I lie, cringing at the need to meet his concern with deception. Does he believe my explanation? Eager to distract him, I pull out a strand of honeysuckle from the bunch, inhaling the warm, fresh scent. Then I put the sprig in my hair, which is undone, combed long and full around my shoulders. "They're lovely. Thank you."

He nods formally, then takes his hat and turns to go. Behind him fireflies blink in the darkness.

"Wait." Setting the flowers on the table inside the doorway, I step out onto the street. The damp pavement releases its smells of earth and stone and waste.

He turns back, eyes hopeful. "Would you like to take a walk?"

"You shouldn't be walking anywhere in your condition."

"Nonsense. Come." I follow him down the dimly lit street. The air is more summer than spring now, any hint of a chill gone. Crickets chirp unseen and water trickles down the gutter along the roadside. "I love to walk at night," he adds.

I nod. I've often felt the pull from my open window to stroll the deserted streets and hear all of the noises so buried in the chaos of the day. I haven't done it, of course; for me alone, it wouldn't be safe. But walking beside Georg, I feel somehow protected. We pass a church and I peer up at figures carved in stone that stare down piously, demanding our repentance. The streets hold their breath, as if at any moment someone might step out and apprehend us.

We reach the park at the end of the street, the pavement fading into a dirt path that runs along a stream. Georg offers his arm and I hesitate. Then I reach out and wrap my hand around his thick forearm, the material of his uniform scratchy under my fingertips, skin warm beneath. We walk in silence for several minutes. The stream grows wider until it opens into a small lake with untended banks, flush with high curved reeds.

"Look." He points upward. I follow his hand, amazed at the bed of stars that unfurls above us. On the streets, the lights and tall buildings make it hard to see the sky properly. But in the shrouded darkness of the park nothing stands between us and them save a gentle canopy of branches and leaves. "Orion's Belt. The stars can be a kind of navigation tool when you are at sea. We have more modern equipment, of course, but in past centuries sailors navigated the world by the stars. As long as I could find Orion's Belt, I wasn't lost. The stars helped center me." There is a kind of hollowness to his voice, as though longing for such a centering now.

"I'm sorry I couldn't come to you these past two nights." I do not elaborate on my argument with Papa, knowing his misgivings would be hurtful to Georg. "I hope I haven't set you back too far in your work."

"I wasn't worried about that. I thought you were angry or upset." His voice trails off. He was concerned that I was put off by the things he said the other night. Despite his delirium, he remembers, and that makes his words real and impossible to deny. "You can stop working for me. The position I've put you in is untenable." My breath catches. Does he know somehow about Ignatz and the missing document, after all? For a moment, it is as if I am transparent, exposed. "I would understand if you didn't want to upset your father." I relax slightly. It is Papa's concerns he's picked up on intuitively. But I hate how that makes me sound like a child.

I consider what he has said. It had not occurred to me to stop working for him. I could even ask Papa to let me return to Berlin. It would solve many problems—Papa would no longer be angry and Ignatz, if he believed my termination involuntary, would have to accept that I could no longer help. But it would feel like giving up. And seeing Georg every day is the last thing I want to forgo.

No, I do not want to leave him. "Not at all," I say finally. "I won't give up on what we are doing."

His shoulders drop perceptibly with relief. "Good. I wanted to see you, too, because I have exciting news."

"Oh?"

"I received a new file from Berlin, one that had been lost in the archives—or so they thought. It belonged to a diplomat called Leimer, who had so many ideas similar to ours about how the German ground forces could partner with the West in peacetime. But then Germany signed the alliance with Russia and it was all moot. Leimer killed himself in protest."

"How awful!"

"Indeed, but his notes may have some suggestions about how to combine the strengths of the two militaries that could be most helpful by analogy for our work."

"Have you gone through it yet?"

He shakes his head. "The file is massive and it only came late today." Yet he had broken from working on it to come find me. "I thought that perhaps if we divided it, we could get through it more quickly. Of course, the documents are already in German, but I thought that if we worked together it might go faster." Though, there was no need for translation, Georg was taking me into his confidence with the materials, treating me as his partner.

I think of the document I'd taken for Ignatz, seemingly disappeared. I do not know where it has gone, the extent of harm it might do in the wrong hands. Georg has not noticed it is missing, at least not yet. I look at him helplessly. I want to tell him everything. But I would have to admit what I had done and then he would despise me. And what could he do? Best to say nothing.

I shiver. Georg starts to remove his coat. I wave him off. "I'm not cold, thank you." My voice comes out more harshly than I intended. We are at a precipice, a place where one more step will make return impossible. I cannot bear to have him closer to me—even if it is only his coat.

"Oh..." He falters. "I'm sorry," he apologizes, mistaking my reticence for offense. Suddenly we are talking about something much larger than a coat. "If I said or did something..." He thinks I'm angry. The truth is just the opposite—it is my feelings and attraction to him that made me push him away.

Unable to bear the notion that I have hurt him, I reach out and touch his arm. "It's not that." Our eyes meet.

"Margot..." He lowers his head and suddenly his lips are lightly on mine, a question. I hesitate for a faint breath and then I am kissing him back, harder, swept away by things I had not dared to imagine. His hand cups my cheek. His mouth tastes of the sea and sand and faraway harbors, of longing and loneliness and loss, a wave pulling back from the shore, threatening to drag me along with it. Stefan has kissed me before but it was nothing like this...

Stefan. His face appears in my mind. I put my hand on Georg's chest, then pull away. "I can't." I struggle to catch my breath and right the world that wobbles around me. My cheeks burn. This is wrong. What kind of horrible woman am I, kissing another man while my husband lies wounded in a hospital bed?

Georg's embrace holds everything I have ever needed, though I had not known until this very moment it existed. But it doesn't matter—I made a promise that I will honor. "I can't," I repeat.

His face crumbles. "I mistook your intentions and I apologize."

I reach for him. "Not at all. It's just that things are very complicated right now."

He pulls his arm from my grasp and steps away. "You needn't worry," he says. His voice is as stiff and formal as the day we met, all traces of the familiarity and closeness we've built up since then. "I understand now. You don't regard me in that way. It doesn't matter if it is about position or religion or something else. I accept it, and I won't bother you about it again…"

No, I want to shout. I have never cared about those societal things and the notion that I do not like him, well, nothing could be further from the truth. But his logic makes sense—we are two young people and both, he thinks, single. There is no reason we could not be together if we chose. He smiles ruefully. "I should thank you. It has been a useful reminder of why I do not dabble in affairs of the heart." He turns abruptly. "I should see you home."

"Georg, wait…" I do not want to leave or to let go of this moment, the most real of my life. But he has already started from the water, back toward the garden path. I reach for him again. Suddenly the ground shifts beneath me. The bank. I've gone too close to the edge and the earth, softened by the recent rains, begins to give way. I fall backward as if in slow motion, my hands reaching toward Georg and closing around emptiness.

I sail through the air for what feels like several seconds before crashing into the water, icy as it engulfs me, seeping through my clothes. I flail my arms and try to kick, but my legs become tangled amid my skirt. The water begins to close over my head.

Georg is beside me then, pulling me to the surface, one arm

around my neck and the other my waist as he guides me to shore. "Are you all right?"

"Quite." I tremble, as much from my terror at encountering the water as from the night air, frigid against my wet skin. "I told you I wasn't much of a swimmer."

He laughs as we reach the bank. "That's an understatement. The water is hardly deeper than you are tall, though panic can make things seem much worse." Then his expression grows serious. "You're soaked," he says, apparently heedless that he is wet, as well. He wraps me in his coat and this time I do not protest. "We need to get you back to the hotel."

I stand, holding my soaked skirt aloft so as not to trip. "I'm fine." But I am unable to stop my teeth from chattering. "I'll just head home."

"Come back to the hotel and while your things are drying out, I can show you the Leimer file."

"Fine," I relent, my curiosity about the new documents piqued. It would be better, too, to avoid seeing Papa and Celia like this and facing their questions.

Ten minutes later, we reach the hotel and he leads me up the back stairs to avoid the lobby. Inside, I wait uncertainly in his sitting room until he reappears, producing a soft, gray dressing gown. "Put this on." I walk to the water closet and come out a few minutes later, his oversize robe swimming around me. He takes my dress from me and hangs it by the fire he's started. "This should dry in no time."

He looks toward the desk, piled high with his papers, and I expect him to pull out the file. But instead he hands me a cup of tea. "Sit." I hesitate. Talking to him in such a state is ridiculously awkward and improper. But there is something strangely delicious about being swallowed by his oversize robe, the familiar smell of his aftershave wafting up from the collar. I wanted to come here tonight, I realize, and it had nothing to do with the new documents or avoiding Papa. I draw my knees up close beneath me as he adds wood to the fire.

He stands and walks into the bedroom once more, then returns a moment later with a small tube. "Let me see your wrist," he says firmly, kneeling in front of me. He squeezes some salve from the tube and rubs it into the wound where Ignatz had grabbed me, the warm pleasure of his touch mixing with dull pain, stirring something deep inside me.

Finally, he sits across from me, then stares into the fire, not speaking. Is he thinking about our kiss, or the fact that I pushed him away? I stop, flooded by regret, feeling Georg's lips so full on mine. The kiss was like nothing I have ever experienced. Live for the moment, Krysia would have admonished. It was all any of us had anymore. But I had turned away, letting as ever all of my self-doubts ruin the kiss. Surely there would not be another.

I notice for the first time the sword that is on the mantelpiece. A shiver runs through me. "They permitted us to keep our weapons," he says. "I do not, of course, carry mine here."

"Have you ever used your sword?"

"Technically, it's a saber." Though his tone is not unkind, I am embarrassed, as though I should have known. "No." His jaw sets grimly. "I haven't used it, but the destruction I've caused is no less egregious. I hate war."

"But you're still in the navy. Isn't that something of a contradiction?"

He shakes his head. "I'm a sailor and I can't abandon that. And I'm proud to serve Germany, even now. I believe that a military, properly designed, can be a deterring force, a valuable part of international relations and peace."

We sit in silence for a few minutes. We should be working. There is much to be done. I realize then that I am not just helping Georg. It has become my mission, too. "You mentioned the Leimer file?"

"Oh, yes," he said, as if while we were talking, he had forgotten. He goes to the desk once more and pulls out a file several inches thick. "They don't appear to be in any particular order," he notes, dividing the stack in two and handing half to me. I begin to page through the materials, noting on a separate paper a few pages of interest. We work alongside each other in silence.

"Your dress should be dry," he concedes some time after midnight, an unmistakable note of reluctance to his voice. "Perhaps if you'd like to take some of the documents, you can review them while I'm meeting with the delegation tomorrow."

"Certainly," I reply, marveling at the ease with which he gives me access to the material. How can I possibly betray him again?

"Is something wrong? You look so sad."

"I'm fine," I say, searching for a plausible explanation. "I just get a bit lost sometimes."

He reaches over and I freeze. Will he try to kiss me again? But he just brushes a smudge of dirt from beneath my right eye, the edge of his finger grazing the lashes before pulling away.

I carry my dress into Georg's room and loosen the robe. I pause, standing unclothed in the center of his room, seized with the urge to lie down in his bed, just inches away. "Margot?" he calls from the sitting room. Hurriedly, I put on the dress. The material is a bit scratchy from the quick drying and a faint pond smell lingers.

I step back out into the sitting room. "I should get home before Papa begins to worry." His brow furrows.

"Does he mind your being out with me?" His question asks something deeper: Does Papa know of the feelings that have transpired between us?

"I don't know." A frown flickers across Georg's face, disappointment, perhaps, that I have not been more forthright with Papa about what is transpiring between us. But how could I have possibly? It's been mere days and whatever has grown between us is too fledgling and strange to understand myself, much less explain. Even without Stefan and the other complications, I could not have told him. "That is, he's been so busy. I haven't had the chance to speak with him about things." It is a lie, I think, remembering our fight about Georg and our conversation just hours ago.

But Georg holds up his arm, warding off my excuses. "Of course not. No explanation needed. How silly of me to have thought... Your father would want someone Jewish, and a learned man to be sure."

"It's not that," I protest quickly. "I would never care about such matters, if things were right."

"If things were right," he repeated slowly, eyes meeting mine with more hope than I have ever seen. Guilt rises. I am leading him on and I cannot stop myself. His face brightens. "I never should have expected you to tell him. You go home now. I should not have had you come here like this. First thing tomorrow I will see your father and ask his permission to call on you formally."

Panic floods my brain. If Georg goes to Papa, he will learn the truth about everything. "Georg, no." He blanches with apprehension that all of his original concerns of not being good enough to be accepted are in fact true. "Papa's just so preoccupied with the conference work right now. It is taxing his health, which is already in a dreadful state." I curse myself for using Papa's heart condition as an alibi. "If we just wait until after the plenary session next week, we can have you around for dinner and then you can ask." I cringe inwardly at the lie. It will never be okay for Georg to ask Papa to court me. But at least this will buy me some time.

"Fine," he says, somewhat mollified.

"I should go," I say again, picking up the documents.

"I'll walk you home."

"Really, that isn't necessary." I am not keen to be seen with him at this hour and my excuses will be so much easier to make if I can be caught alone.

He raises his hand, unwilling to be dissuaded. Neither of us speaks on the short walk down the street to our apartment building. He stops a few meters from the doorway, a concession to the secret I've asked him to keep for now. There is a moment of silence that seems eternal. Our eyes meet uncertainly. Will he try to kiss me again?

But he nods and tips his hat formally, grasping the present limitations—a tactical retreat. There is a moment of awkward hesitation as we watch one another uncertainly. "We'll resume work tomorrow, then?" For everything that has transpired between us, there is still the work.

"Good night," I manage, my voice barely a whisper. Everything has changed between us in a way that cannot be undone. I turn and walk into the apartment building without looking back, feeling his eyes on me.

CHAPTER TWELVE

The next night when I walk into the hotel library, it is dark and empty, with a stale smell that suggests Georg has not yet been there this evening.

Carrying the documents I've brought back with me, I walk down the hall and knock on the door to his room. "Hello?" There is no answer. I turn the handle and push open the door. But his rooms are still, as well. Six forty-five, the clock on the wall reads. He must be in meetings with the delegation. I had not planned to come early, but since I have…my eyes travel across the room to the desk and the pile of papers I'd searched the night he was ill. Perhaps if I look again, I can find another report that details the information Ignatz wants. Of course, it is risky—Georg could return at any second. But time is running out and there's no reason to believe I will have another chance to search the apartment alone. I have to try.

I move toward the desk, peering over my shoulder. Then I lift the stack to the midpoint, separating it close to where I found the original map. There are cables, but they reference other matters, seemingly unrelated to military installations in the east. I page deeper.

The door creaks suddenly. I jump back and the documents scatter like falling leaves. "Georg," I manage, as I kneel hurriedly to pick them up. "You startled me. I was early," I add. I'm babbling now. "I came in here looking for the rest of the Leimer file."

He bends and takes the documents I've collected from me in one fell swoop, then sets them back on the desk. "It's in the library." I follow him down the hall. He does not sound suspicious or annoyed. But when we reach the library, his brow is furrowed, bottom lip drawn in consternation. He looks tired and there are dark circles under his eyes. Perhaps the strain of our walk the previous night was too much.

"What is it?" I ask, putting my hand on his forearm instinctively.

"A document is missing." My breath catches. Easy, I think. There are thousands of documents. It could be something else. "A map of weapons depots to the east." Now I cease breathing entirely. "I received a call from the delegation saying that they needed that document and when I went to fetch it from the file, it was gone."

My pulse quickens. The very paper I had stolen was the one that they sought. What are the odds? It is almost as if someone knew. But how is that possible? "Don't worry," he soothes, seeing my distress. "It wasn't in the binder you took, or even the ones you've reviewed here." No, it is from the pile I riffled while you were semiconscious with fever. "But it's terribly disturbing."

"Perhaps it was a mistake and it was missing before you came to Paris?"

"I'm afraid not. All of the documents were meticulously catalogued." Georg was far too orderly to leave such things to chance. "And I've seen this particular one since coming here.

It is definitely missing." He drops into a chair. "And that is disastrous."

"Surely they won't think you lost it intentionally."

He jumps up again. "Perhaps not. But it could cause problems. You see, there are deep factions within the delegation." I nod. Papa had alluded to as much. "As with any political group, there are different views. The hardliners—mostly the older members— feel that there is no reconciliation with the West, that even in defeat we should hold our ground and remain an island." He is pacing now, one hand at the back of his neck. "They regard my views of possible collaboration on future military endeavors as too liberal. The only reason they tolerate me at all is because of my military service record. And if they think I've lost a document, perhaps even on purpose, it will seriously undermine the credibility of my position and my work will be jeopardized."

Suddenly my violation of his trust seems more egregious than ever. "There has to be something that we can do to mitigate the damage."

"It's more than that, actually. The document did not just contain the German information. I have an ally, you see." I cock my head. "In the ministry is a young French lieutenant, partially of Russian descent. I had the opportunity to make acquaintance with the officer several years ago before the war on a joint training exercise and we stayed in touch. Lieutenant Bouvier believes, as I do, in the future of joint cooperation. So we've been, *ahem*, sharing information where it could be beneficial to that cause."

"I see." Georg has a contact inside the French foreign ministry. I had no idea. All of this time I've been so preoccupied with my own secrets, it never occurred to me that he might have one or two of his own.

"I'm so sorry I didn't tell you, Margot. At first, I didn't know you all that well. It's one thing to tell you about my work, but to jeopardize someone else is another matter. And then it didn't seem to matter as much."

"It's fine." I am hardly in a position to be holding grudges over secrets.

"I need to get word to Lieutenant Bouvier that our information has been compromised. But it hasn't been safe for us to talk for months, and I don't dare call the ministry or go there for fear of attracting attention."

"I can do it," I blurt without thinking. "That is, I can deliver a message to Lieutenant Bouvier for you."

"Margot, no. I couldn't ask." But I can see his mind working, the solution forming even as he protests it.

"I'm familiar with the ministry." It is perhaps an overstatement, but I was inside a handful of times with Papa when we stayed in Paris. And no one is likely to question a young woman such as myself who might easily be a courier. "Write the note," I instruct, with more force than I thought I would have dared.

The next morning at nine, I step out of the taxi in front of the foreign ministry. I cross the street quickly, fighting the urge to run and attract attention as I make my way to the entrance at the side of the massive building. Time is of the essence, Georg had said the previous evening, and I would have gone then and there, had the late hour not made it impossible. Instead, I had lain awake most of the night, plotting how I could get to Lieutenant Bouvier. At the gate, I stop, steeling myself. The arched entranceway is a swirl of bodies, diplomats arriving, couriers setting out on errands, visitors claiming appointments and waiting to be seen. I weave through the horde authoritatively. I do not stop at the gate, but wave airily the visitor badge I'd found in our apartment, hoping that the guard will not notice from this distance that it expired months ago.

Inside, the West Entrance Hall is quiet by contrast, just a few groups of suited men clustered on the red velvet couches talking. My heels echo conspicuously as I cross the marble floor.

"Mademoiselle?" a voice says behind me as I reach the base of the wide staircase.

I freeze and turn back, certain that I have been caught. *"Oui?"*
Standing before me is a uniformed guard who cannot be
more than eighteen or so himself. "You look lost. Can I help?"

"I'm trying to find my father, Professor Rosenthal, who is an
advisor to the conference."

"I believe they're presently in the salon on the second floor."
I continue two flights up the staircase. When I reach the landing, I start down the high-ceilinged corridor, which is lined
with framed tapestries. Thick velvet curtains, held back with
gold brocade, frame the windows.

At the end of the hall, I find a narrower, back stairway. Looking over my shoulder, I walk down to the floor below. Away
from the ceremonial halls, the decor is less ornate: there is a row
of simple oak doors with brass nameplates beside them, modest
lighting instead of chandeliers. Following the instructions Georg
had given me, I reach a door marked "E. Bouvier" and knock.

"Oui?" a female voice calls. I push the door open. Inside, a
woman in a navy skirt and blouse sits behind a desk.

"I'm looking for Lieutenant Bouvier."

"That's me."

I falter. I had never considered that Lieutenant Bouvier might
be a woman. She is beautiful with a short tight cap of black curls
and bright blue eyes. "I'm sorry, I had not expected…"

"A woman?" She smiles wearily. "I was in the nursing corps.
Lieutenant was my military title." Taking in her button nose
and perfect lips, which form a pout without the help of makeup,
I am flooded with jealousy. How well does she know Georg?
Had they been involved? "Can I help?" she prompts.

"Captain Richwalder sent me," I say.

"Georg?" A flash of intimacy crosses her face, confirming
everything I feared about the two of them. "I haven't seen him
in years."

"He wanted me to give you this." I hold out the note. She

unfolds it and as she reads, her eyes widen with alarm. Then she crumples the note in her fist. "Thank you."

"He wanted you to know so that he could offset any damage from the loss," I say, eager to show her that I am not just a messenger but a partner in Georg's work. An idea begins to form. "Georg mentioned that you might have a copy of the map that was lost."

Her eyes narrow. "Did he want it?"

I nod. "A mimeograph, yes." I hold my breath, waiting for her to ask why he had not requested the copy in his note. But she turns and disappears through another door. My heart begins to pound. If I can get her to give me a copy of the map, I can pass it on to Ignatz as I had originally intended.

Several minutes later, she returns carrying a piece of paper and starts to hand it to me. Then she hesitates, leaving my hand outstretched midair. "Be careful with this. Many—including Georg—could be hurt if it falls into the wrong hands."

I swallow as she seems to see right through me. "I shall." Outside the office, I pause, shaking. Then I walk down the hallway to the wide marble staircase, folding the paper as I walk.

As I round the bend, Papa appears several steps below. "There you are." Hurriedly, I jam the paper into my bag. "The guard rang that you were here and asking for me, but you never appeared. Margot, what is it? Are you ill?"

"Not at all." I search for an explanation. "I was in the city and I wanted to check if you were free for coffee."

He studies me, not quite believing the lie. I meet his eyes, willing him not to look down and notice the paper sticking out of my half-open bag. The realization that I had come on an errand for Georg and had become so involved in his work would surely be the final straw. "I'm afraid I can't," Papa says. "Do you mind?"

"Not at all. I'll go visit Krysia instead." I kiss him on the cheek and continue past him on the stairs, warding off further discussion.

Outside, I walk to the bank of the Seine, eager to get as far from the ministry as possible. I start along the quay, trembling. I had done it, delivered Georg's message and even gotten the document I need for Ignatz. I pull it from my bag, holding it tightly against the sharp breeze that comes off the water. I study the map, an exact duplicate of the one I had lost. I can give it to Ignatz right now and be done with this once and for all. I gaze across the river toward the Eiffel Tower, remembering the pain as Ignatz grabbed my wrist. Once he has the map, I will be free.

Two hours later, I return to Versailles and enter the hotel. I knock on the door to the conference room across the hall from the library where the German delegation meets. "Captain Richwalder, please," I say to the aide. A moment later, Georg appears. "Margot, what are you doing here?" he asks, closing the door behind him.

I peer over my shoulder to make sure no one is listening. "I got through to your contact," I say, deliberately omitting her name. Relief crosses his face. "And here." I pass him the document. His eyes widen. Having the map will solve many problems for him. I had walked the riverbank for nearly an hour, trying to figure out what to do and to work up the nerve to give the map to Ignatz. But in the end, I could not bring myself to surrender it to him. For even as I had stood on the quay, seeing his glowering eyes, Georg's trusting face had appeared above his. The document that could have satisfied Ignatz would also save Georg. I could not take it from him.

Seeing his gratitude and relief now, I know that I made the right choice. "Margot, I cannot thank you enough."

"Lieutenant Bouvier is a woman," I remark, hating the jealousy in my own voice. "You had not mentioned."

He looks up from the paper. "Does that matter?"

"Not at all," I reply quickly. "She's quite beautiful, though."

"I suppose, though I really had not noticed." The explanation sounds implausible, but his voice is sincere. "It's funny, isn't it, how we feel that way about some people and not others?" I do not answer. Behind him a door opens and an older man peers out expectantly. "I must return to the meeting."

"Of course."

As I turn away, he clasps my forearm. I freeze, caught off guard by the unexpected touch, the warmth of his fingers against my skin. "Margot, wait…" He looks down, as if he has surprised himself. But he does not let go. Several seconds of silence pass between us. "Let me show you my appreciation. Dinner in Paris, tonight? I'll get a pass and the car and we'll have a nice meal. No talk about work or the conference or the treaty, I promise."

I hesitate. *Walk away,* a voice inside me says. The kiss last night, spontaneous and unplanned, seems somehow less culpable than a planned deception. "How can we possibly spare a night of work?"

He considers the question, torn between wanting to take me out and needing to press forward. "Dinner first, then we can come back and work late."

My stomach flutters. "That would be fine," I say in spite of myself.

"You'll go out with me, then, a proper date?" He repeats the question, not quite believing my response the first time.

"Yes." I shouldn't, but I will.

His face brightens, hopeful as a boy's. "Shall I pick you up at seven?"

An older man appears behind him suddenly in the door frame then. "Captain Richwalder, I apologize, but we really must…" He stops midsentence, noticing Georg's hand on my arm.

But Georg does not pull away, and in that moment, everything between us is out in daylight, exposed. The man clears his throat and disappears back into the room.

"Tonight, then," Georg whispers. Then he steps away and closes the door between us, leaving me alone in the hallway, shaking.

CHAPTER THIRTEEN

That night at seven I stand before the mirror putting the final touches on my outfit, a dress of simple blue satin, adorned only by my mother's necklace and the bracelet Georg had given me. I study my reflection, fretting. Georg had remarked once that he disliked the stiffer, more ruffled fashions, but perhaps my choice is too plain for a Saturday evening in Paris. If only I had something a bit more womanly to wear, or perhaps some more of the things Celia always tried to press on me, such as a pencil to darken my brows or a bit of rouge.

The doorbell rings and I press the buzzer. "Come in," I say when Georg reaches the landing. He wears the same dress uniform as the night of the dinner party, epaulets at the shoulder, three gold bands around the jacket forearms.

But he stands awkwardly inside the doorway. Though we have been alone any number of times at the hotel, it is somehow different here and he is reluctant to enter. "Your father isn't here," he observes. I cannot tell if he is disappointed or relieved.

I notice an envelope lying on the table by the door. It is a letter I received earlier from Stefan and I had opened it hurriedly, barely scanning the scrawl. It sits now just inches from where Georg stands, the photograph Stefan had included facing upward on top. I hold my breath, waiting for Georg to ask about the man in the picture, to come to the realizations I will not be able to deny. A brother, I imagine claiming, if he asks. A cousin. Then I stop, mortified. How far will my lies go?

But he does not look down, instead staring only at me. "Shall we?" I ask. He clears his throat, nods.

The sky is still bright forty-five minutes later, as the car winds its way into Paris, the late-day sun lingering like the patrons drinking coffee at the sidewalk cafés. Georg stares out the window eagerly in spite of the disinterest he'd professed when we first spoke. He has only been into the city once since arriving, I realize, and that was the night he collapsed at the dinner. The car pulls to a stop by the river, just beneath the Louvre. "Do you feel like walking for a bit?" Georg asks after he had come around to offer me his arm. There is an air of formality about him not present the other times we've been together.

We stroll along the quay, past the slanted carts where merchants sell used books and other wares. The waters of the Seine high and brackish. At the base of a bridge, a group of small children hide, pretending to shoot one another with imaginary guns. Georg shakes his head. "How can they still play at war after all that has happened?"

A few minutes later we turn from the river and climb toward the Champs-Élysées. As we pass one of the hotels, lively music seeps out through the open window. Inside, couples glide elegantly across the floor. The Saturday night dances have become something of an institution in the city, persisting even through the darkest days of the war. I've always been curious about the waltzes and other more modern steps, the way that the couples move so easily in tandem. I imagine then Georg taking me in his arms and leading me across the floor. "Not much of a dancer, I'm afraid," he says, noticing my interest.

"Me, either," I reply quickly, wanting to put him at ease. It is not just the dancing that is off-putting to him. The parties are sponsored by the British and he would not be welcome there.

We continue, navigating the sidewalks crowded with other pedestrians enjoying the summer evening stroll. Several women in fashionable dresses give Georg sidelong looks, but he does not seem to notice. A few minutes later, he stops before Maxim's. "I thought we'd eat here," he says. It is a mistake, I decide instantly as we pass beneath the red-and-gold awning through the double oak doors. Georg has not spent enough time in the city to realize that the once-elegant restaurant has changed since the deluge of foreigners arrived. But I do not want to hurt his feelings.

Inside, the front room is packed thick. A group of American officers stands by one of the high tables, enjoying a champagne dinner, great quantities of alcohol and not much else. They are bantering loudly with two women at the bar, who with their heavy makeup and skimpy outfits make no effort to conceal the fact that they are prostitutes. Through another doorway, dance music blares and bodies press together, twirling as gaily as though it were midnight. Something is different from the few other times I've been. Though the conference continues apace, there is a sense of it all ending. In days or weeks, the treaty will be announced and then the conference will be over. There is an intensity to the revelers, as though they need to drink it all in before it is gone.

"Perhaps somewhere quieter," Georg frets as we squeeze between tables in the bar, inching toward the restaurant seating. "One of my colleagues recommended it, only..."

"It's fine," I reassure. He has put much thought into the evening and I don't want to disappoint him.

He wrinkles his nose as a plume of smoke drifts up from one of the tables. "Does it bother you?" I ask.

"Living in such tight quarters on the ship, I inhaled enough of others' smoke for a lifetime." He raises his voice slightly to be heard above the din. "Not a major matter. But it's funny, isn't it, the way that living somewhere else can change you? For example, the officers' quarters on the ship were quite nice, but the food ran scarce and once when we were stranded and unable to make it in to port the only thing we had to eat for two weeks were turnips. I've not been able to swallow one since."

I laugh knowingly. Living abroad had changed me, too, not as profoundly as the war had Georg, but in a dozen more subtle ways. Across the room, the banter has picked up, the soldiers now openly catcalling to the women at the bar. Georg scowls. "This is most improper. I'm so sorry."

"Not at all."

Georg takes my arm without asking and draws me close. As he scans above the crowd for the maître d', a large-bellied man jostles into him. "Excuse me," Georg says reflexively, though the fault is not at all is.

"No excuse, you peacock. Your uniform," the man jeers drunkenly. "It is a relic." I picture then the stares Georg attracted on the street. Perhaps it was not admiration at all, but anger at his audacity for openly identifying himself as a German soldier.

"We are at peace, sir," Georg responds stiffly, his cheeks flushing as though he has been slapped.

"It is still an offense," the man retorts. Georg winces. To him, the uniform is second skin, the only thing he has known. What future has he without it? He cannot—will not—deny who he is to appease the social and political sensibilities of the day. Without provocation, the man spits in Georg's direction. I can feel Georg's arm tightening in anger and I press on it, willing him not to respond, and pull him toward the exit.

"I'm sorry that you had to see that," he says when we've reached the street, wiping the spittle from his lapel.

"Does it happen often?"

"Quite, I'm afraid."

"Have you ever thought about not wearing the uniform?"

"To avoid trouble, you mean?" I nod. "I considered it in the beginning. But I'm an officer of the German navy. It is a question of honor."

Honor. Everything Georg does is about honor. Not stubbornness, but something born of a deeper, more principled place. And me? I've lied to him about Stefan, deceived him by taking the document. No, I'm the furthest thing from honorable. "I'm sorry," he says again.

"Perhaps we should just return to Versailles." His eyes betray his disappointment as he looks out across the river where a ribbon of pink sky sits atop the roofs like icing on a cake.

I shake my head, set upon saving our evening in Paris. "I have an idea. Come." It is my turn to lead now, taking his hand and retracing the route toward the nearby neighborhood where our hotel had been. I stop in front of a crémerie. "Wait here." A few minutes later I emerge with a basket. "We're not done," I say playfully, and dutifully he follows me farther down the road to the bike shop I frequented when we lived here. I pay the shopkeeper for the bicycle rentals and wheel them out onto the pavement.

"Bicycle riding?" he asks in disbelief as I push one in his direction. "That hardly seems…"

I fasten the basket to the handlebars. "You don't ride?"

"Well, perhaps a few times as a boy. And horses, of course."

"It's not that different." Then I stop. He seems so well and happy now, it is easy to forget that just a few days earlier he had been gravely ill. "Perhaps the strain will be too much."

"I'm fine." He squares his shoulders, rising to the challenge.

I mount my bike. "Then catch me if you can." I navigate carefully down the street in the direction of the park.

"Margot…" Georg's voice has grown fainter as he falls behind in the distance. I glance over my shoulder, smiling at the sight of him wobbling uncertainly on his bike, shaky as a newborn calf. When we reach the entrance to the park, I pedal faster. I've not ridden since our move to Versailles and I savor the familiar burning in my legs.

Georg is beside me then, grabbing the handlebar of my bike to slow me. "Mercy!" He laughs and topples his bike sideways to the grass, falling with mock dramatics, more playful than I've ever seen him.

Reluctantly, I set mine down beside him. "We'd best pull farther off the path, so we're not made to leave at dusk." We turn the bikes into a clearing set apart by tall bushes. Suddenly it feels as though we are miles away from the city.

"That's better," he says. He means the two of us alone, freed from the congestion of the restaurant and the streets. Alone together is the only place this seems to work. "Though we should have a blanket." He frowns. "Your dress will get soiled."

I run my hand along the soft, dry patch of moss beneath us. "Nonsense." I pull from the basket the food I purchased. "Just an assortment of cheese and some pâté. I hope you like them."

"I'll eat anything as long as it's not pickled. I had enough of the canned and the salted on the ship to last me a lifetime."

"And turnips," I tease, "don't forget those." Hungry after the bike ride, I spread some chèvre, thick and salted, on a piece of baguette and take a bite. As I chew, I peer through the trees. Though I cannot see it from here, I know that just on the other side of the brush sits the pond where I saw Krysia watching the children that first day.

"What?" I am suddenly aware of Georg's eyes upon me.

"You eat with such gusto," he remarks, and I can feel myself blush. My failure to be ladylike coming back yet again to haunt me. "I mean that as a good thing. You just seem to grab life and shake it like a tree, finding all that falls from it."

I laugh and for a moment it is as if we are any other young couple, in love and carefree, shed of all the secrets and unspoken things that stand between us and the future. "So have you had the chance to look through any more of the Leimer file?" I ask as I pull the bottle of chardonnay from the basket and hand it to him to uncork.

"I went through it last night," he replies as he deftly inserts the corkscrew and turns.

"I left so late it must have been this morning, really."

"Perhaps. Anyway, it's fascinating. Leimer's ideas about how to synchronize the strengths of the various militaries could be very useful and..." He breaks midsentence and smiles sheepishly. "I promised not to talk about work tonight."

"I don't mind," I reply. It is the truth. Work is so much a part of who we are together. *We.* "I'm the one who brought it up."

I lift a glass for him to fill. But when I raise the second glass, Georg shakes his head. "I've decided to stop drinking for a time."

It must be a very recent decision, I think, remembering the wine on his breath a few nights earlier. "Because of your illness?"

"Because of a lot of things. It just gets too easy at sea—beer when the water is fetid, wine with dinner, brandy after." Though his tone remains even, there is a scratch to the underside, like a phonograph record played too many times. "The evening before the battle was something of a celebration." Though he does not specify, I know he means Jutland. There is a care to his voice, a thoughtfulness to the way he forms the words, that tells me he has not shared this story before. "There had been word of a victory, which was becoming increasingly rare. We'd opened the last of the meat stores and the better champagne. I drank more than usual and had retired. If I hadn't I might have heeded the warning signs, seen the way the British ships were amassing. By the time I'd awoken, the *Pommern* had already been hit." He blames himself for not being able to stop the battle that had taken his brother's life.

"Georg, there was nothing you could have done. Even if you'd sensed it..."

But he shakes his head, unwilling to accept any account that does not accord with the narrative he has told himself for so long. "Perhaps I could have signaled for some reinforcements or perhaps repositioned the fleet." What is it about ourselves that makes us believe we can change great events with our thoughts and deeds? It feels a kind of hubris. "And then they made me into some kind of hero. I protested, tried to tell them the truth, but they said it was needed for the morale of the men. It was a lie."

It was the dishonesty, perhaps more so than anything else, that Georg found impossible to bear. I understand so much more about him now, his solitary nature, the way part of him always seems to be elsewhere. What would he say if he knew the truth about me and the things I have done?

He looks up as though he has forgotten I was there. "You must think me a terrible coward."

"Not at all." I reach out and take his hand, not caring now about the propriety as I try to wash away his self-loathing. It takes courage, I want to tell him, to speak the truth. I am the coward here.

"I'd like to leave," Georg says. For a minute, thinking he means our date, I am hurt. Did I say something to offend him? "Head south perhaps, to the Mediterranean." He is referring to the conference and the city. But he seems so intent and driven by the work he is doing here. I nod, recognizing his desire to flee the stifling confines of the city. "Let's do it," he says. "There are places, you know, located by the mountains as well as the sea. Places we could both love." He's serious.

"Georg, what about the conference? And your work?" And my father and my husband and a dozen other reasons I cannot say.

"Perhaps when the conference is over and we are both back in Germany..." he begins, trying again. I do not respond. Berlin means Stefan and the future that inevitably awaits me, the end of all of this. Then he breaks off. "Of course, I'm not presuming that you would want to be with me." He has mistaken my hesitation for demurral. I take his hand, uncertain what to say. Paris is something of a vacuum, so many people brought together in this odd little whirlwind where none of the rules apply. Back home life is stratified, divided, and Georg and I come from different worlds, religions, politically and socially. Even without Stefan, our lives in Germany would be so disparate. But I would transcend all of that for the chance to be with him. Could every day be exactly like this, glorious and sparkling? An image comes into my mind then of Georg as an old man, sharing a cup of tea in our parlor, long after the children have grown and left. I stop, struck by the vision. It is so different from the life I usually envision for myself and yet in that moment I know it is exactly what I want. We could be this good every single day, waking up side by side laughing and talking.

"Margot," he says, squeezing my hand. "We can be together. Why do you resist?" He does not know, as I do, that our days are numbered, that each passing night brings us closer to the fated end.

What will you do after the war? Krysia's words echo in my mind. The answer is so different now. I'm not just running *from* Stefan but *to* Georg and yet at the same time there's an inevitability to the fact that it must end. Is that what makes it so good, the knowledge that these few moments we have together are stolen? No, I decide, looking across at Georg. There's a connection between us, a spark that would burn through the decades, through the everyday, and all of the great hurts and triumphs. I imagine a child then, a boy, with Georg's strong features. My stomach jumps.

"Shh." I lean in, desperate to silence the questions, to stop my head from whirling like a carousel. This time I kiss him, my lips mashing clumsily against his. I wait for him to pull away and tell me it isn't proper. But he presses into me, meeting the intensity of my mouth, probing, upping the stakes. The voices of wrong and right fade in my mind, drowned out by a low moan that sounds foreign escaping my lips as he presses me back toward the ground.

From the far side of the bushes comes a loud noise, an explosion tearing us abruptly apart. "What on earth?" Georg leaps to his feet, reaching for his waist and the weapon that is not there.

The noise comes again, a succession of popping sounds. "It's all right," I soothe, standing hurriedly. But he remains in front of me as we step from the grove onto the path, arm around me protectively.

Fireworks begin to erupt in the distance behind the Eiffel Tower. "Oh!" I exclaim, and we stop to admire the spectacle as great dazzling bursts of green and red and blue fire light up the night sky.

"But why?" he asks, more puzzled than delighted. He has a point—there is no holiday or other reason for them. "Something has happened. We should go." I repack the basket hurriedly and start toward the bicycle shop. When we've returned the bikes, we walk in the direction of the river. The fireworks display has ended then, the sky cloudy with their dust. The faint smell of gunpowder hangs in the air. The streets are crowded, as nearly filled with people as the day Wilson arrived, buzzing excitedly.

Georg takes his hand and mine and places them in my pocket for warmth. He stops unexpectedly and turns to me and his lips are upon mine then and suddenly it is as if the crowds around us have disappeared. "I'm sorry. But I had to do that one last time, before…"

"I understand." Before the fireworks and whatever lay beyond them change our world forever.

He takes my hand once more and leads me in the direction of a newsstand, hands the boy a few coins for a paper, which gives off the smell of fresh ink. "It's the treaty," he says, scanning the headline. "The terms have been announced." As he reads, his eyes widen with disbelief. I lean in over his shoulder. Millions of marks in reparations, the German military to be disbanded immediately.

"This is not peace," he says, struggling to maintain his composure. "This is a crucifixion. I must get back to Versailles at once."

"Yes, of course." I cannot help but be disappointed at our evening ending so abruptly.

Holding tightly to my arm, Georg cuts a path through the crowd. "Across the river," he says, pulling me toward the bridge. On the other side, he hails a taxi, handing the driver several bills once we are inside. "Versailles, immediately." He does not speak as we leave the city. His face is a stony mask, and in the storm clouds of his eyes there is a darkness I had not imagined possible. An hour earlier, we were laughing and coming up with new strategies for work. How had everything changed so quickly?

As we reach Versailles, I can hold back no longer. "Georg, we can still do something about this." The car pulls up in front of the apartment building, any notion of working tonight seemingly forgotten. Georg walks me hurriedly to the door, head low. Then, he climbs back inside the car and a moment later is gone.

CHAPTER FOURTEEN

Sunrise comes as it always does over the fields to the east, illuminating the town below in pale yellow like the lights coming up on the set of a play. I cross the bedroom and pick up my dress, which lies where I'd dropped it to the floor the previous evening. The giddy anticipation with which I'd prepared for my date with Georg seems like another lifetime. I see his face, happy one moment and broken the next. He had pinned so much on the peace process, but those dreams are gone now.

I raise my hands to my lips, which are tender and swollen from our kiss. Guilt rises in me. Once could be seen as an accident. But this time I had kissed Georg and it was deliberate, prolonged. I replay the moment in my mind, wondering what might have happened if we had not been interrupted by the fireworks. How can we ever go back from here as though nothing has happened?

Of course, there is no back, I reflect, as I dress. The world Georg and I had known, of quiet evenings working together, had come to an end last night with the issuance of the peace treaty.

Papa had been gone when I'd come into the apartment the previous night. But he is here this morning, and up uncharacteristically early, hunched over his desk. "Papa, the treaty…"

He straightens and turns toward me. His face is gray and dark circles ring his eyes, as though he has not slept at all. "You've heard." His voice is heavy and cracked around the edges. He is nearly as devastated as Georg, I realize. Papa had been cautious about the scope of Wilson's plan, but he'd held out hope for a world that could be put together after the war a bit better somehow. That world seems not to be. He holds up some papers.

"Is that it?" I ask.

He nods. "The official treaty won't be presented to the conference until later this morning, but I received an advance copy by courier." I walk to the desk, lean over his shoulder. "It's a disaster. Millions of marks in reparations. We're losing Alsace-Lorraine and the Sudetenland. It's hard to fathom the country making it through this." I wait for him to offer his usual moment of hope, or attempt to shield me from the harsh reality of what has happened. But he does not. "I should go today and see about booking our passage home."

"No!" I cry. His eyes widen at my outburst. "I mean, the conference isn't over." But my explanation does little to lessen his surprise. I have always complained about having to be in Paris and I can see him trying to comprehend as to my changed demeanor, why I might be upset to be leaving it now.

"My work is done here, darling. There's no reason for us to stay any longer."

"But Georg's work…if we can just offer an alternative proposal. It doesn't have to be this way."

"Captain Richwalder is fooling himself, my dear. It's over." And I know that he is right. So does Georg, I think, remembering how he slumped in such defeat on the ride back from Paris. "So we will be returning to Berlin." His declaration should hardly be a surprise. With the work of the conference largely done, there is no reason to stay.

"I've contacted Greta about reopening the house," Papa adds. I had not thought of the sweet-faced maid in months. With all of our moving about over the years, life sometimes seemed like a movie set, places and people ceasing to exist once we'd left them behind.

He could not have contacted Greta so quickly, I realize now. He must have done so even before the treaty terms were announced. Though he has spent a good deal of his time with the German delegation the past few weeks, his work at the ministry must have given him a strong indication that the end was near and it wasn't good. This explains his troubled looks and his caution that I not become too invested in Georg's work.

Home. The idea prickles at me like a cactus. I knew that sometime this would have to end. Paris has been a buffer between me and the life that awaits. It could not go on forever. But Germany, with the political chaos and rioting, feels dark and dangerous, a country no longer our own. "Will it be safe for you in Berlin, with everything you've written?" I ask, recalling what Ignatz had said months earlier about Papa not using a pseudonym.

"I'm not worried," he replies, stopping somewhere short of answering my question.

Krysia's voice comes back to me: *Now or never.* "Papa…" I lick my lips, preparing to tell him that I'm not going back. "Remember when we spoke of my studying abroad? I'd like to go when we've finished here, perhaps back to London."

"But with the war over, I thought you'd be eager to return."

"It needn't be a formal degree," I offer, retreating. "Perhaps language classes."

"But you can do that in Berlin."

"It would be so much better to study in the native tongue." Unable to lie to him anymore, I drop all pretense. "I need to see a bit of the world. I can't go back. Not now."

"But Stefan…" He stops as he grasps that my fiancé is the very reason I cannot go. I watch as he wrestles with the conflict. Papa is not a young man and his deepest desire is to have his only child settled and taken care of before he is gone. Not just for financial reasons—Uncle Walter would always make sure that I want for nothing. Rather, he wants me to have the companionship he has lacked since my mother died, to be with someone I love. But doesn't he understand that there are worse things than being alone?

"We can stay a few days longer," Papa offers as a concession. "Perhaps a trip to the south."

"No, that's not necessary." If we are going to leave, best to face the inevitable quickly.

"Georg is from Berlin, too, isn't he?" he asks, sidestepping his real question.

I shake my head, looking away. "Hamburg." The cities are only hours apart by train but it doesn't matter. Once I am back in Berlin and married to Stefan, our separate worlds might as well be on different planets.

"Liebchen," Papa says gently.

I turn back. A single tear runs down his cheek. "Oh, Papa!" I rush to him. I throw my arms around him. Great sobs rack his body, a dry, unfamiliar wheeze. "I won't go. How thoughtless of me to even mention it today…"

He straightens, wiping his eyes. "I'm terribly sorry. It wasn't that at all." Then what? He pulls out a handkerchief and walks to the mirror to compose himself. A moment later, he turns back. "Sometimes we want things that we cannot have. We must accept that." I hold my breath waiting for him to bring up Georg. Should I deny it or tell him the truth, whatever that is? But he is skating just shy of the issue, talking to me in generalities at a more abstract, safe level. "It isn't always possible…"

"But you've always said I must be true to myself," I protest, borrowing his favorite Shakespeare quote. "And that's how you live."

"I try. But it is like the peace conference—sometimes the things that we want and aspire to must coexist within the realm of what is possible." There is a look of longing in his eyes and I want to ask him what he has been forced to compromise. There is a silent gulf between us I have never been able to cross, though, a place in him that for all of our love I cannot reach. I do not press, knowing that he will say no more.

The doorbell rings. He hesitates, not wanting to interrupt our conversation. "That's my car. We can continue this later."

I nod and walk back to my room, peering out the window in the direction of the hotel. *Georg.* I see his face last night, hollow as he read for the first time the draconian terms of the peace treaty, crushing to a pulp everything for which he's worked. I want to go check on him and reassure him. But I suspect he's withdrawn to a place too far and dark for me to reach.

When Papa's car has pulled away, I walk back to the sitting room and cross to the desk, searching for a copy of the peace treaty. Maybe if I can understand it better, I can find a glimmer of hope in the details. Papa has taken the documents with him, but perhaps there is something in the press. I search the desk for *Le Journal*, which I often read after Papa has left it scattered across his desk. But today it is nowhere to be found. He must have taken it with him, as well, in order to digest the treaty coverage.

I walk downstairs to the newsstand at the corner. *"Le Journal,"* I request.

She shakes her head. *"Non."* With news of the treaty, the paper must have sold out quickly. I pick up instead a copy of the *Paris Herald*, curious what the foreign press will have to say. As I pay the seller, she smirks, as though the harsh treaty terms are to be imposed on me personally. Averting my eyes, I carry the paper back up to the apartment. The front-page story carries most of the details I already know from the previous evening. I flip to the inside, searching for more.

At the bottom of the second page, there is a photograph of a beautiful woman that seems oddly placed with the treaty. It is an unrelated story: *Fatal West End Fire,* the headline reads. A massive blaze had broken out at one of the London theaters shortly before showtime. The play had been political in nature and some of the exits had been locked to keep out the protesters. A half-dozen people, including the pictured actress resting in her dressing room before the performance, had been killed.

Papa and I had been to the West End once to see a show before the travel restrictions on Germans had been imposed, an Oscar Wilde play whose title I cannot remember. The century-old theater, with the balconies and ornate carvings around the stage, had been beautiful. But the plush curtains and wooden stage would have made the place a tinderbox, escape from a fire difficult with the narrow aisles and shrouded doorways.

I study the photo again. The woman's large luminescent eyes leap out at me, as familiar as my own. Suddenly it is as if I am looking in a mirror. I scan the caption. The actress was Lucinda Rose, formerly of Berlin. A chill runs up my spine. My mother had been an actress, too, before she had married. But she had died years ago.

My eyes travel from the photograph in the newspaper to the one that sits over the mantelpiece. Though the woman in the paper is older, the heart-shaped face is unmistakably the same. "Oh!" I cry aloud, bringing my hand to my mouth.

There is a noise at the door, footsteps behind me. "I forgot some papers..." Papa's voice is difficult to hear over the roaring in my ears. "Darling, are you...?" He stops midsentence as he leans over my shoulder and sees the newspaper.

I do not look up. "It's her, isn't it?"

I hold up the paper, waiting for the denial. Silence. I turn in time to see his face crumple. His earlier tears had not been about the conference. He had seen the article, taken the newspaper to hide it from me. "Margot, wait..." he calls as I stand and walk to my bedroom, slamming the door behind me.

He raps on my door, then opens it slightly. "Let's talk about this."

"What is there to say? She's my mother, isn't she?"

I wait for him to deny it, to offer some explanation that would make the past ten years something other than a lie. "Yes, she is. Or I should say *was*." His voice cracks on the last word.

"But, Papa, why?"

He sits at the end of the bed, suddenly looking very tired and much older. "I thought it would be easier for you to accept that she had died." Rather than the truth—that she had left us. "When I met your mother she was a rising star of the stage, poised for greatness. I wooed her and convinced her to leave it all for me." A married woman never would have been allowed to continue to act and tour. She would have been expected to choose between the footlights and family.

He continues. "She was always restless, though, and resentful of me for taking the greatness that might have been hers. The story I told you was partially true. She did have the flu and she very nearly died, but when her body healed her spirits didn't. She was morose after that, and said she felt a prisoner." She felt trapped by a husband and baby. *Me.* "She wanted to leave and I couldn't stop her."

So she had left us, whether driven by her depression or something else, I do not know. I picture the elaborate headstone erected in the cemetery in Berlin. It was all a ruse, intended for my benefit—and hers. Better a cherished memory of a mother who had died than hatred for one who had abandoned me. "I planned to tell you when you were old enough." I'm twenty— why isn't that old enough? He continues. "So that way you could make your own decision, maybe even meet her..."

But that opportunity had been taken from me. The article

said the show she was in had toured Paris just months earlier. We were in the same city, might have passed each other on the street. If only I had known.

"Did you suspect she would leave?"

But he shakes his head. "Never. I knew she was discontented, but when I pressed her as to what she wanted, she would not say." *Because the thing she wanted was not something you could have given her—freedom.* "I'm not sure I could have stopped her—she was suffocating." Papa had always regarded my mother as a fragile object, one too perfect and beautiful to be his, a prophecy that had proved to be true the day she left.

Could I have done something differently? If I'd been a neater child, with combed hair and clean dresses and good manners, instead of always knocking things over and throwing fits and climbing trees. In an instant I am nine again, reliving the abandonment. But this loss, coupled with rejection, is worse—death from flu was without choice. She could have stayed, but she chose not to.

An image pops into my mind long forgotten. I rushed into my mother's room having just lost a tooth. She jumped up, hurriedly blocking her armoire from view. I waited for her to rebuke me for not knocking. But instead she took the bloody tooth from me in her elegantly manicured hand with none of the usual revulsion, closing a drawer behind her when she thought I could not see. She was hiding something, I realized.

Later as she napped, I crept back into her room and opened the drawer that she had closed so quickly. Money, great stacks of bills banded neatly together, filled the drawer. Why would she hide it? She could simply ask Papa for anything she needed.

She had stirred then. "Margot," she said, unable to keep the uneasiness from her voice.

"What is all of the money for?" I asked with a childlike trust that my questions would be answered.

"A present for Papa." She winked, making me her coconspirator. Was it to be something practical like a hat, or something grand for all of us? The gift never materialized and I later forgot about it. I know now that the money was for her escape. Nearly eighteen months before she was gone, my mother had been squirreling away funds to disappear. Suddenly I am infused with guilt. If only I had told Papa...

"We could not have stopped her," he says, reading my mind. "Freedom was like oxygen to her and we could not have stopped her from leaving any more than one could stop breathing."

I think of all of her possessions, the jewelry and clothes left as neatly hung in the armoire as though she had just gone out for coffee. It had been easy enough to believe she died because everything remained in place exactly as it had been. Now I see that she left it all and just walked away, not wanting any of her old life to interfere with the escape upon which she was so intent.

His shoulders slump. "I thought you would be angry with me for having not been enough."

"Oh, Papa." He had stayed, doing the work of father and mother taking care of me, just the two of us, because there could not be more children. That was a lie, too, I realize now. My mother had found even one child more than she could bear. Papa would not have insisted upon more for fear of what it would have done to her. "I could never feel that way. But if you had told me..."

He pats my cheek. "Such a beautiful girl. She could not have imagined."

For a moment, I savor the warmth of his hand on my face, his love strong and protecting as it had been every day of my life. Then I pull back. "You lied," I say, the air suddenly cold and distant between us. Every fond memory I have of the two of us over the past decade seems tainted, premised on a fabrication.

"Margot, please."

But I turn away, unwilling to be consoled. His betrayal is worse than my mother's in so many ways because I believed in him. He steps back, defeated. "I'm afraid I must get back to the delegation. We can talk more this evening."

What good will talking do? I want to ask. It won't bring her back, give me a chance to speak with her before it is too late. But he has already closed the door. I lie across my bed, studying the newspaper picture once more. Tears form in my eyes, splashing onto the paper like great raindrops. We might have been sisters, or even friends. No, not friends. I cannot forgive her what she did. What would I say to her if she were here now? I would have liked to ask her why she had gone. Now I won't have the chance.

An hour later Celia rushes into the apartment. "You know." It is not a question. Papa must have rung her and asked her to comfort me in his absence. "Don't judge him for this," Celia pleads. Though she means well, trying to bridge the conflict between Papa and me, I am flooded with anger. Who is she to tell me about my parents? "He loved her…" Hurt washes across her face as she acknowledges the depth of his feelings for her sister, a love that she will never own. "And he tried, really tried." She is asking for him, not for herself.

I raise my hand. "Stop, please."

"Don't blame your father," Celia presses, more forcefully than I have ever heard her speak. "It would be easy to say that he had been inattentive or too preoccupied with his work. But he is the most loving man I have ever known." I cringe at the proprietary tone of her voice. "The truth is no man would have been enough for Lucy. She was like that as a girl, always hungry, always wanting more. It was a curse." Is my own restlessness, always searching for more and never finding it, somehow passed on from her? Maybe that is why I am dissatisfied with Stefan—not because of who he has become, but because of who I really am.

Unable to bear Celia's explanations any longer, I walk from the apartment and downstairs. Though it is midmorning, the streets are somber and hushed, curtains drawn. At the corner, the fountain in the center of the tiny square is still. The smell of the stale water stirs a memory in me. I am standing in the park at the Tiergarten wearing the pink coat that means I could not have been more than four or five at the time. Papa was abroad at one of his conferences and it was the nanny's day off, giving my mother and I a rare few hours alone. She kept us in perpetual motion at times like that, walking parks and streets, as though she could not bear to be home and still, just the two of us. I'd wandered off toward the duck pond, captivated by the proud white swans that Papa had always cautioned me to avoid. Suddenly I turned around. I was alone, lost among a sea of unfamiliar trouser legs and coat hems.

I screamed, a high desperate wail, and the crowd parted as though whatever misfortune I was suffering might be contagious. Finally, a vendor took pity on me. "What is your name?" He led me through the park, calling out, "Has anyone lost a child named Margot?" mispronouncing it with a soft *g*. At the fountain, I recognized my mother's coat and leaped from the man's arms and ran to her. She turned absently, as though she hadn't noticed I was gone. I waited for her to scold me for disappearing, but she simply gave the vendor a mark for his troubles and led me away. I wonder now if she was sorry to have found me again.

My vision clears. All of the time I had been so obsessed with my own secrets, I had not stopped to think. But now everything Papa had told me, the entire fabric of our lives, was premised on a lie.

I walk heedlessly down the street, not realizing where I am going until I am standing on the steps of the hotel. As the door buzzer rings, granting me access, I am flooded with self-doubt. I should not bother Georg now. Inside the corridor, I knock on his door. There is no answer. I turn the knob, push the door open. "Hello?"

He is not at his desk but in a chair by the window, slumped

to one side. "It's over," he says, voice slurred. I notice then the empty wine bottle on the floor, his resolution of temperance quickly abandoned with the crisis. Had he been drinking last night or this morning or both? He is still wearing his uniform from the previous evening. The jacket, usually so neat, is unbuttoned and there is a red wine stain on the lapel of the white shirt that peeks out from beneath.

Concern rises, eclipsing my own problems. "Have you slept at all?"

"They handed us the treaty," he says, ignoring my question. "Three days to say yes or no. They didn't even adopt Wilson's Fourteen Points," he adds glumly. "Studies of the navy?" he spits, knocking down a binder that had been sitting on the windowsill. Papers scatter across the floor. "There is to be no navy. We've been betrayed." He buries his head in his hands. It breaks my heart to see him so deflated by the one thing about which he cared so passionately.

"The conference isn't over. They still might." But even as I speak I know that it isn't likely. Wilson and his delegation were packing up, according to the papers. "Perhaps if we review the notes, we can think of a counterproposal," I venture, but then I stop. It is moot now and I will not insult him by pretending otherwise.

He looks up. "Margot," he says, as though just realizing I am there. He starts to reach for me then hesitates, glancing down at his stained, wrinkled uniform. "I'm terribly sorry. If you'll excuse me a moment..." He stands and walks into the bedroom.

A few minutes later, he returns. His eyes are somewhat clearer now, face washed and shaved. "I'm sorry you had to see me like that, it's just that everything..." He breaks, noticing for the first time the redness of my eyes. "Margot," he repeats, crossing the room and kneeling before where I sit. "Are you all right? Is it the treaty?"

"Georg..." I hate to burden him further at a time like this. But I cannot hold back—I tell him the story.

His jaw drops slightly. "She didn't die from the flu?"

"No, she was alive this entire time, until just now." My voice cracks. "Only I had no idea."

"That's madness!" he flares, his own distress about the treaty momentarily forgotten.

"My whole life has been a lie," I lament.

He puts his arms around me and draws me close. "Not at all. There's nothing worse than when someone close to us betrays our trust." Thinking of the document I stole from him, my stomach turns. "But your father did what he thought was best to protect you. This doesn't change his love, or who he raised you to be."

"And my mother?" I demand, pulling back. "Did she do what she thought was best?"

He turns his palms upward, his expression helpless. "I don't know. But your mother gave you the best of her traits. There's much of her in you, I think. Your curiosity, the desire to see the world." I open my mouth to protest. I want to be nothing like her. But he is right.

What had my mother been thinking in those final moments as she lay dying? Had she thought of me, wished she had done something differently when she'd had the chance? Or was she quite content with her choices?

A giant hole opens up and threatens to engulf me. "Oh, Georg!" I move closer, heedless of the tears that stain the front of his uniform. Our roles have switched suddenly. All of this time, it has been me doing the comforting. But now he holds me in his arms and I am vulnerable as a child. I have been self-sufficient for so long and to lean on someone, to need him for strength, terrifies me beyond anything I've ever known.

"Forgive me," I manage a moment later, straightening. "It

was wrong of me to come here like this, especially now with the treaty…" I gesture to the papers strewn across the floor.

"You have been there for me so many times in moments of need. It is my pleasure to reciprocate." But he shrugs. "None of it matters anymore. I'm just glad you're here."

"It was such a waste…all of that time." Papa had kept secrets from me for years, stopping me from having a chance to know my mother. But am I any better, denying the truth about my feelings for Georg, not living life? Once it seemed to me that if I did the right things, I would be able to stay safe. Now I understand that there is no such thing. All of the rules and conventions, the things that I believed and knew to be right and true, are now gone. But these things, even as they held me in the place I detested so, gave my world structure and order. I am staring over the edge of the abyss.

"It's more than that," I say, realizing as I speak that I had not come to Georg merely for comfort. Papa had kept the truth buried for years. I do not want to waste time like that in my own life anymore. "You and I…" I falter.

"I understand. We had discussed my speaking with your father. But after all that has happened, I have no such expectations that you would still want…"

"No, it's just the opposite," I say, cutting him off. "You see, I know now that we must." Unable to find the words, I lean forward, bringing my lips to his. Joy surges through me. This is where I was meant to be and where I want to be now, whatever the cost. His mouth is on mine then, his hands hesitant at my waist.

"Margot…"

Impatiently, I grab his hand and bring it lower, urging him forward with a sureness despite my lack of experience. I slide from the chair to the floor, papers crushing beneath us.

Even as desire rises in me, though, a voice nags in my head: *not like this.* It is not the impropriety of what is happening—I want Georg too much to stop for social norms. But this is the beginning of something great; it cannot begin with a lie.

"Georg..." I put my hand on his chest to slow him down, then sit up.

He pulls back. "I'm so sorry. I never should have taken such liberties."

"No, it isn't that. I want to." His eyes widen. "But there is something that I must say first." I will tell him about Ignatz and the document. About my marriage. About everything. I steel myself, but before I can speak, he leans in for one more kiss.

Outside something crackles loudly, lightning striking a tree. The noise comes again, closer now. A knock at the door. I kiss him harder, this moment a dream from which I do not want to awake. If we do not stop, then none of this will ever end. But Georg, still practical, pulls back. "I'm so sorry, but with everything that has happened I must..."

I stand and straighten my skirts. Through the narrow window beside the door, I can see the edge of Papa's hat, its worn brim unmistakable. My mind races. What is he doing here? I fleetingly consider remaining hidden. Then, remembering my resolution to proceed without lies, I step forward to face him.

"Papa?" I open the door, then stop, motionless. There, standing beside my father, is Stefan.

CHAPTER FIFTEEN

"Stefan?" I am incredulous. What is he doing here? He stands in the hallway with only the aid of a cane, but it is apparent from his wobbly stance and the way he grasps the door frame that he still needs a good deal of support. He wears his old and tattered uniform, as though no one had told him he is no longer a soldier. His hair is wheat-blond now, perhaps bleached by the sun, but the change looks permanent, brought on by the trauma he has been through. His eyes dart anxiously from side to side.

Papa sent for him, I realize. He was worried about my closeness with Georg. It was so unlike him—in all other areas of life Papa encouraged my independence and tried to let me make my own decisions. But Georg threatening the security of my future was more than Papa could bear and so he intervened. Even as I curse his choice, I cannot be angry with him for doing the thing he thought was right.

Stefan and I stare awkwardly at each other. It has been four years, and though I recognize him as the wan veteran from the photos he has sent, he is a stranger, any inkling of the boy I knew in Berlin long gone. His face searches mine hopefully. I should embrace him, or at least reach out. But my feet are rooted as though in concrete.

"Margot," Papa prompts gently. "Stefan has come all the way from Berlin to see you."

"Stefan." I say again. Through my panic I see him having hopefully traveled thousands of miles in spite of his wounds to find me. The guilt opens up into a chasm, threatening to suck me in. I step forward and kiss the once-wide expanse of his cheek, now sunken. "It is a *wonderful* surprise." He smiles then, basking in my drops of affection, as though my few words have made the struggle of coming here worthwhile. "You're looking so well," I add.

He drinks me in hungrily. "And you, beautiful as ever." The words sound rehearsed, as if he practiced them a hundred times on the journey here. "At first I thought, just a visit," he manages, and his voice is thinner than I recall, a papier-mâché replica of the strong baritone that had sung so richly in the school chorus. "But with the treaty concluded..."

"Stefan is here to accompany us home," Papa finishes for him. *Home.* This is the nightmare I have had a dozen times. If I open my mouth to scream will I wake up?

"Margot...?" My breathing stops, the warmth of Georg's hand on the back of my elbow where no one can see. His touch is reassuring yet bittersweet, because I am certain it will be the last time I feel it. I look from Stefan to Georg, want and need, duty and desire personified in the men that stand before me. Georg smiles at Papa. "Professor..." His tone is affable, only mildly puzzled. "Is something amiss? Beside the wretched treaty, I mean." The air is thick and humid.

Papa watches me expectantly. Only hours have passed since we argued, since I discovered the truth about my mother. Now his lie and mine lie together, juxtaposed. I swallow, clearing my throat. "Georg, may I introduce Stefan Oster." I cannot bring myself to say more, to reveal the full truth of my deception. "Stefan, this is Captain Richwalder." Stefan's eyes dart to Georg's shoulders and, seeing the rank insignia, he straightens and raises his arm to salute. But Georg, unaware of the significance of the introduction, reaches out and shakes his hand. "A fellow member of the Imperial military. A pleasure."

"Margot has been helping Captain Richwalder in his work for the delegation," Papa offers, trying to ease the tension. "Translating documents."

Stefan looks from Georg to me and then back again, and in that moment I am sure he will realize everything. Will he try to strike Georg? But Stefan nods. "A noble endeavor." I study his face for some sign of suspicion, but find none. Is it so hard to believe that another man might desire me? No, Stefan has always seen the world in the very simplest of terms, accepting things at face value. My wanting to be with Georg, or he with me, is beyond Stefan's comprehension. "I'm glad you've found something to occupy your time," he says to me, "besides planning for the wedding."

Wedding. The word echoes through the thick air. Georg's weight shifts almost imperceptibly and, though I cannot bring myself to look up, I feel his gaze upon me, questioning, wanting me to deny it.

Papa steps in, speaking when I cannot. "Stefan is Margot's fiancé," he explains pleasantly. I feel Georg rock back slightly on his heels, as though he has been hit.

I hold my breath, waiting for Stefan to correct Papa and deliver the final blow, announcing a marriage that not even Papa knows exists. I stare at him, willing him to be silent and keep the secret of our vows intact.

Georg clears his throat, the survival instincts of a soldier taking hold. "Well, if you'll excuse me, I must return to my work in the library. Good evening." He cannot bear to say my name. As he walks down the hall, I try to catch his eyes, to speak to him without words as we have so often. But he fixes his gaze over my head, refusing to meet mine and see the explanations and pleading there.

The door to the library closes behind him with quiet finality, the lone click signaling that I will not set foot inside there again, that the pleasure of sitting among the dusty stacks and listening to Georg breathe beside me is gone forever.

I turn back. Stefan stands with a bright, hopeful smile on his face, either not seeing or choosing to ignore the scene that has played out before him. "I'm well now," he says. "Well" for him means able to stand and at least walk a bit with assistance. There is a hesitation to his words, a way that he searches for the simplest terms of expression that speaks volumes about the damage he suffered, the absence of the wit and humor he'd once possessed. "I've been discharged. It's so wonderful to see you. All these years, this is what kept me going." Shame washes over me as I picture Stefan, lying in the hospital bed longing for me. My short, occasional letters, filled with the most basic of pleasantries, had been a lifeline. And as soon as he was able he had gotten out of bed and come to me when I would not go to him.

Stefan takes my hands in his. "Now we can get married." He continues the pretense that we are not already wed for my benefit as well as Papa's.

"Yes," I manage, forcing a smile, acknowledging the long outstanding bill, now come due. "Let's go home."

"How ever did you get here?" The next afternoon Stefan and I stand on one of the terraces at Versailles. We'd spent the better part of the day touring the palace, which I had not taken the time to see properly since we'd moved here. It had seemed an easier activity than trying to venture into Paris. But Stefan had moved with painstaking slowness and the guide tired of us quickly. So we had explored the gilded drawing rooms on the ground floor at a glacial pace, not daring to navigate the steps to the chambers above.

Now we stand on the Northern Parterre of the palace, gazing out over the rolling lawn to the flowered gardens. Below sits a round fountain as big as a pond. Water arcs gaily from the elaborate sculpture at its center.

"A veterans' transport," he replies. "Soldiers being returned home."

"You traveled among the French soldiers?" My tone is incredulous.

"Yes, they were quite friendly, actually, now that the war is over." How ironic that on the streets of Paris, the hatred was as thick as ever, while among the wounded, friendship bloomed. Perhaps it was the commonality of the experiences they had endured.

I study Stefan out of the corner of my eye. He is standing on his own using two canes. Still, his limp is formidable. When we'd left the apartment earlier, he had stepped out heedlessly into the street. I grabbed him and pulled him back as a bus roared by, horn blaring. But he had seemed oblivious to the near crash. Despite being able to get around somewhat, there is a lack of awareness that makes him almost helpless. It is remarkable that he made it to Paris unscathed.

I contemplate the green lawns that fan out endlessly below. I carry a small basket of food we'd hoped to enjoy as a picnic dinner. But a half-dozen steps separate us from the nearest garden spot. "Let's just picnic here," I say, gesturing implausibly to the hard marble patio.

"Nonsense," he says, shuffling toward the stairs and taking a tentative first step downward. I reach for his arm, but he shakes me off. "I can do it myself." But then he stumbles and falls three steps to the landing below.

"Stefan!" I rush to him. He is not hurt but his face has crumpled, reflecting his wounded pride. Without speaking, he allows me to help him over to the lawn.

We are silent as I spread the blanket on the grass, warmed by the late-afternoon sun. I take out the sandwiches I'd packed and hand him one, swatting at the gnats that hover between us. I take a bite of my sandwich, then swallow hard. I cannot help but think of my evening picnic with Georg in the Jardin des Tuileries. Longing rises within me. How can things have changed this much in just a few days?

"It's so good to see you," Stefan says, his voice full and sincere. "All of these months waiting for you to return home…"

I search for the rebuke in his voice, but he is simply stating a fact. "I'm sorry about that. I wanted to come, but Papa had to come directly to Versailles."

"I understand completely. I'd resigned myself to waiting to see you when the conference ended. But when I received word from Celia—"

"Celia?" I interrupt him.

"Your aunt sent a telegram inviting me to come," he says, sounding pleased. "She thought it would be good for you to have me here."

Bile rises in my throat. So it was Celia who had summoned Stefan. I should have known that Papa, for all of his concern, never would have interfered in such a way. But Tante Celia had become so vested in my marrying Stefan. She had worried about the scandal of my association with Georg and had taken matters into her own hands.

"I heard about your mother," he offers, "the truth, I mean."

"Papa told you?"

He nods. Stefan was there for the first funeral when we were children, the one that had been a lie. He has to know how much this hurts. "I'm very sorry." I wait for him to offer something more, some insight from our shared history. But he does not. Georg, who had not known my mother at all, at the height of his own distress, had been better able to help me make sense of it all. The gulf between the two men has never seemed larger.

"I'm living back in the city now," he says.

"Oh?"

"Yes, Father had the front steps modified and put a bedroom in where the study once was." He watches me hopefully and I try to smile. But living on the ground floor of the Osters' crowded house sounds unappealing, like life in a goldfish bowl. "It's so much nicer than being at the convalescent center," he adds.

"Of course," I reply quickly, feeling like an ungrateful child. "So you've heard about the treaty?" I switch the conversation to a more neutral topic.

He nods. "We received word on the train just as it reached the French border."

"There's talk that the Americans aren't even going to sign." He does not respond. We never talked about politics, I realize now. Our conversations before the war had been about practical matters or light things like the cinema. Though we both loved to read and Stefan enjoyed listening to Papa discuss his work, there had never been debate or discussion of the issues like I had with Georg or Krysia, the spark of exchanging ideas I'd come to love since coming to Paris. And once he'd gone off to war, our letters had been brief and conversational. I'd written about Oxford and our life there, always keeping things very general and noncritical in case it was read by the censors. He'd been similarly vague, perhaps wanting to spare me the harsh realities of life at the front. Once I had not minded. Only now, after my months in Paris talking about these bigger ideas, can I appreciate how superficial and unsatisfying our conversations have been. How could Stefan care about me, without caring about my opinions and what I thought? But perhaps he hadn't thought much about his own, either.

Maybe I am being unfair. After everything he has been through, it is understandable that he does not want to discuss the treaty. To him it represents all he had fought for—and failed. "So we'll have to set a date for the wedding," he says brightly.

I falter. We are married but, of course, there will need to be a ceremony to maintain the pretense that we waited with our families. "Let's say September."

"Why so long?" he presses. "Now that you're coming back, I thought we should be married right away."

Coming back. The words reverberate in my head. "We women need at least a few months to plan. For Celia to have her wedding," I joke feebly. "Plus, the weather will be cooler and it will give you some time to heal."

"Time to heal," he repeats slowly, as if not believing the words. "Darling, what if it never gets any better than this?"

"It will," I say.

But he shakes his head. "Don't you see, Margot? This is my life now." He gestures with frustration toward his canes. "I can't join your family's business. And likely I can't even have children."

I had not stopped to think about this possibility. As I had told Georg, I'd always wanted a large family. To Stefan, this is even more of a blow, because he would not be able to carry on his family name, which he needed to do as the only son. "There are other ways," I persist. "We can adopt." He shakes his head angrily, unwilling to be consoled.

Disillusioned, I begin to repack the picnic basket. When I'm finished, I stand. "Come," I say with forced brightness, extending my hand down to him. Suddenly the prospect of another slow walk is less wearisome than further conversation. "There's still time to see some of the fountains before nightfall."

It is nearly eight o'clock when we return to the hotel. Exhausted now, he does not protest as I help him up the narrow flight of stairs to our apartment. Inside, the sitting room is still. "Papa must have gone to Celia's," I say. Stefan stares at the divan, now a makeshift bed. We are husband and wife, alone together, and I can see the hopeful light in his eyes for some affection, even if he is not capable of true intimacy. "I'm terribly tired," I add, "and Papa might return."

"Of course." He recovers quickly. "Best to wait until after the wedding." He turns away, trying to conceal his disappointment.

"Stefan, wait." I walk to him and wrap my arms around him awkwardly. His body slumps into me as he drinks in the affection he has craved for so long. "It will be fine," I say, but the words are more to convince me than him. Why can't I help him? I've helped Georg in a sense, or so he said once. Perhaps I could be good for Stefan, too, and help him find hope. But to do that I would have to believe in us.

A moment later I break away from his now too-tight grasp. "Good night," I say, then walk to the door of my room and close it.

"So you're leaving," Krysia says the next afternoon, when I have finished my story. We are seated on the bench by the pond, watching Emilie and her friends, who have set up a game of croquet on a lush green patch not far from the water. When Krysia had not been at her apartment, I guessed where she had gone. I found her here, standing a bit closer today, out in the open, not obscured by the trees.

As she watches Emilie, I think of my own mother, a woman who did not care enough to stay, much less spy from afar to make sure I am well. Krysia abandoned her child just as mine had done. Should I be angry with her? No, Krysia had no choice and had done the best she could for the child. Even now she lingers, watching and worrying. Whereas my mother had every reason to stay but had chosen not to—she had gone and never looked back.

"Yes, the day after tomorrow."

"I suppose the party had to end sometime." I brace for her

disappointment that I am returning to Berlin as is expected of me, failing to make a life of my own. But her voice is detached in the way of one who has seen much in a lifetime, worlds fallen and rebuilt, people lost and found and lost again. Her words reverberate through my mind. Paris, for all of the gaiety, had never seemed a party to me but a sojourn from who we were expected to be in our regular lives. Sojourns, like parties, had to end, too, didn't they? Or the exception would become the rule. But what, I wonder as the memory of Georg's touch makes me suddenly warm, would be so wrong about that?

"What about Ignatz? He's still expecting me to deliver the documents." I had not told her about the second map I'd gotten from Lieutenant Bouvier, the one I might have given to Ignatz but had not.

"He won't know that you've gone until it's too late." Her mouth twists. "And I think the authorities will be showing some new interest in the backroom gaming activities at the bar. Sorting that out should keep him busy for the foreseeable future."

I stare, bowled over by the audacity and brilliance of what she had done, reporting Ignatz as a means of deterring him. "Thank you."

A croquet ball, hit too hard with a mallet, breaks loose and shoots in Krysia's direction and Emilie runs toward her to retrieve it. Krysia freezes uncertainly, an animal trapped beyond the safety of her nest. Will she run? But she bends down and picks up the ball and hands it to the girl, their long, nearly identically shaped fingers brushing.

Krysia puts the ball into the girl's hands and in that motion I imagine she is feeling all of the birthdays and triumphs she will not witness, the inevitable tears she will never dry. She presses so hard that for a moment I fear the girl will be alarmed by the intensity of the strange woman's touch. But Emilie turns and runs away, unburdened by a sadness she does not know. Krysia stands with her arms still outstretched before her, reaching. I walk up behind her and take her hand. "Come. It's time to go home."

The midmorning sun warms the earth the next day as I tend to my garden plot one last time. I take a sprig of fern from the earth and place it in the tiny pot I've brought with me, no bigger than a teacup. Three days is all that is required to undo the life we've built here. I've taken charge of the packing, a rote, mindless task fit to occupy my hands if not my heart while Papa wraps up his work for the conference and Stefan tours the city with a hired driver and his copy of *Baedeker's Paris*, avoiding the battlefields. I pat down the earth with my index finger, tucking the cutting into the tiny round bed. I'm going to plant it back home, if it survives the journey.

"Liebchen," Papa calls from the garden gate. The car, loaded with our belongings, idles at the curb. Stefan is already seated in the rear, eyes fixed firmly on the road ahead. I stand, brushing the dirt from my hem. My eyes travel in the direction of the hotel. I have not seen Georg since the night Stefan arrived, not even glimpsed him coming or going, though I looked out my window for him constantly. I had half expected that he might call around to see Papa under pretense of finalizing business. But that would be too awkward, not at all his style. No, he had sequestered himself in the study undoubtedly, burying himself in what remained of his work as a way of shutting out the hurt.

After Stefan had retired last night, exhausted from his tour of the Louvre, I'd gazed down the street at the light in the library, worrying. The treaty had been such a blow, and now this on top of it. Had Georg eaten, slept? I debated briefly slipping from the flat and going to the hotel. To say what, exactly? There was no way to explain my betrayal. Georg stood for loyalty and honesty above all that. Through my actions, I epitomized the opposite.

I walk to the taxi and climb in, not meeting Papa's eyes. We have not spoken again about my mother and the secrets he kept from me all of these years. They remain an open wound between us.

Out the back window of the taxi, I take a last glance at the hotel. The once-blossoming apple trees bow sadly now. As we drive from Versailles, I stare up at the palace, its darkened windows looking back like a hundred gaping eyes, reproaching me for all that we had tried to do at the conference and failed. Above the sky is gray and repentant. I imagined the signing we wouldn't be here to see, Georg facing the inevitable reality he had tried so hard to change. "They say the Germans are going to shoot themselves at the signing," I'd overheard a woman say on the metro when I'd gone to see Krysia, her voice hushed with excitement. My stomach turns. Could she possibly be right?

Forty five minutes later, as we reach Gare de l'Est, I am surprised to find Krysia waiting by the door to the station. "You didn't have to come. It's so early." But I am touched.

She holds out an arm to me. "Come."

I follow her into the station while Papa and Stefan supervise the unloading of our luggage by two porters in red jackets. "You have time for a coffee," she says, leading me through the arched station entrance to the kiosk and buying two cups. The food here is Germanic, beer and sauerkraut, as if prematurely signaling that we have somehow already left Paris.

I sit across from her at the counter, playing with my spoon. "You didn't have to come," I say again. She had told me once that she despised farewells.

"I had to see about tickets, anyway," she announces. I tilt my head, curious. "We're leaving, too."

"Where will you go?"

"Home. For the first time in my life there's a country called Poland again and I'm eager to see it." I search her voice for the real reason for her finally assenting to leaving Emilie and going home as Marcin wanted. Could it possibly have to do with my departure? More likely, with the conference winding down and

Elsa Maxwell and her kind setting sail for the next great city, the work for musicians here would be less plentiful and exciting by far.

"But your flat here in Paris. Marcin's touring…"

"Travel is a younger person's game," Krysia replies wearily. "Now I just want to go home." She pauses, sipping her coffee. "Marcin has a family home in the countryside outside Krakow where we can live. We can teach music at the university." She smiles and I can tell that she is finally going to give herself a chance to be happy.

"What about Emilie?" It is the real question that I wanted to ask in the first place.

"You were right, about letting her go. It's time for me to move on. Here," Krysia says, clearing her throat. She sets down her cup and opens her bag. "I knitted this for you." It is a scarf, flecks of something gold interwoven with deep purple wool. She must have been working on it for weeks. "To remember me by."

I take the gift from her, touched. "Thank you."

"We have beautiful mountains near Krakow," she says. "Come visit and we'll go hiking."

I do not answer. Once I am back in Germany with Stefan, ensconced in family and wedding plans, traveling will be difficult. Neighboring Poland, a long train ride from Berlin over rail lines largely decimated by the war, might as well be another planet.

We look out at the sea of travelers crossing the station in all directions, not speaking. "You wanted to leave Paris," she reminds me.

Once I did. If only I had known what that meant, how it would feel. "But what now?"

"You'll find your way," she says, so firmly that for a second I almost believe her. "Each does, in her own time. One door closes, another opens." What will I do without her wisdom?

"At least now I'll be done with Ignatz and the spying," I say.

Before she can respond, an announcement crackles over the speakers, calling our train. "We should go."

We walk to the platform where Papa is helping Stefan into one of the carriages. I turn to Krysia. "You should tell her," I say abruptly, meaning Emilie. She looks at me helplessly as if to ask, *How can you say that when I have just made my peace?* "She should have the chance to know you." Before it's too late, I add silently, thinking of my own mother.

"Margot…" Papa calls from inside the carriage.

I hesitate, the moment I have been forestalling inevitably here. I glance over my shoulder, making sure Stefan is out of earshot. "Krysia, there's one other thing. About Georg…" It nags at me that I did not get to say goodbye, that his last memory of me would be a moment of betrayal. "If you see him…" Then I falter. What can I tell her that would begin to convey my feelings in a way that is not wholly improper with my wounded husband just steps from us?

But Krysia nods, seeming to understand exactly what I mean without my having to say. "I will tell him." For all her dislike of Georg, she will find a way to deliver my message of farewell and regret, finding the words that I cannot.

"Come see me," I plead as I hug her goodbye.

She does not answer, unwilling to make promises she may not keep. Instead, she places her cheek against mine. "Godspeed." I am unable to answer. There was no expectation of permanency to our friendship, two ships flagged by different nations, briefly stopping at the same port of call. Still, I shall miss her.

I climb the steps to the train and enter the carriage where Stefan waits. I turn to say goodbye to Krysia once more through the window. Behind her, I glimpse a tall, familiar figure behind one of the stone balustrades. My breath catches. *Georg.* He is wearing civilian clothes publicly for the first time I've seen, an attempt perhaps to remain unrecognized, though I could pick him out of a mass of thousands. Our eyes meet and I hold my breath, waiting for him to run up and declare his love and beg me to stay. But he remains in place, hidden from sight and a second later he is gone, swallowed by the crowd.

Stefan is by my side then, his arm tugging me downward, urging me to take my seat. "Come, darling," he says, and I fight the urge to scream, knowing that the nightmare I've lived a thousand times in my sleep has at last come true.

PART THREE

BERLIN, AUGUST 1919

CHAPTER SIXTEEN

"More coffee?" A footman hovers expectantly to my right. *"Bitte."* A hint of pomade from his trim blond hair mixes with the aroma of the coffee as he bends to pour. I gaze beyond the head of the table, where Papa and Uncle Walter are debating something in low voices, through the French doors. The terrace behind the villa leads down to the lake, the late-summer water still as glass. A swarm of gnats hovers above it.

It has been over three months since we returned from the peace conference. We had no other choice but to come home. Papa's visit at Oxford had "concluded without possibility of renewal," according to the letter he'd received while we were in Paris, and other universities were similarly unaccommodating. Living abroad had become prohibitively expensive, anyway, and Uncle Walter had informed Papa that he could no longer afford to support "our lifestyle." I had boiled with anger when Papa had shared that conversation with me, thinking of the long hours Papa kept at the conference, taxing his health and energy to the brink. We had not been on holiday, but in Paris at Uncle Walter's request.

So we had returned to Berlin, or more accurately to the villa at Grunewald. Our own house was in disrepair, Papa told me. Though the bombings had left our neighborhood intact, the gangs that had taken to the street after news of Germany's defeat had broken the windows and looted everything. Papa had been evasive when I'd asked about the extent of the damage, or a possible date by which we might expect to return. Instead, he talked about the difficulty in getting the roof replaced, given the lack of young men able to do that sort of work, as well as the scarcity of lumber needed to repair the rotten floorboards.

I've not been into Berlin proper since our return and after more than four years, I'm eager to see it. But Papa forbade my going, even arranging a separate car to take Stefan home from the station the day we arrived so that we could proceed directly to Grunewald. "It's dangerous," he replied with uncharacteristic bluntness, refusing one of my repeated requests to go into the city. "There are riots and strikes." The country, angry at a government that betrayed its own people, is tearing itself apart, like a dog gnawing off its own leg to get free from a trap.

Not that one would know it from Uncle Walter's house, I reflect, as the smaller china dishes are set for the sweets course. The sprawling lakeside mansion on the water is worlds away from the chaos of Berlin, a perpetual holiday. The newspapers depict lines at the markets for food that would never come, buckets of deutschmarks that will not buy a loaf of bread, ration cards that might as well be burned for fuel. But here the food approaches a prewar bounty, as evidenced by the fruit stacked high in a bowl at the center of the table, the soups thick with meat.

My gaze drops from the terrace to the far end of the table, where Papa and Uncle Walter are speaking loudly now, debating something political. As Papa takes off his glasses and rubs at his eyes, my concern grows. Papa returned from the conference a broken man. He once believed in a brotherhood, that his common interests with other scholars would prevail over militarism and national identities. But that belief was shattered by the betrayal at Versailles. We are still—and presumably always would be—the enemy.

Our return to Berlin has been equally unsettling. There is disillusionment about the people here—they understand now that it was not a war of self-defense, but one of aggression. But instead of blaming the government that had lied to them, people have improbably reserved their bile for those who negotiated its end. Papa's position at the university was filled, he was told, a rare exception to the life tenure that should have rightfully been his. So he potters about the house at Grunewald, organizing his notes and talking about writing a book.

"The Jews are giving them ample fodder by allying with the communists," Uncle Walter declares, straightening the pince-nez that balances precariously on his wide nose. It is an argument I have heard him make a dozen times. "We need to be part of the system in order to reform it."

In sharp contrast to Papa, Uncle Walter is looking better than ever, a new ruddiness to his cheeks and girth to his waist beneath the white linen suit. Uncle Walter had been one of the engineers of the war effort—his great skill in maintaining supply and production lines kept the German army going longer than anyone thought possible. Without him Germany might have surrendered two years earlier and thousands of young men might still be alive. Yet he had come out without blame, more powerful and successful than ever, a key player in the Weimar regime. Some talked that he might attain a cabinet post.

"Walter, I'm not sure that even if we completely assimilated they would be ever..." Papa corrects gently. "If you read..."

Uncle Walter raises his hand. "Nonsense. Of course, as an academic, you would take that theoretical view." The two men eye each other icily. My mother's older brother had made it clear from the day she married Papa that the professor from the Jewish quarter was never going to be good enough for his sister and that the situation could not end well—a prediction which he now viewed as having come true. He blames Papa for the unhappiness that had caused her to leave, and now that he does not need to maintain a charade for my benefit, his disdain of Papa is less veiled than ever.

"What a lovely bracelet," Tante Celia observes from my left side, trying to break the tension. She touches my wrist. I cringe at the attention she has drawn to Georg's gift. I have worn the bracelet constantly since our return to Berlin, taking comfort from my one last link to him. Neither Papa nor Stefan, who is seated passively beside me, would have noticed on his own.

Now all eyes are upon me. "Just a trinket I picked up at the market," I lie. Celia's brow furrows. She, above anyone else, knows jewelry and does not believe my explanation. I hold my breath, waiting for her to challenge me, but she does not.

Celia followed us back from Paris just days after we left and has been around nonstop since our return, occupying her own suite of rooms at the villa where she had grown up. It is not just her desire to be close to Papa, but also my wedding preparations that draw her like a moth to flame. I had wanted the wedding to be small, a ceremony down by the lake if the weather permitted, or perhaps in the gazebo if it did not, with a modest reception on the terrace. Just close family and friends. To do more felt garish in light of all the suffering that remained from the war—and I wanted to spare Stefan the embarrassment of trying to limp his way down the aisle and navigate a crowded reception.

But Uncle Walter had insisted that a real wedding was needed. "We owe it to the people to show that Germany remains strong and keep the spirits high." It feels like a farce, Marie Antoinette telling the starving proletariat to eat cake. The elaborate wedding is not about German morale, but Uncle Walter, announcing he has reached a certain political station. With Celia behind him, though, and Papa too distracted to weigh in, I had not been able to fight. The wedding has ballooned to three hundred people, including the prime minister. Celia has taken on the role that my mother might have had, planning the shower tea and ordering the invitations and registry—the things that make me want to scream and crawl out of my skin. It is the wedding and the daughter she's never had all at once.

I should be happy that Celia does not choose to press about the bracelet and retreat gracefully. But Uncle Walter's last jab at my father still stings. "Papa's work at the conference was hardly theoretical," I say, unwilling to be dissuaded from his defense.

"Liebchen..." Papa says, his voice carrying silent warning. Though this is my ancestral home as well as Uncle Walter's, we are still very much his guests here.

I am too far gone to stop, though. Now released, the words pour forth unabated. "The war was a disgrace," I say. "I have seen the destruction at Reims, the debilitated young men on the Parisian street corners." Only one such as Uncle Walter, who has not seen the devastation up close, could still think there had been a purpose to it. "So many lives lost."

"It is pacifist views like yours that cause the German people to distrust the Jews," he retorts.

"Would having no views make our position somehow more tenable?" I demand. Uncle Walter's eyebrows rise. He has never approved of a woman's forthright speech. But this is more than my former childish impertinence. There is a quiet confidence to my argument now, as if I am channeling Krysia's style in debating with the artists at the café in Montparnasse.

"I'm only saying..." He pauses, thrown back on his heels. "Until things settle down, neutrality may be the wisest policy."

I meet his eyes levelly. "A great pity, then, that you didn't discover that four years ago. Hindsight must be lovely," I add. "Especially for those who stayed in Berlin." I can hardly believe my own nerve. I stand up. "Excuse me."

"That is the problem with how you have raised her," I hear Uncle Walter say as I walk from the room. "And now with women's suffrage passed…"

"Indeed," Papa replies. "To have my daughter vote will be the proudest day of my life."

I flee down the corridor, shaking. Why hadn't these things bothered me so before? Or perhaps they had and I just hadn't noticed. Just like Georg's experiences on the ship had reshaped him, I was also changed by my time abroad, unable to fit back into the old forms and strictures.

My heels echo against the marble floor of the high-ceilinged foyer. The house is quiet as I climb the steps beneath the somber oil portraits of our ancestors, set against dark wood paneling, and walk to our apartment. These had been my mother's rooms as a child, a cavernous space occupied by her and a governess, though the girlish pink decor has been repainted a suitable beige and the furniture replaced. The ivory lace wedding gown hangs on the armoire, having arrived from Paris two weeks earlier. Looking at it now, my stomach sinks.

I drop onto one of the velvet-covered divans in the sitting room, still seething from my encounter with Uncle Walter. More so than his conservative politics, it is his constant obsession with assimilation that infuriates me. It is as if he would like us to forget we are Jews entirely in order to fit in. My mind reels back to a Friday afternoon shortly after our return from Paris. I'd come downstairs to the dining room, expecting to see the usual Sabbath preparations, the table set with a fresh white cloth, candlesticks polished. But the air was dry, the smell of freshly baked challah conspicuously absent. I'd made my way into the kitchen. "Elsa…"

"*Ja, fraulein.*" The sallow-skinned maid did not smile. There had been a thinly veiled resentment among the household staff since our return, I assumed. Was it because we had not been here during the war and did not share in the suffering?

"What time is Sabbath dinner? I thought it used to be at seven…"

But Elsa shook her head slightly. "I'll have a tray sent up to the apartment of anything you would like. But Herr Rappaport is away in the city for meetings." Meetings. On a Friday night, that hardly seemed plausible. "There hasn't been a proper Friday dinner in over a year," Elsa added, her voice a note lower. Sabbath dinner at Uncle Walter's had never been a particularly religious affair, a quick lighting of the candles and blessing over the wine and challah before sitting down to a sumptuous roast turkey repast. Afterward, there were glasses of schnapps and conversation long into the night. He used to say it was a break from all of the noise of the week. "It's like that all over the place," the maid added, forgetting to guard her speech. "My brother says it's because of the war, the Jews being ashamed at their part, not fighting."

My anger burned white-hot and I wanted to tell her then about Stefan and the terrible price he paid fighting for Germany. But there was no conviction in her words; she was simply parroting what she heard elsewhere.

"Not anymore," Papa replied when I ran to tell him about the lack of a Sabbath dinner. "Jews like Uncle Walter just want to fit in, to have people forget. They consider themselves Germans first and Jews a distant second."

Are you German or Jew? Krysia's words haunted me. There was an otherness now to our lives in Berlin, in the way people looked at us, that made me understand what she was talking about. We were somehow being asked to choose.

"Surely you don't feel that way?"

He pressed his lips together. "No, but everything has changed. Jews here seem to be either Orthodox, more separate than ever, or assimilationist, like your uncle. There's no middle anymore." He brought his fingers to his chin, deeply troubled. "I just don't know what our future looks like here. I'm too old of a man to relocate permanently. Of course, if you and Stefan want to go to Israel or even America..." I heard the conflict in his voice as it trails off.

"No," I said quickly. I could not leave Papa and I felt no connection to those distant lands. But his question nagged. What would my life be like if I stayed here?

"Would dinner with me suffice?" he asked with a half smile. He was chiding me, reminding me in not so many words of a time when I detested Sabbath at Uncle Walter's, the long trek out to Grunewald, the formality and stiffness a sharp contrast to our quiet dinners in our house. But it was a part of our old world, the one that seems to have disappeared with the war, and I was digging through the sand, searching for any shred of that old life to cling to, a time before Paris when I didn't know enough to be unhappy.

My eyes travel now to the fern from my garden in Versailles, which sits potted on the vast expanse of windowsill. Despite my care, it struggles to survive its transplant to strange surroundings. I water the plant, then walk to the table by the door and riffle through yesterday's post. I have only heard from Krysia once since our return, a hastily scrawled postcard indicating that she and Marcin had reached Krakow safely. I sent her an invitation to the wedding but, given the unreliability of the post, have no real hopes of receiving a response.

My thoughts turn to Georg and I see his face as I have so often since leaving Paris. Each day I check the mail as though there might be a letter from him, though, of course, it would not be proper for him to write or call. I have thought about writing to him, but to say what exactly? I cannot stop thinking of the hurt expression on his face when he saw Stefan and realized the truth.

What would have happened if Stefan had not come to Paris? Would the few happy days Georg and I shared have stretched endlessly? At some point the conference would have ended and we would have had to leave. No, the Fates were decided before we ever met, and those few weeks were a respite, an exception that could not bend the rule.

Of course, it might have never happened at all. If I hadn't broken the heel of my shoe and come home early from the party that night, I would not have spoken with Georg. It all seems so random now—a turn to the right instead of the left at an intersection and lives are different than they might once have been.

Georg would have retreated from Paris now, ostensibly to his family home in Hamburg. I imagine him somewhere close to the water, staring out at the North Sea. He said he would never return to the navy. But perhaps he's fulfilled his dream to leave and not look back. Does he think of me, and if so, is it with longing or hate? He had looked so sad and disbelieving as he realized I had lied to him. Would he even still want me now if I was free?

There is a knock at the door. "Darling?" Stefan pushes it open and limps through, now using just one cane. I study his face. His eyes are still hollow with the things he has seen, ringed with dark circles from the nightmares that deny him sleep. No group has been more ostracized than the Jewish soldiers, branded traitors who had somehow stabbed their Gentile brethren in the back by not fighting hard enough. I wonder if he minded all of the war talk at lunch, and whether the constant references to suffering and loss were too painful for him to bear. "I wanted to come and see you before I head back to the city, to make sure you aren't too upset. I just have a moment before the car comes. Your aunt has arranged another fitting for my tuxedo."

I smile weakly at him. "Tante Celia has become consumed with the wedding, I'm afraid. You don't mind, do you?"

He shakes his head. "Not at all. It is good to give people something to celebrate again. I only wish that I could properly walk down the aisle with you." He is self-conscious about his limp, but prepared to withstand the scrutiny of our friends and family for the privilege of marrying me publicly.

I take a deep breath. "But maybe we are rushing things? We could wait until you are stronger. And I was thinking about taking a course in the meantime…"

He blinks twice. "Here, you mean? Or did you want to leave again?" His voice trembles.

"No, of course not." I feel the shackles begin to tighten. "I just thought that some more time for you to get stronger…"

"Being with you will make me strong. I will be standing for our vows," he promises, his eyes wide with determination.

"Of course you will." I manage to sound convinced.

"You have the marriage certificate?" Stefan asks, dropping his voice as though we are not alone. "Perhaps we should go to get another just so the dates match up."

Guilt rises in me as I remember throwing our certificate in the fireplace when I believed Stefan had been killed, watching the corners curl under glowing embers. I hadn't known. But what kind of unfeeling woman would do such a thing just after learning that her husband had died? I should have kept it, treasuring the fact that we had been connected in such a way—as I had with Georg's bracelet.

"I—I don't know where it is," I lie. "With all of the moving around, it must have become misplaced among my things."

A look of consternation crosses his face. "Not to worry," he replies brightly. "We can get a duplicate."

"But the fire…" Six weeks earlier, rioters had set fire to the Rathaus and many records had been destroyed.

"Then we shall just get a new one. I would love to marry you again. Unless you don't want…" Suddenly we are talking about something larger than the certificate. "You can go," he says with difficulty. He is releasing me from the promise of a life together, setting me free. "I would understand."

In my mind's eye I can see the door he's opened and I imagine walking through it, making a life for myself and perhaps even finding Georg on the other side.

But then my vision clears. Stefan's eyes are inches from mine, the clearest I have seen them since his return. He is quite literally holding his breath, waiting for my response. The door closes quietly with a click. I take his hand reassuringly. "Of course not."

"I'm going to make you happy," Stefan says, a note of desperation in his voice. He is squeezing my fingers with more strength than I thought he could muster.

"Shh, don't be silly, you already do."

But he shakes his head. "It won't always be like this." I sense his helplessness these past months, his awareness on some level that things between us have irreversibly changed. But it isn't his broken body or spirit that is the problem. It is me.

"Oh, darling." I reach to embrace him.

There is a ringing at the door then. "That must be my car." He kisses me lightly, then stands with effort.

Watching him leave, I am filled with sadness. Stefan and I were friends and easy companions once, but without spark or passion. Had I not met Georg, that might have been enough. I might have accepted that romance fades and peaceful coexistence is as much as two people can expect through the years. But now I understand the difference and it makes this stifling and insufferable.

My eyes travel to the photograph of my mother that still sits above the mantelpiece, Papa's reverence for her unchanged by all that has happened. Her ashes were returned to us from London, placed in the Berlin grave that had been made for her years ago with a small ceremony I had attended reluctantly to support Papa. He had not cried, and I thought perhaps as he joined the rabbi in saying Kaddish with a quiet, raspy voice that he might not take it so badly because he had in fact grieved her years earlier when she left. But later that night I heard him sobbing through the closed door to his room. Though she had been gone for over a decade, my mother's death was now real. He mourned, too, the loss of his fast-held, improbable dream that she might change her mind and return to us.

There is a shuffling at the door and I look up. Had Stefan forgotten something? But it is the maid, Elsa. "May I?" She slips in and begins to freshen the sheets without speaking. The intrusion of the household staff is just one of the things to which we've had to become reaccustomed at the villa.

Not wanting to remain in the apartment with Elsa, I walk down the steps and out the back terrace to the path around the lake. From this vantage point I can see that the dining room has cleared. Papa must have gone to his study, without checking on me as he surely would have in the past. There is a quiet tension between us that is worse than our fight in Paris. Papa had kept the truth about my mother from me. I had lied to him about Georg. How had we gotten to this place?

The good thing—if there is to be one—from our return to Berlin is that I have gotten out from under Ignatz and his threats. I imagine his anger at discovering I have escaped his grasp.

I gaze out across the lake to where swans glide across the surface of the water. My days revolve around walks such as this and visits to the massive library on the first floor with shelves so high a wheeled ladder is needed to reach the upper shelves. I imagine my mother walking this path as I do. The villa is luxurious in every sense of the world, but to a young woman wanting to see the world, the quiet lifestyle, with its rigid expectations of marriage and family, must have seemed stifling. Suddenly it is as if we are one person. The desire to leave—whether it is mine or hers I do not know—looms inside me, larger than ever.

I consider a bicycle ride into town, something to break free of the smothering quiet of the villa. But clouds are beginning to gather to the west and a mist begins to pool over the lake, signaling a strong likelihood of rain. I start back toward the house.

Inside, I pass by Uncle Walter's office. Hearing several voices, I stop. It is unusual for Uncle Walter, who keeps a strict office schedule, to have business visitors to the villa, much less on a Sunday. Amid the muffled conversation, a foreign accent emerges. Russian, I realize. I shiver, reminded of Ignatz by the strange inflection.

Then I hear another man speaking, German this time, deep and familiar. I freeze.

The voice is unmistakably Georg's.

CHAPTER SEVENTEEN

The door to the study begins to open. Panicking, I turn in the opposite direction and run down the hallway, fleeing to the terrace once more. Outside I stop, trembling for several seconds in the now-dense fog. *Georg's voice.* It cannot be!

A minute later, the terrace doors creak. "Margot." Georg, who must have broken abruptly from the gathering, steps from the mist and crosses the patio in long strides. He halts before me, tall and magnificent, the shock on his face mirroring my own. It was not a dream. Our eyes meet and hold.

I freeze, barely able to breathe. What on earth is he doing here? Georg was the last person I'd expected to see again, much less in this house. Excitement and dread and terror and joy rip through me as I drink him in, pulling me in a thousand different directions at once. For a fleeting second, I wonder if he has come for me. But I can tell from his puzzled expression that he is surprised, too. In the hallway behind him there is a gathering of suited men. Georg is here for a meeting. Of course, it makes sense that Uncle Walter in industry and Georg's family in ship-ping might have business together.

We stand staring at each other, too surprised for formal greet-ings. "I didn't know you were in Berlin," I offer, suddenly angry. Why hadn't he told me he was going to be in the city? It would not have been proper for him to contact me; still, the idea that he has been so close by, and that he might have come here and gone again without seeing me, as my mother had in Paris, cuts through me like a knife.

"I returned only a few weeks ago." His voice is hollow. "I had hoped I might hear some news of you. But seeing you here..." He clears his throat. "It is so much more than I imagined."

"Oh, Georg!" I want to run to him and fling my arms around him, breathe him in as though this is Paris and nothing has changed. But everything has changed, I remind myself. "We're staying with Uncle Walter while our house is repaired." I strug-gle to keep my voice even.

"You had not mentioned that Walter Rappaport was your uncle."

"You didn't ask." Of course, our last name is Rosenthal so there's no reason he would have guessed. "We are the lesser Rappaports," I joke. He does not rise to the humor, but searches my face hungrily.

"I never dreamed..." I watch his face expectantly as he strug-gles to find the words. He doesn't hate me. For everything that happened before I left Paris, it is all still there in his eyes, as real as the last night we were together. Something swells up in me, threatening to burst. "That is, to see you again..."

"Margot!" Uncle Walter booms behind us, having seen out his other guests. He claps Georg on the back as though he is a boy and not a foot taller. "You've met my niece." He uses a voice more affable than the one he usually reserves for me, giv-ing no indication of either our earlier disagreement or the ac-rimony that is our default state. But behind his smile, his eyes are filled with trepidation. Ever since I was a girl and disrupted one of his dinner parties with a potful of frogs I'd caught in the lake, Uncle Walter has given me wide berth, wary of the havoc I might wreak on his guests.

"Margot and I came to be acquainted in Paris, actually. But I hadn't realized the relation, or that she was staying here."

"My brother-in-law's house is being renovated. I'm afraid the thugs left it uninhabitable." Georg nods with understanding. Our situation was not unique—wide swaths of Berlin neighborhoods had been destroyed by the war and subsequent rioting. "And since the wedding is to be here in less than a week, it is most convenient that they are staying with me." I watch Georg's face. Will the news that Stefan and I are proceeding to get married so soon be a shock? But his face is impassive, no longer vulnerable to such blows.

Papa appears at the terrace door then. "Walter, I..." Seeing Georg standing beside me, he stops. "Captain Richwalder?"

"You also know my brother from Paris," Uncle Walter says.

Georg nods. "*Natürlich*. A pleasure, Herr Ambassador."

"It's back to professor now," Uncle Walter corrects, eager to strip Papa of his once-prestigious title.

"No matter," Papa says mildly, struggling not to convey his displeasure that Georg has once again entered our lives. "So you are working for the government now?"

Georg nods. "In munitions."

"Really? With the terms of the treaty, I wouldn't have thought there would be a need."

"There will be a German military again," Georg says, a hardness to his voice I have not heard before. "And it will need to be stronger than ever so we can resolidify our interests abroad."

"That sounds quite different from the role you envisioned when we were in Paris," Papa observes. "Has your point of view changed?"

"Everything," Georg says slowly, "has changed."

Uncle Walter, though, is oblivious to the subtext. "A fine young man," he says, speaking as if Georg isn't there. "Smart, hardworking. There's likely a real future for him in government. Some have even suggested politics." Georg, a strong and handsome war hero, would make the ideal candidate.

But Georg demurs. "I don't have the words for politics." He's more comfortable with charts and diagrams than speeches.

"It will be a short while until the report we discussed is ready," Uncle Walter says to Georg, his voice businesslike once more. "Margot, would you mind entertaining the captain while I attend to some other matters?" Not waiting for an answer, he disappears back into the house. Papa hesitates before retreating inside once more.

When we are alone again on the terrace, Georg turns to me. He does not speak, but swallows me in his gaze.

I clasp my hands to resist reaching for him. "You are well?" I manage. The lines in Georg's face are more deeply etched, giving him a depth that only makes him more handsome.

"As I told your father, I'm working for the government in munitions now." The answer, focused on his job, is not the one I was seeking. And it surprises me. Georg had said that he hated Berlin and had no time for politics. But something had changed in him since the treaty was signed. "The government is in more dire straits than ever. We need strong leadership if we are to avoid anarchy." I wait for him to launch into one of his speeches about making a difference in the new world. But that dream died at Versailles. He wears his saber again, I notice. Is it ceremonial or a precaution against the violence and chaos that has swept the city?

"Munitions? But I thought…" My surprise echoes Papa's. The peace treaty demilitarized Germany, left any notion of a standing army or equipment for one inconceivable. Then I remember the Russian voice in Walter's study. New allies, allowing us to do on their soil what we cannot do on our own, because there will always be armies and weapons and war. "So you're staying in Berlin, then?" My stomach tightens, an odd combination of excitement and dread.

"Just for a time. I've taken a place at the Grand until I decide what to do next."

I nod, recognizing the famed boardinghouse with its handful of rooms and stately gardens. Even if Georg intended to stay, permanent housing in the city is in notoriously short supply. But I had not been asking about his job. I want to know if he is all right, how he is managing now that the conference is over and his dreams for cooperation as equals in tatters. "Will you go back to sea?"

He shakes his head. "That's a younger man's dream." There is something different about him. The honor and principles are there, but they have been worn down by political realities, grooves in a piece of driftwood. We are all older now.

"And how was the rest of your time in Paris? I heard the weather became most stifling." I am babbling now.

He shrugs. "I hadn't noticed. But I was ready to leave. Nothing was the same after you…that is, after the conference was over." I blink against the burning in my eyes. He clears his throat. "It's beautiful here. You must hate it."

I laugh aloud then, wiping away a lone tear that spills from my right eye. Only Georg, who shares my distaste for formality and pretense, would understand my visceral dislike of our Grunewald villa. "It's good to see you, Margot." It is good to see him, too, more so than I might have imagined. "You cut your hair," he says abruptly.

"Yes." I pat the sleek bob, bits framing my face. The dampness has drawn my curls tight, making it seem shorter than ever. It is a sharp contrast to the long locks I'd worn in Paris. Georg reaches toward my temple, as if he's forgotten all that has happened between the last time he had done that and now.

Then his hand stops midair and flounders before retreating

to his side. "I like it. It looks more sophisticated." Neither of us speak for several seconds. "Margot…" Despite his hardness, I can sense the intensity of his feelings for me.

"I'm so sorry, Georg," I blurt, the words spilling forth. "I never meant to lie to you." Then I falter. *Sorry that I could not tell you about my marriage, because I did not want it to be true, for reality to stand between you and I and all that I wanted for us.*

"I should have known," he laments. "And maybe on some level I did. I assumed that you were standoffish because of the difference in our ages and positions. Still, I never thought…" He never thought that I would have lied to him so. Even now he cannot believe the worst in me and struggles with the truth. "Your friend Krysia came to tell me that you had gone," he adds.

So she had honored her promise. Of course he had already known, I think, remembering the glimpse of him at the station as our train pulled from Paris. "I wanted to come myself. But I thought you must hate me."

"Hate you? I could never." Unconsciously, I reach up and touch his arm. He smiles then, all tension dissipating, and for a moment it is just the two of us, as we always were. "The bracelet." His eyes grow wide. "You're wearing it."

"Always," I say solemnly. "But you should have it back." I reach down and undo the clasp.

He shakes his head, refusing to take it. "It gives me great comfort, knowing that some part of me is with you."

Uncle Walter steps onto the terrace once more and hands Georg a file. "It is good to have you working with us. Would you like to stay for tea?"

Georg's eyes dart involuntarily in my direction and I can see the conflict that pulls him two ways at once, the inches between us suddenly an ocean. Nothing has changed. Our feelings are as real and strong as in Paris. But with Uncle Walter here and my wedding looming over us, there is simply nowhere for them to go. "That's very kind of you, but my driver is waiting. I really should return to the city."

Uncle Walter nods. "I'll see you out."

"Good day, Margot."

I watch with disbelief as Georg turns and starts for the door. *Don't go!* my mind screams, willing time to stand still so I can hold on to this moment for just a few seconds longer. I want to run after him. But I stand motionless as the terrace door closes. A moment later, I hear the roar of a car engine, the whisking of tires against gravel and dirt.

As the sound fades into the distance, I sink to one of the wrought-iron garden chairs, racked with disappointment. How could he simply go, to walk away so quickly after we had just found each other again? He could have stayed, but he had chosen to leave at the earliest possible moment. Despite his feelings, there was some part of him that had not forgiven me for Paris. And now the moment that I had dreamed of a thousand times but had never thought possible actually had happened. But it was over just as quickly.

I fling open the front door and walk into the house. The driveway is empty, a lingering cloud of dust the only proof anyone had been there at all. Unable to stand the containment of the villa any longer, I walk down the driveway. Picturing Georg's face in my mind, my cheeks burn beneath hot tears. It is not just the unexpectedness of seeing him again here of all places. No, my feelings for him are all still there, as real as ever. They aren't going away with time lessening or fading. Desire and pain tear through me.

At the end of the driveway, I retrieve my bike and start to ride, not down the lake path as I customarily do, but toward the main road. I pedal faster now, trying to outrun my thoughts and feelings. But the image of Georg standing on the terrace presses into my mind. I thought my prayers had been answered. I thought he had come for me.

It is not until I reach the station that I realize where I am going. I chain the bike and purchase a ticket and board the train, which soon arrives, largely empty at midday The worn wooden seating is unchanged from my last ride years ago. A handful of other travelers, spread at respectful distances throughout the car, look straightforward. The conductor comes down the aisle and eyes my ticket but does not ask for it.

As we near the city, I peer out the window, eager to glimpse the familiar skyline. Through the dirt-clouded windows, though, I can tell that everything is different. Berlin has become a behemoth on the scale of Paris but with none of the grace of its older sister, like an awkward adolescent growing too quickly for its own body. Construction projects sprawl across fields and streets, cranes hovering over gaping holes in the ground.

We cross over the wide expanse of the Spree where the barges have begun to flow again, the much-needed goods trickling into the city, an intravenous drip. The train slows, weaving between the apartment buildings like a clattering snake. On either side, people in their flats eat lunch and read papers and iron clothes, as indifferent to being on display as the animals at the Tiergarten.

The train screeches into Alexanderplatz and I step off into the swarm of travelers moving haphazardly in all directions. Outside the station, I stop uncertainly, overwhelmed by the bright lights and noise after the months in bucolic Grunewald. The square is choked with motorcars and hackney cabs and omnibuses that have worn the cobblestones flat.

Struggling to breathe in the exhaust-filled air, I begin to walk, past the beer halls and Aschinger's restaurant belching forth sausage fumes and cigar smoke from its open windows. At the corner, a young Romani boy sits on the ground playing an accordion, its open case turned hopefully upward like an outstretched hand. I wind right and then left, feeling my way toward the Jewish quarter as if propelled by a force outside myself. Away from the square, the streets are narrow, tall four-

and five-story row houses lean upon one another, giving off a claustrophobic feel. New wooden poles climb high, wires lashing the sky overhead.

As I near our old neighborhood, the streets grow narrower still and the smell of onions and cabbage overtake those of petrol and exhaust. I turn onto Hirtenstrasse and stop. It is as if I have been transported back a century. The pavement is thick with bodies, women and children clustered by the vegetable carts, men queuing outside the Jewish community building for work or assistance. Foreign languages, Russian and others similarly eastern, fill the air. Refugees, I realize. The pogroms had always sent small groups of immigrants to Berlin, tiny ripples in our pond. But now with the war and the borders redrawn hundreds of thousands have been displaced, the ripple becoming a giant wave that threatens to engulf the entire quarter.

I am suddenly mindful of the eyes watching me, my pressed skirt and blouse so clearly out of place. I do not belong here anymore. Quickly I press onward. Our house sits in the middle of the next block, the overgrown garden beside the front steps like something out of a forgotten dream. My eyes travel to the upper floors. Though the broken glass has been cleared little is left but the shell. There is no sign of the work Papa had told me was taking place in anticipation of our return. He had lied to me, kept the dream alive, but in truth even if the house could be restored, the neighborhood is changed forever.

Despite the devastation, I see ghosts of myself as a girl everywhere, memories of games of hopscotch on the pavement, watching eagerly out the window for Papa to return. They seem tainted now, though, by a sad dark-haired woman who had not wanted to be there with me, and later, hushed whispers about her designed to conceal the truth. I turn and walk from the house with a sense of finality, a door closing.

A sharp breeze blows down the street, sending the newspapers scuffling along the pavement. The sun has begun to set sooner than I expected, the shortening of the days as summer runs into fall a trick that I seem to forget each year anew. It's getting late and Papa will be worried. I turn my back on the neighborhood and start toward the station.

It is evening now and as the train crosses the canal, I gaze out the window to the water where moonlight dances on the surface. Why had I come? There is nothing left here. I was searching for myself, or the girl I had once been. Could I find her if I returned to Paris or London? But retracing my steps will not provide the answers I seek.

A breeze ripples the surface, shattering it into a thousand fragments of light. I am dying inside, like that poor sprig of plant I brought back from Versailles, unable to survive in a cup of hard earth. Perhaps I always have been. But the time in Paris changed me, brought it to the surface, and it's as if I am drowning once and for all. I understand what Krysia was trying to tell me, that I am not living my own best life if I am not being true to myself.

I cannot stay with Stefan and live the rest of my life as a lie. For too long, I have blamed Papa, society, anything and everything but myself. But the truth is that this is a predicament of my own making. I should have been honest with Stefan that I was not ready to be married before the war, honest with Georg that I was married, honest with Papa about my feelings. Honest with myself.

I can start being honest now.

When the train reaches Grunewald, I cross the platform and climb on my bike, pedaling toward the villa with new resolve. I will talk to Papa, tell him again, firmly this time, that I'm not ready—perhaps a sojourn to England, some more time to study before settling down. It would not be a life with Georg, something far short of that. But I would be free.

At the villa gate, I stop. Papa will be angry, Stefan devastated, the family scandalized. But I have to do it. The relief of my decision is like air whooshing out of a balloon. I am sud-

denly energized, empowered. I walk in the house, race up to
the apartment.

I stop again. Opening this door will be irreversible, no chance
of going back. But I already pried it ajar in Paris; now I am just
flinging it wide. There is little to be afraid of anymore, so little left to lose. Scandal will hardly bother me, or Papa who has
already been so decimated by the aftermath of the conference.
Uncle Walter will be livid, of course, perhaps withhold support.
But I've never needed much to get by.

At the entrance to our rooms, I stop again, bracing myself to
open the door to my future. I walk through. Papa is standing
at the desk, leaning over some papers. I wait for him to rebuke
me for not leaving word that I had gone out, for the questions
that will necessitate a confession of my trip into the city. But
he remains still.

"Papa, if you have a moment I'd like to tell you…" I stop.
He isn't reading, I realize, but leaning over, grasping the desk
for support and trying to breathe. "Papa…"

He turns toward me with a sudden lurch, then collapses to
the floor.

CHAPTER EIGHTEEN

I do not remember screaming.

The moment I saw Papa fall to the floor I was back in the hotel elevator in Paris, the one that used to make my stomach jump. Only the bottom had dropped out and I was falling through the darkness. My mind reeled. It was August 24. It couldn't happen on August 24, not on a Sunday, not with our dinner sitting uneaten on the tray, the eggcups giving off that funny little smell. "Please," I said aloud, once, then over and over again. "Please." Papa was my entire world. Not like this. Not so soon. I would do anything, give anything. Was God punishing me for my transgressions, for stepping out of line and being unfaithful? I promised to never see Georg again, to stop even thinking about him. I would be a better daughter, woman, person—anything for a second chance.

One of the servants heard my screams, Tante Celia later told me, and called an ambulance. I rode to the hospital with Papa, sitting back from the gurney, pressed against the cold metal side

of the vehicle to allow the medic to minister to him, but holding his fingertips all the while. Then, when Papa disappeared
from sight behind the clinic doors, I collapsed onto Uncle Walter, who had somehow appeared beside me.

That was three days ago. Papa lies in a hospital bed, his face
as white as the sheets beneath it. He was not dead as I originally
feared, but had a heart attack. I've been at his bedside since then,
hours bleeding into days, the antiseptic smells and whirring ma-
chines now as familiar as my own breath.

My mind now recalls our Sabbath meal in our apartment last
Friday, less than a week ago. It was a routine affair just the two
of us. Had that unremarkable occasion been our last? Parents
leave first, or are supposed to, anyway. That is the way of the
world and no one knew it better than I, the lesson imprinted
young and deep at the age of nine. But Papa was everything and
he could no more cease to exist than the sun not rise.

Stop. I push the thoughts from my head. There will be time
for memories later. Right now he is still here.

I gaze out the wide window at the courtyard where nurses
wheel patients who are well enough to sit. It must be midafter-
noon, I judge from the way the sunlight angles onto the stone
path, trying to center myself from a place where time has ceased.
The hospital is one of the finest in Germany. Papa has a private
room with round-the-clock care, better food than most Berlin-
ers are enjoying these days.

On the far side of the bed, Celia dozes in a chair, mouth
agape. She, too, has scarcely left Papa's side since she ran into
the hospital and threw herself across the stretcher. "Darling,"
she cried, no longer concerned with propriety or who might
hear. Observing her hold his face and run her fingers through
his silver hair as though they were young lovers, I realized then
how little I knew of my father's other life. He had kept me, or
I had chosen to remain, a naive child.

Watching Celia hover by his bedside, I cannot help but think of Georg and how I cared for him when he was ill. If only he were here with me. Just a few hours ago I was about to tell Papa everything and make my bid for freedom. The gulf between that recent time and the present is a lifetime. How simple and silly that plan seems now. I thought that I had nothing left to lose. I had not understood how far there was still to fall.

"Margot?" Stefan is at my side then, holding out a cup with a shaking hand. "I thought you might like some tea." His hand is damp, I notice as I take it from him, and drops of pale brown liquid stain the front of his shirt. He still struggles gamely through the simplest of tasks, like carrying a drink while using his cane.

"Thank you." He stands above me as I take a sip, looking uneasily around the room. Does he mind coming here after his own months of convalescence? He has been with me without complaint each day, trying to help, though there is nothing to be done. "You should go home and rest," I say.

Relief crosses his face. "Are you certain?"

"We'll be fine. I'll ring you if there is news." I watch as he retreats down the hallway, guilty that his is not the comfort I seek.

I turn back to my father. "Papa?" I should let him sleep. He has awoken a handful of times, only to fall back into the long, deep slumber that the doctor assured us is so good for his recovery. But I am suddenly desperate to hear his voice. He does not respond and I am flooded with panic, hurtling back to the moment when I found him on the floor. "Papa?" I reach for the bell to summon the nurse.

But then his eyes flutter open. *"Liebchen?"* At the sound of his voice, Celia sits upright, her always perfect hair flattened to her forehead.

I lean forward. "Are you in pain?"

He shakes his head. "Not at all."

Celia stands. "I'll get the nurse," she says, unpersuaded.

When she has gone, Papa swallows. "I want to tell you…"

He pauses for breath, licks his lips. "If I should..." His voice trails off. He is not struggling to speak, but to find the words.

"No, don't say it. Don't even think it." I squeeze his hand, the need to touch him more acute now.

"I'm not giving up, I promise. I wouldn't leave you alone with Walter and Celia." Tears fill my eyes as he smiles gamely. "But someday it will happen. And when it does, take comfort in the fact that we've had everything."

I nod. Papa and I have lived closely and loved well, had years of conversations and shared meals and moments. It is the beauty of our relationship that makes the idea of losing him so hard to bear. There is nothing left to ask for but more time.

"About your mother," he says. "I want to explain." He speaks as though the revelation about her leaving had occurred days and not months ago. For a moment I wonder if he is confused. But his eyes are clear.

"It's fine. I understand." And I do. Even if he had told me and I had gone to find her, nothing would have changed. She would still have been the person who wanted to leave, and the rejection would have been worse if she had seen who I had become and turned her back, anyway. He lied all of these years to spare me that pain.

"Before I collapsed, you were going to tell me something."

I press my lips together. I had been standing on the precipice, staring into the abyss, about to tell him the truth and shatter something that could never be made whole again. But all of that changed when he collapsed. Papa needs the peace of knowing that I am cared for—it is the one thing I can give him by marrying Stefan. "I don't remember what I was going to say." In his weakened state, he seems to believe me. "I'm sure it was nothing important."

"Everything you say is important," he says, and in that moment I have never loved him more.

I take a deep breath. "Papa, about Paris... I'm so sorry." I am still steering well clear of the truth. "I never meant to cause you any embarrassment or difficulty."

He shakes his head, squeezing my fingers. "You are young and were lonely. But what if it's more than that?" He pauses to catch his breath then stares deep into my eyes. "It was more, wasn't it?" I look down. "With Georg, I mean."

I open my mouth to tell him that it is too far gone, that the world that was destroyed in Versailles that night cannot be rebuilt. But before I can respond, Celia returns with the doctor in tow.

We sit silently while the doctor examines Papa. I watch Celia. She was the one who summoned Stefan to Paris and I might hate her for it. But instead, I find myself regarding her now with pity—these stolen moments with my father are all she has, not a family or husband of her own. Did she want more or didn't she think she deserved it? And she'd tried, really tried. She would have done anything to see that the marriage went through, that the family honor remained intact. I suppose in some way she was protecting Papa from yet another blow.

"He should be fine," the doctor pronounces. Celia exhales audibly and my whole body goes slack with relief. "He can go home in a day or so."

"That seems soon," I remark.

The doctor shrugs. "He just needs rest." Papa's condition cannot be treated, but will always loom in the background, a ticking clock.

"We should postpone the wedding," I say, too eagerly, when the doctor has gone. Celia's right eyebrow arches. "Just until you are better, Papa. I won't get married without you."

"Of course not," he soothes. "The wedding is still a few days away. I would be there even if I was on a stretcher. But I won't be—I will walk you down the aisle." I nod, not placated by his response.

"But perhaps we should widen the aisle, in case you need

a chair," Celia frets, her preoccupation with the wedding returning.

"We can discuss that later. He needs his rest," I say protectively.

"So do you," Papa replies, his voice quiet but firm. "You should go home and sleep."

"I can stay," Celia offers.

I eye her uncertainly. Her goodwill toward my father is undeniable, but it is still a battle over territory.

"Fine," I relent, reluctantly acknowledging her place and sharing the responsibility for his well-being with her at last. I kiss Papa's cheek. "I will come back later."

I walk from the hospital, then hesitate. The sun is high above the buildings now, the Kurfürstendamm bustling with shoppers. The bucolic scene is a seeming interlude to the chaos that has recently grasped the city. Electric streetcars glide silently down the middle of the wide thoroughfare. I stroll past the terrace at Schwanneckes, filled with diners enjoying the lovely weather, the waiter offering newspapers to well-heeled coffee drinkers whose world has not been stopped by illness.

Watching the couples laugh over drinks, my longing for Georg is stronger than ever. After we'd left Paris, when I assumed he was there or had perhaps returned to Hamburg, it was easier somehow, picturing him in a faraway city. I imagined him in Versailles, sitting in the hotel library or walking in the park. But now knowing that he is here in Berlin, just miles away—the fact that we cannot be together is somehow even more unbearable.

Suddenly weary, I walk to the corner and get into a Renault taxi. As we speed from the city, I slump against the seat, overwhelmed. Papa nearly died. Georg is not far away, but he might as well be across an ocean since I cannot go to him.

At the villa, I walk up the darkened stairs. At the door to our apartment, I stop, remembering the moment I stood here just days earlier, planning to tell Papa the truth. Of course, that is impossible now. My plan to free myself from marrying Stefan begins to fade and blow away like dust.

I throw myself across the bed, sobbing.

CHAPTER NINETEEN

The next morning I am awakened by the chiming of the doorbell. I open my eyes. Sun slants brightly through the filmy lace curtains, creating patterns that dance on the cream bed linens. Through the open window, I hear a familiar voice on the doorstep below. Krysia!

I jump up and dress hurriedly, then run from the apartment. Krysia stands in the foyer looking uneasy in the grand, unfamiliar surroundings. "You came!" I cry as I fly down the stairs. I throw my arms around her, forgetting in my excitement the proper kiss on each cheek.

She removes her hat. "I'm sorry to arrive unannounced. I sent a response, but only just days ago when I was certain I could come." I'd sent her a wedding invitation on a whim, with no real expectation she'd actually make it. "With as slow as the post is these days, I suppose I arrived before it did. I just got off the train," she adds, gesturing apologetically toward her dress.

But she appears fresh and unwrinkled, her hair immaculately in place. "I can book a room."

"Nonsense, there's plenty of space here." I turn to the butler. "Charles, you'll have the one next to mine readied please?"

"Straight away, *fraulein*."

"Marcin sends his congratulations," Krysia says when the butler has left. "He would have come but he's working on a new piece."

"So he's composing again?"

"More so than ever. He thinks it's the peace of the countryside, but I'm sure all of the energy from Paris helped."

I drink Krysia in, the familiar sight of her righting my topsy-turvy world. With the trains still in disrepair and the border heavily guarded, it was no small feat to get from Poland to Germany these days. No, she had moved mountains to be here. She had come for the wedding, despite knowing that it was a farce— or perhaps *because* it was a farce and I would need her support more than ever to get through it.

"I'm so glad you're here," I say, meaning it. I did not realize before Krysia how lonely for company I was, but since she had filled the space and gone again I'd felt the emptiness acutely. "Let's get you settled." I lead her up the stairs and show her to the room closest to mine. "There are grander suites in other parts of the house," I say, an apologetic tone to my voice. "If you'd like something with a better view of the lake..."

She shakes her head. "This is lovely."

I exhale quietly. I picked the room because I wanted her close to me. "I'll let you freshen up." I go downstairs to the sitting room, sink into one of the plush velvet chairs. It has been a week of reunions—first Georg, and now Krysia. Suddenly it is as if all of Paris has followed me here. I am very glad to see her, though.

Twenty minutes later Krysia comes downstairs, wearing a fresh cotton dress I do not recognize from Paris. "Are you hungry?" I ask.

"No, I tend not to eat much after traveling. But I'd love to stretch my legs after so long on the train." I lead her through the foyer. "So this is your familial home," she remarks as we reach the terrace.

"My great-great-grandfather built the original house in the early nineteenth century," I say, feeling like a tour guide. "And then his sons added to the structure." The house, built over the course of a century, has a patchwork feel, a variety of architectural styles thrown together at random.

"It must have been a fun place to play as a child."

Was that true? The house had always seemed so quiet. Uncle Walter, married to his work, had no family. I'd been the only child and I'd had to invent my own games. "There were certainly a lot of places to explore," I concede.

"Oh?"

"There are underground tunnels, built during the Franco-Prussian War to ferry supplies from market back to the house."

"How interesting. Are they still used?"

We follow the path around the lake. A brackish smell wafts upward from the murky water. "I don't know. Perhaps by the servants in winter if the weather is poor. But enough about the house—tell me about Krakow."

Her face widens into a smile. "It's beautiful, just as lovely as I remember from when I was a girl. We have an apartment in the city center and then the house in the countryside where Marcin likes to work. I join him there for weekends." Then her eyes grow cloudy. "Of course, I miss Paris." She means Emilie. "Nothing is ever quite the same after you've been elsewhere, is it?"

I shake my head, recalling my visit to our old neighborhood in the city. The Berlin of my childhood, our town house with its secret corners and garden, is gone. But even if our block in the Jewish quarter had not been marred by the vandals and changed by immigrants, it would not have been the same. There is a hollowness about it now that comes as much from me and the places I've been as the things that have happened here.

"And your father, is he enjoying his work away from the conference?"

I stop and turn to her. "Oh, Krysia!" I'd been so overjoyed at her unexpected arrival that I had nearly forgotten the events of the past few days. Quickly I tell her about Papa's collapse.

"He's going to be fine," she reassures firmly.

"I know. He should be coming home tomorrow."

She puts her arm around my shoulders. "Your father is strong—and he has you to live for."

Me, I think, and the wedding. My heart sinks. "I just feel so lost."

"Then so much the better I am here."

I look down, kicking at a rock with my shoe. "I saw him."

"Georg? I thought he went back to Hamburg. Does he have an apartment here?"

"He's taken a room at the Grand. I didn't even know that he was in Berlin. But he showed up here for a business meeting with Uncle Walter. It's almost like fate..."

"Nonsense. You can't attach some sort of higher meaning to it. It doesn't matter why he was here. The question is what you do about it."

"I almost told Papa that I was canceling the wedding," I offer. "But then he collapsed." There is a plaintive note to my voice, a student asking for credit for an answer that is partially correct.

But Krysia does not award points for effort. "And now?" The fact that I was going to tell Papa means nothing—only the result and how it changes my life matters.

"There's nothing to be done. I'm marrying Stefan. Or remarrying him, I should say. With Papa recuperating, there's no other choice."

She opens her mouth and I brace myself for the lecture. "Perhaps it is for the best," she says, surprising me. "Georg is surely much changed, after everything that happened."

I want to tell her that, beneath his disappointment over the treaty and the way I have hurt him, he is still the same man with whom I fell in love.

"Would you like me to play at the wedding?" she asks, before I can respond.

"Oh, Krysia…" I am touched by her gesture, her willingness to support my marriage, even though she believes it is a mistake. "I'd love that. But you're a guest."

"Perhaps just a few songs, then."

"That would be lovely. Though I'd much rather—" I pause "—you stand up with me." I wait for her to refuse to be witness to the deception.

"I'd be honored."

We walk for several minutes in silence before reaching the low footbridge that bisects the lake into two ovals. She stops, staring out across the water where a moored rowboat bumps against its docking. "I never told her, before leaving Paris. Emilie," she adds, though, of course, I knew whom she meant. Her faces searches mine, asking for confirmation that she had done the right thing.

"You did what you thought was best," I say, offering the absolution that is not mine to give. At least Krysia tried to do the right thing. Did my mother think she had done what was best for me, leaving me to those who actually wanted to raise me? Or did she just not care? Krysia nods, my answer enough.

A few minutes later, as we near the house, a bell chimes, signaling lunch. "You must be hungry by now," I say.

"A bit," she concedes. In the dining room, the side bar has been set with cold dishes: cured meats, herring in cream, smoked salmon, freshly cut fruit. We fill our plates and start for the table on the terrace. In the long gravel service driveway that runs along the right side of the house, a truck has pulled up and is unloading tables and chairs from the back. It is only two days until the wedding and the preparations have begun in earnest. My throat tightens.

Uncle Walter sticks his head out of the door. "Have you seen Noel?" he asks, referring to his aide.

I shake my head. "Uncle Walter, may I present Krysia Smok? She's come from Krakow for the wedding."

Krysia rises and Uncle Walter takes her hand absentmindedly. "Welcome." Then he turns to me. "I'm sure you've seen that the deliveries have begun."

"Yes. And the chuppa?" It was one of my few requests for the wedding that we procure the same canopy from the synagogue that I had seen in my parents' wedding photo.

Uncle Walter shakes his head. "Destroyed, I'm afraid, during one of the ransackings of the Jewish quarter." He pronounces this last part firmly as though it proves everything he has been trying to tell Papa about the danger of keeping to our own kind. I want to respond that the Jews have not been the target of the violence. Rather, they have just been caught up in the general melee of the city, their belongings destroyed when in the path of the protesters just the same as their Gentile neighbors, any affluence a target of equal opportunity.

Knowing further political debate is pointless, I decide to focus on the chuppa. "And there's none other like it to be had?" Uncle Walter hesitates. "It needn't be a fancy one," I press. The Jewish wedding canopy need only have four poles, a piece of cloth. But it isn't about the difficulty of procuring it. He views the chuppa as an embarrassment, a sign that we are somehow different from our non-Jewish friends and that assimilation is not quite complete. Krysia pats my hand under the table reassuringly, signaling not to make a fuss. But I cannot pull back now. "I'll not be married without a chuppa," I declare, drawing my line in the sand. This is the last strain of who we are, our lives as Jews before the war.

"I'll see what I can do," he says, a tactical retreat. "Though with Celia still at the hospital and your father coming home to-morrow, you'll have to take more of a role in making sure the wedding deliveries are done properly. The flowers will be here in the morning, so you'll want to be here when they arrive."

"But I'm going to the polls tomorrow and I want to get an early start." Parliamentary elections are the next day, yet another hapless attempt to construct a coalition government among the Social Democrats and their allies. It is the first election since we've returned to Germany and my first chance to vote.

"The polls? Surely you aren't planning to go."

"Women have the right to vote now."

"I know. It's a right that I lobbied for and spent a great deal of time and effort securing." He sounds as though he is per-sonally responsible for women's suffrage. "It is a great victory in principle. But you can't be seriously considering venturing down into that fracas." He had never understood Papa's choice to remain in the crowded urban neighborhood where he had grown up rather than at the villa. He has a point, of course—the polling places are dangerous, elections being a flashpoint in an already tumultuous political atmosphere.

"I am not just thinking. I'm going to do it." I set my jaw stubbornly.

"It's not as if one vote will make a difference." Easy enough for a man to say—he has always had the right. But I remember Papa's words: *the proudest day of my life,* he had said when speak-ing of my exercising the vote. I have to go through with this for him as much as for myself.

"I can supervise the deliveries," Krysia says gently, stepping in. I had nearly forgotten she was beside me. I am embarrassed to have her witness all of this play out. Uncle Walter shrugs in-differently and retreats back into the house.

The sky is just growing pink over the lake the next morning as I slip from the villa. Outside, I yawn, more tired than I usu-

THE AMBASSADOR'S DAUGHTER

ally am at this hour. Krysia and I had sat up talking late into the night, jumping easily from one topic to the next, making up for all of the months since Paris. I make my way to the train station by bicycle, my growing anticipation clearing exhaustion like a broom to cobwebs. Grunewald is still asleep and even the sellers at market have not yet come to set out their wares. But when I step off the train at Alexanderplatz, the city is at full bustle, as though it had never bothered to rest. Businessmen in suits mix with revelers making their way from the bars to the steam baths or home, dressed in the previous night's clothes.

It is not yet eight o'clock as I approach the crumbling brick municipal building close to our old neighborhood, my official residence from which I am required to vote. My excitement fades to nervousness. The street in front of the polling place is chaotic—political demonstrators from all parties, held back by police, choke the pavement, exhorting the hordes of voters that shuffle toward the polls to take a particular view. Taking a deep breath, I wade into the crowd, pushing toward the municipal building. I am the only woman, I realize as I join the queue. As I near, the men who had been jostling and talking grow quiet, eyeing me as if I am a foreign creature. For a moment I wonder if I was mistaken about the suffrage bill actually passing.

The line creeps forward up the damp stone steps to the municipal building. Through the open door, the smell of stale coffee drifts out. Suddenly I am five years old, coming here with Papa to register for school. My stomach tugs with longing. He should have been here with me for this moment.

"Such chaos," a man in front of me laments. "Not like the good old days." Inwardly, I laugh. The good old days of totalitarianism, of kaisers and kings. There were people who would always find comfort in being told what to do and in the clear, rigid lines of social division. The world was more chaotic now than it had ever been, but at the same time bursting with possibility.

Behind me, voices rise. Two of the political demonstrators have gotten inside the building and are arguing heatedly with a poll worker who orders them to leave. As they begin pushing each other, the crowd surges backward to escape the skirmish. Strangers press against me from all directions, making it impossible to breathe. I cry out.

A hand grabs me and pulls me through the crowd toward the door. I yelp, struggling to escape, but I cannot wrest myself from the unseen grasp. As I see the open sky, I relax slightly. But I am still being pulled. I wrench away and make it to the street before turning to confront my assailant. Georg stands behind me, breathing hard.

"What are you doing here?" I demand. I find myself staring at his mouth, flung back to our kiss by the pond in Versailles.

"Or, you could say thank you," he replies pointedly, brushing off the sleeves of his uniform.

Annoyance rises up, eclipsing my desire. "For what? I didn't need rescuing." I point toward the crowd at the municipal building, larger than ever. "And now I've lost my place in the queue."

"It was foolish to come," he admonishes, sounding more like Uncle Walter than I would have thought possible.

"You still haven't told me what you are doing here. Are you following me?"

"In a sense, yes." A shiver runs up my spine. "Your father rang me from the hospital, with Celia's help, of course. He knew you were coming to vote and he asked me to check on you." So he had not chosen to come after me, after all, but had done so dutifully at my father's behest. Had Papa softened toward Georg? More likely, he was just concerned about my well-being and saw Georg as being in the best position to help. Georg gazes over the crowd, which has descended into a widespread brawl. "This is madness."

"I'm still going to vote."

A faint smile plays around his lips. "I had no doubt. Come with me." Without waiting, Georg takes my hand and tucks it beneath his arm and walks briskly toward the stairs of the municipal building. I start to protest that I do not need his help. Then, taking in the shoving, fighting men, I decide against it. Georg's hand is warm around mine as he leads me through the crowd. I wait for my anxiety to rise again, but it does not. Here, in this most cramped of places, I feel comfortable and safe. I understand then that my claustrophobia has not really been about closed spaces at all, but about yearning to breathe freely—something I can do when I am with him.

Inside, Georg waves his government identification card to bypass the queue. At the front of the hall, he stops short of the registration table, gesturing for me to go ahead.

"You voted already?"

"Yes, by absentee ballot in Hamburg. I think that the National Socialists are most promising." I stare at him in disbelief. Georg had always been a bit more conservative. I notice then that he wears a cornflower in his lapel, the bright blue signaling his shift to the right.

"But, Georg, they're barbarians." Suddenly we are back in the study at Versailles, quarreling over politics. "How can you possibly support their position?"

"Weimar is weak. The right are the ones who are willing to crush the opposition and make a strong stand for Germany's future." He had been so burned by the treaty that he now sees militarism as the only way.

"Perhaps the Americans..." I begin.

"The Americans?" He cuts me off, his voice is harsher than I have ever heard him speak. I glance anxiously over my shoulder. It is not wise to discuss politics loudly in public these days. But he does not seem to care who hears him. "They came and created this mess and then didn't even ratify the treaty." He has an undeniable point—the Americans are an ocean away, unscathed by the disaster they left behind.

I struggle to find the words to make him understand reason, but find none. Once I'd been able to help him see the right way. *True north,* he'd called me. But Versailles had changed him. We are both less open now, calcified in our respective positions.

I present my identification and the woman escorts me to a booth where there are a dizzying array of choices. I punch the slots on the cards for the candidates. *This is for you, Papa,* I think as I finish.

When I emerge from the voting booth a few minutes later, the melee has mostly cleared, broken up by brown-shirted Frei-korps, the burly police who are known to be quick with a billy club. Outside, Georg leads me away from the crowd to the corner where his car is waiting. I wait for him to suggest coffee, anything to give us more time together so that we do not have to say goodbye as swiftly as we did at the villa. "Shall we?" I offer when he does not, gesturing down the wide, tree-lined Unter den Linden. He hesitates and I brace myself for the rejection of his refusal. But then he nods in assent.

Neither of us speaks as we stroll beneath the bowed branches of the chestnut trees in the direction of the Tiergarten. I study him out of the corner of my eye, searching for some sign that he is glad to see me or eager to get away. But his face is impassive.

A few minutes later, I hear the carousel tinkling unseen behind high bushes. We turn into the park, which is speckled this midweek morning with crisp-skirted nannies pushing prams and children playing hoops in the grass. In the brush alongside the path, a man stoops to gather leaves for fuel. We cross the footbridge over the canal, a thin strip of brown water amid two steep dirt banks. Georg turns off onto a side path, shrouded high on both sides by birch trees and brush. Suddenly it is as if we are back in the Tuileries Gardens the night the treaty was announced, alone in a world made for just the two of us.

He stops then and turns to me. "I was sorry to hear about your father. You must have been terribly frightened."

"He's recuperating slowly but surely. He's a fighter, stronger than he looks."

He smiles. "It runs in the family, no doubt." Then his expression grows serious. "I wanted to come to see you, I mean him, but I feared it would only complicate matters for you." It would have. I had not told Stefan about my encounter with Georg at the villa or the fact that he was in Berlin. A run-in between the two men would have been an unbearable reprise of that night in Versailles. But in my anguish, his comfort was the one for which I had yearned.

"I'm sorry we didn't have more time to talk at the house the other day," I offer. "I was surprised to see you."

"No matter." His lips twist. "You must be quite busy with preparations for the wedding." The last word is clearly distasteful, almost spat. He is angrier than I realized when we last met. Had seeing me again dredged up his feelings of betrayal and hurt, or had I simply been too caught off guard at our encounter the other day to notice?

I reach out and touch his forearm. "Georg, about that..." I debate telling him the truth: that I was about to cancel my wedding to Stefan and come back to him when Papa collapsed. But knowing how close we had come would only make the fact that we cannot be together harder to bear. I swallow, pull my hand back. "The wedding is tomorrow."

"I know." His words are neutral, but there is a pain to his voice he cannot mask. The notion of me marrying Stefan was hard enough when it was in the future. But faced with the immediacy of it, his veneer begins to crumble. Seeing him now, I understand that he had not fled the villa the other day because he was angry about Paris. Rather, being that close to me and unable to be together was simply unbearable.

I swallow, fighting back the urge to throw my arms around him. "Georg, I know how difficult this is..." Then I stop—my words sound condescending and I will not add to his injury. "I will hate your fiancée someday, I am sure," I joke feebly.

But he shakes his head, unwilling to see the humor. "I've no intention of meeting anyone. I'm quite fine alone." He has withdrawn again to the solitary man he was before he met me. His isolation and retreat to a place I cannot reach is almost worse than any jealousy I might feel over another woman. "Anyway..." He clears his throat and turns away and I can see the faintest glisten of wetness at the corner of his right eye. "I'm leaving Berlin," he announces.

"But you can't! What about your position with the new government?" He does not respond. I'm driving him away. Seeing me once or by happenstance was unbearable enough. But we travel in concentric circles, and though the city is large, we are inevitably bound to run into or hear news of one another. Knowing that I am so close, but that I am married and can never be his, is more than he can stand.

"It was too good to be true." He smiles ruefully. "It had to be, didn't it? Congratulations on your marriage," he manages, his voice gruff. "Don't be nervous about the wedding. I'm told that it is just a big party—and a bit about lifetime commitment." He turns away.

"Georg," I cry out, a note of desperation creeping into my voice. I cannot bear to have him walk away and, having felt the fire again, to now have it go cold. He looks back and vulnerability and rage break his face into a thousand pieces. "Goodbye." He kisses me on the cheek, his lips pressing hard against my skin, as if he is trying to give me in that moment all that cannot be. I reach out and cup my hand around the back of his neck, holding him. Everything I have ever wanted is both inches and lifetimes away.

Then I release him and he straightens. "Godspeed, Margot." As he walks away, shoulders low, the air grows empty and cold around me.

Georg disappears, enveloped by the trees. I watch sadly, fighting the urge to go after him. What did I expect? It isn't fair to ask him to stand by and watch as I start my life with someone else. I retrace our route from the Tiergarten, feeling the emptiness of the space beside me where Georg walked. Laughter drifts from an unseen woman on the far side of the trees, her happiness somehow an affront.

As I reach the corner by the municipal building, Uncle Walter's Model T appears and he steps out from the backseat. His face is thunderous and I wait for him to rebuke me for going to vote. "Margot." There is a note of urgency to his voice I've not before heard. "Celia rang. She said it's about your father, and she needs you at once."

CHAPTER TWENTY

The ground shifts sideways beneath me. Uncle Walter steps forward and helps me into the rear of the car. Inside, Krysia sits by the far window, brow knotted. "What happened?" I move closer and she squeezes my hand tight. The car turns not in the direction of the hospital, but winds out of the city on the motorway toward Grunewald. "It has to be all right, doesn't it, if they've sent him home?" There is no response.

Thirty minutes later, we reach the villa and I leap from the car, scarcely waiting for it to come to a stop. As I race down the hallway to our suite, I brace myself for the worst. But when we reach his room, Papa is sitting up in bed, showing no signs of distress. "Papa, what is it? Are you feeling unwell?"

He shakes his head. "Quite the opposite. I feel better just being home. I was worried about you, though. I heard something on the radio about a skirmish at the polling place."

"I'm fine," I say. He should know, having sent Georg after me. "There was a bit of a fight, but then Georg…"

"There's to be another wedding," Tante Celia announces, cutting me off. She sits by Papa's bed, clasping his hand, assuming her rightful place. I cock my head, confused by her outburst. Celia holds up her hand. "We're engaged!"

So that was the emergency. For the first time since Celia's call, I breathe normally. I gesture to Krysia, who has appeared but hangs back near the door. "You remember Krysia?"

Papa smiles. "Lovely to see you again. It is a great comfort to my daughter to have you here." Then he turns back to me. "I'm sorry to have worried you. We wanted you to be the first to know—and to tell you in person."

"Engaged," Celia repeats, waving her hand like a flag.

I cringe, not wanting to look. Had Papa really given her my mother's ring, the one she had left behind when she fled? No, he would not have been so cruel. The band around Celia's fourth finger is a more modern design, just her sort of thing, with lots of stones and detail. I turn to Papa. "How did you…?" He must have bought it in Paris and saved it, waiting for the right time to propose. I remember then how he'd tried to get the three of us to dinner. But then I had learned the truth about my mother and forestalled things once more.

"We're going to get married in the spring," Celia says, giddy as a girl.

I feel Papa watching my face, searching for signs of disapproval. "After all that has happened," Papa adds, "we don't want to wait any longer." It is more than that—all of these years, while my mother was out there still alive, he was still technically married. Finally, he is free. My thoughts turn improbably to Uncle Walter, who has disappeared from the room, and I recall his angry expression when he met me at the polls. What did he think of the relationship, now too public for him to ignore? Would he be furious that Papa had "ruined" one of his sisters before moving on to the next—or relieved to have the long-unwed Celia cared for?

I hesitate. Should I tell them that it is too soon after mother's death? Papa would listen, perhaps persuade Celia to delay. They have waited years, though, caught in a limbo not of their own making. Part of me wants to keep Papa all for myself. But I cannot deny them this chance for happiness that might not come again. I force a smile. "Mazel tov." Their faces break with relief in unison.

A footman enters the room then and sets down a tray of sandwiches. "I'd love for you to stand up with me," Celia says. Not waiting for an answer, she lifts the plate of sandwiches from the tray and offers them to us as though we are at a picnic. "I'm thinking about the spa at Baden for the honeymoon. The waters would be good for your father's health." She really does, in her own strange way, care for him a great deal.

"Celia, would you mind looking over the flower deliveries that arrived this morning?" Krysia asks when we have finished eating. She is pulling Celia away, trying to give me a moment alone with Papa.

I take his hand, staring out the window, not speaking. "You seem troubled, my dear. Is it our engagement? I didn't want to announce it on the eve of your wedding, but Celia…"

"No, it's fine," I reply quickly. I am a bit jealous—Papa and Celia are able to be with the person they genuinely love. But it is more than that: seeing their happiness reminds me of how I should feel about my marriage, and how I do not. "I don't mind. And I'm so glad you're home."

"Then what?" His brow wrinkles.

I look down, running my hand along the edge of his bedsheet to smooth it. I should not be worrying him in his condition. Tears fill my eyes. "It's nothing." But avoiding the truth is what brought us to this place in the first place. I cannot keep it from him any longer. "What if I'm not ready to marry Stefan?"

"I think," he replies, "that you will never be ready. That's what you wanted to talk to me about the other day, wasn't it?" I nod. "Then don't."

I stare at him, mouth agape. "You mean, I don't have to marry him?" Even now, I cannot bring myself to admit to Papa that we are already married.

"This isn't the eighteenth century, darling. You don't have to marry anyone. I'd like to see you settled, of course, while I'm still here. But there are worse things than being unsettled." He is thinking of my mother and the years of loneliness he faced after she left.

"But the wedding is tomorrow."

He waves his hand. "It's just a big party," he says, his words a refrain of what Georg had said earlier. "Now go find him." The emphasis on this last word leaves no confusion about whom he is speaking.

My eyes widen. "You mean that?" It is the first time we have spoken of the situation since Paris.

He nods. "The light in your eyes every time you look at him would be hard for a father to miss—and unfair to deny. Shame on me for pushing what society expected over your happiness." The illness has emboldened him somehow, made him view things more clearly. "Go. Be happy."

My heart lifts. He is giving me his blessing, uttering the words I never thought I would hear. "I appreciate that. But I can't hurt Stefan after all he has been through." Then I picture Georg's face, alienated and alone, as we said goodbye. He could never trust me again. "It's too late, anyway."

"If Celia and I are proof of anything, it's that it is never too late. Never mind, you know best on that front. But, darling, if it truly cannot be, let it go. Don't be a prisoner of the past." Before he can say more, Celia and Krysia are back. He squeezes my hand, silently assenting to whatever decision I make.

"We should let you rest," Krysia says.

I wait for Papa to protest. But he lies back, his face pale from the effort of conversation. "Look after her, will you?" he says, and Krysia, now an old friend, laughs conspiratorially.

"That silly woman, scaring me like that," I say when we are out of earshot.

"You aren't going to change Celia, or anyone else. Why drive yourself mad trying?"

"It was Celia, you know. She summoned Stefan to Paris to keep me from Georg."

"I see." Her tone makes it clear that she regards this bit of information about the past irrelevant. "Did you have the chance to tell your father the truth?"

"I did. He brought it up, actually."

We stop in the hallway, the door to her room on one side, mine the other. "What are you going to do now?"

"There's nothing to be done. It's too late."

"Even if it is too late for you and Georg, that doesn't mean you have to stay here trapped with Stefan. Go to America, see the world."

"I can't leave Papa."

"You aren't your mother," she says gently. "Children are supposed to leave. And he has Celia now." She opens the door to her room and walks inside, closing it behind her.

As I cross the hallway, the phone in our sitting room rings and I rush to answer it before it disturbs Papa. *"Hallo,* Margot *hier."*

"Margot, it's Stefan," he says as though I might not recognize his voice.

I squeeze the receiver hard. "Stefan, is something wrong?" It is unusual for him to ring and I find myself praying for a small catastrophe, nothing too serious, just something that will necessitate postponing the wedding.

"Not at all. I wanted to call you one last time before tomorrow." To confirm that it is real, make sure that I would be going through with it. "How's your father?"

"Home and resting."

"My cousins have tried to arrange a stag night," he confides. "Out in the city, beer and cigars, the works." There is a note of excitement in his voice, joy at being able to do the normal things a groom should do.

"Well, don't strain yourself."

"Perhaps I might call round afterward," he teases. "A preview of the wedding night."

"Don't you dare!" A bit of playful creeps into my voice, reminding me of how we were before war and adulthood crashed down upon us. Perhaps our life together will not be altogether bad.

"But we're already…"

"Shh." I cut him off, suddenly apprehensive, as though it is not just he and I on the line and someone might learn our secret. Though, did it really matter that much anymore?

"Anyway, I just wanted to say good-night." His call is a confirmation that all of this is real and that the wedding will happen as planned.

"I shall see you tomorrow." I set the receiver back in its hook with a click. I might have had a hen night, the bride's equivalent party, if I'd had the friends locally to plan one. But I don't mind.

Restless now, I step from the apartment and make my way down the stairs. The portraits on the wall, solemn-faced men who had walked these corridors for centuries, look down on me piously, whispering. My stomach rumbles, reminding me that I had missed dinner and lunch. I walk through the darkened foyer to the kitchen. It is deserted, the freshly polished stove gleaming in the moonlight. The smell of lemon cleanser hangs in the air.

I stare out the window over the sink into the night, replaying Papa's words in my mind. The notion that he would support my decision to leave Stefan for Georg, despite the fact that he is not Jewish and a thousand other differences, is monumental. But it doesn't matter—I am already married to Stefan and I have taken a vow to stand by him. Even if I could just walk away, I had pushed Georg away, this time for good. There is no going back.

There is a faint rustling, the movement of someone behind me. I turn. "Hello?" But the space is empty. Suddenly the familiar kitchen seems somehow chilling.

No longer hungry, I start back to the apartment. As I cross the foyer, I stop before the open door of the great room. It has been set for the wedding, the rows of chairs divided by a wide aisle. A chuppa, more modern than the lace canopy I'd wanted but a concession by Uncle Walter, nonetheless, stands at the front of the room. An image flashes through my mind of the room set just like this one. But a coffin stands at the front in place of the canopy. I stifle a scream. It is a nightmare that I've had so many times, but could not remember until just now. Tomorrow is not my wedding—it is my funeral.

Upstairs, I walk to the open window in my bedroom, where a gentle breeze blows the curtains inward. Suddenly, seized with the urge to jump, I step back, terrified by the thought.

Don't be a prisoner of those who have gone, Papa said. He was speaking of my mother, I know, and the way he had allowed her memory to stop him from living fully for so many years. But so had I. I'd been so caught up in trying to please everyone and fulfill expectations, I had not lived.

Leave, a voice inside me says. I would not have to marry Stefan. Papa has Celia now. I could, as Krysia had suggested, see the world.

The idea is growing now, gaining strength. Impulsively, I pull out a small travel bag and throw a few things into it. I can buy the rest of what I need once I have gone. I grab the scarf Krysia had knitted for me from the back of the chair and head for the door.

I look across the hallway at the room where Krysia is staying. I cannot go without telling her, not after she has come all of this way. I rap on the door lightly so as not to wake Papa or anyone else. "Krysia?" I whisper. She does not answer. I try the knob, but the door is locked. I will have to leave her a note, and one for my father, as well. I return to our apartment and find two sheets of paper on Papa's desk, then look without success for a pen.

I carry the paper and my bag downstairs, start toward Uncle Walter's study to find a pen. The door is ajar, I notice. How odd. In contrast to Papa's night-owl habits, my uncle has always kept a strict day schedule. I hope Papa hasn't tried to get out of bed to do some work.

I push open the door. The study is empty, lights dark. One of the housecleaners must have left it open. As I turn to leave, a whiff of something familiar tickles my nose. The smell of lilac perfume.

"Hello…" I call into the darkness, a funny feeling tugging at my stomach. There is no answer and for a second I am relieved. But then, as if propelled by a force not my own, I move forward toward Uncle Walter's desk. The papers I'd been holding drop from my hand and flutter to the floor.

There, crouched by a file taken from the safe, is Krysia.

CHAPTER TWENTY-ONE

"What…?" I cannot finish the question. As Krysia slowly stands, I search for a possible explanation. Perhaps she was lost. She turns to me and, unable to mask the truth, her usually impassive face crumples.

"You," I said, disbelief overcoming me. "You're a spy." She opens her mouth, but no sound comes out. The document, clutched in her hand in my uncle's darkened study, makes it impossible to deny. Had she done it for the money? Perhaps Ignatz had been blackmailing her, too.

Then, improbably, she laughs, swiping at the hair that has sprung forth from her usually well-ordered mane. "Spy. That's such a grand term. People think that espionage is some vast sophisticated machine. In reality, it's just lots of little bits, farmers and policemen and housewives living in border towns. There's no giant conspiracy. People feel safer somehow believing such fears because it distracts them from the things they should worry about, harder questions of poverty and justice." She is rambling now, as perturbed as I've ever seen her. Stalling for time. Fine perspiration coats her upper lip.

She has not denied it. "It isn't possible," I say slowly.

"Why? Because I'm a woman?"

"You're a musician. I would not have thought…"

But she does not appear to take offense. "Everyone played a role during the war. Nuns obtained information from prisoners and convalescents. Young girls watched the train routes to detect enemy movement. I was approached early in the war, years before we ever met, by another musician who asked if I wanted to help. I found that I was good at it. Our touring for concerts gave us the perfect excuse to move between countries, to carry papers and information over borders. No one would think to check the lining of a violin case for documents. A piano might become a drop box." Drop box. My head swims. "Even music became a kind of code."

I recall then the man who had come to the piano at the dinner party that night. "The sheet music…"

"An effective way for sharing information," she concedes. "Invisible in plain sight."

"You betrayed me. Got close to me in order to steal information from my father and Georg."

"I never planned it. When you found me and started asking questions, it seemed like an inconvenience. It was only after Ignatz discovered how useful you could be…"

"That you decided to use me for your own purposes," I finish bitterly. I see the past months replayed as a movie but it is all different now, each scene orchestrated like a puppet theater. Every conversation where I had confided and she had listened sympathetically was a setup, her mining each sentence for information. "He said you weren't involved."

"That was a lie. In part, because he wanted to take credit for having found you and persuaded you to help—in part, to protect my leadership." Red Thorn—it is not a man at all—Krysia is the head of the organization. She was not doing this out of desperation or for money. She believed in the work that she was doing.

"I never planned it," she repeats. "Our friendship was real, Margot, you must believe that. I felt a connection to you from the first, even before I realized who you were. But yes, I am involved with intelligence work. No one is watching out for our interests but ourselves. Not now and not a hundred years from now." Is she talking about her interests personally, or her country's? "I'm sorry," she says, but her voice dispassionate, somewhere short of cold. "I was doing what I had to do. You would have done the same."

I would not, I want to tell her. But the point is moot. "And Marcin?"

"Sweet Marcin is a cellist—a very gifted cellist. He knows nothing of this. I cannot burden him with such worries and he would be furious knowing the risks that I have taken. He's a pragmatist, like your father, believing people are neither altogether as good nor as bad as they seem, that everything cycles with time and we cannot altogether make a difference." More composed now, she points at the bag that sits by my feet. "Going somewhere?"

"I..." I falter, instantly on the defensive. "You told me to see the world. Take charge of my destiny."

"There is a difference between going on an adventure and running away." She has a point. I had fled Paris, now Berlin. If I left like this, secretly in the middle of the night, I was somehow always going to be running away.

"The document from Georg's study," I say, unwilling to let her change the subject for long. "You took it, didn't you?" She looks away and in her hesitation I see layers of the onion not yet peeled back. She had brought me the herbs for Georg's tea, perhaps intending to steal the document from him herself. But I had drunk them instead and then, when I had grown drowsy and fallen asleep, she'd made her move. "But why would you go to all of that trouble? I was going to give the document to Ignatz, anyway." Impulsively, I reach down and grab the document that is in her hands. It is a blueprint of the villa, showing entrances to the house, the underground pathways built a century ago between the servants' cottages and the mansion. Access to the house. But she already had access. No, the document was for someone else.

"Krysia…" There is a moment of interminable silence between us. "You aren't working for the communists, are you?" She does not answer. "Then who? The Americans?" I stand up straight, meeting her eyes. "You can tell me or you can tell the police."

"What is it that you want from me?"

"The truth. You owe me that much."

"The West." Her shoulders slump. "The British, to be precise. I really did start working with a musician friend to help the communists. But British intelligence was onto me quickly and they approached me and asked me to work for them. 'Turned me,' I guess is the term. Not that it was hard—I couldn't have continued once they knew. And the communists were in such disarray at that point, all of the turmoil and infighting. Working for the West really did seem like the best way to help the war effort and to secure a future for Poland."

"So you switched sides." She had turned in Ignatz to the police not to protect me, but perhaps he was getting too close to the truth about her.

"I suppose. Or I became, as they call it, a double agent. That sounds very glamorous, doesn't it?" she jokes feebly.

I do not respond. Regardless of whom she is spying for, I am equally betrayed. "You spied on me."

"Not on you exactly." No, of course not. I was inconsequential. But she had used me to gain access and the information she needed to know. "When Ignatz roped you in, it was a bonus— keep tabs on what he was up to while seeing if you were of use.

We didn't actually think you'd have the steel to go through with helping him. We had not expected you to take the document he wanted so quickly. I had to make sure it didn't actually fall into the wrong hands." So she intercepted the document before I could get it to Ignatz.

There are sides, I realize, hearing the triumphant note in her voice, boundaries that make some pieces of friendship untenable. "Why didn't you just ask me to help?"

She leans against the desk, eyes me levelly. "Would you have done it if I had?" I consider the question. "No, you were too smart to follow me blindly, even for our friendship. You would have had the same questions and doubts—only you would have had no one to ask about them. Even if you wanted to help, the very information would have changed how you behaved. We needed you exactly as you were."

Krysia was right. By appearing neutral, a friend and mentor who had only my best interests at heart, she was able to guide me exactly where she wanted me to go—and that was perhaps the greatest betrayal of all.

Or maybe not. An image flashes into my mind then of Krysia in the park, handing the ball back to the young woman in the park. "Emilie," I say slowly, my voice heavy with incredulity even as the truth crystallizes in my mind.

Krysia shakes her head. "No, Emilie is not my daughter. What I told you was true—I did become pregnant almost twenty years ago. But the baby was not born." I am curious, and yet at the same time grateful that she does not elaborate on what really happened. "Emilie is about the same age that my child would have been. She's another operative. When she came to me I recognized so much of myself in her that she might have been... I tried to dissuade her in fact from working with us but she was intent. She volunteered instead of being recruited, and had a real passion and natural ability for the cause."

I sink to the edge of the desk in disbelief. "But you were so worried for her when she was sick. You prayed for her." Or had her excursion to the church been another rendezvous, part of her work?

"Emilie is not my daughter," she repeats, as if trying to remind herself. All of her machinations over whether she had done right by the girl, her inability to let her go, and her worry when she was ill, were nothing more than a fiction. Perhaps she had developed such an affinity for the girl over the years that the story had started to seem true. "But our similar coloring provided a useful cover in case anyone—it just happened to be you—stumbled upon us." So Krysia had gone to the park each week not to watch her child nostalgically, but to get or deliver information.

"What else?" I demand. This one report could not have been the total of it. Had she taken other things from Papa or Georg, as well?

But she presses her lips together. Though repentant in having got caught, she is still not willing to divulge all of her secrets. "There is one thing, now that you know—I suppose it is too much to ask, that is, there is still a great deal of work to be done…" She trails off, too embarrassed to finish the thought. My eyes widen. Does she really believe, after all that has happened, all of the betrayal and lies, that I would help her? Once I would have followed her anywhere. For a minute, I am flattered. Krysia thinks me worthy of involvement. Perhaps, that is why she came to Berlin. I shake my head. No, recruiting me was a contingency plan, to be implemented only if I discovered the truth. Otherwise she would have kept me playing the pawn.

She continues, "We believe that the Germans are rearming in spite of the treaty, that they are secretly making plans." It can't be true, though I would not blame them if they were, I think, remembering Georg's disillusion. "You are in a position to help and you have real skills. Perhaps if you agree with what we are trying to do, if you believe…"

I shake my head. Once, I might have thought that Krysia and

her friends had the answers. I wanted to be included so desperately I would have done anything for their approval. But they are politicians and liars like the rest. Now I just want to be free.

I study her, considering. I could scream and Uncle Walter and the servants would come running and summon the police to arrest Krysia. She deserves no better for her betrayal. But the scandal and everything that would be revealed would implicate Papa as surely as it had in Paris. There's more to it, though, than concern for my father: Krysia had changed my life that night in Montparnasse when she challenged me to be something more. And there is part of me that wants to spare her, to save her as surely as she had saved me.

"I think," I say with great difficulty, "that it is time for you to go."

"Go? You mean you aren't…" Krysia assumed that, knowing she had been behind everything, I would have her arrested. Her body goes slack with relief. Then she straightens. "I hope someday you'll understand." She starts for the door, then turns back. "Margot, there is one other thing…you must be careful about Georg. He's broken and a bit off center since Versailles. With everything that has happened, there's no telling what he might do."

I stare at her, dumbfounded. Is she really purporting to offer advice after what she has done? Perhaps this is just another attempt to manipulate me. There's nothing left for her to gain from it, though, and her expression is one of genuine concern. But I cannot trust her again.

"Goodbye, Krysia." I turn away, understanding that I have seen her for the last time. A moment later, the door shuts with a click and she is gone.

CHAPTER TWENTY-TWO

I turn back and stare at the space where Krysia once stood, wondering if it had been a dream. The wool scarf she knitted for me hangs around my neck, one of the few things I'd cared enough to take in my flight. It now feels like a scratchy noose. I remove it and study the patterns in my hand, its beauty a mockery. I am tearing it apart in my hands then, ripping each stitch from its moorings.

When I am done, I stare remorsefully at the great pile of kinked purple thread on the desk before me, still shaking. Now I know why Krysia had come to Berlin. It wasn't about the wedding or supporting me. She had come with her own motives, to continue the deception.

But what had she been searching for? Pushing down the emotions that threaten to swallow me, I pick up the file of documents she had dropped on the floor. Like the paper I'd grabbed from her, they are blueprints and maps of the grounds. I remember then her questions about the layout of the villa, the tunnels leading into the house. Why had she wanted to know?

I see the great room, with the rows of chairs in straight lines. My wedding. A guest list of hundreds, with dozens of ambassadors and government officials, including the prime minister. It would be the perfect opportunity for an assassination attempt, if one could bypass security.

Considering my theory, doubts bubble anew. Krysia works for the British government. Surely they were not in the assassination business. But those in power will stop at nothing to achieve their aims. If they could send millions to die in the trenches, why not one or two more? And if it could be made to appear as if the right people did it—the communists, for example—the German government would come down on them with great force. Perhaps, it was not about the assassination at all, but about the repercussions after.

Of course, they will not dare to attempt the assassination at the wedding now that I know. But they will try again another way. I have to tell someone. Georg. I pick up the blank paper on which I'd intended to tell Krysia I was leaving. Should I use it instead to write to Georg? A letter would not be enough— any assassination plot, if they still dared to go through with it, might take place too soon, the damage done before my missive arrived. No, I have to tell him in person.

I grab my bag, then run from the house and climb onto my bicycle. I begin to pedal, straining to see the darkened road ahead. The night air is thick and humid. Thunder rumbles in the distance. As I near the center of town, I stop. It is well after curfew, and there will be no taxis or trains. The omnibus, I recall, making my way to the side of the train station. A dilapidated bus sits idling at the curb, belching fumes. I pay the driver, ignoring the curious stares of the two other passengers, laborers who are likely making their way to the city to begin night shifts.

As the bus bumps over the rough road leading from town and

turns onto the motorway, I lean my head against the window and stare out into the darkness, unable to shake Krysia from my mind. She was like an older sister to me, and the closest I had to a friend. She had used me, betrayed me for her own version of good. Had it all been an act? But Krysia is not the only one guilty of deception. I lied to Georg as she had lied to me. None of it is clear anymore.

Forty minutes later, the bus stops at Potsdamer Platz and I step out into the night. It is raining now, thick drops that splash against my face as I make my way from the gritty square, winding in the direction of Georg's hotel. The streets are deserted and ominous, and a strange burning smell permeates the air. I move swiftly, glancing over my shoulder every few seconds. In the distance, there is a loud popping sound. Gunfire, I think instinctively, stopping. It is followed by the sounds of shouting and sirens. Is it a political protest, or some sort of crime?

Struggling to breathe against the wet smoke that scratches my nose and throat, I press forward. Soon I reach the Grand. I stop, peering up at the front of the terraced hotel uncertainly. I do not want to face the questions the lobby clerk will surely have about the arrival of a strange woman caller in the middle of the night. In a second-floor window to the right of the entrance, a light burns. Rain falls harder now as I step closer. Through the crack in the curtains I can see Georg sitting at a desk working, and in that moment it is as if I am transported back to Paris, to a time when I could go inside and be with him.

I brush a tear from my eye and walk closer. "Georg," I call in a loud whisper, through cupped hands, tilting my head upward. But, of course, he cannot hear me from this distance. Desperately, I search for a way to get his attention. I grab a few pieces of gravel from the pavement, throw one in the direction of the window, ajar despite the rain. But it misses by a meter and falls back to the pavement. I eye the front of the hotel. The ground-floor windows are covered by an iron grating, intended per-

haps to stave off potential rioters. I hitch up my skirt and lift
my foot onto the grating, climbing as I had on the cannon in
Paris the day Wilson arrived. Despite the slickness of the wet
metal, I find my footing and reach higher. My childhood years
of scaling trees, to the distress of my mother and later Celia,
now serve me well.

There is a precarious creak. I reach higher with my left hand,
praying at the same time that the grating will hold and that no
one will see me on the street below. With my right hand I hurl
the second stone at Georg's window, trying to hit the glass. But
it flies through the open window and a moment later I hear a
squawk.

"Georg." I cringe at the volume of my voice this time, certain that it will attract attention from the neighboring rooms.

He comes to the window, rubbing his head. "Margot?" Disbelief and confusion cross his face as I scamper down from the
grating, wet hair plastered to my face. Then he walks away and
the curtains fall closed behind him. My heart sinks in despair.
Is he really so angry that he would turn his back on me?

The door to the hotel opens. Georg stands shoeless in a white
shirt and trousers, silhouetted against the golden light that burns
behind him. A faint stubble covers his jaw. I have never seen
him look so handsome. My breath skips.

He blinks twice, as though checking if the image he had seen
through the window was a dream. "Margot?" he says again, his
voice hollow. We had parted so badly that he had not expected
to see me again at all, much less on his doorstep in the middle
of the night.

"I'm so sorry to come here like this." I could have called. Just
rung the hotel and asked to speak with him. It would have been
quicker that way. But instead I had to come.

"Is something wrong?"

"No, I mean, yes…" I falter. The rain continues to fall around
me, though I am soaked to the point where it no longer mat-

ters. "May I come in?" He does not answer right away and, for a moment, I wonder if he will refuse. But then he steps back and ushers me upstairs to the room where he had been working. I stand in the entranceway, water dripping onto the parquet floor. "Thank you," I say as he hands me a towel. I avert my eyes from the rumpled bed in the far corner, cringing at the half-empty bottle of liquor on the nightstand.

He clears a chair by the desk for me, but I do not sit. "Tea?" I shake my head. I have not come for a social visit. "What's wrong? Is it your father?"

"No, I have to tell you something." I take a deep breath. "There's a man from Paris who was blackmailing me to spy on you." His eyes widen. "You remember the assassination attempt on Clemenceau's life that happened before you came to Paris?" I do not wait for an answer. "I'd said something in public that I shouldn't have about Papa's work and it prompted the man who tried to kill Clemenceau to act. And after, well, this other man was blackmailing me to get information from you. If I didn't, he was going to blame everything on Papa. Anyway, I thought it was all done with in Paris. But then I discovered this." I hold up the blueprint of the villa. "They were planning some sort of assassination attempt at my wedding, I think."

"Who are 'they'?" he asks. I hesitate. I've told the story in a roundabout way, jumbling Ignatz's role in it with Krysia's. But it is not until I have spoken that I realize what I am planning to do. "The man who asked me to take documents from you is called Ignatz Stein. He's a Ukrainian and he used to run a bar in Montparnasse that has been shut down by the police. He's working for someone, the communists or the British, maybe."

He is quiet for several seconds, processing. "The map?"

I lower my head. "That was me. But it went missing before I could give it to him." I stop, unable to say more without involving Krysia.

"Wait here," Georg instructs, then disappears through the

doorway. I hear him making a call, speaking in a low voice. I glance around his hotel room, as spare as the one in Versailles. What is it that makes him unable to call anywhere home?

I drop to a chair, shaken. I have told Georg about my deception and implicated Ignatz, but steered clear of Krysia and the full truth. Even now, after everything that has happened, my instinct is still to protect her. Will the half-truth I've told be enough to stop Krysia and those she works for from what they are trying to do?

A moment later, Georg returns. "Your suspicions were right. Our intelligence had picked up the possibility of an attempt on the prime minister's life, but we hadn't known where or when—until now. It would have thrown the country into total anarchy. We've alerted the police and the border patrol." I exhale slightly. I should tell him about Krysia, too, but I cannot.

"Georg…" We stare uncertainly at each other, the full extent of my deception laid naked between us. "Say something, please. You must understand, they had threatened my father's reputation…"

"So instead you decided to risk mine."

"It wasn't like that." But it was exactly like that. Papa was my blood and I had chosen him. "Papa's health never would have withstood the scandal."

He is not mollified. "You should go."

"Georg, please. I'm sorry. I did take the document from you. I knew you trusted me and I hated myself for doing it. The second time, though, when I got the document from Lieutenant Bouvier, I might have turned it over. But I didn't. I chose you."

His eyes search my face and something in him seems to give. "You were just protecting your father. You had no other choice." My shoulders slump with relief. Georg has forgiven me, at least for the one transgression. But he had opened himself up to me and he had gotten burned. It is a mistake, I can tell by his grimly set jaw, that he will not make again.

"I'm only sorry that being close to me put you in such a position." He is talking about something deeper than the materials.
"And you risked a great deal coming here to tell me. I want to
tell you that you shouldn't have, but thank God you did. Margot…" He falters and the room is instantly cold and cavernous
around us.

His eyes drop to my travel bag, which I'd forgotten I was still
carrying. "You're leaving?" His voice is hollow with disbelief.

"Yes," I reply. His face looks as though he's been slapped. In
that moment, I realize for the first time the depth of his feelings. He loved me—still does—and although until recently we
had not seen each other in months, the feelings are there, as real
and intense as in Paris.

"When Ignatz was blackmailing me to get information from
you, I thought that leaving was the only way to avoid hurting
Papa—and you." I watch the conflict on his face as he processes
the information—that I cared about him enough to leave to protect him, but might have left without saying goodbye.

"But now that he is to be stopped, surely you needn't go."

"It's more than that." I turn away, unable to finish. Even in
these final moments, I cannot bring myself to tell him everything.

"Oh?" I can hear him struggling to keep the hope from his
voice. "But you are to be married tomorrow."

I stand up. "Exactly."

"You would rather go on alone?"

I nod. "Rather than live a lie, yes."

"And what about…?" He waves his arm in between us, unable to finish the thought.

I stare at him, wordless and stunned. How is it possible, after
all of the lies and everything I have done, that Georg still wants
me?

"You are to be married tomorrow," he repeats. I take a step
toward him. He stares at me unabashedly now.

I swallow. "But I am here with you tonight." And suddenly there is no other moment than this. I pull him close and he surges forward. His lips miss mine, crashing hastily against my chin. He kisses my neck and then my shoulder, his stubbled cheek grating against my skin, inflaming it. I cup his face and draw it upward.

His hands drop to my waist and I arch against him, the wetness of my clothes seeping through to his as I mold myself to the shape of his caress. Then he stops. In his hesitation I can feel it all, his concern about my marriage, his not wanting to get hurt again. This time, there will be no return. "Margot," he whispers, "I think…"

"Don't." I urge him on, taking his hands and moving them where I need to be touched. His hands inch lower, raising my skirt, and it is exactly as I've dreamed a thousand times. But now, after all of the betrayal, it is the one real thing. I press against him harder, losing myself.

He lets out a low growl, lifting me off the ground with the intensity of his embrace. I pull his shirt above his head, then rip off my own and the buttons burst and scatter across the floor. His skin is hot and damp against mine as I draw him down to the floor with me, his hands cushioning me from the hard wood. My whole life I have played it safe and have in fact protected nothing. Now I am going to live. He lifts me onto his lap and I bite hard against the saltiness of his shoulder, his cries mingling with my own.

And then I surrender.

Afterward, I lie in his arms, waiting for the shame that does not come. "Margot," he murmurs against my shoulder. "I never should have…"

"No. Don't be sorry. I'm not."

"Don't marry him, Margot," he pleads, turning to me, brushing a lock of damp hair from my face. All of the realities of the outside world come rushing back, intruding on the haze of desire. "We'll do it all," he promises. "We'll take the railway to China, see Africa. It will be a wonderful adventure. Just break your engagement to him."

"But…"

"Goddammit, Margot," he says, and I start, unaccustomed to hearing him swear. "For everything that has happened, I still love you." His words echo and hang in the air between us: *love you*. If only it were that simple.

He rolls over on his back, clasps his arms behind his head. Watching the muscles in his arms flex, I am seized with the urge to reach for him once again. "We could elope," he persists. An image forms in my mind, Georg and I hopping on a freighter and traveling the world, never looking back. We would be happy, I know in that instant. "Or if you want to be close to your father, we could live in Berlin. I could bear the city in the long term if I was with you." I do not answer. I cannot marry him or anyone else. I am already wed to Stefan.

There is a knock at the door. *"Ja?"* Georg calls, a note of irritation in his voice.

"Pardon me for interrupting," the voice on the other side of the door, presumably a clerk, replies. "But you have a caller downstairs." I sit up. Who could be here at this hour?

Georg turns to me. "I'm not expecting anyone, but it could be about the call I just put in to the ministry." He pats my arm reassuringly. "You stay here." He dresses and walks from the room. Uneasily, I climb from bed and pull on my clothes, closing my top as well as I am able. Then I peer into the corridor and down the stairs.

There, at the door to the hotel, stands Stefan.

"Margot!" he bellows over the rain. How had he found me? Had he made good on his joking promise to come see me after the stag night and somehow followed me here?

I hear Georg's voice at the door, low and pleading for calm. "Corporal Oster, please."

"I know that she's here," Stefan bellows, his words slurred from liquor. He wears his tattered army uniform, the one I have not seen since returning to Berlin. Georg does not counter the statement. "Margot!" Stefan bellows again, louder this time. For a moment, I consider remaining hidden. But I cannot ask Georg to lie for me. I take a deep breath and walk from the apartment.

"Margot," Stefan says, his voice rising with disbelief. Taking in my disheveled hair and the unbuttoned top of my dress, his face crumples and he leans harder on his cane. "Your friend Krysia rang and said she was concerned. But I never thought..." So she had tipped him off, hoping to forestall my telling Georg the truth about her by sending Stefan after me.

Seeing the confrontation between the two men—it is Paris all over again. Only this time in redux, Stefan understands everything. The full extent of my betrayal, which he had not wanted to acknowledge in Paris, is laid out before him, impossible to deny.

"There's been a misunderstanding," Georg says, persisting in the attempt, however implausible, to preserve my honor. He steps outside. "Young Margot works as my translator, that is all." He tries to make his voice paternalistic. Even knowing my deception, he is still trying to protect me. But his explanation falls so far short of explaining matters—why I am here in the middle of the night, months after our translation work was done. Georg extends an arm to Stefan. "Why don't you come inside out of the rain and we'll sort all of this out." Other guests have trickled from their rooms now, and a few people from the neighboring buildings have come into the street, drawn in spite of the rain by the commotion.

Stefan looks from Georg to me and then back again. He has been through hell and is a remnant of his former self, but he isn't a fool. "Draw your weapon, sir." The sky crackles white with lightning behind him.

Georg, of course, is half-dressed and not wearing his saber.

"I challenge you to a duel," Stefan declares. An audible murmur passes through the crowd that has assembled. It sounds silly, like something out of a nineteenth-century romance novel. But Stefan's tone is deadly serious.

Georg shakes his head, then exhales slowly. "I'll not raise arms against another Imperial soldier." He turns away.

"Coward! I spit blood in the trenches while you sailed around on a cruise ship. It's an affront to have you say we are the same." There is a whistling sound as Stefan draws his saber. Georg spins and puts his arm across my midsection in a protective gesture. Stefan's stunned expression explodes into rage. "Take your hand off my wife," he snarls, weapon in one hand, cane flailing wildly in the other. Lightning crackles in the distance, a second too late to obscure this last word.

Georg turns to me, his face stunned. "Wife?" Processing the information, shock and sadness cloud his face. His hand drops from my side as though hot to the touch.

"Georg, no, it isn't..."

But Stefan is charging him awkwardly now with as much speed as he can manage, taking advantage of Georg's shock to attack. He raises his saber high, the blade glinting silver in the streetlights. Before Georg can react, Stefan lunges toward him, swinging wildly. Georg cries out angrily as the blade slashes against his face.

"Georg!" I shout, starting forward, but hands unseen grab me from behind, holding me back from the fight. He is all right, I realize with relief. Though blood pours through his fingers where they press against his face, he is still standing. I brace myself, expecting him to go after Stefan, to seek the retribution now so rightfully his. But he shakes his head and growls, unwilling even in his pain to attack a fellow soldier, especially one who is still half-lame.

Angered to see Georg still standing, Stefan lunges forward once more. "Georg!" I cry again. But his reaction has been slowed by the pain and he does not move as Stefan charges to-ward him, blade aimed at his midsection, intended this time not to maim but to kill. Desperately, I push Georg out of the way, turning my shoulder to deflect Stefan as he nears.

Stefan slams into me and his cane sails through the air, slip-ping on the wet step and losing his footing. I reach out, but before I can grab him, he flies backward, seeming to remain suspended in midair for several seconds before falling down the stairs. For the rest of my life, I will wonder about the angle of his arm, the odd way in which his saber fell under him, blade running his midsection through.

"No!" I start toward the spot where Stefan lays motionless on the wet pavement. "Call an ambulance!" His eyes are open, gaz-ing blankly toward the sky, and I know he is seeing not the rain-soaked Berlin sky, but clouds over the battlefield of the Marne.

Someone, not Georg, is beside me then, wrapping me in a blanket and spiriting me from the street. "Come, you should not be seen here." As I am led away, I look back for Georg, but the crowd had closed in around him and sirens cry out in the distance.

Early morning fog hangs thick above Hamburg harbor as I step from the bus before the passenger terminal. I search for a porter among the stevedores unloading freight from ships. Finding none, I start forward. My valise is heavier than I expected and I struggle to walk evenly under the weight, my footsteps kicking up clouds of dust.

I walk through the building and check my bag, then a few minutes later step out onto the other side. A winding expanse of water unfurls before me, adorned with boats of every size, tall-masted ships and cargo freighters. Looking down the dock at the people bidding one another farewell, I am suddenly lonely. Celia had offered to come with me when I'd said goodbye the previous evening, standing in Papa's stead for the journey to the coast that would be too much for him. But life on my own was the bargain I had made, and I was intent on beginning it as soon as possible.

Our last night together had been a quiet wine-filled meal at which Papa forbade tears. "Go," Papa said. "There's no life for you here anymore."

"You are my life." After Stefan died I had told Papa the truth about our wedding. There were no secrets between us anymore.

But he shook his head. "That's not enough anymore. That's what you were trying to tell me in Paris. You need to make something for yourself."

I was glad that I had not snuck away in the middle of the night like a thief, but was going with his blessing. It was Papa who had in fact secured my position as a governess for two young children with a family in North London he'd come to know during our stay there. He'd made the arrangements quickly after I asked, leaving an envelope on my pillow with the ferry tickets to England. It was his silent apology for Celia bringing Stefan to Paris and all of the misery it caused.

The family in England offered a room as part of my pay but I declined, asking instead for extra money to let a place of my own. Though I am excited about the prospect, I suspect I will not stay there long before moving on—the boat will take me to a train and a train to a path, perhaps with a bicycle. At some point perhaps the path will grow tiring and I will decide that I have seen enough and it is time to come home. Or perhaps I will just keep going. But this trip is about more than just escape. It is time to figure out who I am, the direction of my life.

Celia had insisted on riding with me as far as the train station, and I was very touched by her parting gift of a new parasol, pale pink but not at all frilly, for the trip.

"Take care of him," I said as I started from the car.

"I shall. We will see you for the wedding. And, Margot, I want to apologize, if I've sometimes overstepped." She turned away. "When I invited Stefan to Paris, I never meant to hurt you." She blamed herself for everything that happened, as if she and not I had set in motion the terrible events that had resulted in Stefan's death. "I only wanted what was best."

I raised my hand. "There's no need to apologize. The fault is all mine. It is I who should ask for forgiveness, for not being kinder to you and more grateful for everything you have done for Papa and me. We really are very lucky to have you in our family. I'm so glad to know you'll be here caring for him."

She beamed, basking in my words, and it was only then I realized how much my approval meant to her, how long she had been waiting for my true acceptance. "Then let's not either of us ask and just part as friends. Your mother, she would have been very proud."

"And you?"

She looked flustered, unused to my caring about her opinion. "Very much so."

"Then that is more than enough for me." But in truth I am not seeking Celia's approval, or even Papa's anymore.

Alone now, I gaze across the shoreline, past the massive ship with its three freshly scrubbed decks to the east where the shipping canal opens to a wide expanse of sea. The air is cool and crisp, an early hint of the autumn that is to come. The water is as dark and deep as ever, fanning out endlessly to the horizon. Once I would not have thought of taking a sea voyage by myself. But now the unknown holds a kind of promise. I feel a tug, as though out there another world is beckoning to me.

I take a step toward the ship. "Margot!" I turn in disbelief to see Georg running down the dock. The wound on his face, a bright red line from temple to chin, is fresh and unbandaged, the stitches demarcating a scar that will always be his. But it makes him even more handsome somehow, rugged and tragic.

"How did you know?" I had not told Georg I was leaving, had not seen him since the night Stefan was killed. He was taken by the police that night for questioning as the opponent in a duel that had ended with a fatality. But he was quickly let go, a war hero and government official who had been weaponless and acted in self-defense. The story was all over the newspapers, a high-ranking German killing a soldier in a heated quarrel. Somehow my name was kept from the press, for which I am eternally grateful—I don't think Papa could have withstood the additional strain. No one ever questioned me or suggested that I might have had a role in Stefan's death—that I had pushed him down the stairs, hurtling toward his death was as unfathomable to those who saw it as it was to me. And Georg never said a word.

But for all of his protection, Georg could not absolve my guilt. I had killed Stefan, as surely as if I had run the saber through him myself. It is not so much that I blame myself for pushing him away as he charged or for choosing to protect Georg in that fleeting moment. But I had set our feet on the course of events that brought us to the steps of the hotel and the tragic events that unfolded that night. If I had told Georg the truth, if I hadn't gone there that night…so many ifs—it was impossible to go back and see where the turning point was that had made things go so terribly wrong, like trying to put together a shattered glass.

I had not heard from Georg after that night. I could hardly blame him. Surely after learning that I had lied to him about being married, he would not want to speak with me again.

Yet here he is. Papa had told him about my departure, I realize, one desperate last concession and an apology for keeping us apart. "I'm very sorry," I say. "I should have told you that I was married to Stefan. We wed secretly the night before he left for war, just to give him hope. Not even Papa knew. That is why there was to be a wedding now. But we never…" I stop, trying to find the words. You were my first, I want to say. *My only.* "Anyway, it doesn't matter now. It was wrong of me and I'm sorry I lied to you."

"You owe me no explanations. And I'm sorry, too."

"Georg, it wasn't your fault."

He shakes his head, haunted by the memory of Stefan's death. "It was the worst moment of my life. I could have done something to defuse the situation, but I was caught off guard." His face is haunted and I can tell that the formal acquittal has done little to ease his guilt. "Seeing him lying there…" He does not use Stefan's name.

"Stop, I beg you…" I cannot bear to relive the moment.

But he is too far gone now, needing to process what happened. "And then to see your face…"

He keeps talking, but I do not hear. My mind reels back to Stefan's funeral, a small affair with a military trumpeter and two Jewish veterans among those who bore his casket. The photo atop it, a smiling, confident man in uniform, was one I remember faintly. His dignity restored, he seemed at peace. Standing beside the casket, I realized that the dreams I'd had about a funeral were somehow a premonition. I sobbed openly and others nodded their heads approvingly and offered soothing platitudes. Papa looked quietly puzzled at the depths of my sorrow for a man I had not wanted to marry. My sadness was genuine, for though I had not loved Stefan in the way he had wanted, he was an inextricable part of my life and I cared for him deeply. Part of me—perhaps the best, most innocent part, that had never known war or deception or pain—had died that night on the hotel steps with him.

"Please," I say again, holding up my hand to ward off my memories as well as his words.

Georg glances over his shoulder. "My hometown," he says wistfully. "I would have liked to show it to you." His words are a proxy for so many things that we might have done if given the chance.

A horn sounds long and low. "I must go." I gesture to the boat where the last of the passengers ahead of me have boarded.

"You aren't still leaving, are you?" Even now, as I am about to board the ship, he is in denial about my departure. I understand what he is saying, though—after we had given everything to each other, how could I possibly walk away? That moment, beautiful and perfect, seemed to hold all of the answers. But then Stefan had come and everything had been shattered in an instant. "With all that has happened, I thought that perhaps…"

I look away, biting my lip. I need to leave behind Berlin and its painful memories.

See the world, Krysia said, and though she had betrayed me most deeply, in this one regard she was right. The old me would have stayed, taken the certain route, but I have to take this chance while I can. I recall her suggestion, seemingly long ago, that I become a writer. Then, I knew so little. But I have seen lifetimes these past months—the world broken, then rebuilt, my own shattered anew. Perhaps, after a bit of travel to gain perspective, I may have something to say, after all.

Krysia. I'd been surprised a week earlier to receive a postcard of the Krakow skyline, a broad, turreted castle nestled among cathedral spires, a winding river beneath. It was blank and unsigned, but the faint hint of lilac that lingered on the paper throughout its journey told me everything. Though she would not write anything out of fear of implicating herself, she was asking for forgiveness.

Reliving the betrayal now, my heart aches anew. Why had she done it? I had thought about going after her, hopping a train east and making for Krakow. The wife of a famous musician, she wouldn't be hard to find. But even if I did, she would not give me the answers I seek. No, I will choose to remember her at the battlefield at Reims or swaying over her piano. Those parts of our friendship I know were real. A tiny piece of the anger I've been holding inside breaks off and I begin to forgive her.

Georg looks uneasily from me to the ship, then back again. "You'll be all right on the boat?"

"Yes." Fear, I've learned, does nothing to stave off the inevitable truth. It is time to make my peace with it.

"What about your father?" He is desperate now, trying anything to keep me from going.

It is a question I have thought about a great deal these past few days. "Papa is not alone now. He has Celia."

"I wish…"

I hold my breath waiting for him to say something, to ask me even not to go. But he will not. He does not have the right without offering me a reason to stay, a fresh start, and that possibility disappeared the night he killed Stefan.

"Let me come with you," he says, taking my hand impulsively. In the distance, a seagull calls out as if joining his entreaty.

"Georg," I protest with a laugh. He has a life and a future here. Yet he is willing to give it all up for me. Suddenly I feel the weight of our feelings, undiluted by the time that has passed and events that have transpired. But I cannot allow him to come. I've spent my entire life in the shadow of a man and I need to do this on my own. I think of the sprig of fern from Versailles, which sits still on the windowsill of the villa. There are some things that we cannot take with us, things that must be left behind. "I have to go."

He presses his lips together and stares out across the horizon. "Here." He reaches down and hands me a box. Inside is a small travel set, mother-of-pearl mirror and brush. "A parting gift. I knew I could not change your mind. I had to try, of course." He does not like my decision to go. But he respects it, and I love him for that.

I will return, I want to say. I bite my lip, unwilling to give him false hope.

"How long?" Georg asks, as if reading my mind. His face brightens.

"I don't know."

"One month, one year?" he presses.

I shake my head. "Until it is time to come home." The only answer I can offer, it seems to come from a place deep in me, strong and firm. The words sound like Krysia's but the voice is my own. Perhaps I have learned enough from her to carry forward, after all.

"You feel it, though, as I do?" he presses. I look away, unable to deny it. Then I nod and his face breaks into a smile. "Six months," he pronounces, as though it has been agreed upon and, with those words, he is setting me free. Whether the deadline is a real expectation, or simply a way to make farewell bearable for both of us, I cannot say. "I will be standing right here in six months, waiting for you."

I nod. Six months will be just before Papa and Celia's wedding. Georg is not likely aware of that, though, and I will keep that secret tucked in my pocket for now, in case I change my mind. In my heart, I know that I will be here, striding down the gangplank into his arms. I could not stay away from Georg any more than I could myself. But I have to do this first.

A gull cries out in the distance, again, reminding me that it is time to go. If I don't leave now, I never will. "Goodbye, Georg."

He takes my hand. *"Auf wiedersehen." Until we meet again.* He lowers his head to kiss my hand. But I lift his chin and bring my lips to his, full and hard. Then I turn and start up the gangplank. If I stop, I will not have the strength to start again. Tears stream down my cheeks. Six months. It is not so long, but the world can change in an instant.

I step onto the deck of the ship and a deckhand closes the gate behind me. Only when we have pushed from shore and I can no longer change my mind do I turn around. Georg stands motionless, one hand raised to shield his eyes, the other outstretched.

I take one last look at the dock, imagining our reunion there. I am carried, by his love, and Papa's, and even Krysia's, as I go. This time, leaving is my choice. I wave and blow him a single kiss. Then, squaring my shoulders, I turn and face the water ahead, taking the first step toward the life that is waiting for me.

★ ★ ★ ★ ★

ACKNOWLEDGMENTS

The Ambassador's Daughter represents joy on so many levels to me. First, it gave me the chance to return to some of my beloved characters and themes from *The Kommandant's Girl,* something that I—and many of my readers—have been hoping would happen for several years. It also allowed me to explore Europe after the First World War, an era that has fascinated me since I wrote about it in my thesis at Cambridge nearly two decades ago. Writing a story in this era required extensive research about historical events as well as the social and political climate at the time. As always when writing historical fiction, I had to make some judgment calls about when to remain historically accurate and when to "bend" history, melding fact and fiction for the sake of story (a creative indulgence for which I hope my readers will forgive me).

This book brought me back to the incomparable publishing team at Harlequin MIRA, including my wonderful editor, Susan Swinwood, and the many brilliant folks in editorial, marketing, publicity and sales, and Kim Young and the marvelous team at MIRA U.K. I am so grateful for your time and talents, and overjoyed to be working with you again! Big thanks as always to my agents Scott Hoffman and Michelle Brower at Folio Literary Management for all of your keen insight and tireless work on my behalf. Thanks also to my colleagues at Rutgers for your interest and support.

Even as it is joyous, writing this book has been bittersweet. When I began *The Ambassador's Daughter,* a book that examines among other things the parent-child relationship, I had no idea that my own beloved father would not be here to see the finished project. With each book I always recognize the "village" that makes my writing life possible. However, this time I need to express even more deeply my gratitude for those closest to me: my husband, Phillip, mother, Marsha, brother, Jay, as well as my in-laws Ann and Wayne, dear friends, and of course, the three little muses who sustain and inspire me every day, Benjamin, Charlotte and Elizabeth. I love you all.

THE AMBASSADOR'S DAUGHTER

PAM JENOFF

Reader's Guide

PARK
ROW
BOOKS

1. As the story opened, Margot appeared to be an independent and confident young woman. How do you think her character changed throughout the story, and what caused those changes? What do you feel was her greatest strength and weakness?

2. How do you think the loss of her mother affected Margot? How did this change throughout the book, particularly when she learned the truth?

3. Georg and Margot developed feelings for one another after mere days. What did you see in their time together that attracted them so powerfully? Do you believe it is possible to fall in love so quickly and for such a relationship to last?

4. How was it possible for Margot to keep secrets from those she professed to love most? How did it affect her relation-

ships with her father, with Georg? Do you think that Margot's choices were justified by her intentions?

5. Margot and Krysia became such close friends despite significant differences in age and circumstances. What do you think it was that drew them together, and what did each of them provide for the other? Have you ever found yourself in such a close but unlikely friendship?

6. Margot was a very young woman dealing with situations that most of us today would find completely overwhelming at age twenty. What do you think it was that Margot really wanted out of life?

7. What did you think about Margot's relationship with Stefan? Could you sympathize with her, being torn by an old promise to a man she didn't know anymore and her love for a man that offered her a promising future? What would you have done in her shoes?

8. Margot experienced anti-German sentiment from those around her who saw her as the enemy. Do you think this was a fair judgment, given the political climate of the time? Do you think this type of mentality still exists today?

9. The post-WWI era is less familiar to some readers than WWII and other historical time periods. What did you like about a novel set during this time? Did you identify with any symbolic items, people or places throughout the book? What did they represent to you?

10. Do you agree that Margot's relationship with her father improved over the course of the novel? How so, or how not?

11. What do you think happens six months after the end of the book? Six years?

12. *The Ambassador's Daughter* is the prequel to two of Pam Jenoff's other novels, *The Kommandant's Girl* and *The Diplomat's Wife*. If you have read those, how did you feel this book compared? Did knowing what happens twenty years down the line color your reading of this book?

Read on for a sneak peek from The Lost Girls of Paris,
*Pam Jenoff's captivating tale of courage and survival inspired by true
events from World War II.*

CHAPTER ONE

GRACE

New York, 1946

If not for the second-worst mistake of Grace Healey's life, she never would have found the suitcase.

At nine twenty on a Tuesday morning, Grace should have been headed south on the first of two buses she took to get downtown, commuting from the rooming house in Hell's Kitchen to the Lower East Side office where she worked. And she *was* on her way to work. But she was nowhere near the neighborhood she had come to call home. Instead, she was racing south on Madison Avenue, corralling her corkscrew hair into a low knot. She quickly removed her coat, despite the chill, so she could take off her mint green cardigan. She didn't want Frankie to notice it was the exact same one she had been wearing at work the previous day and question the unthinkable: whether she had gone home at all.

Grace paused to study herself in the window of a five-and-dime. She wished the store was open so she could buy some

powder to hide the marks on her neck and sample a bit of perfume to conceal the stench of day-old brandy mixed with that
delicious-but-wrong smell of Mark's aftershave, which made her
dizzy and ashamed with every inhale. A wino sat on the corner,
moaning to himself in sleep. Looking at his gray, lifeless pallor, Grace felt a certain solidarity. From the adjacent alley came
the banging on a trash can, a sound marching in time with the
thudding in her own head. The whole city of New York seemed
green and hungover. Or perhaps she was confusing it for herself.

Sharp gusts of February wind cut across Madison, causing the
flags that hung from the skyscrapers above to whip furiously.
An old crumpled newspaper danced along the gutter. Hearing
the bells of Saint Agnes's toll half past nine, Grace pressed on,
her skin growing moist under her collar as she neared a run.
Grand Central Terminal loomed hulking ahead. Just a bit farther and she could turn left on Forty-Second Street and catch a
bus downtown on Lexington.

But as she neared the intersection at Forty-Third, the street
ahead was blocked. Police cars sat three across, cordoning off
Madison and preventing anyone from going farther south. A car
accident, Grace suspected at first, noting the black Studebaker,
which sat jackknifed across the street, steam billowing from the
hood. More cars clogged the Midtown streets than ever these
days, jockeying for space with the buses and taxis and trucks
making deliveries. There did not appear to be another vehicle
involved, though. A lone ambulance sat at the corner. The medics did not rush about urgently, but stood leaning against the
vehicle, smoking.

Grace started toward a policeman, whose paunchy face pushed
up from the high collar of his uniform, navy with gold buttons. "Excuse me. Will the street be closed for long? I'm late
for work."

He looked out at her disdainfully from under the brim of his
hat, as if despite all of the women who had worked dutifully in

the factories to take the place of the men who had enlisted and gone overseas during the war, the notion of a woman holding a job was still laughable. "You can't go this way," he replied officiously. "And you won't be able to anytime soon."

"What happened?" she asked, but the policeman turned away. Grace took a step forward, craning to see.

"A woman was hit by a car and died," a man in a flat wool cap beside her said.

Taking in the shattered windshield of the Studebaker, Grace suddenly felt sick. "Such a shame," she managed finally.

"I didn't see it," the man replied. "But someone said she was killed instantly. At least she didn't suffer."

At least. That was the phrase Grace heard too often after Tom had died. At least she was still young. At least there had not been children—as if that made it somehow easier to bear. (Children, she sometimes thought, would not have been a burden, but a bit of him left behind forever.)

"You just never know where it will all end," mused the flat-capped man beside her. Grace did not answer. Tom's death had been unexpected, too, an overturned jeep on the way from the army base to the train station in Georgia, headed to New York to see her before he'd deployed. They called him a casualty of war, but in fact it had been just another accident that might have happened anywhere.

A flashbulb from a reporter's camera popped, causing her to blink. Grace shielded her eyes then backed away blindly through the crowd that had formed, seeking air amid the cigarette smoke and sweat and perfume.

Away from the police barricade now, Grace looked over her shoulder. Forty-Third Street was blocked to the west as well, preventing her from cutting across. To go back up Madison and around the other side of the station would take at least another half an hour, making her even later for work than she already was. Again, she cursed the night before. If it weren't for Mark, she wouldn't be standing here, faced with no other choice than to cut through Grand Central—the one place she had sworn to never go again.

Grace turned to face it. Grand Central loomed before her, its massive shadow darkening the pavement below. Commuters streamed endlessly through its doors. She imagined the inside of the station, the concourse where the light slatted in through the stained glass windows, the big clock where friends and lovers met. It was not the place she couldn't bear to see, but the people. The girls with their fresh red lipstick, pressing tongues against teeth to make sure the color hadn't bled through, clutching purses expectantly. Freshly washed children looking just a bit nervous at seeing a father who they could not remember because he had left when they were scarcely toddlers. The soldiers in uniforms rumpled from travel bounding onto the platform with wilted daisies in hand. The reunion that would never be hers.

She should just give up and go home. Grace longed for a nice bath, perhaps a nap. But she had to get to work. Frankie had interviews with a French family at ten and needed her to take dictation. And after that the Rosenbergs were coming, seeking papers for housing. Normally this was what she loved about the work, losing herself in other peoples' problems. But today the responsibility weighed down heavy upon her.

No, she had to go forward and there was only one choice. Squaring her shoulders, Grace started toward Grand Central.

She walked through the station door. It was the first time she had been here since that afternoon she'd arrived from Connecticut in her best shirred dress, hair perfectly coiffed in victory rolls and topped with her pillbox hat. Tom hadn't arrived on the three from Philadelphia, where he should have changed trains, as expected and she assumed he had missed his connection. When he didn't get off the next train either, she became a bit uneasy. She checked the message board beside the information booth at the center of the station, where people pinned notes in case Tom had come early or she had somehow missed him. She had no way to reach him or check and there was nothing to do but wait. She ate a hot dog that smudged her lipstick and turned sour in her mouth, read the newspaper headlines at the kiosk a second, then a third time. Trains came and emptied, spilling onto the platform soldiers who might have been Tom but weren't. By the time the last train of the night arrived at eight thirty, she was frantic with worry. Tom never would have left her standing like this. What had happened? Finally, an auburn-haired lieutenant she'd recognized from Tom's induction ceremony came toward her with an expression of dread and she'd known. She could still feel his unfamiliar hands catching her as her knees buckled.

The station looked the same now as it had that night, a businesslike, never-ending stream of commuters and travelers, undisturbed by the role it had played so large in her mind these many months. *Just get across*, she told herself, the wide exit at the far side of the station calling to her like a beacon. She didn't have to stop and remember.

Something pulled at her leg strangely, like the tearing of a small child's fingers. Grace stopped and looked behind her. It was only a run in her nylons. Had Mark's hands made it? The tear was growing larger with every step now, an almost gash across her calf. She was seized with the need to get them off.

Grace raced for the stairs to the public washroom on the lower level. As she passed a bench, she stumbled, nearly falling. Her foot twisted, causing a wave of pain to shoot through her ankle. She limped to the bench and lifted her foot, assuming that the heel that she had not had fixed properly had come off again. But the shoe was still intact. No, there was something jutting out from beneath the bench she had just passed that had caused her to trip. A brown suitcase, shoved haphazardly beneath. She looked around with annoyance, wondering who could have been so irresponsible as to leave it like that, but there was no one close and the other people passed by without taking notice. Perhaps whoever owned it had gone to the restroom or to buy a newspaper. She pushed it farther underneath the bench so that no one else would trip on it and kept walking.

Outside the door to the ladies' room, Grace noticed a man sitting on the ground in a tattered uniform. For a fleeting second, she was glad Tom had not lived to fight and return destroyed from what he had seen. She would always have the golden image of him, perfect and strong. He would not come home scarred like so many she saw now, struggling to put a brave face over the brokenness. Grace reached in her pocket for the last of her coins, trying not to think about the coffee she so dearly wanted that she would now have to do without. She pressed the money into the man's cracked palm. She simply couldn't look away.

Grace continued into the ladies' room, locking herself in a stall to remove her nylons. Then she walked to the mirror to smooth her ink-black hair and reapply her Coty lipstick, tasting in its waxiness all that had happened the night before. At the next sink, a woman younger than herself smoothed her coat over her rounded belly. Pregnancies were everywhere now, it seemed, the fruits of so many joyous reunions with the boys who came home from the war. Grace could feel the woman looking at her disheveled appearance. *Knowing.*

Mindful that she was even later now for work, Grace hurried from the restroom. As she started across the station once more, she noticed the suitcase she had nearly tripped over moments earlier. It was still sitting under the bench. Slowing, she walked to the suitcase, looking around for someone coming to claim it.

When no one did, Grace knelt to examine the suitcase. There was nothing terribly extraordinary about it, rounded like a thousand other valises that travelers carried through the station every day, with a worn mother-of-pearl handle that was nicer than most. Only this one wasn't passing through; it was sitting under a bench unattended. *Abandoned.* Had someone lost it? She stopped with a moment's caution, remembering a story from during the war about a bag that was actually a bomb. But that was all over, the danger of invasion or other attack that had once seemed to lurk around every corner now faded.

Grace studied the case for some sign of ownership. There was a name chalked onto the side. She recalled uneasily some of Frankie's clients, survivors whom the Germans had forced to write their names on their suitcases in a false promise that they would be reunited with their belongings. This one bore a single word: *Trigg*.

Grace considered her options: tell a porter, or simply walk away. She was late for work. But curiosity nagged at her. Perhaps there was a tag inside. She toyed with the clasp. It popped open in her fingers seemingly of its own accord. She found herself lifting the lid a few inches. She glanced over her shoulder, feeling as though at any minute she might get caught. Then she looked inside the suitcase. It was neatly packed, with a silver-backed hairbrush and an unwrapped bar of Yardley's lavender soap tucked in a top corner, women's clothes folded with perfect creases. There was a pair of baby shoes tucked in the rear of the case, but no other sign of children's clothing.

Suddenly, being in the suitcase felt like an unforgivable invasion of privacy (which, of course, it was). Grace pulled back her hand quickly. As she did, something sliced into her index finger. "Ouch!" she cried aloud, in spite of herself. A line of blood an inch or more long, already widening with red bubbles, appeared. She put her finger to her mouth, sucking on the wound to stop the bleeding. Then she reached for the case with her good hand, needing to know what had cut her, a razor or knife. Below the clothes was an envelope, maybe a quarter inch thick. The sharp edge of the paper had cut her hand. *Leave it*, a voice inside her seemed to say. But unable to stop herself, she opened the envelope.

Inside lay a pack of photographs, wrapped carefully in a piece of lace. Grace pulled them out, and as she did a drop of blood seeped from her finger onto the lace, irreparably staining it. There were about a dozen photos in all, each a portrait of a single young woman. They looked too different to be related to one another. Some wore military uniforms, others crisply pressed blouses or blazers. Not one among them could have been older than twenty-five.

Holding the photos of these strangers felt too intimate, wrong. Grace wanted to put them away, forget what she had seen. But the eyes of the girl in the top photo were dark and beckoning. Who was she?

Just then there were sirens outside the station and it felt as though they might be meant for her, the police coming to arrest her for opening someone else's bag. Hurriedly, Grace struggled to rewrap the photos in the lace and put the whole thing back into the suitcase. But the lace bunched and she could not get the packet back into the envelope. The sirens were getting louder now. There was no time. Furtively, she tucked the photos into her own satchel and she pushed the suitcase back under the bench with her foot, well out of sight.

Then she started for the exit, the wound on her finger throbbing. "I should have known," she muttered to herself, "that no good could ever come from going into the station."

CHAPTER TWO

ELEANOR

London, 1943

The Director was furious.

He slammed his paw-like hand down on the long conference table so hard the teacups rattled and tea sloshed over the rims all the way at the far end. The normal banter and chatter of the morning meeting went silent. His face reddened.

"Another two agents captured," he bellowed, not bothering to lower his voice. One of the typists passing in the corridor stopped, taking in the scene with wide eyes before scurrying on. Eleanor stood hurriedly to close the door, swatting at the cloud of cigarette smoke that had formed above them.

"Yes, sir," Captain Michaels, the Royal Air Force attaché, stammered. "The agents dropped near Marseille were arrested, just hours after arrival. There's been no word and we're presuming they've been killed."

"Which ones?" the Director demanded. Gregory Winslow, Director of Special Operations Executive, was a former army colonel, highly decorated in the Great War. Though close to sixty, he remained an imposing figure, known only as "the Director" to everyone at headquarters.

Captain Michaels looked flummoxed by the question. To the men who ran the operation from afar, the agents in the field were nameless chess pieces.

But not to Eleanor, who was seated beside him. "James, Harry. Canadian by birth and a graduate of Magdalen College, Oxford. Peterson, Ewan, former Royal Air Force." She knew the details of every man they'd dropped into the field by heart.

"That makes the second set of arrests this month." The Director chewed on the end of his pipe without bothering to light it.

"The third," Eleanor corrected softly, not wanting to enrage him further but unwilling to lie. It had been almost three years since Churchill had authorized the creation of Special Operations Executive, or SOE, and charged it with the order to "set Europe ablaze" through sabotage and subversion. Since then, they had deployed close to three hundred agents into Europe to disrupt munitions factories and rail lines. The majority had gone into France as part of the unit called "F Section" to weaken the infrastructure and arm the French partisans ahead of the long-rumored cross-Channel Allied invasion.

But beyond the walls of its Baker Street headquarters, SOE was hardly regarded as a shining success. MI6 and some of the other traditional government agencies resented SOE's sabotage, which they saw as amateurish and damaging to their own, more clandestine, operations. The success of SOE efforts were also hard to quantify, either because they were classified or because their effect would not be fully felt until the invasion. And lately things had started to go wrong, their agents arrested in increasing number. Was it the size of the operations that was the problem, making them victims of their own success? Or was it something else entirely?

The Director turned to Eleanor, newfound prey that had suddenly caught the lion's attention. "What the hell is happening, Trigg? Are they ill prepared? Making mistakes?"

Eleanor was surprised. She had come to SOE as a secretary shortly after the organization was created. Getting hired had been an uphill battle: she was not just a woman, but a Polish national— and a Jew. Few thought she belonged here. Oftentimes she wondered herself how she'd come from her small village near Pinsk to the halls of power in London. But she'd persuaded the Director to give her a chance, and through her skill and knowledge, meticulous attention to detail and encyclopedic memory, she had gained his trust. Even though her title and pay had remained the same, she was now much more of an advisor. The Director insisted that she sit not with the other secretaries along the periphery, but at the conference table immediately to his right. (He did this in part, she suspected, to compensate for his deafness in his ear on that side, which he admitted to no one else. She always debriefed him in private just after the meeting to make certain he had not missed anything.)

This was the first time, though, that the Director had asked for her opinion in front of the others. "Respectfully, sir, it isn't the training, or the execution." Eleanor was suddenly aware of every eye on her. She prided herself on lying low in the agency, drawing as little attention as possible. But now her cover, so to speak, had been blown, and the men were watching her with an unmasked skepticism.

"Then what is it?" the Director asked, his usual lack of patience worn even thinner.

"It's that they are men." Eleanor chose her words carefully, not letting him rush her, wanting to make him understand in a way that would not cause offense. "Most of the young Frenchmen are gone from the cities or towns. Conscripted to the LVF, off fighting for the Vichy collaborationist militia or imprisoned for refusing to do so. It's impossible for our agents to fit in now."

"So what then? Should we send them all to ground?"

Eleanor shook her head. The agents could not go into hiding. They needed to be able to interact with the locals in order to get information. It was the waitress in Lautrec overhearing the officers chatter after too much wine, the farmer's wife noticing changes in the trains that passed by the fields, the observations of everyday citizens that yielded the real information. And the agents needed to be making contacts with the *reseau*, the local networks of resistance, in order to fortify their efforts to subvert the Germans. No, the agents of the F Section could not operate by hiding in the cellars and caves.

"Then what?" the Director pressed.

"There's another option..." She faltered and he looked at her impatiently. Eleanor was not one to be at a loss for words, but what she was about to say was so audacious she hardly dared. She took a deep breath. "Send women."

"Women? I don't understand."

The idea had come to her weeks earlier as she watched one of the girls in the radio room decode a message that had come through from a field agent in France with a swift and sure hand. Her talents were wasted, Eleanor thought. The girl should be transmitting from the field. The idea had been so foreign that it had taken time to crystalize in Eleanor's own mind. She had not meant to bring it up now, or maybe ever, but it had come out nonetheless, a half-formed thing.

"Yes." Eleanor had heard stories of women agents, rogue operatives working on their own in the east, carrying messages and helping POWs to escape. Such things had happened in the First World War as well, probably to a greater extent than most people imagined. But to create a formal program to actually train and deploy women was something altogether different.

"But what would they *do*?" the Director asked.

"The same work as the men," Eleanor replied, suddenly annoyed at having to explain what should have been obvious. "Courier messages. Transmit by radio. Arm the partisans, blow up bridges." Women had risen up to take on all sorts of roles on the home front, not just nursing and local guard. They manned antiaircraft guns and flew planes. Why was the notion that they could do this, too, so hard to understand?

"A women's sector?" Michaels interjected, barely containing his skepticism.

Ignoring him, Eleanor turned to face the Director squarely. "Think about it, sir," she said, gaining steam as the idea firmed in her mind. "Young men are scarce in France, but women are everywhere. They blend in on the street and in the shops and cafés."

"As for the other women who work here already…" She hesitated, considering the wireless radio operators who labored tirelessly for SOE. On some level they were perfect: skilled, knowledgeable, wholly committed to the cause. But the same assets that made them ideal also rendered them useless for the field. They were simply too entrenched to train as operatives, and they had seen and knew too much to be deployed. "They won't do either. The women would need to be freshly recruited."

"But where would we find them?" the Director asked, seeming to warm to the idea.

"The same places we do the men." It was true they didn't have the corps of officers from which to recruit. "From the WACs or the FANYs, the universities and trade schools, or in the factories or on the street." There was not a single résumé that made an ideal agent, no special degree. It was more of a sense that one could do the work. "The same types of people—smart, adaptable, proficient in French," she added.

"They would have to be trained," Michaels pointed out, making it sound like an insurmountable obstacle.

"Just like the men," Eleanor countered. "No one is born knowing how to do this."

"And then?" the Director asked.

"And then we deploy them."

"Sir," Michaels interjected. "The Geneva Convention expressly prohibits women combatants." The men around the table nodded their heads, seeming to seize on the point.

"The convention prohibits a lot of things," Eleanor shot back. She knew all of the dark corners of SOE, the ways in which the agency and others cut corners and skirted the law in the desperation of war. "We can make them part of the FANY as a cover."

"We'd be risking the lives of wives, daughters and mothers," Michaels pointed out.

"I don't like it," said one of the other uniformed men from the far end of the table. Nervousness tugged at Eleanor's stomach. The Director was not the most strong-willed of leaders. If the others all lined up behind Michaels, he might back away from the idea.

"Do you like losing a half-dozen men every fortnight to the Germans?" Eleanor shot back, scarcely believing her own nerve.

"We'll try it," the Director said with unusual decisiveness, foreclosing any further debate. He turned to Eleanor. "Set up an office down the street at Norgeby House and let me know what you need."

"Me?" she asked, surprised.

"You thought of it, Trigg. And you're going to run the bloody thing." Recalling the casualties they had discussed just minutes earlier, Eleanor cringed at the Director's choice of words.

"Sir," Michaels interjected. "I hardly think that Miss Trigg is qualified. Meaning no offense," he added, tilting his head in her direction. The men looked at her dubiously.

"None taken." Eleanor had long ago hardened herself to the dismissiveness of the men around her.

"Sir," the army officer at the far end of the table interjected. "I, too, find Miss Trigg a most unlikely choice. With her background…" Heads nodded around the table, their skeptical looks accompanied by a few murmurs. Eleanor could feel them studying her, wondering about her loyalties. *Not one of us*, the men's expressions seemed to say, *and not to be trusted*. For all that she did for SOE, they still regarded her as an enemy. Alien, foreign. It was not for lack of trying. She had worked to fit in, to mute all traces of her accent. And she had applied for British citizenship. Her naturalization application had been denied once, on grounds that even the Director, for all of his power and clearances, had not been able to ascertain. She had resubmitted it a second time a few months earlier with a note of recommendation from him, hoping this might make the difference. Thus far, she had not received a response.

Eleanor cleared her throat, prepared to withdraw from consideration. But the Director spoke first. "Eleanor, set up your office," he ordered. "Begin recruiting and training the girls with all due haste." He raised his hand, foreclosing further discussion.

"Yes, sir." She kept her head up, unwilling to look away from the eyes now trained upon her.

After the meeting, Eleanor waited until the others had left before approaching the Director. "Sir, I hardly think..."

"Nonsense, Trigg. We all know you are the man for the job, if you'll pardon the expression. Even the military chaps, though they may not want to admit it or quite understand why."

"But, sir, even if that is true, I'm an outsider. I don't have the clout."

"You're an outsider, and that is just one of the things that makes you perfect for the position." He lowered his voice. "I'm tired of it all getting mired by politics. You won't let personal loyalties or other concerns affect your judgment." She nodded, knowing that was true. She had no husband or children, no outside distractions. The mission was the only thing that mattered—and always had been.

"Are you sure I can't go?" she asked, already knowing the answer. Though flattered that he wanted her to run the women's operation, it would still be a distant second-best to actually deploying as one of the agents in the field.

"Without the paperwork, you couldn't possibly." He was right, of course. In London, she might be able to hide her background. But to get papers to send her over, especially now, while her citizenship application was pending, was another matter entirely. "Anyway, this is much more important. You're the head of a department now. We need you to recruit the girls. Train them. It has to be someone they trust."

"Me?" Eleanor knew the other women who worked at SOE saw her as cold and distant, not the type they would invite to lunch or tea, much less confide in.

"Eleanor," the Director continued, his voice low and stern, eyes piercing. "Few of us are finding ourselves where we expected at the start of the war."

That, she reflected, was more true than he possibly could have known. She thought about what he was asking. A chance to take the helm, to try to fix all of the mistakes that she'd been forced to watch from the sidelines these many months, powerless to do anything. Though one step short of actual deployment, this would be an opportunity to do so much more.

"We need you to figure out where the girls belong and get them there," the Director continued on, as though it had all been settled and she'd said yes. Inwardly, Eleanor felt conflicted. The prospect of taking this on was appealing. At the same time, she saw the enormity of the task splayed before her on the table like a deck of cards. The men already faced so much, and while in her heart she knew that the women were the answer, getting them ready would be Herculean. It was too much, the kind of involvement—and exposure—that she could hardly afford.

Then she looked up at the photos on the wall of fallen SOE agents, young men who had given everything for the war. She imagined the German security intelligence, the Sicherheitsdienst, at their French headquarters on the Avenue Foch in Paris. The SD was headed by the infamous Sturmbannführer Hans Kriegler, a former concentration camp commandant who Eleanor knew from the files to be as cunning as he was cruel. There were reports of his using the children of locals to coerce confessions, of hanging prisoners alive from meat hooks to withdraw information before leaving them there to die. He was undoubtedly planning the downfall of more agents even as they spoke.

Eleanor knew then that she had no choice but to take on the task. "Fine. I'll need complete control," she added. It was always important to go first when setting the terms.

"You shall have it."

"And I report only to you." Special sectors would, in other circumstances, report through one of the Director's deputies. Eleanor peered out of the corner of her eye at Michaels, who lingered in the hallway. He and the other men would not be happy about her having the Director's ear, even more so than she already had. "To you," she repeated for emphasis, letting her words sink in.

"No bureaucratic meddling," the Director promised. "You report only to me." She could hear then the desperation in his voice, how very much he needed her to make this work.

CHAPTER THREE

MARIE

London, 1944

The last place Marie would have expected to be recruited as a secret agent (if indeed she could have anticipated it at all) was in the loo.

An hour earlier, Marie sat at a table by the window in the Town House, a quiet café on York Street she had come to frequent, savoring a few minutes of quiet after a day of endless clacking at the dingy War Office annex where she had taken a position as a typist. She thought of the coming weekend, just two days off, and smiled, imagining five-year-old Tess and the crooked tooth that surely would have come in a bit more by now. That was the thing about only seeing her daughter on the weekend—Marie seemed to miss years in the days in between. She wanted to be out in the country with Tess, playing by the brook and digging for stones. But someone had to stay here and make a few pounds in order to keep their aging row home in

Maida Vale from falling into foreclosure or disrepair, assuming the bombs didn't take it all first.

There was a booming noise in the distance, causing the dishes on the table to rattle. Marie started, reaching instinctively for the gas mask that no one carried anymore since the Blitz had ended. She lifted her gaze to the plate glass window of the café. Outside the rain-soaked street, a boy of no more than eight or nine was trying to scrape up bits of coal from the pavement. Her stomach ached. Where was his mother?

She remembered the day more than two years ago that she'd decided to send Tess away. At first, the notion of being separated from her daughter was almost unthinkable. Then a bomb had hit the flats across the street, killing seven children. But for the grace of God, that might have been Tess. The next morning, Marie began making arrangements.

At least Tess was with Aunt Hazel. The woman was more of a cousin and a bit dour to be sure, but was nevertheless fond of the little girl. And Tess loved the old vicarage in East Anglia, with its endless cupboards and musty crawl spaces. She could run wild across the fens when the weather permitted, and help Hazel with her work at the post office when it did not. Marie couldn't imagine putting her girl on a train to be sent off to the countryside to a cold convent or God-knows-where-else, into the arms of strangers. She had seen it at King's Cross almost every Friday last year as she made her way north to visit Tess— mothers battling back tears as they adjusted coats and scarves on the little ones, younger siblings clinging to older, children with too-large suitcases crying openly, trying to escape through the carriage windows. It made the two-hour journey until she could reach Tess and wrap her arms around her almost unbearable. She stayed each Sunday until Hazel reminded her that she had best take the last train or miss curfew. Her daughter was safe and well and with family. But that didn't make the fact that it was only Wednesday any more bearable.

Should she have brought Tess back already? That was the question that had dogged Marie these past few months as she had seen the trickle of children coming back to the city. The Blitz was long over and there was a kind of normalcy that had resumed now that they weren't sleeping in the Tube stations at night. But the war was far from won, and Marie sensed that something far worse was yet to come.

Pushing her doubts aside, Marie pulled a book from her bag. It was poetry by Baudelaire, which she loved because his elegant verse took her back to happier times as a child summering on the coast in Brittany with her mother.

"Excuse me," a man said a moment later. She looked up, annoyed by the interruption. He was fortyish, thin and unremarkable in a tweedy sport coat and glasses. A scone sat untouched on the plate at the table next to her from which he had risen. "I was curious about what you are reading." She wondered if he were trying to make advances. The intrusions were everywhere now with all of the American GIs in the city, spilling from the pubs at midday and walking three abreast in the streets, their jarring laughter breaking the stillness.

But the man's accent was British and his mild expression contained no hint of impropriety. Marie held up the book so that he could see. "Would you mind reading me a bit?" he asked. "I'm afraid I don't speak French."

"Really, I don't think…" she began to demur, surprised by the odd request.

"Please," he said, cutting her off, his tone almost imploring. "You'd be doing me a kindness." She wondered why it meant so much to him. Perhaps he had lost someone French or was a veteran who had fought over there.

"All right," she relented. A few lines couldn't hurt. She began to read from the poem, "N'importe où hors du monde (Anywhere Out of the World)." Her voice was self-conscious at first, but she felt herself slowly gain confidence.

After a few sentences, Marie stopped. "How was that?" She expected him to ask her to read further.

He did not. "You've studied French?"

She shook her head. "No, but I speak it. My mother was French and we spent summers there when I was a child." In truth, the summers had been an escape from her father, an angry drunk unable to find work or hold down a job, resentful of her mother's breeding and family money and disappointed that Marie wasn't a boy. That was the reason Marie and her mother summered far away in France. And it was the reason Marie had run away from the Herefordshire manor where she'd been raised to London when she was eighteen, and then took her mother's surname. She knew if she stayed in the house she had dreaded all her childhood with her father's worsening temper, she wouldn't make it out alive.

"Your accent is extraordinary," the man said. "Nearly perfect." How could he know that if he didn't speak French? she wondered. "Are you working?" he asked.

"Yes," she blurted. The transition in subject was abrupt, the question too personal. She stood hurriedly, fumbling in her purse for coins. "I'm sorry, but I really must go."

The man reached up and when she looked back she saw he was holding a business card. "I didn't mean to be rude. But I was wondering if you would like a job." She took the card. *Number 64 Baker Street*, was all it said. No person or office named. "Ask for Eleanor Trigg."

"Why should I?" she asked, perplexed. "I have a job."

He shook his head slightly. "This is different. It's important work and you'd be well suited—and well compensated. I'm afraid I can't say any more."

"When should I go there?" she asked, though certain that she never would.

"Now." She'd expected an appointment. "So you'll go?"

Marie left a few coins on the table and left the café without

answering, eager to be away from the man and his intrusive-
ness. Outside, she opened her umbrella and adjusted her bur-
gundy print scarf to protect against the chill. She rounded the
corner, then stopped, peering over her shoulder to make sure
he had not followed her. She looked down at the card, simple
black and white. *Official.*

She could have told the man no, Marie realized. Even now,
she could throw out the card and walk away. But she was curious; what kind of work, and for whom? Perhaps it was something more interesting than endless typing. The man had said
it paid well, too, something she dearly needed.

Ten minutes later, Marie found herself standing at the end of
Baker Street. She paused by a red post box at the corner. The
storied home of Sherlock Holmes was meant to be on Baker
Street, she recalled. She had always imagined it as mysterious,
shrouded in fog. But the block was like any other, drab office
buildings with ground floor shops. Farther down the row there
were brick town houses that had been converted for business
use. She walked to Number 64, then hesitated. Inter-Services
Research Bureau, the sign by the door read. What on earth was
this all about?

Before she could knock the door flew open and a hand that
did not seem attached to anybody pointed left. "Orchard Court,
Portman Square. Around the corner and down the street."

"Excuse me," Marie said, holding up the card though there
seemed to be no one to see it. "My name is Marie Roux. I was
told to come here and ask for Eleanor Trigg." The door closed.

"Curiouser and curiouser," she muttered, thinking of Tess's
favorite book, the illustrated version of *Alice in Wonderland* Marie
read aloud to her when she visited. Around the corner there
were more row houses. She continued down the street to Portman Square and found the building marked "Orchard Court."
Marie knocked. There was no answer. The whole thing was

starting to feel like a very odd prank. She turned, ready to go home and forget this folly.

Behind her, the door opened with a creak. She spun back to face a white-haired butler. "Yes?" He stared at her coldly, like she was a door-to-door salesman peddling something unwanted. Too nervous to speak, she held out the card.

He waved her inside. "Come." His tone was impatient now, as though she was expected and late. He led her through a foyer, its high ceiling and chandelier giving the impression that it had once been the entranceway to a grand home. He opened a door on his right, then closed it again quickly. "Wait here," he instructed.

Marie stood awkwardly in the foyer, feeling entirely as though she did not belong. She heard footsteps on the floor above and turned to see a handsome young man with a shock of blond hair descending a curved staircase. Noticing her, he stopped. "So, you're part of the Racket?" he asked.

"I have no idea what you're talking about."

He smiled. "Just wandered in then?" He did not wait for an answer. "The Racket—that's what we call all of this." He gestured around the foyer.

The butler reappeared, clearing his throat. His stern expression gave Marie the undeniable sense that they were not supposed to be speaking with one another. Without another word, the blond man disappeared around the corner into another of what seemed to be an endless number of doors.

The butler led her down the hallway and opened the door to an onyx-and-white-tiled bathroom. She turned back, puzzled; she hadn't asked for the loo. "Wait in here."

Before Marie could protest, the butler closed the door, leaving her alone. She stood awkwardly, inhaling the smell of mildew lingering beneath cleaners. Asked to wait in a toilet! She needed to leave but was not quite sure how to manage it. She perched on the edge of a claw-footed bathtub, ankles neatly crossed. Five minutes passed, then ten.

At last the door opened with a click and a woman walked in. She was older than Marie by at least a decade, maybe two. Her face was grave. At first her dark hair appeared to be short, but closer Marie saw that it was pulled tightly in a bun at the nape of her neck. She wore no makeup or jewelry, and her starched white shirt was perfectly pressed, almost military.

"I'm Eleanor Trigg, Chief Recruitment Officer. I'm sorry for the accommodations," she said, her voice clipped. "We are short on space." The explanation seemed odd, given the size of the house, the number of doors Marie had seen. But then she remembered the man whom the butler seemed to chastise for speaking with her. Perhaps the people who came here weren't meant to see one another at all.

Eleanor appraised Marie as one might a vase or piece of jewelry, her gaze steely and unrelenting. "So you've decided then?" she said, making it sound as if they were at the end of a long conversation and had not met thirty seconds earlier.

"Decided?" Marie repeated, puzzled.

"Yes. You have to decide if you want to risk your life, and I have to decide if I can let you."

Marie's mind whirled. "I'm sorry… I'm afraid I don't understand."

"You don't know who we are, do you?" Marie shook her head. "Then what are you doing here?"

"A man in a café gave me a card and…" Marie faltered, hearing the ridiculousness of the situation in her own voice. She had not even learned his name. "I should just go." She stood.

The woman pressed a firm hand on her shoulder. "Not necessarily. Just because you don't know why you've come, doesn't mean you shouldn't be here. We often find purpose where we least expect it—or not." Her style was brusque, unfeminine and unquestionably stern. "Don't blame the man who sent you. He wasn't authorized to say more. Our work is highly classified. Many who work at the most senior levels of Whitehall itself have no idea what it is that we do."

"Which is what, exactly?" Marie ventured to ask.

"We're a branch of Special Operations Executive."

"Oh," Marie said, though the answer really didn't clarify matters for her.

"Covert operations."

"Like the codebreakers at Bletchley?" She'd known a girl who had left the typing pool to do that once.

"Something like that. Our work is a bit more physical, though. On the ground."

"In Europe?" Eleanor nodded. Marie understood then: they meant to send her over, into the war. "You want me to be a spy?"

"We don't ask questions here," Eleanor snapped. Then it was not, Marie reflected, the place for her. She had always been curious, too curious, her mother would say, with never-ending questions that only made her father's temper worsen as Marie progressed through her teen years. "We aren't spies," Eleanor added, as though the suggestion was offensive. "Espionage is the business of MI6. Rather, here at SOE, our mission is sabotage, or destroying things like railroad tracks, telegraph lines, factory equipment and such, in order to hinder the Germans. We also help the local partisans arm and resist."

"I've never heard of such things."

"Exactly." Eleanor sounded almost pleased.

"But what makes you think I could have any part in something like this? I'm hardly qualified."

"Nonsense. You're smart, capable." How could this woman, who had only just met her, possibly know that? It was perhaps the first time in her life that anyone had described her that way. Her father made sure she felt the very opposite. And Richard, her now-gone husband, had treated her as if she was special for a fleeting moment, and look where all that had led. Marie had never thought of herself as any of those things, but now she found herself sitting a bit taller. "You speak the language. You're exactly who we're looking for. Have you ever played a musical instrument?" Eleanor asked.

Though it seemed nothing should surprise her anymore, Marie found the question strange. "Piano when I was very young. Harp in school."

"That could be useful. Open your mouth," Eleanor ordered, her voice suddenly terse. Marie was certain that she had misheard. But Eleanor's face was serious. "Your mouth" came the command again, insistent and impatient. Reluctantly, Marie complied. Eleanor stared into her mouth like a dentist. Marie bristled, resenting the intrusion by a woman she had only just met. "That back filling will have to go," Eleanor said decisively, stepping back.

"Go?" Marie's voice rose with alarm. "But that's a perfectly good filling—just a year old and was quite expensive."

"Exactly. Too expensive. It will mark you as English right away. We'll have it replaced with porcelain—that's what the French use."

It all came together in Marie's mind then: the man's interest in her language skills, Eleanor's concern over whether a tooth filling was too English. "You want me to impersonate a French-woman."

"Among other things, yes. You'll receive training in operations skills before you are deployed—if you make it through training." Eleanor spoke as though Marie had already agreed to go. "That's all I can say about it for now. Secrecy is of the utmost importance to our operations."

Deployed. Operations. Marie's head swam. It seemed surreal that in this elegant town house just steps from the shops and bustle of Oxford Street, covert war against Germany was planned and waged.

"The car will be here for you in one hour to take you to training school," Eleanor said, as though it were all settled.

"Now? But that's so soon! I would have to sort out my affairs and pack."

"It is always the way," Eleanor replied. Perhaps, Marie reflected, they didn't want to give people a chance to go home and have second thoughts. "We'll provide everything you need and give notice to the War Office for you." Marie stared at Eleanor with surprise. She hadn't said where she worked. She realized then that these people, whoever they were, knew too much about her. The meeting in the café had not been by chance.

"How long would I have to be gone?" Marie asked.

"That depends on the mission and a variety of other circumstances. You can resign at any time."

Leave, a voice not her own seemed to say. Marie was into something much bigger and deeper than she had imagined. But her feet remained planted, curiosity piqued. "I have a daughter up near Ely with my aunt. She's five."

"And your husband?"

"Killed in action," she lied. In fact, Tess's father, Richard, had been an unemployed actor who had gotten by on parts as extras in West End shows and disappeared shortly after Tess was born. Marie had come to London when she was eighteen, fleeing her father's home, and had promptly fallen for the first bad apple that dropped at her feet. "He went missing at Dunkirk." The explanation, a morbid lie, was preferable to the likely truth: that he was in Buenos Aires, spending what was left of her mother's inheritance, which Marie had naively moved to a joint account to cover their household expenses when they had first married.

"Your daughter is well cared for?" Marie nodded. "Good. You would not be able to concentrate on training if you were worried about that."

She would never stop worrying about Tess, Marie thought. She knew in that instant that Eleanor did not have children.

Marie thought about Tess up in the countryside, the weekend visits that wouldn't happen if she accepted Eleanor's proposal. What kind of mother would do such a thing? The responsible choice would be to stay here in London, to thank Eleanor and go back to whatever ordinary life was left during the war. She was the only parent Tess had. If she failed to come back, Tess would have no one but aging Aunt Hazel, who surely couldn't look after her much longer.

"The work pays ten pounds per week," Eleanor added.

That was five times what Marie made typing. She'd found the best work she could in London, but it hadn't been enough. Even combined with a second job, the kind that would have kept her from getting up to see Tess at the weekends, she would not have made what Eleanor was offering. She did the calculations. She would have enough to keep up the house even after sending money to Hazel each week to cover Tess's care and expenses, something that simply was not possible now. She imagined a new dress for her daughter, perhaps even a few toys at Christmas. Tess was unspoiled and never complained, but Marie often wished to give her more of the things she had taken for granted in her own childhood. It wasn't like she could be with Tess now while she was stuck working in London anyway. And, in truth, Marie was curious about the mysterious adventure Eleanor was dangling in front of her. She felt so useless sitting here in London, typing endlessly. Might as well do some good, make a real difference in the war effort—if, as Eleanor had said, she in fact had what it took.

"All right then. I'm ready. But I have to phone and let my daughter's caretaker know that I won't be coming up."

Eleanor shook her head firmly. "Impossible. No one can know where you are going—or even that you are going. We'll send a telegram informing your family that you've been called away for work."

"I can't simply leave without saying anything."

"That is exactly what you must do." Eleanor stared at her evenly. Though her expression did not change, Marie saw a flicker of doubt behind her eyes. "If you aren't prepared to do this, you can just leave."

"I have to speak to my daughter. I won't go unless I can hear her voice."

"Fine," Eleanor relented finally. "But you cannot tell her that you are going. There's a phone in the next room you can use. Keep it brief. No more than five minutes." Eleanor spoke as though she was in charge of Marie now, owned her. Marie wondered if accepting had been a mistake. "Say nothing of your departure," Eleanor reiterated. Marie sensed it was some sort of test—perhaps the first of many.

Eleanor started for the door, indicating that Marie should follow. "Wait," Marie said. "There's one thing." Eleanor turned back, the start of annoyance creeping onto her face. "I should tell you that my father's family is German." Marie watched Eleanor's face, half hoping the information might cause Eleanor to change her mind about accepting Marie for whatever she was proposing.

But Eleanor simply nodded in confirmation. "I know."

"But how?"

"You've sat in that same café every day, haven't you?" Marie nodded. "You should stop that, by the way. Terrible habit. Varying one's routine is key. In any event, you sit there and read books in French and one of our people noticed and thought you might be a good recruit. We followed you back to work, learned who you are. We ran you through the cards, found you qualified, at least for initial consideration." Marie was stunned; all of this had been going on and she'd had no idea. "We have finders, recruiters looking for girls who might be the right sort all over Britain. But in the end I decide if they are the right sort to go. Every single one of the girls passes through me." There was a note of protectiveness in her voice.

"And you think I do?"

"You might," Eleanor said carefully. "You've got the proper credentials. But in training you'll be tested to see if you can actually put them into use. Skills on paper are useless if you don't have the grit to see it all through. Do you have any political allegiances of your own?"

"None. My mother didn't believe in…"

"Enough," Eleanor snapped. "Don't answer a question with any more than you have to." Another test. "You must never talk about yourself or your past. You'll be given a new identity in training." And until then, Marie thought, it would be as if she simply didn't exist.

Eleanor held open the door to the toilet. Marie walked through into a study with high bookshelves. A black phone sat on a mahogany desk. "You can call here." Eleanor remained in the doorway, not even pretending to give her privacy. Marie dialed the operator and asked to be connected to the post office where Hazel worked each day, hoping she had not yet gone home. She asked for Hazel from the woman who answered.

Then a warbling voice came across the line. "Marie! Is something wrong?"

"Everything's fine," Marie reassured quickly, so desperately wanting to tell her the truth about why she had called. "Just checking on Tess."

"I'll fetch her." One minute passed then another. Quickly, Marie thought, wondering if Eleanor would snatch the phone from her hand the moment five minutes had passed.

"Allo!" Tess's voice squeaked, flooding Marie's heart.

"Darling, how are you?"

"Mummy, I'm helping Aunt Hazel sort the mail."

Marie smiled, imagining her playing around the pigeonholes. "Good girl."

"And just two more days until I see you." Tess, who even as a young child had an acute sense of time, knew her mother always came on Friday. Only now she wouldn't be. Marie's heart wrenched.

"Let me speak to your auntie. And, Tess, I love you," she added.

But Tess was already gone. Hazel came back on the line. "She's well?" Marie asked.

"She's brilliant. Counting to a hundred and doing sums. So bright. Why, just the other day, she…" Hazel stopped, seeming to sense that sharing what Marie had missed would only make things worse. Marie couldn't help but feel a tiny bit jealous. When Richard abandoned her and left her alone with a newborn, Marie had been terrified. But in those long nights of comforting and nursing an infant, she and Tess had become one. Then she'd been forced to send Tess away. She was missing so much of Tess's childhood as this bloody war dragged on. "You'll see for yourself at the weekend," Hazel added kindly.

Marie's stomach ached as though she had been punched. "I have to go."

"See you soon," Hazel replied.

Fearful she would say more, Marie hung up the phone.